So Long Been
DREAMING

SO LONG BEEN DREAMING

NALO HOPKINSON & UPPINDER MEHAN eds

Postcolonial Science Fiction & Fantasy

ARSENAL
PULP PRESS
Vancouver

SO LONG BEEN DREAMING: POSTCOLONIAL SCIENCE FICTION & FANTASY
Stories and essays copyright © 2004 by the authors, unless otherwise indicated

ARSENAL PULP PRESS
103 – 1014 Homer Street
Vancouver, B.C.
Canada v6b 2w9
arsenalpulp.com

The publisher gratefully acknowledges the support of the Canada Council for the Arts and the British Columbia Arts Council for its publishing program, and the Government of Canada through the Book Publishing Industry Development Program for its publishing activities.

Design by Solo
Cover illustration by Ho Che Anderson
Printed and bound in Canada

National Library of Canada Cataloguing in Publication Data
        So long been dreaming : postcolonial science fiction &
fantasy / edited by Nalo Hopkinson and Uppinder Mehan.
ISBN 1–55152–158–X
        1. Science fiction. 2. Fantasy fiction. 3. Developing countries –
Literatures – 21st century. I. Hopkinson, Nalo II. Mehan, Uppinder, 1961–
PN6071.S33S6 2004808.83'876C2004–900676–2

Introduction   7   Nalo Hopkinson

SECTION I: THE BODY

Deep End   12   Nisi Shawl
Griots of the Galaxy   23   Andrea Hairston
Toot Sweet Matricia   46   Suzette Mayr
Rachel   53   Larissa Lai

SECTION II: FUTURE EARTH

Terminal Avenue   62   Eden Robinson
When Scarabs Multiply   70   Nnedi Okorafor–Mbachu
Delhi   79   Vandana Singh
Panopte's Eye   95   Tamai Kobayashi

SECTION III: ALLEGORY

The Grassdreaming Tree   108   Sheree R. Thomas
The Blue Road: A Fairy Tale   120   Wayde Compton

SECTION IV: ENCOUNTERS WITH THE ALIEN

The Forgotten Ones   140   Karin Lowachee
Native Aliens   151   Greg van Eekhout
Refugees   161   Celu Amberstone
Trade Winds   183   devorah major
Lingua Franca   201   Carole McDonnell
Out of Sync   217   Ven Begamudré

SECTION V: RE–IMAGINING THE PAST

The Living Roots   230   Opal Palmer Adisa
Journey Into the Vortex   243   Maya Khankhoje
Necahual   251   Tobias S. Buckell

Final Thoughts   269   Uppinder Mehan

Introduction

Nalo Hopkinson, co-editor

I met and became friends with Uppinder Mehan when he was still living in Toronto. A little later, he told me that he was about to have an essay published, entitled "The Domestication of Technology in Indian Science Fiction Short Stories" (in *Foundation: the International Review of Science Fiction*, No. 74, Autumn 1998). As a fiction writer, I myself was struggling with what seemed like the unholy marriage of race consciousness and science fiction sensibility, and I was hungry for any critical thought that might shed light on the topic. I got myself a copy of Uppinder's essay, and there was light indeed. In fact, some of his ideas on the development of indigenous metaphors for technological progress influenced me strongly as I finished the novel *Midnight Robber*.

A friend and fellow science fiction writer, Zainab Amadahy, once introduced me to a friend of hers, a black scholar who had recently completed his PhD. We got to talking about my short story "Riding the Red," which does a jazz riff on the folk tale of Little Red Riding Hood. He listened to my description of my story, then asked, "What do you think of Audre Lorde's comment that massa's tools will never dismantle massa's house?"

I froze. Much of the folklore on which I draw is European. Even the form in which I write is European. Arguably, one of the most familiar memes of science fiction is that of going to foreign countries and colonizing the natives, and as I've said elsewhere, for many of us, that's not a thrilling adventure story; it's non–fiction, and we are on the wrong side of the strange–looking ship that appears out of nowhere. To be a person of colour writing science fiction is to be under suspicion of having internalized one's colonization. I knew that I'd have to fight this battle at some point in my career,

7

but I wasn't ready. Hadn't yet formulated my thoughts on the matter. I was still struggling to figure it all out for myself. "What do you mean?" I asked, stalling for time.

He looked at me and said (I'm paraphrasing), "We've been taught all our lives how superior European literature is. In our schools, it's what we're instructed to read, to analyze, to understand, how we're taught to think. They gave us those tools. I think that now, they're our tools, too."

I found I was able to breathe again. And now I had plenty to think about. When I write science fiction and fantasy from a context of blackness and Caribbeanness, using Afro-Caribbean lore, history, and language, it should logically be no different than writing it from a Western European context: take out the Cinderella folk tale, replace it with the crab-back woman folk tale; exchange the struggle of the marginalized poor with the struggle of the racialized marginalized poor.

And yet, it's very different. When I rewrote my story "Riding the Red" in Jamaican creole, all of a sudden I could no longer have a peasant grandmother living in a cottage in Britain's past in the middle of the English woods; how would a Jamaican farm woman have gotten there in the seventeenth century? Not inconceivable, but I didn't want to stop and explain the how. So I brought my Jamaican granny home. She doesn't live in a forest; we don't call them forests, and besides, how is she to feed herself in the middle of a forest? So now she lives on a small hand-hewed farm with the tropical bush not too far outside her front door. Little Red Riding Hood doesn't want to attend soigné Cinderellaesque balls; come Saturday evening, she want feh go a-dance hall. And the scourge of the little girl and her granny can't be a wolf; no such thing in Jamaica. Instead, he becomes that boogie man from Caribbean folklore, Brer Tiger. These are changes that should be superficial, but that end up giving the story a completely different feel. Even the title had to change from "Riding the Red" to "Red Rider," a creole phrase that evoked Caribbean music and sexual innuendo. In my hands, massa's tools don't dismantle massa's house – and in fact, I don't want to destroy it so much as I want to undertake massive renovations – they build me a house of my own.

So, a little while ago, Uppinder approached me about co-editing an anthology of postcolonial science fiction short stories written exclusively by people of colour. The idea excited me. If I were to edit such an anthology on my own, I would likely have chosen to include white writers, since I feel that a dialogue about the effects of colonialism is one that white folks need to have with the rest of us, but I also understand and believe in the importance of creating defended spaces where marginalized groups of people can discuss their own marginalization. I wanted to see what would happen if we handed out massa's tools and said, "Go on; let's see what you build."

What you hold in your hand is the result; stories that take the meme of colonizing the natives and, from the experience of the colonizee, critique it, pervert it, fuck with it, with irony, with anger, with humour, and also, with love and respect for the genre of science fiction that makes it possible to think about new ways of doing things.

Toronto, March 2004

SECTION I
THE BODY

The first four stories in the anthology –
"Deep End" by Nisi Shawl, "Griots of the
Galaxy" by Andrea Hairston, "Toot Sweet
Matricia" by Suzette Mayr, and "Rachel"
by Larissa Lai – explore the close connections
between body and identity. In "Deep End," a
black jailed woman struggles with questions
of identity and community as she hurtles
towards a new planet. Hairston's story
makes literal the figure of the griot as the
embodiment of communal memory. Mayr
appropriates an old Irish folktale in an
attempt to address her postcolonial hybrid
identity. And in Lai's "Rachel," a replicant's
attempt to understand her implanted
memories racializes that neutral but somehow
always white construction, the android.

Most recently, **Nisi Shawl**'s *stories have been published in Asimov's* SF Magazine *and* Strange Horizons; *they also appear in* Mojo: Conjure Stories *and in both volumes of the groundbreaking* Dark Matter *anthology series. With her friend Cindy Ward, she teaches "Writing the Other: Bridging Cultural Differences for Successful Fiction," a class based on her thought-provoking essay "Transracial Writing for the Sincere." A member of the board of the Clarion West Writers Workshop, she lives in Seattle, on a direct bus route to the beach.*

cⱱɔ

Deep End

Nisi Shawl

The pool was supposed to be like freespace. Enough like it, anyway, to help Wayna acclimate to her download. She went in first thing every "morning," as soon as Dr Ops, the ship's mind, awakened her. Too bad it wasn't scheduled for later; all the slow, meat–based activities afterwards were a drag.

The voices of the pool's other occupants boomed back and forth in an odd, uncontrolled manner, steel–born echoes muffling and exposing what was said. The temperature varied irregularly, warm intake jets competing with cold currents and, Wayna suspected, illicitly released urine. Overhead lights speckled the wall, the ceiling, the water with a shifting, uneven glare.

Psyche Moth was a prison ship. Like all those on board, Wayna was an upload of a criminal's mind. The process of uploading her had destroyed her physical body. Punishment. Then the ship, with Wayna and 248,961 other prisoners, set off on a long voyage to another star. The prisoners cycled through consciousness: one year on, four years off. Of the eighty-seven years en route, Wayna had only lived through sixteen. More punishment, though it was unclear whether it was oblivion or the time spent in freespace that constituted the actual punishment. Or maybe the mandatory classes they took there really were intended to be rehabilitative, as Dr Ops claimed.

Now she spent most of her time as meat. When *Psyche Moth* had reached its goal and verified that the world it called Amends was colonizable, her group had been the second downloaded into empty clones, right after the trustees.

Wayna's jaw ached. She'd been clenching it, trying to amp up her sensory inputs. She paddled toward the deep end, consciously relaxing her useless facial muscles. A trustee had told her it was typical to translocate missing controls.

Then the pain hit.

White! Heat! There then gone – the lash of a whip.

Wayna stopped moving. Her suit held her up. She floated, waiting. Nothing else happened. Tentatively, she kicked and stroked her way to the steps rising from the pool's shallows, nodding to those she passed. At the door to the showers, it hit her again: a shock of electricity slicing from right shoulder to left hip. She caught her breath and continued in.

The showers were empty. Wayna was the first one from her hour out of the pool, and it was too soon for the next hour to wake up. She turned on the water and stood in its welcome warmth. What was going on? She'd never felt anything like this, not that she could remember – and surely she wouldn't have forgotten something so intense. She stripped off her wet suit and hung it to dry. Instead of dressing in her overall and reporting to the laundry, her next assignment, she retreated into her locker and linked with Dr Ops.

In the sphere of freespace, his office always hovered in the northwest quadrant, about halfway up from the horizon. Doe, Wayna's honeywoman, disliked this placement. Why pretend he was anything other than central to the whole setup? she asked. Why not put himself smack dab in the middle where he belonged? Doe distrusted Dr Ops and everything about *Psyche Moth*. Wayna understood why. But there was nothing else. Not for eight light-years in any direction. According to Dr Ops.

She swam into his pink-walled waiting room and eased her icon into a chair, which automatically posted a request for the AI's attention. A couple of other prisoners were there ahead of her; one disappeared soon after she sat. A few more minutes objective measure, and the other was gone as well. Then it was Wayna's turn.

Dr Ops presented as a lean-faced Caucasian man with a shock of mixed brown and blond hair. He wore an anachronistic headlamp and stethoscope and a gentle, kindly persona. "I have your readouts, of course, but why don't you tell me in your own words what's going on?"

He looked like he was listening. When she finished, he sat silent for a few seconds – much more time than he needed to consider what she'd said. Making an ostentatious display of his concern.

"There's no sign of nerve damage," he told her. "Nothing wrong with your spine or any of your articulation or musculature."

"So then how come –"

"It's probably nothing," the AI said, interrupting her. "But just in case, let's give you the rest of the day off. Take it easy – outside your locker, of course. I'll clear your bunkroom for the next twenty–five hours. Lie down. Put in some face time with your friends."

"'Probably?'"

"I'll let you know for sure tomorrow morning. Right now, relax. Doctor's orders." He smiled and logged her out. He could do that. It was his system.

Wayna tongued open her locker; no use staying in there without access to freespace. She put on her overall and walked up the corridor to her bunkroom. Fellow prisoners passed her heading the other way to the pool: no one she'd known back on Earth, no one she had gotten to know that well in freespace or since the download. Plenty of time for that onplanet. The woman with the curly red hair was called Robeson, she was pretty sure. They smiled at each other. Robeson walked hand in hand with a slender man whose mischievous smile reminded Wayna of Thad. It wasn't him. Thad was scheduled for later download. Wayna was lucky to have Doe with her.

Another pain. Not so strong this time. Strong enough, though. Sweat dampened her skin. She kept going, almost there.

There. Through the doorless opening she saw the mirror she hated, ordered up by one of the two women she timeshared with. It was only partly obscured by the genetics charts the other woman taped everywhere. Immersion learning. Even Wayna was absorbing something from it.

But not now. She lay on the bunk without looking at anything, eyes open. What was wrong with her?

Probably nothing.

Relax.

She did her body awareness exercises, tensing and loosening different muscle groups. She'd gotten as far as her knees when Doe walked in. Stood over her till Wayna focused on her honeywoman's new visage. "Sweetheart," Doe said. Her pale fingers stroked Wayna's face. "Dr Ops told a trustee you wanted me."

"No – I mean yes, but I didn't ask –"

Doe's expression froze, flickered, froze again.

"Don't be – it's so hard, can't you just –" Wayna reached for and found both Doe's hands and held them. They felt cool and small and dry. She pressed them against her overall's open v–neck and slid them beneath the fabric, forcing them to stroke her shoulders.

Making love to Doe in her download seemed like cheating. Wayna wondered what Thad's clone would look like, and if they'd be able to travel to his group's settlement to see him.

Anticipating agony, Wayna found herself hung up, nowhere near ecstasy. Doe pulled back and looked down at her, expecting an explanation. So Wayna had to tell her what little she knew.

"You! You weren't going to say anything! Just let me hurt you –" Doe had zero tolerance for accidentally inflicting pain, the legacy of her marriage to a closeted masochist.

"It wouldn't be anything you *did!* And I don't know if –"

Doe tore aside the paper they had taped across the doorway for privacy. From her bunk, Wayna heard her raging along the corridor, slapping the walls.

Face time was over.

ᴄᴧᴏ

Taken off of her normal schedule, Wayna had no idea how to spend the rest of her day. Not lying down alone. Not after that. She tried, but she couldn't.

Relax.

Ordinarily when her laundry shift was over, she was supposed to show up in the cafeteria and eat. Never one of her favourite activities, even back on Earth. She went there early, though, surveying the occupied tables. The same glaring lights hung from the ceiling here as in the pool, glinting off plastic plates and water glasses. The same confused noise, the sound of overlapping conversations. No sign of Doe.

She stood in line. The trustee in charge started to give her a hard time about not waiting for her usual lunch hour. He shut up suddenly; Dr Ops must have tipped him a clue. Trustees were in constant contact with the ship's mind – part of why Wayna hadn't volunteered to be one.

Mashed potatoes. Honey mustard nuggets. Slaw. All freshly factured, filled with nutrients and the proper amount of fiber for this stage of her digestive tract's maturation.

She sat at a table near the disposal dump. The redhead, Robeson, was there too, and a man – a different one than Wayna had seen her with before. Wayna introduced herself. She didn't feel like talking, but listening was fine. The topic was the latest virch from the settlement site. She hadn't done it yet.

This installment had been recorded by a botanist; lots of information on grass analogs and pollinating insects. "We know more about Jubilee than *Psyche Moth*," Robeson said.

"Well, sure," said the man. His name was Jawann. "Jubilee is where we're going to live."

"*Psyche Moth* is where we live now, where we've lived for the last eighty-seven years. We don't know jack about this ship. Because Dr Ops doesn't want us to."

"We know enough to realize we'd look stupid trying to attack him," Wayna said. Even Doe admitted that. Dr Ops' hardware lay in *Psyche Moth's* central section, along with the drive engine. A tether almost two kilometers long separated their living quarters from the AI's physical components and any other mission-critical equipment they might damage. At the end of the tether, Wayna and the rest of the downloads swung faster and faster. They were like sand in a bucket, centrifugal force mimicking gravity and gradually building up to the level they'd experience on Amend's surface, in Jubilee.

That was all they knew. All Dr Ops thought they needed to know.

"Who said anything about an attack?" Robeson frowned.

"No one." Wayna was suddenly sorry she'd spoken. "All I mean is, his only motive in telling us anything was to prevent that from happening." She spooned some nuggets onto her mashed potatoes and shoved them into her mouth so she wouldn't say any more.

"You think he's lying?" Jawann asked. Wayna shook her head no.

"He could if he wanted. How would we find out?"

The slaw was too sweet; not enough contrast with the nuggets. Not peppery, like what Aunt Nono used to make.

"Why would we want to find out? We'll be on our own ground, in Jubilee, soon enough." Four weeks. Twenty days by *Psyche Moth's* rationalized calendar.

"With trustees to watch us all the time, everywhere we go, and this ship hanging in orbit right over our heads." Robeson sounded as suspicious as Doe, Jawann as placatory as Wayna tried to be in their identical arguments. Thad usually came across as neutral, controlled, the way you could be out of your meat.

"So? They're not going to hurt us after they brought us all this way. At least, they won't want to hurt our bodies."

Because their bodies came from, were copies of, the people against whom they'd rebelled. The rich. The politically powerful.

But Wayna's body was *hers*. No one else owned it, no matter who her clone's cells had started off with. Hers, no matter how different it looked from the one she had been born with. How white.

Hers to take care of. Early on in her training she'd decided that. How else could she be serious about her exercises? Why else would she bother?

This was her body. She'd earned it.

Jawann and Robeson were done; they'd started eating before her and now they were leaving. She swallowed quickly. "Wait – I wanted to ask – " They stopped and she stood up to follow them, taking her half-full plate. "Either of you have any medical training?"

They knew someone, a man called Unique, a nurse when he'd lived on Earth. Here he worked in the factory, quality control. Wayna would have to go back to her bunkroom until he got off and could come see her. She left Doe a message on the board by the cafeteria's entrance, an apology. Face up on her bed, Wayna concentrated fiercely on the muscle groups she'd skipped earlier. A trustee came by to check on her and seemed satisfied to find her lying down, everything in line with her remote readings. He acted as if she should be flattered by the extra attention. "Dr Ops will be in touch first thing tomorrow," he promised as he left.

"Oooh, baby," she said softly to herself, and went on with what she'd been doing.

A little later, for no reason she knew of, she looked up at her doorway. The man that had held Robeson's hand that morning stood there as if this was where he'd always been. "Hi. Do I have the right place? You're Wayna?"

"Unique?"

"Yeah."

"Come on in." She swung her feet to the floor and patted a place beside her on the bed. He sat closer than she'd expected, closer than she was used to. Maybe that meant he'd been born Hispanic or Middle Eastern. Or maybe not.

"Robeson said you had some sort of problem to ask me about. So – of course I don't have any equipment, but if I can help in any way, I will."

She told him what had happened, feeling foolish all of a sudden. There'd only been those three times, nothing more since seeing Dr Ops.

"Lie on your stomach," he said. Through the fabric, firm fingers pressed on either side of her spine, from mid-back to her skull, then down again to her tailbone. "Turn over, please. Bend your knees. All right if I take off your shoes?" He stroked the soles of her feet, had her push them against his hands in different directions. His touch, his resistance to her pressure, reassured her. What she was going through was real. It mattered.

He asked her how she slept, what she massed, if she was always thirsty, other things. He finished his questions and walked back and forth in her room, glancing often in her direction. She sat again, hugging herself. If Doe came in now, she'd know Wayna wanted him.

Unique quit his pacing and faced her, his eyes steady. "I don't know what's wrong with you," he said. "You're not the only one, though. There are 150 others that I've seen or heard of experiencing major problems – circulatory, muscular, digestive. Some even have the same symptoms you do."

"What is it?" Wayna asked stupidly.

"Honestly, I don't know," he repeated. "If I had a lab – I'll set one up in Jubilee – call it neuropathy, but I don't know for sure what's causing it."

"Neuropathy?"

"Means nerve problems."

"But Dr Ops told me my nerves were fine...." No response to that.

"If we were on Earth, what would you think?"

He compressed his already thin lips. "Most likely possibility, some kind of thyroid problem. Or – but what it would be elsewhere, that's irrelevant. You're here, and it's the numbers involved that concern me, though superficially the cases seem unrelated.

"One hundred and fifty of you out of the Jubilee group with what might be germ plasm disorders; 150 out of 20,000. At least 150; take under-reporting into account and there's probably more. Too many. They would have screened foetuses for irregularities before shipping them out."

"Well, what should I do then?"

"Get Dr Ops to give you a new clone."

"But –"

"This one's damaged. If you train intensely, you'll make up the lost time and go down to Jubilee with the rest of us."

Or she might be able to delay and wind up part of Thad's settlement instead.

As if he'd heard her thought, Unique added, "I wouldn't wait, if I were you. I'd ask for – no, demand another body – now. Soon as you can."

"Because?"

"Because your chances of a decent one will just get worse, if this is a radiation–induced mutation. Which I have absolutely no proof of. But if it is."

∽

"By the rivers of Babylon, there we sat down, and there we wept...." The pool reflected music, voices vaulting upward off the water, outward to the walls of white-painted steel. Unlike yesterday, the words were clear, because everyone was saying the same thing. Singing the same thing. "For the wicked carried us away...." Wayna wondered why the trustee in charge had chosen this song. Of course he was a prisoner, too.

The impromptu choir sounded more soulful than it looked. If the personalities of these clones' originals had been in charge, what would they be singing now? The "Doxology?" "Bringing in the Sheaves?" Did Episcopalians even have hymns?

Focusing on the physical, Wayna scanned her body for symptoms. So far this morning, she'd felt nothing unusual. Carefully, slowly, she swept the satiny surface with her arms, raising a tapering wave. She worked her legs, shooting backwards like a squid, away from the shallows and most of the other swimmers. Would sex underwater be as good as it was in freespace? No, you'd be constantly coming up for breath. Instead of constantly coming.... Last night, Doe had forgiven her, and they'd gone to Thad together. And everything had been fine until they started fighting again. It hadn't been her fault. Or Doe's, either.

They told Thad about Wayna's pains, and how Unique thought she should ask for another clone. "Why do you want to download at all?" he asked. "Stay in here with me."

"Until you do? But if –"

"Until I don't. I wasn't sure I wanted to anyway. Now it sounds *so* much more inviting. 'Defective body?' 'Don't mind if I do.'" Thad's icon got up from their bed to mimic unctuous host and vivacious guest. "'And, oh, you're serving that on a totally unexplored and no doubt dangerous new planet? I just adore totally –'"

"Stop it!" Wayna hated it when he acted that way, faking that he was a flamer. She hooked him by one knee and pulled him down, putting her hand over his mouth. She meant it as a joke; they ought to have ended up wrestling, rolling around, having fun, having more sex. Thad didn't respond, though. Not even when Wayna tickled him under his arms. He had amped down his input.

"Look," he said. "I went through our 'voluntary agreement.' We did our part by letting them bring us here."

Doe propped herself up on both elbows. She had huge nipples, not like the ones on her clone's breasts. "You're really serious."

"Yes. I really am."

"Why?" asked Wayna. She answered herself: "Dr Ops won't let you download into a woman. Will he."

"Probably not. I haven't even asked."

Doe said "Then what is it? We were going to be together, at least on the same world. All we went through and you're just throwing it away –"

"Together to do what? To bear our enemies' children, that's what, we nothing but a bunch of glorified mammies, girl, don't you get it? Remote-control units for their immortality investments, protection for their precious genetic material. Cheaper than your average AI, no benefits, no union, no personnel manager. *Mammies.*"

"Not mammies," Doe said slowly. "I see what you're saying, but we're more like incubators, if you think about it. Or petri dishes – inoculated with their DNA. Except they're back on Earth; they won't be around to see the results of their experiment."

"Don't need to be. They got Dr Ops to report back."

"Once we're on Amends," Wayna said, "no one can make us have kids or do anything we don't want."

"You think. Besides, they won't *have* to make people reproduce. It's a basic drive."

"Of the meat." Doe nodded. "Okay. Point granted, Wayna?" She sank down again, resting her head on her crossed arms.

No one said anything for awhile. The jazz Thad liked to listen to filled the silence: smooth horns, rough drums, discreet bass.

"Well, what'll you do if you stay in here?" Doe asked. "What'll Dr Ops do? Turn you off? Log you out permanently? Put your processors on half power?"

"Don't think so. He's an AI. He'll stick to the rules."

"Whatever those are," said Wayna.

"I'll find out."

She had logged off then, withdrawn to sleep in her bunkroom, expecting Doe to join her. She'd wakened alone, a note from Dr Ops on the mirror, which normally she would have missed. Normally she avoided the mirror, but not this morning. She'd studied her face, noting the narrow nose, the light, stubby lashes around eyes an indeterminate colour she guessed could be called grey. Whose face had this been? A senator's? A favourite secretary's? Hers, now. For how long?

Floating upright in the deep end, she glanced at her arms. They were covered with blonde hairs which the water washed into rippled patterns. Her small breasts mounded high here in the pool, buoyant with fat.

Would the replacement be better-looking, or worse?

Wayna turned to see the clock on the wall behind her. Ten. Time to get out and get ready for her appointment.

∞

"I'm afraid I can't do that, Wayna." Dr Ops looked harassed and faintly ashamed. He hadn't been able to tell her anything about the pains. He acted like they weren't important; he'd even hinted she might be making them up just to get a different body. "You're not the first to ask, you know. One per person, that's all. That's it."

Thad's right, Wayna thought to herself. AIs stick to the rules. He could improvise, but he won't.

"Why?" Always a good question.

"We didn't bring a bunch of extra bodies, Wayna," Dr Ops said.

"Well, why not?" Another excellent question. "You should have," she went on. "What if there was an emergency, an epidemic?"

"There's enough for that –"

"I know someone who's not going to use theirs. Give it to me."

"You must mean Thad." Dr Ops frowned. "That would be a man's body. Our charter doesn't allow transgender downloads."

Wayna counted in twelves under her breath, closing her eyes so long she almost logged off.

"Who's to know?" Her voice was too loud, and her jaw hurt. She'd been clenching it tight, forgetting it would amp up her inputs. Download settings had apparently become her default overnight. "Never mind. You're not going to give me a second body. I can't make you."

"I thought you'd understand." He smiled and hunched his shoulders. "I *am* sorry."

Swimming through freespace to her locker, she was sure Dr Ops didn't know what sorry was. She wondered if he ever would.

Meanwhile.

∽

She never saw Doe again outside freespace. There'd still be two of them together – just not the two they'd assumed.

She had other attacks, some mild, some much stronger than the first. Massage helped, and keeping still, and moving. She met prisoners who had similar symptoms, and they traded tips and theories about what was wrong with them.

Doe kept telling her that if she wanted to be without pain, she should simply stay in freespace. After awhile, Wayna did more and more virches and spent less and less time with her lovers.

Jubilee lay in Amends' Northern latitudes, high on a curving peninsula, in the rain shadow of old, gentle mountains. Bright-skinned tree-dwelling amphibians inhabited the mountain passes, their trilling cries rising and falling like loud orgasms whenever Wayna took her favourite tour.

And then there were the instructional virches, building on what they'd learned in their freespace classes. Her specialty, fiber tech, became suddenly fascinating: baskets, nets, ropes, cloth, paper – so much to learn, so little time.

The day before planetfall she went for one last swim in the pool. It was deserted, awaiting the next settlement group. It would never be as full of prisoners again; Thad and Doe weren't the only ones opting out of their downloads.

There was plenty of open fresh water on Amends: a large lake not far from Jubilee, and rivers even closer. She peered down past her dangling feet at the pool's white bottom. Nothing to see there. Never had been; never would be.

She had lunch with Robeson, Unique, and Jawann. As Dr Ops recommended, they skipped dinner.

She didn't try to say goodbye. She didn't sleep alone.

And then it was morning and they were walking into one of *Psyche Moth*'s landing units, underbuckets held to the pool's bottom, to its outside, by retractable bolts, and Dr Ops unlocked them and they were free, flying, falling, down, down, down, out of the black and into the blue, the green, the thousand colours of their new home.

Andrea Hairston *is a Professor of Theatre at Smith College. She is the Artistic Director of Chrysalis Theatre and her plays have been produced at Yale Rep, Rites and Reason, the Kennedy Center, StageWest, and on Public Radio and Public Television. The flash of spirit in West African and Caribbean performance traditions has offered her much wisdom and inspiration. She has received a National Endowment for the Arts Grant to Playwrights, a Rockefeller/NEA Grant for New Works, a Ford Foundation Grant to collaborate with Senegalese Master Drummer Massamba Diop, and a Shubert Fellowship for Playwriting. Since 1997, her plays produced by Chrysalis Theatre*, Soul Repairs, Lonely Stardust, *and* Hummingbird Flying Backward, *have been science fiction-themed.* Archangels of Funk, *a sci-fi theatre jam, garnered her a Massachusetts Cultural Council Fellowship for 2003. She recently completed a speculative novel,* Mindscape, *excerpted in* Dark Matter: Reading the Bones, *an anthology of African diasporic speculative fiction edited by Sheree Thomas and published by Warner Books in 2004.* "Double Consciousness," *a story from* Mindscape, *will appear in* Future Females of Colour, *edited by Marleen Barr, to be published by Ohio State University Press in 2005. She is currently working on a new speculative novel,* Exploding in Slow Motion.

☙

Griots of the Galaxy

Andrea Hairston

*The Griots of West Africa are musicians, oral historians,
praise singers negotiating community. They stand between us
and cultural amnesia. Through them we learn to hear beyond
our time and understand the future.*

The first thing I knew, I was thigh–deep in swamp scum, strangling a silver and white Siberian husky with ice eyes and dead fish breath. I liked dogs, vaguely remembered being one once, and would have let him go, but he was trying to eat

23

me. I pressed through matted hair and squeezed his windpipe. He gagged, startled out of attack mode by my newfound vigour and the rapidly healing wounds on my neck, wounds he had just made. We wrestled in a jungle swamp, more Amazon than Florida, drenched in a chemical haze. It was high noon, but the trees gobbled up ninety percent of the photons. It might as well have been evening, except for the heavy heat hanging in the mist. A husky could die in weather like this. What was he doing here?

What was I?

He stood on hind legs and looked right in my eyes. I didn't know how tall I was, but that seemed like a lot of dog to me. From the smell of my ripped pants, the body I was in had already lost control of sphincter muscles once – which explained why I didn't piss myself looking at his bloody fangs and intelligent eyes, like people's eyes. What had this body ever done to him, I wondered?

He smacked his six-inch paws against my arms, clawed at my breasts, and tried to shake my hands from his throat, but I didn't feel it. I was pumped from the drop into this body and I had him. That dawned on him too, and with a panicked look, he stopped squirming and whimpered, a tortured sound I didn't want to hear. My new heart banged against ribs and backbone, flushed nerves and muscles with potent stimulants, and obliterated my fledgling compassion. When you dropped into a life, the story of the host body, its impulses and desires, were almost impossible to resist. A body historian, working the soul mines of Earth, but I wanted to resist. What the hell was wrong with me?

The husky lunged. Turning his momentum against him, I plunged his head and shoulders into the water and grunted a cheer through clenched teeth. His struggle splashed swamp in my face. I snorted stagnant muck out of my mouth and nose. It tasted like dandelion and beet greens, like my past lives breaking out on a new tongue. Panicked, I swallowed down this old history. My skinny brown forearms trembled with holding 150 pounds of dog under water, and I wondered just how long my drop-in power surge would last. I'd been wrestling the husky less than a minute, but I dimly recalled entire lifetimes that seemed shorter. I was suddenly terrified:

What kind of life was it going to be in this body?

The lapse of killer concentration cost me a chunk of leg flesh and my balance. The husky could have chewed through bone, so I was lucky. Still, it hurt like hell, and I roared a mezzo-soprano glissando that startled me out of pain. The diva holler was definitely one of my former voices breaking out, and no way should that be happening. Body historians never let the past take over; you were now or nothing.

No time for existential crises. Flailing under water, the husky banged into my wounded leg, and a blues holler burst from my chest. Another old voice. Loudmouth jungle fauna joined in, chattering and hooting like they were on my side. The dog thrashed up to suck in some air, his face just cracking the surface. My hands wanted to shove him back toward the bottom of the swamp, but looking at his soggy snout and mud-rimmed eyes, I couldn't do it. The body I was in had already died once, and I could drop into another dying somebody – if complex enough and within range – risky, but the husky's only life was on the line. I summoned the divas back to my mouth. Singing syncopated rhythms in a minor mode, I forced the hands to let go of his neck. His ears shot up. My blues aria surprised him as much as me. He gulped down air, shook the water out of his fur, and without blinking, watched me scramble away. I couldn't stop singing until the song was done. He cocked his head at the last notes, like he knew the melody. Brown saliva dripped off his tongue as his ears went flat again. I hauled butt for dry land when I saw a plan working behind his eyes.

The mucky bottom grabbed my feet and pitched me against two dead dogs. Buttocks and hind legs dangled in the algae soup, head and shoulders slumped on the slimy shore. Dobermans. I vaguely remembered them trying to eat me too, but I'd managed to waste them before it came to that. They had holes in their heads, and blood was attracting the bugs: crawlers, fliers, and swimmers. I recoiled, glad I hadn't dropped in as a Doberman attack dog. I recoiled again, this time at myself. You didn't get to choose a life; you only had minutes to find what was available. A true historian should be glad for any dying body to ride. Every story offered precious insight.

The dog lowered his head and extended his snout. I knew huskies were quiet, not barkers or yappers. They put everything into the growl. Still, feeling the rumble from his chest forty feet away surprised me in my bones. I glimpsed a pistol just beyond the dead Dobermans, easily within reach, but I hollered out another aria and squashed the urge to grab it. Staring into the husky's eyes, I let the melody fade. This body for his life, it seemed fair.

We both gulped shallow breaths. I ran my fingers across the smooth skin on my neck and remembered the husky ripping out my jugular. Body historians were serial amnesiacs, conscious only of our griot's creed and the Edges, the sliding in and out of a life. I had twice ten thousand Earth years of Edges. That and a griot's loyalty to the soul mines. Dropping in for a quickie then suiciding out to somebody else was a total waste of resources. Griots rode a body as long as possible. In the soul mines, you collected lives; you didn't sacrifice yourself to save one.

The husky came at me like a flash of silver lightning. Dropping out was going to hurt like hell, but I was prepared. I focused on his eyes, not his fangs. The husky was quite beautiful, a strange presence in this jungle world, a special Edge for my memory tatters.... At the last second, with astounding speed and grace, and despite my spark of rebellion, this body reached across the dead Dobermans, grabbed the gun, and shoved it down the husky's mouth. The pistol barked five times, and he was gone before I could think, before I could struggle with my new self to save him. I yanked the pistol out of his mouth, and the corpse slid down my belly into the water, ice eyes gone dull gray, jaws frozen in a deadly grin. My right hand was shaking, but my gun hand was still. I threw up the meager contents of my stomach and tried for a few tears. Nada. This body didn't want me to care about dead huskies or Edges of pain. It swallowed my distress almost before any emotion registered, and directed me toward its Mission. I shivered.

When the husky corpse floated against the other dead dogs, I stopped waiting for it to come back to life and crawled ashore. Now or nothing. I stuffed the pistol in my pants, squeezed water out of my spongy hair, and headed for a tangle of trees and vines. My drop-in power surge had faded. Solid ground wobbled under my legs, even when I stopped moving. The trees threatened to turn upside down and stick the sky under my shaky toes. Blood and white froth spurted out of the puncture wounds in my leg, and one arm looked liked mincemeat. Tatters of a taupe cotton shirt stuck to blood and muck on my belly and breasts. I ripped off a piece of pants that wasn't swampy or piss-yellow and tied it tight around the leg wound. I tried touching myself all over to feel who I was, but I was too raggedy. Settling down in a tree root throne, I watched thin spears of sunlight bounce off my shark navel ring and cut through the haze. Glints of metal among the branches made me blink and squint.

The trees had eyes, and they were watching me. Mechanical worms with camera heads wriggled up branches into blossoms and clumps of foliage. I should have checked them out. Instead I convinced myself I was paranoid, hallucinating, and what I needed was to sit still and gather myself, not chase spooks. Dizzy from the heat, sore and itchy from sweat, bug bites, and dog gouges, I didn't feel excitement for a new life, just fear at a moral chasm opening before me. At each drop-out, specific memories from a finished life slipped beyond consciousness. Body historians dropped into a new life with old lives repressed, except for the Edges, the first and last moments, or there'd be no space for new experiences. Damned serial amnesia was working my last nerve – getting me all caught up in patterns I didn't remember – or why else would I be too lazy for paranoia and morally outraged over a dog killed in self-defense?

Because at a certain point, you get tired of being a gig slut.

I couldn't tell if this thought was griot creed, from past lives, or from my current body. One thing I did remember – if you got too full of life, a historian could unravel into chaos, into a jumble of nothing. That wasn't going to happen to me. I made myself listen to the birds singing squabbles and love songs. Occasionally I heard a war.

Sharp mechanical sounds clashed with the nature music. Bells and whistles mashed together in nagging bursts. My new life was calling. I had to get on with it. Body historians, griots of the galaxy, we didn't diddle ourselves in jungle paradises, we inhabited flesh to gather a genealogy of life. We sought the story behind all the stories. Collecting life's dazzling permutations, however sweet or sour, was our science, religion, and art – nothing nobler in eternity. I peered in the direction of the nasty noise. At the south end of the mucky water where the trees thinned out, I saw a leather jacket, one sleeve inside out, flung across a signpost. The sign read: "Biohazard! No Trespassing!" in English with a vividly drawn skull dead centre.

Damn!

Everything hurt. I'd sat in the tree root throne for quite awhile. Stiff muscles and joints protested as I stood up. At least the ground stayed still and the sky didn't fall. I limped along the shore to the sign and jacket. A cell phone jangled in the breast pocket. I didn't want to answer, especially not knowing who I was or how I wanted to deal. And it seemed like I'd been hating phones for over a hundred years, but you got to start somewhere.

"What's up?" I said in full-throated mezzo irritation.

"If you got the hot sauce, I got the stew," a male basso said in Standard American English. I couldn't fix a more specific point of origin.

"Diablo sauce," I said without thinking. "Sets your mouth on fire."

"You get the recipe?"

"Yeah." I wanted him to mention my name, what I was supposed to be doing, where I was, but somehow I knew it wasn't the sort of operation you discussed on an open line.

"Twenty-six hours or we lose the bonus." His voice tickled the backs of my knees and under my arms. "You're almost inside the white circle. How you holding up?"

I looked at the bloody rag around my leg. Claw marks on my breasts raked over old scars. My hands slid across muscular thighs and buttocks, narrow ribcage and broad shoulders, to a big head sitting on not much neck. I tried to fill the sculpture of this woman. Something in me resisted, not her exactly, but.... Fingertips glided down high cheekbones, broad nose, and full lips to a blunt chin. The supple skin felt good. A middle-aged firebrand in great shape, scarred and battered here and there but.... "Nothing significant."

"You sound … tired."

Did he hear something in my voice or was this just code? "It's the heat, mostly."

"After the dinner rendezvous, can you handle an explosive situation?"

"I can handle anything, as long as the food's good." That seemed the right amount of bravado for this body. "How's the rest of the menu?"

"Out of this world." He chuckled, and the connection went dead.

I felt abandoned. Rubbing my cheek against the phone, I checked through the jacket pockets and found a few ammunition clips for the pistol, a purple beanbag lizard, a fountain pen/flashlight, two packets of extra-strength Frizz Ease, crushed sunglasses, menthol eucalyptus cough drops, and a slip of fortune cookie wisdom:

The Gods who were smiling at your birth are laughing now.

My lucky numbers were two, three, five, seven, eleven, thirteen – and somebody had scrawled "plus five backward."

No wallet, no name, and a pathetic bunch of random clues. I dumped one packet of Frizz Ease into my hair and worked my fingers through tight knots. The frizz didn't ease. Feeling vigilant at last, I scanned the trees for mechanical worms with camera heads. All I saw scurrying along the branches were furry black millipedes squirting stink gland poison at ants. A bug, smudge of mold, blade of grass – they were too simple for a griot drop-in, yet still compelling. The front-runner ants got a blast of lethal funk, curled up into balls, and fell out of the trees. The other ants kept marching forward. The millipedes' stink glands would be empty soon. I smiled. An eye trained on movement, a scientist hooked on bugs, an assassin with murder on the brain – how to read the signs of life and make a story? That was a griot's challenge. That's what I loved: being in a life, discovering the story, no matter how rough the ride.

The dogs had ripped my shirt to shreds, but putting on a jacket in heavy, no-breathing heat seemed mucho loco. The sleeves were several inches too long and an odd combination of black coconut oil and seaweed smells permeated the lining. The bugs having a party on my skin finally drove me inside the leather – at least until I knew what I was doing.

Surveying the area, I realized the swamp was actually flooded land in the oxbow of a stream, not a proper swamp. An endless relief of trees and water in every direction offered no perspective. Which way was the white circle and the damn rendezvous? From the marks in the ground at the Biohazard sign, I could see where my body had fought with the dogs. I traced the footprints to a narrow path that led north through the trees. At a flowering tree split by lightning so that it stooped over the path with innards exposed, I found a brown leather knapsack that matched the jacket. The straps were caught in scorched branches and dead vines. Here the footprint trails diverged. My host and the husky had dashed down the path until the two Dobermans jumped out of the bush, then we all high-tailed it to the water.

Thick white slugs, gorged with wounded tree flesh, oozed through black cracks in the bark, like pus. Looking at the charred trunk and boughs made old scars on my breasts and thighs throb. I stroked the mangled tree and disentangled the knapsack from split branches. It weighed almost forty pounds – heavier than I expected. In the top compartment I found a clean tee shirt, packets of dried fruit, which I gobbled down, and Soya Power Bars, which I saved for later, despite how hungry I was. Three bottles of Fluid Mineral Recharge, bug juice, antiseptics, and bandages made me feel well-prepared. The bug juice smelled like millipedes' stink glands. Remembering the curled-up ants, I sprayed myself liberally.

A thrill danced up and down my nerves as I pulled out a plastic map and an electronic compass. No aimless wandering – I had directions. I longed for a mirror to glimpse what I looked like this time. I took off the jacket and pulled on the tee shirt, which was way too big, then cleaned and bandaged my arm and leg. I splashed antiseptics on the rest of my wounds and squirmed at the sharp pains. One bottle of Recharge was all I'd allow myself before looking over the map. No global context, just local frames of reference – this was a map for somebody dealing in secrets. I wanted to find my way out of secrets. The oxbow and the path I stood on were marked in green. An arrow pointed beyond a "circle of death" and a "forest of ancestors" to "the final shore." I lingered over the map, memorizing its details and imaging the journey before folding it carefully and tucking it into my pants.

The main compartment's zipper snagged on threads from the seam, and after a few half-hearted tugs, I almost gave up. For someone hungry for clues, I was procrastinating, because I just knew.... One sharp tug ripped it open and revealed thin metal cylinders bundled in groups of twelve, each held together by what I guessed were timing devices.

A backpack of explosives with fancy detonators.

I didn't have to follow this body's terror story. I could rebel, invent a new scenario or....

A sound behind me, something splashing in the water, made me spin around, pull the pistol out of my pants, and throw myself to the ground. My raw skin screamed, but I ignored that and the acid sweat dripping into my eyes. In the distance, water sloshed against the swampy oxbow shore, vines swayed against one another, and a breeze in the treetops made spears of sunlight dance through the mist. Shadows played in shadows. The pistol shook in my hands and tears dribbled down my chin. I didn't want to go back and hunt for spooks. I wanted to move forward, get on with the Mission – mine and hers. Griots were storytellers, whatever the story. The detonators and explosives made my heart race. Now or nothing: experience this life, gather its secrets, or in the chaos of memories, cease to exist. I heaved the pack onto my back and started walking the route outlined in green on the map. If I only had twenty-six hours, I shouldn't waste time. There were worse things than being a terrorist, and I'd been them all.

⌒∿⌒

I tried not to think, just walk the trail. No underbrush kept me occupied, no wild animals came out to challenge me. All I had to do was put one foot in front of the other. Maybe it was the heat and swaying vines or the chemical haze that set me adrift, I couldn't say. My feet were still on the spongy ground, but I was lost in bits of memory – from the Edges.

I'd dropped into a tree once, somewhere cooler than this jungle. The first Edge was a sapling, shaken, uprooted, and stripped bare, then a canyon of memories too deep to reach, and finally I was a giant tree – nothing between me and the sky. I didn't have eyes, but I could drink a trillion points of light and stroke out the right vibrations, red and violet vibrations that sent excited electrons dancing with new partners. A gigawatt blast of lightning surged through my body, shattered my woody spine, and set me on fire. Miles of roots smoldered in the dirt. I fell over and burned to death in a rainstorm.

So many fires and storms.

I flashed on a hillside battlefield pummeled by balls of hail. A master samurai had run an enemy through with a sword. I dropped in the body, and his death wounds healed before the samurai's eyes. With hail cracking against my skull, I picked up a curved sword and swung it through the air at no one in particular. The samurai muttered a prayer and chopped off my demon head to make sure I stayed dead. He was safe. No griot could reclaim a body twice. We only got one dance.

"Yes, dance life!" an old priestess in a Sea Island village shouted. I can still feel her voice in my throat. "But if you trip and stumble, then sing life!" She danced down her gods, called them to ride her body, while she healed a sick child. Feet, hands, head, and belly moved to different beats, a polyrhythmic prayer that wore out her heart. With her last breath, she left her story behind, a blessing for the future. I dropped in, ready to ride clear, new flesh, but her last breath caught in my throat. She refused to leave, and we were stuck in one body – she at the edge of death and me on the verge of life. In the final moments, when I was on my way out, the priestess was still with me, a mad woman lost to herself, begging me to let her cross over, to let her be a song on the wind. Suiciding precious resources, I walked her into the sea, headed across the waves to the motherland, and the priestess blessed my future.

Even now, I was blessed with an ache of loneliness for her, for the healing we did: my cool hands on hot cheeks, on the soft heads of newborns pressing into the light; my strong hands clutching the dry fingers of an old man no longer afraid to die and grasping my granddaughter's sticky fingers when she pulled me close to whisper the secret of the tiny bird we'd rescued. "Iridescent hummers are the only ones who can fly backwards."

I stumbled, and the deep memory scattered. My brain was frying and so were my feet. The swampy smell was gone, and the sun blasted the blank earth from a white sky. Behind me the jungle was a thin swatch of black on the horizon. I pulled out the crushed sunglasses and cursed my laughing Gods. Not a sight, sound, or scent of life ahead of me. My nose and throat ached in the hot, dry air, and I could have used six bottles of Recharge. I scooped up a mound of white dirt, not sand. It blew away in my hands. A row of signs planted fifty feet apart warned me to turn around: "Biohazard! No Trespassing!" Still in English, but this time with an atomic symbol at the center. I wondered how contaminated I was.

To the west, where the jungle reached a claw into the white desert, an exploded van still smoldered. Déjà vu brought me up short. The person, the body I'd been before my current terrorist self couldn't be far, couldn't be long dead. Sifting through the fragments of my mind, I didn't find an Edge with an exploding van story. When very full, body historians remembered distant Edges better than one or two lives ago. I made a Mission detour to check out the site anyhow. Pieces of the driver and melted gear spiraled out from the wreck. Naked dog prints crisscrossed human boot shapes. Half of a purple beanbag lizard stared up at me with empty eye sockets. I stuffed the blind survivor in a pocket with the unscathed one. My lips trembled. Rescuing a half-dead toy made no sense.

A coconut-sized ball of mahogany fur tugged a chunk of human gore toward the trees. It paused to gnaw and chew. I didn't want to watch this meal, so I consulted the map. According to it, this expanse of white dirt should have been rainforest for many more miles. Not a root, bone, or fragment of life – whatever happened since the map was drawn had killed even the soil. Using the compass, I got myself back on the map's green path, moving across dead earth toward the 'forest of the ancestors.' I slipped a cough drop in my mouth and took a swig of Recharge. In the whiteness, I thought I would go blind.

The cell phone jangled in my breast pocket. When it hadn't stopped after ten chimes, I pulled it out and answered. "What's up?" I whispered, like somebody was spying on me.

"Renee, I got a message for you from deep time." A female answered, American contralto with inner city chop. She was breathless and hoarse. "Are you ready?"

So maybe I was Renee. "Who is this?"

"If you're alive again." She talked on top of me in a gurgling voice.

"What?" I walked faster. This barren landscape made me an easy target.

"Don't answer, just watch out for the landmines at the Edges of things."

"I think you've got the wrong...."

"Two, three, five, seven, eleven, and thirteen. Memories spilling out? Are you tired of dropping into lives and not committing to them? It's our choice, you know." She talked on top of me again, wheezing and chasing her words like they'd get away from her before she got everything said. "You're bouncing across the desert, a baby in your mother's arms, reaching for her breast, when she thought her little boy was already dead from whatever war does to babies. She couldn't bear to leave your tiny body behind and now you're alive again, a miracle in her arms. You feel her joy spurt hot milk onto your tongue. A taste you'll never forget."

Indeed I remembered a stream of sweetness and salty sweat from under her breasts, mixed with the tangy thrill of being a miracle in someone's arms.

"Of course you drop into the mother, she's so close, so deliciously complex. What griot could resist her story? The drop-in heals her shattered flesh and then you're running again, clutching a dead miracle against throbbing breasts." She paused. "You're a terrorist now, Axala."

"Axala?" I stopped so quickly, my muscles cramped. How could she know me when I didn't?

"A righteous murderer in a war that never makes the news. Griots of the galaxy dance in the dark. How long can we run around with dead miracles and do nothing? Amnesiacs – most of who we are, we don't even know. What good is the story behind all the stories if you never really get to live fully? Never your story...." The woman struggled for breath. "What am I saying? Look, I've gathered the griots in the forest for the rendezvous with the mother ship.... Follow the signs and don't get blown up by mines. Across the water and you're home." She'd talked herself out of a voice, just a gurgling wheeze.

"Who are you?" I walked a circle in white dirt. "How do you know...." A single note droned in my ear. A dead line. "Shit!" I said to the phone and turned it off. Rendezvous with the mother ship meant life on Earth was almost over.

My body didn't know enough to be scared of a voice from deep time, praise singing my former lives, questioning my future ones. For the Mission, my muscles ignored the weighty backpack and wounded leg, and shifted to top speed – as if racing through clouds of white dust would save me from a fucking griot minefield or human bombs buried in the ground. Part of me was dead certain there was nowhere to run except into a trap, but I ran until....

Crouching on the white expanse, sparkling like dragons with diamond-crusted backs, I saw purple beanbag lizards, red felt tongues dragging in the dust. Hundreds of them, a stop–action collage, crawling in my direction. Was this toy parade a joke? I considered stepping on one, but couldn't bring myself to crush its cheery face into the white dust. Moving carefully through them, nothing exploded under my feet. Markers. In a minefield, what more could you ask?

The barren plain slipped into a valley. I ran down to a skinny stream. Fractals of white dust swirled out from crumbling banks, occasionally clouding the middle. The opposite shore of the fast–moving water was brilliant green. In one bound, I crossed out of the circle of death back into jungle. Standing under a tiny waterfall tributary, I swallowed a stream. As I shook the water out of my ears, I thought I heard panting and footsteps behind me, but of course when I turned to look, nada. Somebody chasing me in the white wasteland would have been visible for miles. Fear made phantoms of wind and dust. I walked on.

Under the trees, I closed my eyes and savoured the cool darkness, the pungent odours of life and decay, the branches and vines drumming with the breeze. It felt like family gathering me into her bosom. After wandering for millennia, I was home. When I opened my eyes, a lanky man with a shaved head and a few days growth on chiseled cheeks stepped out of a vine–covered hole in an enormous trunk. Without a word, he yanked me inside the tree cave, put his rough hands over my lips, and nodded toward the direction I'd been heading. Squinting through a hole in an abandoned nest, I saw a squad of soldiers hacking through dense new growth 100 yards away. Somebody's private army and I knew they were gunning for us.

My companion and I crouched in the dark of the tree trunk and watched the squad cross the stream and walk up the side of the hill toward the minefield. We sat cramped against one another for several minutes, sweat and breath mingling, then explosions from the minefield knocked us on our faces.

"Dead," he sighed, "And we didn't even have to kill them." I recognized his voice, the dinner–rendezvous man. He patted the knapsack. "You're packing a lot of heat. Perez made the transfer. She give you the map, the code?"

I nodded, looking at myself in his deep–set eyes.

My mind flashed on another woman warrior blowing up her lover and herself in a tight spot like the tree cave, only outside was white hot, not cool green. She'd sacrificed herself to save her community from. . . .

"Hey, don't worry!"

I'd mumbled something upsetting. His hands hovered close to my cheeks. They exuded a damp heat and made the hair on my face stand on end. I closed my eyes, relaxed into his caress, feeling myself under his rough fingers. He jerked away from me.

"What's the matter?" I said without opening my eyes, pressing my face into his hand, my body against his.

"What are you doing?" He tried to pull away from me, but I sensed he didn't want to.

And I wouldn't let him go. "What do you *think* I'm doing?"

"It's been ... a long time." He was trembling.

I slid my hands along his smooth scalp. "Too long." The whisper of growth on his head made my fingertips ache. I sucked in a breath of him through nostrils burned and blistered from the white heat and chemicals. Even that didn't dampen the flow of passion.

"You miss my hair?" His voice tickled the inside of my thighs.

"I miss all of you." I undid his shirt to feel my face against the wiry hairs on his chest. His skin shivered and puckered under my lips.

He lifted my face toward his. "Look at me, Renee." I felt the words more than heard them, his chest vibrating mine, notes so low as to resonate backbone and heart. "Look at me."

A deep ache I didn't understand, something from his and Renee's past threatened to override my passion before I felt it. I opened my eyes slowly, not wanting to blur this moment with tears, Renee's tears or twice ten thousand years of. . . . "We don't have time for. . . ." He trailed off.

"I *am* looking at you." A weathered, moody face with high cheekbones, full lips, and prominent chin. For an instant, Renee's memories came so vividly to me.

The smell of jasmine incense filled a cramped apartment. An elevated train smashed through the night just beyond the window, shaking the floorboards under our naked bodies. Before the disaster in Juba ... I ran my fingers through thick black hair that fell below his shoulders. Sharp brown eyes smiled at me from under bushy brows raised in question.

"Is this what you like? Tell me. I want you to feel happy."

And Renee could say nothing to him. Too shy, too uncertain for words.

"You can still see all that?" he said, holding back tears.

I'd been talking again, without knowing what I was saying. "Of course."

"Is this what you want?" His words moved through my skin and opened me up, like a voice from deep time singing my code. I was flooded with ancient memories.

I had a horse's head, feet of a jaguar, leaves sprouted from my fingers, wings broke across my back, my mouth was in bloom, the kick of a machine gun bruised my ribs, I swallowed a harpoon, and sang with elephants on the stage of a great hall.

"I want your best self," I said and fell into him. Delicious images exploded across my body, yet I wasn't overwhelmed. He didn't mean to set me off. I was not who he expected at all, not his Renee. I was Axala, a griot from the stars, come for the story of life, now in the body of a dead terrorist. And who was he? What was his story? A new beard covered his coppery skin like morning frost. My fingers slid through the hard little hairs up to the lines that broke apart the edges of his eyes. I didn't care if this moment was a lie.

"Are you sure?" he murmured. "You're hurt." His fingers were tentative, careful. "There's no time…."

"We'll steal the time. This is what I want."

His lips nudged mine open. My body knew exactly what to do.

⚬⎋⚬

We snatched long moments out of nowhere and then –

"I'm not your Renee." He was still inside me when I said this. I felt his shock and embraced it. "I only remember bits and pieces of your Renee."

I flashed on Renee and her man, his long hair pulled tight against the skull, his face smooth. They were flattened against a rough wall, waiting for a blast in the village beyond, then they ran along a broken walkway.

"Blowing up shit … the only thing I ever got a chance to get good at," Renee shouted.

"Not the only thing," he argued.

"And I was gonna do something noble…." Renee muttered as they dropped into dung and mud for a second explosion. She closed her eyes on a stream of blood.

"Are you having one of your episodes?" He tried to pull away from me. I was stronger than he expected. "We don't have time for you to snap out."

What did he mean? He had offered me his best self. I wanted him to know my story. Body historians didn't usually reveal themselves or get involved, certainly not with pure natives. Just grab the dead miracles and run. Well, not any more.

"My name is Axala." I released him. "I'm from…." I didn't remember my specific griot life, before Earth. Damn serial amnesia. "Light-years from here…."

"Stop it!"

We stuck together where I had started bleeding again. I winced as he moved out of my body and rolled against a tree root arching up at the entranceway.

"You can't snap on me, not now, not on this job." He jerked his sweaty clothes back on his body. Clots of dirt clung to the hairs on his chest. "We could retire after this job."

"I'd like that." I wanted to wipe my blood off his stomach, do something, anything, instead of waiting for him to curse me out for playing games, going insane, fucking with him.

"You'd consider retiring, just living our lives, putting the shit behind us?" He sounded desperate.

"Look, I don't know how to be straight with you." I pulled on clothes. Cool, slimy bugs crawled across my ribs. "Some of Renee is still in me. She loves you." Stalling for time, I brushed away the bugs. They made Renee's skin crawl. "Despite … whatever … has happened between you."

"What hasn't happened? I don't know how much more I can take." He pressed himself further into the darkness of the tree, but I could still see his eyes, like the husky's eyes watching the wounds on my neck heal. A freak-show glare, foam at the corners of his mouth. I turned away, before he started howling.

"What I'm saying is … I know I can handle the memories. Everything I've been."

He shook his head. "But I can't handle all that."

"What do you mean?" I dug my fingers into the dirt. *The head of a whale breaching on a rocky beach, the hands of a samurai clutching a sword, the feet of a Maasai cow herd running from demons, the oxygen breath of an orange tree.… I was lost.*

"We don't have time for this." His voice found me. "Cut it!"

I moved close to him, felt his breath on my cheeks, smelled his sweat. We had the same smell now. That brought me back for a moment. "What's your name, tell me your name," I pleaded, wiping my blood off his stomach.

A stream of gibberish, a hundred tangled languages, gestures from around the world, from sequoias, bald eagles, deep-sea divers, hostages, and nuns, all broke out of me and I was nobody, flailing inside a tree. He grabbed my shoulders and shook me like an hysterical woman who could be jerked back to reality.

"We have a job to do, remember?"

I found Renee and held on. Twice ten thousand years of history wouldn't swallow me.

"I didn't screw myself." He stopped shaking me. Even in my anger, I could taste his best self. "I want to hear your name."

"All the fucked up things that happened to you aren't my fault, Renee."

"I know that."

"For years, you don't even let me touch you." His grip on my shoulder softened. "And now in the middle of a job … you come on so strong…."

I dragged him down in the dirt. It smelled of us, of lovemaking. "I just want to know your name, hear you say it."

"I lost my name after Juba … somewhere in the goddamned desert." He rubbed his hands against sweaty pants. "We don't have names, causes, just a price tag. We're gig sluts now. Not freedom fighters like in Juba, just terrorists for hire."

"Gig sluts?" I got a face full of sticky spider web and clawed it away. "Are you saying we're not committed to anything?"

"For a long time now." He spit web from his lips also. "From the Juba fiasco on, I did every crazy revenge thing you wanted."

"You don't think we're going to make it today, do you?" Inside the tree was getting claustrophobic.

"What difference if we do?" He stood up. "It just goes on and on…."

"Yes, yes, but it doesn't have to." I crawled over to my knapsack, to the griot Mission, a praise song to life. "You may be pointless. I am not."

"Oh, yeah? You're fine now?"

"On top of the world." I couldn't tell who was talking anymore. Axala, Renee, an angry tree….

"When you lost yourself before…." He picked up his bag. "The amnesia thing after Juba, after they … after they…." He couldn't say what *they* had done to me in Juba.

"It's not your fault," I murmured, sucking mucous down my throat and scratching my nose. "Let's get out of this hole. Do the job. I can't breathe."

He blocked my way. "In Juba when they jumped you, I hid in the back of the plant, where they'd stashed the stolen weapons. Listening. I didn't do anything!"

"What could you do?"

"They had guns, six of them. But I didn't even…."

I tried to wriggle past him. "So?"

"Don't interrupt me, let me say this!"

My mouth clamped shut.

"You never let me say this." He clutched at several stringy vines.

"Say it." I set my face hard to listen to what Renee didn't want to hear from him.

He was spread-eagled against the vine mass, silhouetted by pink twilight. "They had you. I was afraid. I should have done … anything. But I didn't want them on me too. I thought, please god, don't let her tell them I'm here, don't let them find me. You were screaming and screaming, but you told them nothing, then they gagged you, and I prayed, don't let them hurt me. Praying not for you, still just about me."

The scars on my breasts and thighs throbbed with old pain, but I couldn't see Juba, the story he told. Renee was suddenly desperate. She wanted to know. I balled up my fist and pounded his chest. "Tell me what I forgot."

"I can't," he whispered, fighting tears.

"You're all the memory I've got."

"I don't know what they did." He hung in the web of vines.

"Tell me what you know or I swear to god, I'll blow us up now." I pointed my pistol at the explosives in the knapsack. Several vines snapped from his weight and he staggered toward me. I pointed the pistol at him. For a moment Renee wanted to shoot him down like a dog, but I didn't. "Tell me."

"After they worked you over I remember you screaming my name … like a prayer, but you never betrayed me." He stared at the gun until I finally lowered it. "For a time you forgot everything, but if somebody touched you, it was the rape happening again." He looked far away though I was close enough to smell his fear. "Doctors said you might never remember. It was a miracle you got out alive."

"You call that a miracle?" My voice was hollow. I felt like a spirit unhinged, floating above this body.

"Your mind came back without those memories, but you couldn't stand to be touched – until now." He shivered. "I would have told them anything, but you…."

He waited for me to say something. He pleaded with his eyes, with all the tiny muscles of his face for contempt, forgiveness, something. I teetered at the edge of chaos, vertigo claiming my senses. "I gotta get out of this hole, now." I pushed through him and the vines. The air outside was a welcome relief. I drew myself back into Renee's flesh. The sun had disappeared behind distant hills. Birds sang love suites and battle sonatas. I took out a Soya Power Bar and chewed at it furiously.

After a few moments he emerged from the tree, mumbling something about the Perez woman and the damn Mission. I forced myself to listen. "Blowing up a bunch of trees. She could've done this bizarre shit herself."

Shop talk. I could do that too. "Perez is a biologist or something. These trees are old souls, a couple thousand years even. Maybe Perez didn't have the heart to blast millennia of living into nothing."

He stared at me. "You sounded like her just now. That was exactly her little speech, when she hired us."

I shrugged. "Good memory."

"You weren't there."

"You told me."

"Right. But you sounded *just like her.*"

"Your mind is playing tricks on you. How could I sound just like Perez?" Unless I'd been her, but I couldn't share that suspicion with him.

"Of course." Methodically, he pulled explosives out of my pack, fussed over detonators, and every hundred feet buried a bundle in the roots of a giant tree. He didn't ask for my assistance and I didn't offer. So much history behind and between people, one moment was always a nasty echo of another time, most of who you were already scripted. That was Renee. Axala was outside of history, dropping in for samples, but not really taking part. Not committing to the lives she became. More of a gig slut than Renee could ever be. And sick to death of it.

"Are you setting us up?" He looked up from the last detonator, hand on his pistol, eyes frantic. "You and Perez, setting me up? Some kind of final revenge?"

"What are you talking about?"

He stared at me, fighting with something inside himself. I touched his hand. "Sorry. You'd lay down your life for me, I know that. I'm just being paranoid." He brushed his lips across my damp palm and headed for the dense new growth beyond the trees. "You got the map to 'the final shore'?"

"Like I told you." I started after him, but stumbled over roots and fell back against a tree. The impact knocked the wind out of me, slapped my brain against its skull, and I lay a moment plastered against smooth bark, seeing stars.

"What's the matter? Come on!"

I couldn't speak or move. The tree wouldn't let me go. It snagged me in a magnetic field, lined up my electrons, and started generating current. Energy rushed from my toes out through the fuzzy ends of my hair, like a lightning bolt sparking into the ground. The tree was a body historian, this rain forest, a jungle of galactic griots, roots intertwining underground, branches interwoven above, and their fields all lined up. Perez had gathered all the griots in the forest! I was in the home grove, the bosom of family, connected to deep time, praise singing life. All of our griot experiences, a polyphony of memories rushed through me. Together the trees and I made meaning and broadcast twice ten thousand years, the incredible story of life on Earth out to the stars. Imbedded in this polyrhythmic history, I remembered everything, the story I'd become. Axala of Earth.

Renee's man watched my hair catch fire and my hands and feet turn white–hot. I saw myself in his eyes. I heard his voice rumble out a warning, a prayer, I didn't know which. His body was a blur of impulses – his legs tearing away from me, his hands reaching for mine. I wanted to share the spectacle of Earth with him, despite the danger, but I couldn't move the inches it would take to touch him. I was caught in deep time, with all the ancestors walking through my body, making sense of the present moment from so many gone by. I felt the mother ship leave the shores of our birth world to wander through star systems and collect the genealogy of life in the galaxy. We body historians were a Diaspora of ghosts living only in borrowed bodies, collecting the wisdom of others, slaves to their appetites, lost to ourselves. After twice ten thousand years on this watery outpost, we were so full of life, the past broke out all over us. Earth had made us aliens to our former selves. We had no desire to be spirits in perpetual exile; we longed to make Earth our story.

I heard the reply of the mother ship, as it gathered the polyphony of memories we broadcast. Renee's man grabbed my hand. I risked his life and my griot existence and channeled our field into him. The praise song we made of his world passed through his body. He knew my story. What he made of griot longing, our love, I couldn't say, but his mouth was in bloom, wings broke out on his back; he sang on the stage of a great hall surrounded by elephants and sequoias, and he carried me to safety:

In Juba, Renee's man, a coward who had abandoned her, who trembled in the shadows while six terrorists violated her, fell on his face at the first explosion. The terrorists scattered past him, grabbing more weapons and screaming. After the second explosion he crawled toward Renee. When he reached her, she was barely breathing. He scooped up her broken body and carried her through the desert to safety, certain he was too late. Certain she had died in his arms. Everybody said it was a miracle she got out alive. And he was a hero.

A terrible ache for cowards and heroes passed amongst all the griots. We grieved for the lives we had collected, for the Earth beings we had studied and become. Embodying wisdom was our art, science, and religion. Yet endless new adventures on distant planets no longer excited our old souls. After eons of wandering, of losing ourselves again and again, we griots longed to make these beautiful and painful memories, this particular world, this Earth home. How would we bear a final death and the desolate flight to yet another star after being ripped from the body of our beloved Earth?

Large projectiles slammed into the tree. Its crown crashed into neighbouring trees, slicing away branches and vines. Renee's man cried out in pain. In an instant the magnetic web connecting the jungle of body historians was broken, and the light went out of my eyes. My hair fell in ashes to the ground. I slid down the trunk, my limbs locked, my backbone frozen. I thought I would die, once and for all.

"I can't move," I murmured.

Renee's man covered my body with his. A charred mercenary charged down the path from the minefield. She hadn't stepped on a beanbag lizard and exploded. Falling branches knocked a massive weapon from her hands and ripped flesh from her face. She pulled out a handgun.

"Jay Silver Feather," he whispered in my ear as he stood up to run toward her. His name. My stiff body rolled against his feet, and he stumbled down to one knee. He fired several shots and my ears stopped hearing, but the lock on my muscles eased.

This body for his life, it seemed fair.

I was trying to stand up in the line of fire when bullets smashed in one side of his chest and out the other. He fell down on me again in a river of blood. The rainforest screamed, all the griots calling his name. I couldn't move.

"Jay Silver Feather," I whispered. Cold and shivering, he put his arms around me, around his Renee. "Your great–grandfather was a Seminole, a black Indian, and he told you swamp stories, about stealing slaves into freedom, hiding with trees, making new world communities from the swamps to … across the border, and never letting white folks catch you at anything. He called you his Silver Feather, because you had a spirit that nobody could beat down. I remember your stories, even if I didn't live them. Your spirit is safe with me."

Jay, his eyes a burst of light, smiled at me, Axala/Renee, and then his head lulled against my shoulder. I listened carefully to his last breaths. The mercenary stood over us with a gun at my temples, telling me to get up or die on the ground, because it didn't matter to her. Perez wanted us alive, but it didn't have to be that way if I had some crazy cowboy notion.

"My limbs are paralyzed."

Perez hired Jay and me, Perez hired her. Neat. Another gig slut like all of us. I couldn't even hate her. "Kill me here. Kill me now. Get it over with." I started singing a Seminole song for Jay.

"Stop that singing." She kicked Jay's gun out of reach and stepped back to consider my twisted limbs. "Paralyzed? Cut the crap. A trick like that won't work on me."

It was a huge branch, but she never saw it coming. She never had time to be shocked by death. A few inches to the right and the bough of the tree would have flattened me as well. But I was so lucky.

Jay's body leaned against my chest, the fuzz on his head soothing my cheeks. I waited for him or the mercenary woman to come back to life. But the griot tree she had blasted was only wounded. There was no free body historian to drop into their lives – not enough luck for that. And then I wasn't waiting for them to come back to life. It was too late anyhow. Sitting on bloody ground, separated from the griot family and no longer remembering everything, I didn't know what to do. My eyes settled on the detonator in Jay's bag, the one connected to the bombs nestled in our roots. Grief overwhelmed me, muddled my impulses. Maybe I should just blow up the forest of ancestors, and we griots could fly back to the mother ship and be done with Earth. That was Renee and Axala's Mission, after all.

cℵ∂

The husky found me sleeping on the ground between two dead bodies. He licked my face awake. A spark of energy passed between us, then he stepped back while I sputtered and wiped his doggy spit into my shirt. It was night. The moon was up, almost full in a cloudless sky. The chilly air forced me back inside the jacket. The husky grumble–growled, but didn't frighten me. A griot spirit on his way to the rendezvous had dropped into the dog I shot. He was the shadow that had tracked me. Every body historian was present and accounted for. Perez had managed to collect us all. I reached out my arms, and the husky ran toward me, his silver hair and ice blue eyes easy to catch in the moonlight. Why couldn't it have been Jay come back to life? I buried my face in the dog's fur. A deep rumble in his chest soothed me. I pulled myself up and caressed the tree, hoping to re–establish a connection with the other griots. Nada. These crotchety old giants were waiting to see what I'd do since I could move again. They had shared their insights and feelings, written truth on my body. We were one story now, and the choice of ending was up to me. An endless quest or committing to Earth?

Renee didn't want to go anywhere, but if nothing else, Axala would see where Perez's Mission took us. I checked Jay's watch. We had six hours. I drank the last two bottles of Recharge and scanned the map with my fountain pen flashlight. The dog looked over my shoulder, panting in my ears. I gazed into his intelligent eyes and wondered at the Earth lives he'd led. Dogs couldn't talk but....

The husky/griot guided me through the night to my destination.

The sun had been up several hours when I stood at "the final shore." Other eyes would have seen only a shallow pond, a rocky hillside, and a plain covered by enormous satellite dishes, radio telescopes listening to deep space for extra–terrestrial intelligence. I knew they were soul collectors, ready to transport griots to the mother ship when I blew up the forest of ancestors. Cut off from other complex life forms by the lifeless white desert, no griot would be enticed by a dying body to stay on Earth. Shattering the tree bodies, snuffing out a trillion points of light would release all the body historians to the stars. The mother ship would catch us on a beam of light. An elegant plan. I should have rejoiced at the approaching rendezvous, but I felt listless, a sleepwalker waking up from a journey of bad dreams.

The husky stood on hind legs and tapped his nose against a portal set in the hillside. It rolled open, and he trotted inside. No private army prevented me from walking behind him. Inside was dim and cool: concrete, metal, and plastic held the jungle at bay. I could have been in any office/ science installation in the world. The husky led me through an empty security station to a door labelled "control room." It was unlocked but the hinges wouldn't budge. I squirted my last packet of Frizz Ease on the rusty metal, and the door opened with a touch.

The strong smell of black coconut didn't surprise me, nor did the clutter of video monitors, computers, and receivers. A photo of a fifty-something woman with wiry grey hair, light brown skin, and high cheekbones drew me to what I surmised was the main workstation. The woman wore a leather jacket, carried a matching knapsack, and was hugging a husky. The back of the photo read: "Crystal and Max up North." I sat down. Several purple lizards grinned at me from atop a coffee machine. Shells, seaweed, and green memo-paper with "From the desk of Dr Crystal Perez" were scattered everywhere. Her handwriting was unreadable except for EXOBIOLOGY in block letters. I crumpled up the notes and let my head drop onto the desk. Using biotech weapons and nuclear death, Dr Perez had corralled the griots of the galaxy into the forest of the ancestors, making ready to send us home.

The husky shoved his cold nose against my neck. I sat up. Beside me, a computer monitor blinked, asking for someone to press ESCAPE to execute or ENTER for abort. The program was labelled with the first six prime numbers. One simple key, ESCAPE, and I could blow the jungle of griots and twice ten thousand years of living sky-high. Jammed with poignant memories of Earth, we'd ride long radio waves back out to the mother ship. Dr Crystal Perez stared at me from snowy hills up north and waited. I turned her picture face down.

The phone in my jacket pocket jangled. I answered it after one ring. I knew who it would be. "Yeah?"

"Renee? Tell me you're alive again. Tell me the numbers." A hoarse, gurgling voice near death.

I didn't say anything.

"Renee? Tell me you're alive again. Tell me the numbers." It was a recording, asking for the code.

When it repeated for the third time, I answered. "I'm alive again. Two, three, five, seven, eleven, thirteen." The first six prime numbers.

Silence for a moment, like the machine was waiting for something else.

"Thirteen, ninety-two, thirty-two, ninety-one, seventy-one." Remembering the handwritten scrawl, I quickly added the next five primes as backwards as I could.

The entire control room came alive, whirring and hissing. The husky banged his paws against the bottom row of monitors as a close-up from a videotape dated yesterday popped on.

"This is Axala." The wheezing contralto spoke from Dr Perez's body. Crumpled up by a smoldering van at the edge of the white desert, she recorded this message as life slipped away from her. "I don't know what to tell you." She sputtered. "A year into Crystal Perez and deep memories, not just Edges started breaking out."

"A year? Deep memory started breaking out of Renee the first hour...." I muttered.

"The griots were getting too full and ... I thought I had it all figured out," Perez/Axala continued.

"Oh yeah?" I walked from the desk over to the monitors to confront the image.

"None of the griots wanted to leave this planet, but that always happens. You leave anyhow." Perez/Axala coughed and spit something out of the frame. "But even I couldn't do it, couldn't separate us from the body of Earth, couldn't send us on our endless journey. I just didn't have the heart to blast millennia of living into nothing."

I gasped at the words I had spoken to Jay.

"So...." The sun made her eyes look white. She closed them slowly and gathered her last few breaths. "So I hired Jay and Renee to explode me and the tree griots, and release us all from life on Earth."

The map, the lizards, the guards blown up. An inside job to kill yourself and get back to the mother ship.

"Renee surprised me. Blew up the van before I was ready ... when Max and I got out to pee. Max didn't like that. Chased her down."

Renee probably thought the good doctor would double-cross her.

"Perez's body is almost finished." Perez/Axala opened her eyes and squinted at something off camera. "And from what I can see, Max is chewing up Renee, so...." She looked right into my eyes. "I guess I'm talking to myself." Axala had jumped into Renee.

"Each body changes us. We are the sum of all the bodies we have joined," I said out loud. "I'm not the same Axala that you were."

On a second row of video screens, the husky lunged at Renee's throat. The metal worms with camera eyes captured their fatal encounter from every angle. I switched off the screens just as he would have ripped her throat out.

"One last blast and we body historians are free to download the burden of Earth and start again." Perez/Axala chased after her words, hoping to get everything said before it was too late. "You can release the griots and get to the mother ship or...." She looked away from me, at the ruin of her body.

"Or stay.... And what the hell will that be?" I argued out loud with the ghost on the screen, with the body I had been yesterday. "If we don't blow up shit and run away to the stars.... What the hell do we do here?"

"A great mystery. It's up to you." Perez/Axala fell against a purple lizard and her image exploded on nineteen monitors, but one screen froze on a close-up, as Axala dropped out of Perez and into Renee. I had never seen myself abandon a body, never looked back at a finished life, always rushing to the next body.... I switched off the monitors.

Jay's watch had run down to a row of zeroes. Rendezvous time. The mother ship was calling. I stumbled back into the chair at Perez's workstation. Max put his head in my lap, his chest rumbled, his eyes searched mine. My left hand hovered over ESCAPE – one touch would blast us to the mother ship. Two right hand fingers rested on ENTER – one touch and we were Earthbound. Paralyzed, I flashed on the forest of ancestors holding Jay and me, on hot milk flowing, humming birds flying backwards, Jay inside of me, and miles of roots holding up a mountain. After twice ten thousand years I wanted to do something impossible, something noble. Instead of chasing down infinity, we could contribute our souls to Earth. A blessing on this future, not now or nothing. The voice and the body and the history.

Axala of Earth.

ENTER

Suzette Mayr *is the author of two novels,* Moon Honey *and* The Widows, *and a poetry chapbook entitled* Zebra Talk. The Widows *was shortlisted for the 1998 Commonwealth Prize Best Book in the Canada-Caribbean region and was translated into German. Her third novel is being published by Arsenal Pulp Press in 2004. She lives and works in Calgary.*

֍

Toot Sweet Matricia

Suzette Mayr

The legend goes like this:

A lazy horny fisherman, classy as a goat and smelling as good, finds what he thinks is a seal skin. This fisherman is not very clever – no one on land would ever marry him.

These are the rules.

The selkie sunbathes naked on the rocks; her skin tucked away in what she thinks is a good hiding place. The fisherman hides the seal skin from her, and the selkie is forced to be his wife.

The selkie makes a wistful but loyal wife and no one in the neighbourhood asks questions. She dutifully suckles her babies, her husband, but her eye is always on the sea, or the lake, or the plastic swimming pool, or the goldfish bowl where Darth Vader, the 75-cent feeder goldfish, blows "I love you" over and over.

Her two-year-old's fingerprinted glass of lemonade makes her so homesick she wants to puke. All her children and her children's children have webbed fingers and toes.

But the day comes when the selkie decides to give all the clothes in the attic to the Salvation Army, or sweep up the mouse turds in the basement once and for all, or clean out the ancient dirt in the upstairs closet, and then she finds the trunk, or the canvas sack, or the plastic Safeway bag and inside, where her husband's hidden it, her selkie's skin. Suddenly she's gone out to her yoga lesson and strangely enough forgotten her yoga mat.

The horror is, she never looks back.

Crueler men burn the skins. These wives are doomed. Prozac, scotch on the rocks, varicose vein strippings, house renovations, feigned and real illnesses can't stop the mourning, the inner burning. These are the kinds of wives who one day set their houses on fire with themselves inside, or in a matter of hours turn into lesbians, or slash themselves with their husband's razors just so they feel something.

৩৬

I feel something.

Putting on the skin when it's not really yours is like putting both arms into a bog and drawing up pieces of corpse. Ring fingers still wearing rings, arms, palms, and hands (these are harder to identify), legs severed at calf and mid-thigh. I have found no heads yet, not yet felt the horror of hair twine around my fingers, the yawn of a mouth, a thick flapping tongue. Body bits perfectly preserved.

I look in the mirror at the skin around my shoulders, draped over my head. I look like my grandmother.

Matricia said that with the chemical straightener, my hair felt like the strings on the bow of her violin. The afro roots of my hair winding and colliding from my scalp, the straightened ends down my shoulders, dry and crisp as winter twigs. She fingered and stroked my hair, buried her hands in its coils while I kissed her breasts. I tugged at her nipples with my teeth through the layers of her sweater, her blouse, her bra. Her armpits seaweed-fragrant.

Her body smells like perfume and sweat. Matricia is a very black woman, much blacker than me, her hair scraped back from her face and into an elaborate coil, and I picture the excruciating smoothness of her inner thighs. I dragged her up piece by piece from the bogs of memory and horror. The smell of her. The smell of her hair and my skin.

৩৬

I try to lose myself to the river by filling my pockets with stones from my mother's rock garden.

You'll only rip the seams of the pockets, my sister says. It'll never work.

Detergent foam, empty pop cans, floating cigarette butts swirl around my ankles. The denim of my jeans sucks at my thighs.

Don't think you're getting out of washing the dishes! my sister calls.

∾

I smell tears; they smell the same as water–fear. That horrifying lurch when my head is pulled under and a long fluid gasp fills my lungs. My mother drags my sputtering body through unnaturally bright pool water, and when she lets go I sink and inhale the water like rose petals. For years we did this every Sunday, she teaching me how to swim, me foundering, flailing, my hair afroed from my head in all directions, dry even under water and strung–out from chlorine, my eyes bitter–red and bulging.

I have watched too many television documentaries about the *Titanic*. This is why I hate the water. The documentaries never show the body remains; pieces of bodies just outside the picture, inedible chunks of skull, the flat, silver eyes of fish ogling the newly sunk banquet, the flat, silver lips shredding and tearing away at the sad skin under the soaked fabric, the taut necks, the soft flesh of human bellies. The camera focuses instead on a well-preserved shoe. A barnacled chandelier. A brooch filled with hair in the shape of flowers.

The TV camera never shows the people who live where the *Titanic* sank. The ones who stare up through the water's surface with the faces of the drowned, the ones who crunch through bones like sharks.

I look into a cup of tea and see my eyes flat, silvered with salt–water cataracts. Submersion, immersion, mouth an open, wavering cavity. There is even danger in dish–water. Drowned angry children hissing through the drains sing me to sleep.

∾

The water licks and licks at my sister's boots. Every step she takes swirls whirlpools. My body floats face–down in the river, stopped by the branches of trees caught on my clothes. The stones in my pockets don't hold me down.

You can stop faking it, my sister says.

She watches my blue lips sputter awake when the paramedic with prematurely grey hairs in his nose gives me mouth–to–mouth.

He's gay, you dummy, she says. He's gayer than Paree.

A year later, I marry the paramedic. On our wedding night at the Royal

Wayne Hotel, he pushes the skin away and says, Phew! That reeks!

I get up from the bed and pretend to steal another motel soap. When you have webs between your fingers, you can't cry.

⌘

And what if you are the kind of woman who slips from world to world, slides through sewers and between the walls, propelled by will alone? This is not just a metaphor for a black woman with a white father, a lesbian who likes a little cock now and then, a vegetarian who craves Alberta beef. This is a question of heredity.

If you are the kind of woman who slips from world to world, slides through sewers and between the walls, propelled by will alone, the more you travel the in-betweens, the more you play an either/or tourist, the more you realize home was never really home.

⌘

When Matricia reached the shore, pulled her blubbered body up onto the jagged rocks, she peeled off her skin. Not like a banana because you can't peel banana skin back on. More like the ripping of a membrane, a hymen; a hymen can be unripped. Her skin tears from her body; the grey silver black speckles of her slick skin rip away like so much sausage pelt and there she stands. Her black skin, not black like coal or chocolate or velvet, her black skin, black.

Matricia pulls on her pants-suit and Italian shoes. Tucks her skin in her bag. My blackness in the middle of the white prairie makes me an easy target. My marriage, job are water-soaked; panic flush, slip of fingers, suck of whirlpool. Vulnerable desire.

Matricia paints her nails algae green.

⌘

But then there are the other women in my family.

Never before in the history of this family, says my grandmother, have the women had to fake orgasms.

My grandmother strokes the scaly patch of skin on her wrist. The scales glitter like seed-pearls, scratch like sand-paper against our faces. She also has scales behind her ears, in the small of her back.

Eczema, says my mother. She will not believe anything not in the science books.

Selkie blood, says my grandmother, and she lights another cigarette, her mouth pursed fish–like against the paper tube.

Of course, my mother won't believe this either. There's no ocean where she comes from. She was born in Saskatchewan. Grandmother's skin is the colour of the teak coffee table.

The scaly patches prove love, my grandmother says.

What they never talk about in that selkie story, says my grandmother, is the bed. How important the bed is. If the man's nonexistent in bed, then why would you stay?

According to the rules, if my grandmother, being a selkie, ever retrieved the skin, she would leave immediately. But she's the one who left the water, saw the liquid muscles of her future lover's forearms, the silver bubbles trapped among the hairs. Watched her fisherman up through the waves and fell in love with the vibrations in his throat, the cracked skin on his fisherman's hands. And he stared back at her in water, couldn't believe his eyes.

Mixed marriages never work, people say, but my grandmother stumbled up into air, her addiction to cigarettes and wearing men's trousers more a problem than the fact that she enjoyed her fish still gasping. Scales, gut, and open fish mouth pulled down her throat.

Toot sweet, she says, and smacks her lips.

She kept her skin like a wedding gown wrapped muslin, stored in cedar to keep away the bugs. Kept the key on a chain around her throat and as far as we could tell, never opened the chest again for as long as she lived.

I, on the other hand, open her chest again. And again. And again.

⌀

Matricia slides in and around and among the neighbourhoods like a crocodile in a sewer looking for me. Too much time in the world and she looks at her watch.

Matricia comes for me. She smells exactly like the ocean.

We were the only two black kids in the junior high school, Matricia and I, and then her father kidnapped her and I was the only one. Or so the legend went.

The legend goes like this: We are the only two black girls in the school. Matricia wants to be my friend, but this is against the rules. I ignore her. She disappears. Her father stole her, everyone says. My horror mouth open because I didn't save her. I remember the dandruff flecks in her hair, the green tinge on her fingernails, the seaweed smell of her skin.

⌀

I will eventually be kidnapped by water for good. This is how all women in my family die. When the water finds me, when it inflates my lungs, it will be crammed with the faces of drowned relatives. Women in our family avoid river banks, cliffs, wave pools, backyard fish ponds, sinks too full of water, they move to the centre of islands, high on mountains, buy dishwashers, but water always finds us.

I am not safe anywhere.

I kick my rubber boots hard against the polished floor of the museum, the security guards run, their basset-hound jowls and full bellies bouncing, navy-blue security jackets streaming past glass cases, marbles of naked women, paintings of ornate gardens, and they try to grab me by the collar of my shirt, my sleeves and legs, try to pull me from the canvas-painted oily storm. I will hang in the water for hours before they can retrieve my body. My pockets filled with priceless, deformed pearls.

I die for love. Matricia, body sleek in waves. I die for love.

ᐤ

Her skin is the same. Her skin is the same as mine. She is my ghost. Digging for treasure, I found mismatched pieces, assembled and resuscitated her. She tastes like licorice. Water beings always have the faint aftertaste of licorice. I have tasted licorice myself on their lips when they come up from between my thighs to kiss me.

.   ᐤ

I wanted to steal her skin. Force her to marry me.

ᐤ

When Matricia left, I got up from my bed and pretended to steal another motel soap.

They say fish never blink; selkies don't cry. I wait for the diamonds to come trickling from my eyes. I have not been a maid since I was sixteen and she stole my maidenhead.

In love with the ocean through my rubber boats.

Asthma returns with a splash on the cheek. I am allergic to hairy animals. This is how I know she is for real.

And how girls can say *No Thanks* from the safety of their mermaids' tails or selkie skins. Dust sifts through the air. A desire for the parts of other women. Skin brown even in the womb, eyes grey until they ripen into Caribbean brown. An appetite for other women. I pull her up piece by piece from the muck and memory. Assemble her into the ex-lover who gave the clothes to the Salvation Army, swept up the mouse turds, cleaned out the closet, who left with my heart in the trunk. Of her car. She comes to life in the prairies, in the murky river that drowns prize begonias.

Toot sweet Matricia. I stretch my lips and blow.

Larissa Lai *was born in La Jolla, California, grew up in Newfoundland, and lived and worked in Vancouver. Her first novel,* When Fox Is a Thousand *(Press Gang, 1995), was shortlisted for the Chapters/*Books in Canada *First Novel Award. She has an MA in Creative Writing from the University of East Anglia in Norwich, England, and is working on a PhD at the University of Calgary. Her second novel,* Salt Fish Girl *(Thomas Allen Publishers, 2002) was shortlisted for the Sunburst Award, the Tiptree Award, and the W. O. Mitchell Award. In 2003, TVO's Imprint named her one the Top Ten Writers to Watch Under 40. Arsenal Pulp Press will release a new edition of* When Fox Is A Thousand *in 2004.*

∽

Rachel

Larissa Lai

When the policeman says I'm cold, my father tells him about the figure skating accident. "She was a beautiful skater. She could execute a perfect quadruple lutz by the time she was thirteen. But the previous skater had really worked over the ice. It was perilously uneven before Rachel ever set foot on it. Or should I say blade."

"In short, I fell," I tell him. I eye the officer nervously. My father doesn't trust policemen and neither do I.

"And you hit your head," the policeman says, evenly. I can't tell whether or not he is being sarcastic. His speech is steady and uninflected.

"Yes, officer," I say. "On the ice. It knocked me out cold."

"She was an extraordinarily emotive child before that," my father says. "Her mother is Chinese, and very circumspect. And I'm a man of science myself. I don't know where her passion came from. Or where it went. But doctors say this happens sometimes."

53

"I don't know where it went myself," I say, somewhat earnestly. "But it's gone. That's for sure."

I don't want to take the test, but my father and I had agreed beforehand that I should. That I would. And that I should volunteer before the policeman asked, so there would be no question of coercion. I hadn't expected to feel nervous. There is nothing to be nervous about. My father is here. I know who I am. There is no question of failing.

I sit down opposite the policeman at the long table and let him shine his nasty light into my eye. I can feel him scrutinizing me. There is something about him that stirs me in a way I can't describe. It's not exactly pleasant.

"You're given a calf skin wallet for your birthday," he says. The test has begun.

"I'd return it," I say. Since 2017 it's been illegal to slaughter any living thing on Earth. "Also, I'd report the person who gave it to me."

✺

My childhood memories are extraordinarily vivid. I remember my mother giving me an empty egg box one day when I was playing in the sand. I filled the box with sand and packed it down tight. When I turned it over there were two neat rows of six identical little houses with round tops. I imagined that if I were really small, I could stroll the alleyways between them.

I remember piano lessons. I was never very good at music, but it was something my mother valued a great deal, so I made the effort. Recitals made me terribly nervous. When I had to get up to play, I'd be shaking so badly I could barely hit the keys. I played at a tremendous speed with no attention at all to feeling or dynamics. My mother told people I played beautifully at home. I don't remember that, but that's how memory works, isn't it? Selectively.

I liked to dress up. I remember once making an elaborate Indian Princess costume which I wore for the Halloween dress-up contest at school. I brushed my long black hair straight and darkened my skin with cocoa powder mixed with water. I expected to win, since all the other kids wore costumes that were obviously store-bought. I was devastated when the boy in the Darth Vader mask won. It seemed the teachers placed no value whatsoever on creativity and imagination.

✺

"You are reading a magazine and you come across a picture of a naked woman. You show it to your husband and he likes it so much he wants to hang it in your bedroom."

"Is this testing whether I'm a replicant or a lesbian, sir?" The question annoys me. I am now sure that I don't like the policeman. Or his test. There is a subtext to it I don't understand. Is he coming on to me, or does he know something about me that I don't? I want to look at my father but I don't dare.

When the test is over, I am inexplicably angry. At my father or at the policeman, I'm not sure. What I want more than anything is to see my mother, but she died shortly after my skating accident. I remember little about her death. My father says I've repressed it because it was so traumatic. He says when I'm older, I can have hypnosis therapy to try and retrieve the memories. Right now all I know is that I miss her. I get up from the long table and leave the room quickly, rudely. I don't care. I just want to get to the music room where there is a large portrait of my mother over the piano.

But I am still within earshot when I hear the policeman say, "How can it not know what it is?"

ᴄⱴᴏ

How can it not know what it is? I barely heard the words, but now I can't stop them from echoing in my head. I have failed. My father has been lying to me. But how much? I run to the music room and sit down at the piano. It is the one place where I feel most comfortable. Or should I say it is the one place where I feel closest to my mother. I try playing the most famous of Schumann's *Songs from Childhood*, the sweet, sad *Traumerei*. It uses four octaves at once and requires large hands, but mine are small. It was my mother's favourite piece. I love it too, but she always complained that my rendition was too mechanical.

Playing comforts me. I don't know if I'm playing well, but I play the piece over and over until my fingers ache.

My father had first seen my mother in a catalogue of women in China who wanted to marry Western men. He said he liked her sad eyes. They began a correspondence and fell in love. After six months she agreed to marry him. He went to Shanghai and paid for her to fly down from her small northern Chinese village. They were married a week after they first met. Sepia photographs of the wedding, framed in elaborate pewter, adorn the music room. They could easily have taken colour photographs, or holographic ones for that matter, but my mother was the nostalgic, sentimental sort, and sepia was all the rage in fashionable Shanghai at the time of their marriage. There are also sepia photographs of me and my brother on the walls and the sideboards: playing in the yard at our New England house, running on the beach during a holiday in Southern California, screaming during the sudden drop of a rollercoaster at Disneyland.

My brother died at the same time as my mother. I think it's strange that I don't remember what happened. My father says that the memories will return in time, and that I should tell him when they do so he can help me through the process of mourning. But it's been five years and I still don't remember a thing.

It comforts me to be surrounded by these photographs, these certain memories. *How can it not know what it is?* Whose memories are these?

I can't think of myself as one of them. *Replicants like photographs,* the policeman had said. Did my mother put these photographs here, or did I?

I must have fallen asleep while playing because I don't hear my father enter the room. He is not a sentimental man, and he says nothing to comfort me, though he does put his hand on my shoulder.

"Rachel," he says. "I want you to offer the policeman your help. I think you can be of service to him."

"No," I say. "Don't you know what you're asking of me?"

"Please do as I ask, child," he says. "One of the escaped androids is the same model as you. You could really make a difference." He gives me a set of photographs, not nostalgic, sepia-stained images, but holographic cards identifying the escaped replicants. He turns abruptly and leaves the room.

My cheeks are wet. It is the first time I've cried since my mother and brother died.

⚘

The policeman calls me from a sleazy bar near Chinatown. He looks a little drunk on the vidphone screen, and I detect self-loathing behind his impenetrable eyes.

"I'm at Taffy Lewis's," he says. "Why don't you come down and join me for a drink?" There is a lot of movement in the background behind him.

"That's not my kind of place," I say. Right now I hate him more than anyone. I turn off the vidphone without saying goodbye, and go upstairs to bed.

⚘

I can't sleep. As the night progresses, the object of my fury slowly moves from the policeman to my father. At around three, our artificial owl flies past my window. I see its dark shape and hear the rapid pulse of air and feathers. I don't know what my father is playing at. I have to know what the policeman knows. I go downstairs and dial the police station on the vidphone. I tell them I am his estranged sister and that our parents have been in a terrible accident. They give me his home address. I take a skycab to his building and give the doorman the same story. He lets me into the elevator. But the policeman isn't home. It's cold, so I pull my collar up and wait.

∞

It must be close to daybreak when he finally steps out of the elevator, though these days the rain and smog are so constant that the presence or absence of the sun makes little difference. He isn't just a little drunk anymore. He's tanked. His eyes are dark and there is blood on his coat. By the looks of things, he's been working. I wonder if he's just retired one of the androids. I wonder if it was the one that looks like me.

"I need to talk to you," I say, stepping out of the shadows. If he's startled, he recovers quickly. In his line of work, I guess he has to. But he doesn't seem worried to see me.

"Talk to your father," he says.

He punches in a code and presses his thumb into the printreader. His door clicks open. I follow him in.

"I want to talk to you," I say. From inside my coat I pull out a photograph I carry with me everywhere. "Look. It's me and my mother." I show it to him.

"Do you remember when you were ten?" he says. "You and your brother were going to play doctor. You broke into an abandoned building and went down to the basement. Your brother showed you his, but when your turn came, you chickened and ran. You ever tell anyone that?"

"Yes," I say, though to be honest, I'm not sure.

"You're lying," he says. "You remember the orange and green spider that spun a web outside your window one spring?"

I nod slowly.

"She laid a huge egg and nursed it all summer. In the fall...."

"Hundreds of little baby spiders came crawling out. And they ate her," I finish. I've never told anyone that. So it's true. "I'm a replicant," I say. For the second time in years I feel tears well up.

He looks at me. I hate that I can't read him, can't tell what he's thinking. Is it pity in his eyes?

"Implants," he says. "The manufacturer's niece...."

He continues to stare. I'm uncomfortable. Finally he says, "Look, I'm sorry. Your father told me ... that he had you hypnotized...." He puts his hand on mine. I don't like it and pull away. "What about a drink?" he asks. "I'll get you a drink. I could use a drink."

When he turns to reach for a glass, I bolt out the still open door.

⤸

Until this morning, my father was my best and only friend. The only one who understood. The only one who accepted the strangeness that came over me after my mother's death. The only one who could see that I'm not cold, only sad.

I don't know what to think. The feelings have become stranger, uglier. The only one who understands now is this policeman, this murderer.

I wander the streets, drift through the banality of another grey Los Angeles day with my collar around my ears and my hands in my pockets. Hours pass before I see a man who looks like one of the escaped replicants. I check the holographic cards my father gave me. I follow him, half out of curiousity to know what replicants on the street are like and half out of some emotion I can't name. It has something to do with the policeman, and the uncomfortable sensation of his hand on mine, which lingers, though I don't will it.

The android walks up and down the residential streets in a neighbourhood that used to house garbage collectors and rat catchers. The buildings were all five and six-storey walk-ups, mildewed, dilapidated, and identical. Occasionally, he breaks into one. He emerges moments later looking frustrated and worried. He's looking for something.

I realise we're in the policeman's neighbourhood. The replicant slips into an alley and I slip into one just behind him. The policeman, wearing a coat identical to the one he was wearing last night but without the bloodstain, walks toward us. From the alley, the replicant steps out behind the policeman and grabs him in a headlock. The policeman thrashes, but isn't strong enough. The replicant puts a gun to his temple. My heart is beating fast. I don't fully understand why, but I don't want my policeman to die. I reach for my own gun and empty a round into the back of the replicant's head.

The policeman picks himself up and looks at me. He's been roughed up. He has a black eye and a bleeding lip. He offers me his arm. I take it.

⤸

When the policeman tells me what he wants, I can only reflect his desire back to him. Is that because I am eighteen and inexperienced or because I am nothing more than a wind–up doll? He treats me like a wind–up doll. He pushes me against the wall. It hurts but I don't say anything. I don't struggle. "Say kiss me," he says.

"Kiss me," I say. I like his mouth and the taste of alcohol on his breath.

∽

Lying in the policeman's bed, contemplating what it means to be a machine, I begin to remember the day of my mother's death. I was thirteen. There was a skating competition. I'd been practicing a sweet, melancholic choreography to music from *Swan Lake*. I had a white dress, covered in feathers.

On the drive to the skating rink, my mother and father fell into a bitter argument about the identity of a young woman in one of their wedding photographs. I knew exactly which picture they were talking about. It was a side profile of a young, dark–haired girl, who, on the day of the wedding must have been about my age. It was one of those strange photographs where you can't tell what race the person is. My father insisted it was his niece – his older brother's only daughter, and, in fact, the only child in the family until the arrival of my brother and me some years later. My mother said that it was obvious the girl was Chinese, and that she was, in fact, the daughter of her friend who had left the village to marry a Shanghainese businessman some years before. They fought bitterly and angrily. I was sure that there was something important about that young girl, though I didn't know what. Either that, or there was a subtext to the argument I didn't understand. My brother and I sat quietly in the back of the car, frightened and worried. My mother said that my father didn't know her and that she should never have married him. My father said that maybe she shouldn't have. After that, there was a dreadful silence in the car. It lasted all the way to the rink.

I remember skating to the dramatic strains of *Swan Lake*. I remember falling. But I didn't hit my head. I threw my arm out in time and managed to land on my hip and elbow. They were badly bruised but I had no concussion. The trauma came later.

When the competition was over and first prize had been awarded to a pale gold girl in a green tutu, only my father came to comfort me. "You'll always be number one in my eyes," he said, and I believed him. We went to the bleachers to collect my mother and brother, but they weren't there. A security guard said he had seen them leaving halfway through the show. I wondered whether or not they had seen me skate.

The police had taken photographs of the crash site and the mangled bodies. My father said I shouldn't look at them, but I opened the folder when my father was led to the morgue to confirm their identity. That was when I blacked out and hit my head.

∽

My policeman stirs in his sleep. I nudge him and his eyes blink open. "I dreamt I heard music," he says. He looks like a child.

"I dreamt about my parents," I say.

He nods, as though he's understood something. He reaches for his gun.

"I heard them say there's a man and a woman left."

"That's right." His face settles into a killer's mask.

"I heard the woman looks like me."

He nods.

"You don't have to do this," I say. I touch his cheek.

"You don't have to remember," he says.

"All I want is for someone to know me," I say. "Do you think that will ever be possible?"

"Yes," he says. "I do think it's possible."

Then he and his gun are gone. I move to the piano to see if I can really play, or if those music lessons were just the product of a stranger's love for another stranger. I'm not sure which way I'd have it, if I had a choice.

SECTION II
FUTURE EARTH

The next four stories give us extrapolations from the present that take our human histories of colonization into account; given our belligerent past, what kind of futures might we create? Eden Robinson's "Terminal Avenue" explores a future Canada where First Nations peoples face an increasingly apartheid life. "When Scarabs Multiply" by Nnedi Okorafor-Mbachu follows a young African girl as she puzzles through the bonds of love and hate in a reborn society that quickly degenerates into patriarchal stagnation. The protagonist of Vandana Singh's "Delhi" searches for meaning now that he wanders between a past and future Delhi. And in "Panopte's Eye," by Tamai Kobayashi, the world's ecological survival is set against an apocalyptic landscape of warlords and slave gangs.

Eden Robinson wrote "Terminal Avenue" in Vancouver, Canada on the number 9 Broadway bus between Commercial and the University of British Columbia over a period of two months. It was the third anniversary of the Oka Uprising, the salmon wars had just heated up, and the B.C. television helicopters were scanning the Fraser River looking to catch native fishermen "illegally" fishing. She is the author of a novel, Monkey Beach, *and a collection of short stories,* Traplines. *She is currently working on another novel,* Blood Sports, *and the screenplay adaptation of* Monkey Beach.

ᴄᴎᴐ

Terminal Avenue

Eden Robinson

His brother once held a peeled orange slice up against the sun. When the light shone through it, the slice became a brilliant amber: the setting sun is this colour, ripe orange.

The uniforms of the five advancing Peace Officers are robin's egg blue, but the slanting light catches their visors and sets their faces aflame.

ᴄᴎᴐ

In his memory, the water of the Douglas Channel is a hard blue, baked to a glassy translucence by the August sun. The mountains in the distance form a crown; *Gabiswa*, the mountain in the centre, is the same shade of blue as his lover's veins.

She raises her arms to sweep her hair from her face. Her breasts lift. In the cool morning air, her nipples harden to knobby raspberries. Her eyes are widening in indignation: he

62

once saw that shade of blue in a dragonfly's wing, but this is another thing he will keep secret.

∾

Say nothing, his mother said, without moving her lips, careful not to attract attention. They waited in their car in silence after that. His father and mother were in the front seat, stiff.

Blood plastered his father's hair to his skull; blood leaked down his father's blank face. In the flashing lights of the patrol car, the blood looked black and moved like honey.

∾

A rocket has entered the event horizon of a black hole. To an observer who is watching this from a safe distance, the rocket trapped here, in the black hole's inescapable halo of gravity, will appear to stop.

To an astronaut in the rocket, however, gravity is a rack that stretches his body like taffy, thinner and thinner, until there is nothing left but x-rays.

∾

In full body-armour, the five Peace Officers are sexless and anonymous. With their visors down, they look like old-fashioned astronauts. The landscape they move across is the rapid transit line, the Surreycentral Skytrain station, but if they remove their body-armour, it may as well be the moon.

The Peace Officers begin to match strides until they move like a machine. This is an intimidation tactic that works, is working on him even though he knows what it is. He finds himself frozen. He can't move, even as they roll towards him, a train on invisible tracks.

∾

Once, when his brother dared him, he jumped off the high diving tower. He wasn't really scared until he stepped away from the platform. In that moment, he realized he couldn't change his mind.

You stupid shit, his brother said when he surfaced.

In his dreams, everything is the same, except there is no water in the swimming pool and he crashes into the concrete like a dropped pumpkin.

∾

He thinks of his brother, who is so perfect he wasn't born, but chiselled from stone. There is nothing he can do against that brown Apollo's face, nothing he can say that will justify his inaction. Kevin would know what to do, with doom coming towards him in formation.

But Kevin is dead. He walked through their mother's door one day, wearing the robin's egg blue uniform of the great enemy, and his mother struck him down. She summoned the ghost of their father and put him in the room, sat him beside her, bloody and stunned. Against this Kevin said, I can stop it, Mom. I have the power to change things now.

She turned away, then the family turned away. Kevin looked at him, pleading, before he left her house and never came back, disappeared. Wil closed his eyes, a dark, secret joy welling in him, to watch his brother fall: Kevin never made the little mistakes in his life, never so much as sprouted a pimple. He made up for it though by doing the unforgivable.

Wil wonders if his brother knows what is happening. If, in fact, he isn't one of the Peace Officers, filled himself with secret joy.

cho

His lover will wait for him tonight. Ironically, she will be wearing a complete Peace Officer's uniform, bought at great expense on the black market, and very, very illegal. She will wait at the door of her club, Terminal Avenue, and she will frisk clients that she knows will enjoy it. She will have the playroom ready, with its great wooden beams stuck through with hooks and cages, with its expensive equipment built for the exclusive purpose of causing pain. On a steel cart, her toys will be spread out as neatly as surgical instruments.

When he walks through the door, she likes to have her bouncers, also dressed as Peace Officers, hurl him against the wall. They let him struggle before they handcuff him. Their uniforms are slippery as rubber. He can't get a grip on them. The uniforms are padded with the latest in wonderfabric so no matter how hard he punches them, he can't hurt them. They will drag him into the back and strip-search him in front of clients who pay for the privilege of watching. He stands under a spotlight that shines an impersonal cone of light from the ceiling. The rest of the room is darkened. He can see reflections of glasses, red-eyed cigarettes, the glint of ice clinking against glass, shadows shifting. He can hear zippers coming undone, low moans; he can smell the cum when he's beaten into passivity.

Once, he wanted to cut his hair, but she wouldn't let him, said she'd never speak to him again if he did. She likes it when the bouncers grab him by his hair and drag him to the exploratory table in the centre of the room.

She says she likes the way it veils his face when he's kneeling.

In the playroom though, she changes. He can't hurt her the way she wants him to; she is tiring of him. He whips her half–heartedly until she tells the bouncer to do it properly.

A man walked in one day, in a robin's egg blue uniform, and Wil froze. When he could breathe again, when he could think, he found her watching him, thoughtful.

She borrowed the man's uniform and lay on the table, her face blank and smooth and round as a basketball under the visor. He put a painstick against the left nipple. It darkened and bruised. Her screams were muffled by the helmet. Her bouncers whispered things to her as they pinned her to the table, and he hurt her. When she begged him to stop, he moved the painstick to her right nipple.

He kept going until he was shaking so hard he had to stop.

That's enough for tonight, she said, breathless, wrapping her arms around him, telling the bouncers to leave when he started to cry. My poor virgin. It's not pain so much as it is a cleansing.

Is it, he asked her, one of those whiteguilt things?

She laughed, kissed him. Rocked him and forgave him, on the evening he discovered that it wasn't just easy to do terrible things to another person: it could give pleasure. It could give power.

She said she'd kill him if he told anyone what happened in the playroom. She has a reputation and is vaguely ashamed of her secret weakness. He wouldn't tell, not ever. He is addicted to her pain.

To distinguish it from real uniforms, hers has an inverted black triangle on the left side, just over her heart: asocialism, she says with a laugh, and he doesn't get it. She won't explain it, her blue eyes black with desire as her pupils widened suddenly like a cat's.

The uniforms advancing on him, however, are clean and pure and real.

⌇

Wil wanted to be an astronaut. He bought the books, he watched the movies and he dreamed. He did well in Physics, Math, and Sciences, and his mother bragged, He's got my brains.

He was so dedicated, he would test himself, just like the astronauts on TV. He locked himself in his closet once with nothing but a bag of potato chips and a bottle of pop. He wanted to see if he could spend time in a small space, alone and deprived. It was July and they had no air conditioning. He fainted in the heat, dreamed that he was floating over the Earth on his way to Mars, weightless.

Kevin found him, dragged him from the closet, and laughed at him.

You stupid shit, he said. Don't you know anything?

When his father slid off the hood leaving a snail's trail of blood, Kevin ran out of the car.

Stop it! Kevin screamed, his face contorted in the headlight's beam. Shadows loomed over him, but he was undaunted. Stop it!

Kevin threw himself on their dad and saved his life.

Wil stayed with their father in the hospital, never left his side. He was there when the Peace Officers came and took their father's statement. When they closed the door in his face and he heard his father screaming. The nurses took him away and he let them. Wil watched his father withdraw into himself after that, never quite healing.

He knew the names of all the constellations, the distances of the stars, the equations that would launch a ship to reach them. He knew how to stay alive in any conditions, except when someone didn't want to stay alive.

No one was surprised when his father shot himself.

At the funeral potlatch, his mother split his father's ceremonial regalia between Wil and Kevin. She gave Kevin his father's frontlet. He placed it immediately on his head and danced. The room became still, the family shocked at his lack of tact. When Kevin stopped dancing, she gave Wil his father's button blanket. The dark wool held his smell. Wil knew then that he would never be an astronaut. He didn't have a backup dream and drifted through school, coasting on a reputation of Brain he'd stopped trying to earn.

Kevin, on the other hand, ran away and joined the Mohawk Warriors. He was at Oka on August 16 when the bombs rained down and the last Canadian reserve was Adjusted.

Wil expected him to come back broken. He was ready with patience, with forgiveness. Kevin came back a Peace Officer.

Why? his aunts, his uncles, cousins, and friends asked.

How could you? his mother asked.

Wil said nothing. When his brother looked up, Wil knew the truth, even if Kevin didn't. There were things that adjusted to rapid change – pigeons, dogs, rats, cockroaches. Then there were things that didn't – panda bears, whales, flamingos, Atlantic cod, salmon, owls.

Kevin would survive the Adjustment. Kevin had found a way to come through it and be better for it. He instinctively felt the changes coming and adapted. I, on the other hand, he thought, am going the way of the dodo bird.

✧

There are rumours in the neighbourhood. No one from the Vancouver Urban Reserve #2 can get into Terminal Avenue. They don't have the money or the connections. Whispers follow him, anyway, but no one will ask him to his face. He suspects that his mother suspects. He has been careful, but he sees the questions in her eyes when he leaves for work. Someday she'll ask him what he really does and he'll lie to her.

To allay suspicion, he smuggles cigarettes and sweetgrass from the downtown core to Surreycentral. This is useful, makes him friends, adds a kick to his evening train ride. He finds that he needs these kicks. Has a morbid fear of becoming dead like his father, talking and breathing and eating, but frightened into vacancy, a living blankness.

His identity card that gets him to the downtown core says *Occupation: Waiter.* He pins it to his jacket so that no one will mistake him for a terrorist and shoot him.

He is not really alive until he steps past the industrial black doors of his lover's club. Until that moment, he is living inside his head, lost in memories. He knows that he is a novelty item, a real living Indian: that is why his prices are so inflated. He knows there will come a time when he is yesterday's condom.

He walks past the club's façade, the elegant dining rooms filled with the glittering people who watch the screens or dance across the dimly–lit ballroom–sized floor. He descends the stairs where his lover waits for him with her games and her toys, where they do things that aren't sanctioned by the Purity laws, where he gets hurt and gives hurt.

He is greeted by his high priestess. He enters her temple of discipline and submits. When the pain becomes too much, he hallucinates. There is no preparing for that moment when reality shifts and he is free.

∽

They have formed a circle around him. Another standard intimidation tactic. The Peace Officer facing him is waiting for him to talk. He stares up at it. This will be different from the club. He is about to become an example.

Wilson Wilson? the Officer says. The voice sounds male but is altered by computers so it won't be recognizable.

He smiles. The name is one of his mother's little jokes, a little defiance. He has hated her for it all his life, but now he doesn't mind. He is in a forgiving mood. *Yes, that's me.*

In the silence that stretches, Wil realizes that he always believed this moment would come. That he has been preparing himself for it. The smiling–faced lies from the TV haven't fooled him, or anyone else. After the Uprisings, it was only a matter of time before someone decided to solve the Indian problem once and for all.

The Peace Officer raises his club and brings it down.

cvs

His father held a potlatch before they left Kitamaat, before they came to Vancouver to earn a living, after the aluminum smelter closed.

They had to hold it in secret, so they hired three large seiners for the family and rode to Monkey Beach. They left in their old beat–up speedboat, early in the morning, when the Douglas Channel was calm and flat, before the winds blew in from the ocean, turning the water choppy. The seine boats fell far behind them, heavy with people. Kevin begged and begged to steer and his father laughingly gave in.

Wil knelt on the bow and held his arms open, wishing he could take off his lifejacket. In four hours they will land on Monkey Beach and will set up for the potlatch where they will dance and sing and say goodbye. His father will cook salmon around fires, roasted the old–fashioned way: split down the centre and splayed open like butterflies, thin sticks of cedar woven through the skin to hold the fish open, the sticks planted in the sand; as the flesh darkens, the juice runs down and hisses on the fire. The smell will permeate the beach. Camouflage nets will be set up all over the beach so they won't be spotted by planes. Family will lounge under them as if they were beach umbrellas. The more daring of the family will dash into the water, which is still glacier–cold and shocking.

This will happen when they land in four hours, but Wil chooses to remember the boat ride with his mother resting in his father's arm when Wil comes back from the bow and sits beside them. She is wearing a blue scarf and black sunglasses and red lipstick. She can't stop smiling even though they are going to leave home soon. She looks like a movie star. His father has his hair slicked back, and it makes him look like an otter. He kisses her, and she kisses him back.

Kevin is so excited that he raises one arm and makes the Mohawk salute they see on TV all the time. He loses control of the boat, and they swerve violently. His father cuffs Kevin and takes the wheel.

The sun rises as they pass Costi Island, and the water sparkles and shifts. The sky hardens into a deep summer blue.

The wind and the noise of the engine prevent them from talking. His father begins to sing. Wil doesn't understand the words, couldn't pronounce them if he tried. He can see that his father is happy. Maybe he's drunk on the excitement of the day, on the way that his wife touches him, tenderly. He gives Wil the wheel.

His father puts on his button blanket, rests it solemnly on his shoulders. He balances on the boat with the ease of someone who's spent all his life on the water. He does a twirl, when he reaches the bow of the speedboat and the button blanket opens, a navy lotus. The abalone buttons sparkle when they catch the light. She's laughing as he poses. He dances, suddenly inspired, exuberant.

Later he will understand what his father is doing, the rules he is breaking, the risks he is taking, and the price he will pay on a deserted road, when the siren goes off and the lights flash and they are pulled over.

At the time, though, Wil is white-knuckled, afraid to move the boat in a wrong way and toss his father overboard. He is also embarrassed, wishing his father were more reserved. Wishing he was being normal instead of dancing, a whirling shadow against the sun, blocking his view of the Channel.

This is the moment he chooses to be in, the place he goes to when the club flattens him to the Surreycentral tiles. He holds himself there, in the boat with his brother, his father, his mother. The sun on the water makes pale northern lights flicker against everyone's faces, and the smell of the water is clean and salty, and the boat's spray is cool against his skin.

Nnedi Okorafor–Mbachu *is a writer and journalist from Chicago. Her novel,*
Zahrah the Windseeker *(Houghton Mifflin), is scheduled for release in late 2004. Her
short story "The Magical Negro" and her essay "Her Pen Could Fly: A Tribute to Virginia
Hamilton" were published in* Dark Matter II: Reading the Bones *(Warner Aspect),
and her short story "Asuquo" was published in* Mojo: Conjure Stories *(Warner
Aspect). In 2004, her short story "The Ghastly Bird" will be published in the* Other Half
Literary Magazine. *She is currently working on her PhD in English at the University of
Illinois, Chicago.*

⤬

When Scarabs Multiply
Nnedi Okorafor-Mbachu

I was only twelve years old when Srauniya Jaa, the Red
Queen of Niger, returned to my town wanting to cut off my
father's head. But I don't hate her. I don't fear her either. But
I feel … something. Something strong. And that's why I plan
to do this.

Kwàmfà was a great town because of Jaa. It was she who
came and organized it, and then ran it. Though she'd left
Kwàmfà a year before I was born, I'd been hearing about her
all my life. From my mother I had always heard about how
good life was because of her, before she left.

"It was relaxed here," my mother said. "Even after the
bombs fell and everything changed."

Jaa came decades ago with her nomads, when Kwàmfà
was just a tiny dying village. Under Jaa's guidance, Kwàmfà
became a booming town of palm and monkey bread trees,
old but still useful satellite dishes, and neatly built mud brick
houses with colourful, Zulu–style geometric designs and

conical thatch roofs. The streets filled up with cars, motorbikes, and camels. Kwàmfà became known for its exquisite carpets and after the great change, also for its flying carpets.

But after Jaa hopped onto her camel and rode into the Sahara, my mother said, things changed yet again. And it was all due to my father.

My father was wealthy, influential, and highly respected. When he spoke, people listened. My mother said he was born with a sugared tongue. And also he had always been quite popular amongst the women because he was very lovely.

"When we were younger, I didn't mind," my mother said. "Your father was strikingly beautiful. How could I expect others not to notice? You know, when he was in his twenties, he was the winner three years in a row of the Mr Sahara beauty contest." She smiled and shook her head. "It was those eyes. He could make them go in two different directions. The judges loved that. It's a shame that stupidity took over his heart."

My father did very well selling and buying houses, but he had always been interested in politics. He never missed a town meeting, and he was most attentive when Jaa was speaking. My mother never thought anything of it. Mother was also interested in politics and liked attending the meetings.

Nevertheless, the same day Jaa left, my father did too. And he refused to tell my mother where he was going. He returned a month later riding a bejewelled camel and wearing a golden caftan and turban and an equally golden smile on his handsome face. My father was somewhat light in skin tone, the colour of tea and cream, but Mother said that day he looked much darker, as if he'd been out in the sun for weeks. Probably bargaining for the camels and jewels. Behind him marched more camels, freshly brushed, ridden by several of his close friends. They threw naira notes to the gathering crowd and the crowd gathered faster.

"Jaa is gone, but no need to worry!" he shouted in his booming voice as he smiled and winked at the women in the crowd. "In her absence, I can make sure Kwàmfà remains the great town she built! Make *me* your chief and there will be no need to worry about greedy shady men destroying her council!"

My father was playing off of people's fears that without Jaa, our world would crumble back into corruption. They followed him because he promised to keep things as they were.

In a matter of months, Kwàmfà had a chief, my father. And only a few months later, after throwing a lot more money around, flashing his pretty smile, making sure he had the right people on his side, making even more promises, and silencing Jaa's most devoted devotees with money or indirect threats, my father succeeded in making many changes to Kwàmfà.

My mother said that before, when Kwàmfà was Jaa's town, everyone learned how to shoot a gun, ride a camel, take apart and rebuild a computer. My father made it so that only the boys got to do these things.

"Women and girls are too beautiful to dirty their hands with such things," he told the people with a soft chuckle. The women and girls blushed at his words and the men agreed with them. My father also thought us too beautiful to be seen, so he brought back the burka.

He cut off several food and housing programs, which left many starving and destitute.

"Soon we won't *need* such programs," he told the people with a wink. Most people backed him in his iron-fisted fight against even the smallest crime. Kwàmfà was safe, but no place is free of all crime. My father wanted absolute perfection. Soon there were public whippings, hands cut off, and in the rare cases of murder, public executions. All was in the name of Jaa, he constantly said, although Jaa would never have approved of these things.

He was so confident in himself that he didn't fear Jaa's wrath, so sure he was that she would never return. My mother watched him become a different man. It must have been most painful when, to top it all off, he started marrying more wives. The better to look the part of the "big man."

He was like one of those wild magicians who goes astray in the storyteller's stories. Talented, self-righteous, and power-drunk. He used the shadowy magic and spells of politics to pull together a mountain of power. But like every magician of this kind, it was all bound to come back to him.

It's no wonder Sarauniya Jaa wanted to cut off his head.

Even before she returned, everyone knew the legend of Sarauniya Jaa, Princess of the New Sahara. On clear nights when the full moon made streetlights useless, the storyteller would come out of his hut and sit under the ancient monkey bread tree and wait for the children to gather around him. As he waited, that tree would tell him what stories to tell; or so my mother said. He usually recited Jaa's tale last. And he told it in Hausa, not English, and spoke loud enough for his voice to echo high up into the Aïr Mountains. By this time, I was always tired and the story was like a vivid dream.

cło

She isn't the daughter of the prophet as her name suggests.

No, no. "Fatima" was just what her parents named her. Her true name is Sarauniya Jaa, Queen of the Red. She is the dreamer. Simply call her Jaa. Whenever she storms into the cities and towns here in Niger, she's draped in a long red dress and a red silk burka so sheer that you can see the smile on her face.

Her sword is thin as paper and strong enough to cut diamond, and it bears the scent of the rain-soaked soil. It's made of a green clear metal that has no earthly name because it doesn't come from earth, but from the body of another place called Ginen, where Jaa often travels to when her Sahara queendom is calm. Years ago, she left our town to go there.

Jaa is always accompanied by her two wild and sword-swinging husbands, Buji and Gambo; ask me for their stories and I will give them to you on another day. Jaa is a tiny woman, small like a worldly child. But size is deceptive. You do not want to be the enemy of her sword.

Her voice is high-pitched and melodious. Sometimes when she speaks, red flowers fall from the sky. Legend has it that when she was a young woman, she was stolen by a group of New Tuareg nomads called the Lwa. They claimed that the reason for the kidnapping was because she was their queen.

They were right.

Soon, the queen in her awakened, and before they knew it, she was laughing loudly and telling men to straighten up their clothes, women to learn to ride camels, and whoever would listen, the stories of her past life as a daydreaming medical student. This was just after the Sahara was no longer the Sahara and the world had changed. Soon Jaa was ruling the new land with her army of devoted nomads. She feared none of the talking sandstorms, flocks of carnivorous hummingbirds, or the nuclear fallout that drifted from countries away. The subsequent return of magic to the world didn't bother her.

I tell you, if it were not for this woman, death and blood would have run through the irrigation lakes and soaked the sands. No empire would have thrived. But it is not Jaa's wish to rule.

Whenever things grow calm, she has her group of nomads settle in a town. This last time, it was our town, Kwàmfà. I myself was one of those nomads who traveled with her and settled here. When we were comfortable, Jaa and her husbands rode off into the desert. She hasn't been seen since.

But Jaa always knows when to return.

☙

The storyteller usually recited the last line with a knowing look on his wrinkled shiny face. Then he'd glance in the direction of my father's big house. I always wanted to ask him why, but I never found the right moment. I knew the answer anyway.

It was during the New Yam Festival. I was twelve years old. It had been thirteen years since she'd left and my father took over. My father liked to have an opening ceremony where he gave a speech and ate the first piece of yam. The festival was set up in the centre of town. There were booths made of thatch where food and jewelry would be sold and performances would take place. As always, the wrestling match would be held next to the giant monkey bread tree. I'd always wanted to go watch, but women could only attend if they wore the full veil. The matches were always in the middle of the day under the hottest sun, so few women ever attended.

My father made sure that there was a specific spot next to the stage for plenty of journalists. He loved to be seen and talked about. He also wanted to "put Kwàmfà on the map." They brought their digital cameras, and the footage and photos would be posted on the Naija Net News and talked about on the even more popular net radio stations. My mother said that Jaa would have been disgusted, for she viewed the yam festival as a private Kwàmfà affair.

A stage was set up in the center of all the booths and festival spaces for my father to give his speech. A high golden top covered it, and around it were several bushes and a palm tree. The stage floor was covered with a thick red cloth – Jaa's colour – and decorated with red and gold pillows. The air already smelled of palm oil and the pungent aroma of pepper soup, sweat, and cologne. It was going to be a fun day.

I sat on some of the gold pillows with my half brothers and sisters. Today I wore my yellow veil. It was light, so although I had on a long blue dress underneath (blue was my favourite colour), I wasn't too hot.

"Look at this goat girl who thinks she should be here," Baturiya said to Azumi. She whispered, but she must have known that she was loud enough for me to hear. She screwed up her nose. "I hate smelling her."

"I know," Azumi replied. "Papa's heart is too soft. I guess he doesn't mind the smell of goat shit."

"I don't know why she comes." Baturiya sucked her teeth, looked me in the eye, and said, "She should be ashamed."

They could say whatever they wanted; we were still related. My mother sat in the audience, though. Even if she hadn't divorced him, she still would have refused to sit with the other wives who were all closer to my age than hers.

My mother was pregnant with me when she decided to divorce my father.

"Get out then! You mean less than goat shit to me!" my father shouted that day for all the neighbours to hear when he caught my mother trying to sneak out with her bags. "I don't want you if you can't support me!" He was shouting so loudly that his voice cracked and his entire body shook. My mother said he had tears in his eyes, that it was the only time she'd ever seen him shed tears.

She was several months pregnant and still she was trying to carry those bags. It's hard for me to get that image out of my mind. But so desperate she was to leave him quietly. He grabbed her bags from her and threw them out the door. Then he pushed her out, too.

"But not hard enough so that I would fall," she said, looking at me and knowing my thoughts.

Over the years, my father didn't visit me. And only during public appearances did he acknowledge me indirectly by sending a messenger to tell me my presence was demanded. The entire town knew I was his daughter and he'd look silly pretending that I was not of his blood. He went on to marry three very young wives. I think he did it to spite my mother. When they were married, he loved her dearly and exclusively and never spoke of marrying any other women. His wives have since blessed him with five sons and four daughters. So what does he need me for, really?

As I sat there onstage, a light blue scarab beetle climbed up my sandal. I brought out my magnifying glass to look more closely at it. I liked insects, especially these kinds of scarabs, so I always carried the magnifying glass in my pocket. As I looked, I knew to tilt the magnifying glass with great care. One move in the wrong direction and the inspected insect would fry.

Sometimes these blue scarabs would spontaneously multiply. My mother said that they weren't native to earth, that they came from that other place. Still, for thousands of years, scarabs have been the sign of rebirth here in Niger. So what does it mean when such a sign multiplies?

I dropped my magnifying glass when I felt the rhythm vibrate through the stage, like a heartbeat.

"In the new year," my father was saying. He was draped in the red cape that he always wore for speeches. "As chief of Kwàmfà, I will make sure elections run smoothly, and that every man running has his say. In the name of our nurturing queen, Sarauniya Jaa, I will...."

"You *dare* speak my name?!" said a voice high–pitched like the sound of a bamboo flute. "You dare say your words are in the name of *Jaa*?!"

A whisper flew through the audience and the sound of camel feet on sand grew closer. With my peripheral vision, I saw my half–siblings all running in different directions. But I stayed where I was, too terrified to move. I looked at my father. His eyes were wide and his upper lip quivered as he stared at his fleeing audience. From somewhere in the crowd came the sound of galloping camels.

"Kwàmfà is mine now," I heard my father say, his voice sounding as if he were being strangled. "You won't take it, you witch!"

There were shouts of surprise as people jumped and threw themselves aside. Behind us, gutsy journalists continued taping and snapping pictures. My mother remained where she was, her eyes wide. Only my father and I now stood onstage. Even his wives had run off!

I have seen many camels. People ride them and use them to carry burdens. They smell like desert wind and have long eyelashes, rough fur, soft lips, and knobby knees. They roar with protest when mounted and many of them can speak in human languages, usually to complain. But I have never seen camels of this size. I don't know how such a small woman was able to climb onto such a great beast, let alone ride it. Her two husbands were not much taller, their camels equally as huge.

The camels wore no gold or silver and had no saddle or reins. And their eyes were wild. But they traipsed through the crowd with swift agile care. Not one person was trampled. I could see her face clearly through her sheer red burka as she approached. Jaa was very very dark, her skin almost blue – like mine. She had a smile on her round face, just like in the stories.

Once everyone was out of the way, she picked up speed and unsheathed her sword as she barked something to her husbands. They say she speaks ten languages. Hausa, Igbo, Yoruba, English, Efik, Arabic, all those I know. This language she spoke was foreign to me. Her husbands stopped their camels, but she continued, with her sword held high.

A guttural grunt came from my father's throat that was probably meant to be a scream. He swayed slightly, paralyzed by indecisiveness, awe, and fear. Jaa's camel leapt onstage and ran past my father. I could hear the thumps of its hooves on the stage floor.

At the same moment, the scarab beetle landed right on my shoulder. It made a soft popping sound as it multiplied into two, the second beetle appearing on my other shoulder. I didn't brush them off. I was barely even aware of them because of what happened next.

Shhhhooooomp. With a swipe, she took his head right off.

I opened my eyes and mouth wide, all the blood rushing to my head, but no scream came. Later I would see that several small veins had burst around my eyes and on my chest.

The camera flashes made the scene even more gruesome, lighting up the shade and highlighting the blood and bone. I smelled urine as my father's head fell onto the red cloth, leaving a redder trail, and rolled off the stage and onto the sand. His eyes were still open as his head rolled and sand must have gotten in them. It stopped underneath a bush. I felt sick.

I didn't want to look at the rest of my father's body, which was still standing, swaying, bleeding, dribbling, and would fall at any moment. I knew my father had done bad things, but that didn't change the horror of what I witnessed. Someone screamed, but I was focused only on Jaa. Her camel had leapt off the other side of the stage. Now it had climbed back onstage and was approaching me!

I still didn't move, though at this time I was shaking. I heard a crunch. Her camel had stepped on my magnifying glass. She reached down and pulled off my veil. I felt naked in my blue dress.

"Are you his daughter?" she asked me in Igbo.

A red flower fell from the sky, bounced on my head, and fell to my feet.

"Y–y–yes," I said.

"What is your name?"

"Ejii Ugabe," I said.

She chuckled. "Chief Ugabe, indeed," she said. "I hope *you* are nothing like him."

I stood there looking at the smear of blood on her sword and the strange blue eyes of her camel.

"Where is your mother?" she asked.

I looked around. People were running and screaming. A few were staring. Her husbands, Gambo and Buji, shouted for everyone to calm down. Some stopped, but few were listening. My mother was still standing there. I pointed and Jaa looked toward her. She looked at her for a long time. For a moment I was afraid she'd raise her sword and behead my mother too.

"It's time that you, Gambo, and Buji have come back, Sarauniya Jaa," my mother said with a bow. When she looked up, her face was sad and she wiped a tear from her cheek. But that was all.

Jaa laughed as if my mother were an old friend; no longer did she look like a crazed warrior. I stood there trying to figure out her age, not wanting to look beside me at my father's body. She appeared both ancient and the age of my mother.

"You will handle this town when I'm next gone," Jaa said.

My mother nodded.

And that is how my mother became Kwàmfà's Councilwoman who answers only to Sarauniya Jaa. I think it was also the moment I made my decision.

We never found my father's head. The bush it rolled under was one of the new type, the carnivorous ones. It was several minutes before anyone thought to search for it, enough time for one of these bushes to devour flesh and bone. So my father was buried without his lovely head. I still have the flower that fell when Jaa spoke to me. I planted it and over the years it has grown into a tree next to my window. I also still have nightmares about that moment. Sometimes I hear the sound of her camel's hooves, other times I see my father's head roll. Other times I see my father and he's winking at me. He never winked at me when he was alive. But I don't cry as much anymore.

I don't want to be a councilwoman like my mother, though I respect her job. There's something I need to learn. I keep thinking about how the scarab beetle, the sign of rebirth, landed on me moments before my father's life was taken. And how it multiplied. What does that mean? It must mean something. Something always comes out of horror, my mother says. She also says that nothing is ever a coincidence.

I hate Jaa because, though my father did what he did, I loved him. Without him, I would not exist. One is only born with one father. And she killed him. Right in front of me. But I love her because she too gave me a life. If she hadn't returned, I wouldn't have been able to go to school and learn and read and think. Still, I want to know why Jaa couldn't have found another way. Why did she have to *kill* him?

It's been five years since the day Jaa returned to our town and killed my father. For five years, she's been mentoring my mother and the group of men and women she appointed to work with my mother in the town's government. Things are running smoothly now, so she is leaving tomorrow. And I'm going to follow her.

Vandana Singh *was born and raised in India, which is on the planet known as the Third World. She currently lives in the United States with her family, where she teaches college physics, writes, and wears her green skin and antennae with pride. Her interests include women's movements, Indian classical music, and the environment. Her stories and poems have appeared in* Strange Horizons *and the anthologies* Polyphony *and* Trampoline. Younguncle Comes to Town, *her first book for children, has just been published in India by Zubaan Press.*

⌒

Delhi

Vandana Singh

Tonight he is intensely aware of the city: its ancient stones, the flat-roofed brick houses, threads of clotheslines, wet, bright colours waving like pennants, neem-tree lined roads choked with traffic. There's a bus going over the bridge under which he has chosen to sleep. The night smells of jasmine and stale urine, and the dust of the cricket field on the other side of the road. A man is lighting a bidi near him: face lean, half in shadow, and he thinks he sees himself. He goes over to the man, who looks like another layabout. "My name is Aseem," he says.

The man, reeking of tobacco, glares at him, coughs, and spits, "Kya chahiye?"

Aseem steps back in a hurry. No, that man is not Aseem's older self; anyway, Aseem can't imagine he would take up smoking bidis at any point in his life. He leaves the dubious shelter of the bridge, the quiet lane that runs under it, and makes his way through the litter and anemic street lamps to the neon-bright highway. The new city is less confusing, he thinks; the colours are more solid, the lights dazzling, so he can't see the apparitions as clearly. But once he saw a milkman going past him on Shahjahan road, complete with humped white cow and tinkling bell. Under the stately, ancient trees that partly shaded the street lamps, the milkman stopped to speak to his cow and faded into the dimness of twilight.

When he was younger, he thought the apparitions he saw were ghosts of the dead, but now he knows that is not true. Now he has a theory that his visions are tricks of time, tangles produced when one part of the time-stream rubs up against another and the two cross for a moment. He has decided (after years of struggle) that he is not insane after all; his brain is wired differently from others, enabling him to discern these temporal coincidences. He knows he is not the only one with this ability, because some of the people he sees also see him, and shrink back in terror. The thought that he is a ghost to people long dead or still to come in this world both amuses and terrifies him.

He's seen more apparitions in the older parts of the city than anywhere else, and he's not sure why. There is plenty of history in Delhi, no doubt about that – the city's past goes back into myth, when the Pandava brothers of the epic Mahabharata first founded their fabled capital, Indraprastha, some 3,000 years ago. In medieval times alone there were seven cities of Delhi, he remembers, from a well-thumbed history textbook – and the eighth city was established by the British during the days of the Raj. The city of the present day, the ninth, is the largest. Only for Aseem are the old cities of Delhi still alive, glimpsed like mysterious islands from a passing ship, but real nevertheless. He wishes he could discuss his temporal visions with someone who would take him seriously and help him understand the nature and limits of his peculiar malady, but ironically, the only sympathetic person he's met who shares his condition happened to live in 1100 AD or thereabouts, the time of Prithviraj Chauhan, the last Hindu ruler of Delhi.

He was walking past the faded white colonnades of some building in Connaught Place when he saw her: an old woman in a long skirt and shawl, making her way sedately across the car park, her body rising above the road and falling below its surface parallel to some invisible topography. She came face to face with Aseem – and saw him. They both stopped. Clinging to her like grey ribbons were glimpses of her environs – he saw mist, the darkness of trees behind her. Suddenly, in the middle of summer, he could smell fresh rain. She put a wondering arm out toward him but didn't touch him. She said: "What age are you from?" in an unfamiliar dialect of Hindi. He did not know how to answer the question, or how to contain within him that sharp shock of joy. She, too, had looked across the barriers of time and glimpsed other people, other ages. She named Prithviraj Chauhan as her king. Aseem told her he lived some 900 years after Chauhan. They exchanged stories of other visions – she had seen armies, spears flashing, and pale men with yellow beards, and a woman in a metal carriage, crying. He was able to interpret some of this for her before she began to fade away. He started toward her as though to step into her world, and ran right into a pillar. As he picked himself off the ground he heard derisive laughter. Under the arches a shoeshine boy and a man chewing betel leaf were staring at him, enjoying the show.

Once he met the mad emperor, Mohammad Shah. He was walking through Red Fort one late afternoon, avoiding clumps of tourists and their clicking cameras, and feeling particularly restless. There was a smoky tang in the air because some gardener in the grounds was burning dry leaves. As the sun set, the red sandstone fort walls glowed, then darkened. Night came, blanketing the tall ramparts, the lawns through which he strolled, the shimmering beauty of the Pearl Mosque, the languorous curves of the now distant Yamuna that had once flowed under this marble terrace. He saw a man standing, leaning over the railing, dressed in a red silk sherwani, jewels at his throat, a gem studded in his turban. The man smelled of wine and rose attar, and was singing a song about a night of separation from the Beloved, slurring the words together.

Bairan bhayii raat sakhiya....

Mammad Shah piya sada Rangila....

Mohammad Shah Rangila, early 1700s, Aseem recalled. The Emperor who loved music, poetry, and wine more than anything, who ignored warnings that the Persian king was marching to Delhi with a vast army.... "Listen, King," Aseem whispered urgently, wondering if he could change the course of history, "you must prepare for battle. Else Nadir Shah will overrun the city. Thousands will be butchered by his army...."

The king lifted wine–darkened eyes. "Begone, wraith!"

Sometimes he stops at the India Gate lawns in the heart of modern Delhi and buys ice–cream from a vendor and eats it sitting by one of the fountains that Lutyens built. Watching the play of light on the shimmering water, he thinks about the British invaders, who brought one of the richest and oldest civilizations on earth to abject poverty in only two hundred years. They built these great edifices, gracious buildings, and fountains, but even they had to leave it all behind. Kings came and went, the goras came and went, but the city lives on. Sometimes he sees apparitions of the goras, the palefaces, walking by him or riding on horses. Each time he yells out to them: "Your people are doomed. You will leave here. Your Empire will crumble." Once in a while they glance at him, startled, before they fade away.

In his more fanciful moments, he wonders if he hasn't, in some way, *caused* history to happen the way it does. Planted a seed of doubt in a British officer's mind about the permanency of the Empire. Despite his best intentions, convinced Mohammad Shah that the impending invasion is not a real danger but a ploy wrought against him by evil spirits. But he knows that apart from the Emperor, nobody he has communicated with is of any real importance in the course of history, and that he is simply deluding himself about his own significance.

Still, he makes compulsive notes of his more interesting encounters. He carries with him at all times a thick, somewhat shabby notebook, one-half of which is devoted to recording these temporal adventures. But because the apparitions he sees are so clear, he is sometimes not certain whether the face he glimpses in the crowd, or the man wrapped in shawls passing him by on a cold night, belong to this time or some other. Only some incongruity – spatial or temporal – distinguishes the apparitions from the rest.

Sometimes he sees landscapes too, but rarely – a skyline dotted with palaces and temple spires, a forest in the middle of a busy thoroughfare – and, strangest of all, once an array of tall, jewelled towers reaching into the clouds. Each such vision seems to be charged with a peculiar energy, like a scene lit up by lightning. And although the apparitions are apparently random and not often repeated, there are certain places where he sees (he thinks) the same people again and again. For instance, while travelling on the Metro, he almost always sees people in the subway tunnels, floating through the train and the passengers on the platforms, dressed in tatters, their faces pale and unhealthy as though they have never beheld the sun. The first time he saw them, he shuddered. "The Metro is quite new," he thought to himself, "and the first underground train system in Delhi. So what I saw must be in the future...."

One day, he tells himself, he will write a history of the future.

⚬ა⚬

The street is Nai Sarak, a name he has always thought absurd. New Road, it means, but this road has not been new in a very long time. He could cross the street in two jumps if it wasn't so crowded with people, shoulder to shoulder. The houses are like that too, hunched together with windows like dull eyes, and narrow, dusty stairways and even narrower alleys in between. The ground floors are taken up by tiny, musty shops containing piles of books that smell fresh and pungent, a wake-up smell like coffee. It is a hot day, and there is no shade. The girl he is following is just another

Delhi University student looking for a bargain, trying not to get jostled or groped in the crowd, much less have her purse stolen. There are small, barefoot boys running around with wire-carriers of lemon-water in chipped glasses, and fat old men in their undershirts behind the counters, bargaining fiercely with pale, defenseless college students over the hum of electric fans, rubbing clammy hands across their hairy bellies while they slurp their ice drinks, signaling to some waif when the transaction is complete, so that the desired volume can be deposited into the feverish hands of the student. Some of the shopkeepers like to add a little lecture along the lines of, "Now, my son, study hard, make your parents proud...." Aseem hasn't been here in a long time (since his own college days, in fact); he is not prepared for any of this: the brightness of the day, the white dome of the mosque rising up behind him, the old stone walls of the city engirdling him, enclosing him in people and sweat and dust. He's dazzled by the white kurtas of the men, the neat beards and the prayer caps; this is, of course, the Muslim part of the city, Old Delhi, but not as romantic as his grandmother used to make it sound. He has a rare flash of memory into a past where he was a small boy listening to the old woman's tales. His grandmother was one of the Hindus who never went back to old Delhi, not after the madness of Partition in 1947, the Hindu-Muslim riots that killed thousands, but he still remembers how she spoke of the places of her girlhood: parathe-walon-ki-gali, the lane of the paratha-makers, where all the shops sell freshly-cooked flatbreads of every possible kind, stuffed with spiced potatoes or minced lamb, or fenugreek leaves, or crushed cauliflower and fiery red chillies; and Dariba Kalan, where after hundreds of years they still sell the best and purest silver in the world, delicate chains and anklets and bracelets. Among the crowds that throng these places he has seen the apparitions of courtesans and young men, and the blood and thunder of invasions, and the bodies of princes hanged by British soldiers. To him the old city, surrounded by high, crumbling stone walls, is like the heart of a crone who dreams perpetually of her youth.

The girl who's caught his attention walks on. Aseem hasn't been able to get a proper look at her – all he's noticed are the dark eyes, and the death in them. After all these years in the city he's learned to recognize a certain preoccupation in the eyes of some of his fellow citizens: the desire for the final anonymity that death brings. Sometimes, as in this case, he knows it before they do.

The girl goes into a shop. The proprietor, a young man built like a wrestler, is dressed only in cotton shorts. The massage-man is working his back, kneading and sculpting the slick, gold muscles. The young man says: "Advanced Biochemistry? Watkins? One copy, only one copy left." He shouts into the dark, cavernous interior, and the requisite small boy comes up, bearing the volume as though it were a rare book. The girl's face shows too much relief; she's doomed even before the bargaining begins. She parts with her money with a resigned air, steps out into the noisy brightness, and is caught up with the crowd in the street like a piece of wood tossed in a river. She pushes and elbows her way through it, fending off anonymous hands that reach toward her breasts or back. He loses sight of her for a moment, but there she is, walking past the mosque to the bus stop on the main road. At the bus stop she catches Aseem's glance and gives him the pre-emptive cold look. Now there's a bus coming, filled with people, young men hanging out of the doorways as though on the prow of a sailboat. He sees her struggling through the crowd toward the bus, and at the last minute she's right in its path. The bus is not stopping but (in the tantalizing manner of Delhi buses) barely slowing, as though to play catch with the crowd. It is an immense green and yellow metal monstrosity bearing down on her as she stands rooted, clutching her bag of books. This is Aseem's moment. He lunges at the girl, pushing her out of the way, grabbing her before she can fall to the ground. There is a roaring in his ears, the shriek of brakes, and the conductor yelling. Her books are scattered on the ground. He helps pick them up. She's trembling with shock. In her eyes he sees himself for a moment: a drifter, his face unshaven, his hair unkempt. He tells her: don't do it, don't ever do it. Life is never so bereft of hope. You have a purpose you must fulfill. He repeats it like a mantra, and she looks bewildered, as though she doesn't understand that she was trying to kill herself. He can see that he puzzles her: his grammatical Hindi and his fair English labels him middle class and educated, like herself, but his appearance says otherwise. Although he knows she's not the woman he is seeking, he pulls out the computer printout just to be sure. No, she's not the one. Cheeks too thin, chin not sharp enough. He pushes one of the business cards into her hand and walks away. From a distance, he sees that she's looking at the card in her hand and frowning. Will she throw it away? At the last minute, she shoves it into her bag with the books. He remembers all too clearly the first time someone gave him one of the cards. "Worried About Your Future? Consult Pandit Vidyanath. Computerized and Air-Conditioned Office. Discover Your True Purpose in Life." There is a logo of a beehive and an address in South Delhi.

Later he will write up this encounter in the second half of his notebook. In three years, he has filled this part almost to capacity. He's stopped young men from flinging themselves off the bridges that span the Yamuna. He's prevented women from jumping off tall buildings, from dousing themselves with kerosene, from murderous encounters with city traffic. All this by way of seeking *her*, whose story will be the last in his book.

But the very first story in this part of his notebook is his own....

⌀

Three years ago. He is standing on a bridge over the Yamuna. There is a heavy, odorous fog in the air, the kind that mars winter mornings in Delhi. He is shivering because of the chill, and because he is tired, tired of the apparitions that have always plagued him, tired of the endless rounds of medications and appointments with doctors and psychologists. He has just written a letter to his fiancée, severing their already fragile relationship. Two months ago, he stopped attending his college classes. His mother and father have been dead a year and two years respectively, and there will be no one to mourn him, except for relatives in other towns who know him only by reputation as a person with problems. Last night he tried, as a last resort, to leave Delhi, hoping that perhaps the visions would stop. He got as far as the railway station. He stood in the line before the ticket counter, jostled by young men carrying hold–alls and aggressive matrons in bright saris. "Name?" said the man behind the window, but Aseem couldn't remember it. Around him, in the cavernous interior of the station, shouting, red–clad porters rushed past, balancing tiers of suitcases on their turbaned heads, and vast waves of passengers swarmed the stairs that led up across the platforms. People were nudging him, telling him to hurry up, but all he could think of were the still trains between the platforms, steaming in the cold air, hissing softly like warm snakes, waiting to take him away. The thought of leaving filled him with a sudden terror. He turned and walked out of the station. Outside, in the cold, glittering night, he breathed deep, fierce breaths of relief, as though he had walked away from his own death.

So here he is, the morning after his attempted escape, standing on the bridge, shivering in the fog. He notices a crack in the concrete railing, which he traces with his finger to the seedling of a pipal tree, growing on the outside of the rail. He remembers his mother pulling pipal seedlings out of walls and the paved courtyard of their house, over his protests. He remembers how difficult it was for him to see, in each fragile sapling, the giant full-grown tree. Leaning over the bridge, he finds himself wondering which will fall first – the pipal tree or the bridge. Just then he hears a bicycle on the road behind him, one that needs oiling, evidently, and before he knows it some rude fellow with a straggly beard has come out of the fog, pulled him off the railing and on to the road. "Don't be a fool, don't do it," says the stranger, breathing hard. His bicycle is lying on the roadside, one wheel still spinning. "Here, take this," the man says, pushing a small card into Aseem's unresisting hand. "Go see them. If they can't give you a reason to live, your own mother wouldn't be able to."

The address on the card proves to be in a small marketplace near Sarojini Nagar. Around a dusty square of withered grass where ubiquitous pariah dogs sleep fitfully in the pale sun, there is a row of shops. The place he seeks is a corner shop next to a vast jamun tree. Under the tree, three humped white cows are chewing cud, watching him with bovine indifference. Aseem makes his way through a jangle of bicycles, motor-rickshaws, and people, and finds himself before a closed door with a small sign saying only, "Pandit Vidyanath, Consultations." He goes in.

The Pandit is not in, but his assistant, a thin, earnest-faced young man, waves Aseem to a chair. The assistant is sitting behind a desk with a PC, a printer, and a plaque bearing his name: Om Prakash, BSc Physics (Failed), Delhi University. There is a window with the promised air-conditioner (apparently defunct) occupying its lower half. On the other side of the window is a beehive in the process of completion. Aseem feels he has come to the wrong place, and regrets already the whim that brought him here, but the beehive fascinates him, how it is still and in motion all at once, and the way the bees seem to be in concert with one another, as though performing a complicated dance. Two of the bees are crawling on the computer and there is one on the assistant's arm. Om Prakash seems completely unperturbed; he assures Aseem that the bees are harmless, and tries to interest him in array of bottles of honey on the shelf behind him. Apparently the bees belong to Pandit Vidyanath, a man of many facets, who keeps very busy because he also works for the city. (Aseem has a suspicion that perhaps the great man is no more than a petty clerk in a municipal office.) Honey is ten rupees a bottle. Aseem shakes his head, and Om Prakash gets down to business with a noisy clearing of his throat, asking questions and entering the answers into the computer. By now Aseem feels like a fool.

"How does your computer know the future?" Aseem asks.

Om Prakash has a lanky, giraffe-like grace, although he is not tall. He makes a deprecating gesture with his long, thin hands that travels all the way up to his mobile shoulders.

"A computer is like a beehive. Many bits and parts, none is by itself intelligent. Combine together, and you have something that can think. This computer is not an ordinary one. Built by Pandit Vidyanath himself."

Om Prakash grins as the printer begins to whir.

"All persons who come here seek meaning. Each person has their own dharma, their own unique purpose. We don't tell future, because future is beyond us, Sahib. We tell them why they need to live."

He hands a printout to Aseem. When he first sees it, the page makes no sense. It consists of xs arranged in an apparently random pattern over the page. He holds it at a distance and sees – indistinctly – the face of a woman.

"Who is she?"

"It is for you to interpret what this picture means," says Om Prakash. "You must live because you need to meet this woman, perhaps to save her or be saved. It may mean that you could be at the right place and time to save her from some terrible fate. She could be your sister or daughter, a wife or stranger."

There are dark smudges for eyes, the hint of a high cheekbone, and swirl of hair across the cheek, half–obscuring the mouth. The face is broad and heart–shaped, narrowing to a small chin.

"But this is not very clear.... It could be almost anyone. How will I know...."

"You will know when you meet her," Om Prakash says with finality. "There is no charge. Thank you, sir, and here are cards for you to give other unfortunate souls."

Aseem takes the pack of business cards and leaves. He distrusts the entire business, especially the bit about no charge. No charge? In a city like Delhi?

But despite his doubts he finds himself intrigued. He had expected the usual platitudes about life and death, the fatalistic pronouncements peculiar to charlatan fortune tellers, but this fellow Vidyanath obviously is an original. That Aseem must live simply so he might be there for someone at the right moment: what an amusing, humbling idea! As the days pass it grows on him, and he comes to believe it, if for nothing else than to have something in which to believe. He scans the faces of the people in the crowds, on the dusty sidewalks, the overladen buses, the Metro, and he looks for her. He lives so that he will cross her path some day. For three years, he has convinced himself that she is real, that she waits for him. He's made something of a life for himself, working at a photocopy shop in Lajpat Nagar, where he can sleep on winter nights, or making deliveries for shopkeepers in Defence Colony, who pay enough to keep him in food and clothing. For three years, he has handed out hundreds of the little business cards, and visited the address in South Delhi dozens of times. He's become used to the bees, the defunct air–conditioner, and even to Om Prakash. Although there is too much distance between them to allow friendship (a distance of temperament, really), Aseem has told Om Prakash about the apparitions he sees. Om Prakash receives these confidences with his rather

foolish grin and much waggling of the head in wonder, and says he will tell
Pandit Vidyanath. Only, each time Aseem visits there is no sign of Pandit
Vidyanath, so now Aseem suspects that there is no such person, that Om
Prakash himself is the unlikely mind behind the whole business.

But sometimes he is scared of finding the woman. He imagines
himself saving her from death or a fate worse than death, realizing at
last his purpose. But after that, what awaits him? The oily embrace of the
Yamuna?

Or will she save him in turn?

⌇

One of the things he likes about the city is how it breaks all rules. Delhi
is a place of contradictions – it transcends thesis and antithesis. Here he
has seen both the hovels of the poor and the opulent monstrosities of the
rich. At major intersections, where the rich wait impatiently in their air-
conditioned cars for the light to change, he's seen bone–thin waifs running
from car to car, peddling glossy magazines like *Vogue* and *Cosmopolitan*.
Amid the glitzy new high–rises are troupes of wandering cows and pariah
dogs; rhesus monkeys mate with abandon in the trees around Parliament
House.

He hasn't slept well – last night the police raided the Aurobindo Marg
sidewalk where he was sleeping. Some foreign VIP was expected in the
morning so the riffraff on the roadsides were driven off by stick–wielding
policemen. This has happened many times before, but today Aseem is
smarting with rage and humiliation: he has a bruise on his back where a
policeman's stick hit him, and it burns in the relentless heat. Death lurks
behind the walled eyes of the populace – but for once he is sick of his
proximity to death. So he goes to the only place where he can leave behind
the city without actually leaving its borders – another anomaly in a city
of surprises. Amid the endless sprawl of brick houses and crowded roads,
within Delhi's borders, there lies an entire forest: the Delhi Ridge, a green
lung. The coolness of the forest beckons to him.

Only a little way from the main road, the forest is still, except for the
subdued chirping of birds. He is in a warm, green womb. Under the acacia
trees, he finds an old ruin, one of the many nameless remains of Delhi's
medieval era. After checking for snakes or scorpions, he curls up under a
crumbling wall and dozes off.

Some time later, when the sun is lower in the sky and the heat not as
intense, he hears a tapping sound, soft and regular, like slow rain on a tin
roof. He sees a woman – a young girl – on the paved path in front of him,

holding a cane before her. She's blind, obviously, and lost. This is no place for a woman alone. He clears his throat and she starts.

"Is someone there?"

She's wearing a long blue shirt over a salwaar of the same colour, and there is a shawl around her shoulders. The thin material of her dupatta drapes her head, half covering her face, blurring her features. He looks at her and sees the face in the printout. Or thinks he does.

"You are lost," he says, his voice trembling with excitement. He fumbles in his pockets for the printout. Surely he must still be asleep and dreaming. Hasn't he dreamed about her many, many times already? "Where do you wish to go?"

She clutches her stick. Her shoulders slump.

"Naya Diwas Lane, good sir. I am traveling from Jaipur. I came to meet my sister, who lives here, but I lost my papers. They say you must have papers. Or they'll send me to Neechi-Dilli with all the poor and the criminals. I don't want to go there! My sister has money. Please, sir, tell me how to find Naya Diwas."

He's never heard of Naya Diwas Lane, or Neechi Dilli. New Day Lane? Lower Delhi? What strange names. He wipes the sweat off his forehead.

"There aren't any such places. Somebody has misled you. Go back to the main road, turn right, there is a marketplace there. I will come with you. Nobody will harm you. We can make enquiries there."

She thanks him, her voice catching with relief. She tells him she's heard many stories about the fabled city and its tall, gem-studded minars that reach the sky, and the perfect gardens. And the ships, the silver udan-khatolas, that fly across worlds. She's very excited to be here at last in the Immaculate City.

His eyes widen. He gets up abruptly, but she's already fading away into the trees. The computer printout is in his hand, but before he can get another look at her, she's gone.

What has he told her? Where is she going, in what future age, buoyed by the hope he has given her, which (he fears now) may be false?

He stumbles around the ruin, disturbing ground squirrels and a sleepy flock of jungle babblers, but he knows there is no hope of finding her again except by chance. Temporal coincidences have their own unfathomable rules. He's looked ahead to this moment so many times, imagined both joy and despair as a result of it, but never this apprehension, this uncertainty. He looks at the computer printout again. Is it mere coincidence that the apparition he saw looked like the image? What if Pandit Vidyanath's computer generated something quite random, and that his quest, his life for the past few years, has been completely pointless? That Om Prakash or

Vidyanath (if he exists) is enjoying an intricate joke at his expense? That he has allowed himself to be duped by his own hopes and fears?

But beyond all this, he's worried about this young woman. There's only one thing to do – go to Om Prakash and get the truth out of him. After all, if Vidyanath's computer generated her image, and if Vidyanath isn't a complete fraud, he would know something about her, about that time. It is a forlorn hope, but it's all he has.

He takes the Metro on his way back. The train snakes its way under the city through the still–new tunnels, past brightly–lit stations where crowds surge in and out and small boys peddle chai and soft drinks. At one of these stops, he sees the apparitions of people, their faces clammy and pale, clad in rags; he smells the stench of unwashed bodies too long out of the sun. They are coming out of the cement floor of the platform, as though from the bowels of the earth. He's seen them many times before; he knows they are from some future he'd rather not think about. But now it occurs to him with the suddenness of a blow that they are from the blind girl's future. Lower Delhi – Neechi Dilli – that is what this must be: a city of the poor, the outcast, the criminal, in the still–to–be–carved tunnels underneath the Delhi that he knows. He thinks of the Metro, fallen into disuse in that distant future, its tunnels abandoned to the dispossessed, and the city above a delight of gardens and gracious buildings, and tall spires reaching through the clouds. He has seen that once, he remembers. The Immaculate City, the blind girl called it.

By the time he gets to Vidyanath's shop, it is late afternoon, and the little square is filling with long shadows. At the bus stop where he disembarks, there is a young woman sitting, reading something. She looks vaguely familiar; she glances quickly at him but he notices her only peripherally.

He bursts into the room. Om Prakash is reading a magazine, which he sets down in surprise. A bee crawls out of his ear and flies up in a wide circle to the hive on the window. Aseem hardly notices.

"Where's that fellow, Vidyanath?"

Om Prakash looks mildly alarmed.

"My employer is not here, sir."

"Look, Om Prakash, something has happened, something serious. I met the young woman of the printout. But she's from the future. I need to go back and find her. You must get Vidyanath for me. If his computer made the image of her, he must know how I can reach her."

Om Prakash shakes his head sadly.

"Panditji speaks only through the computer." He looks at the beehive, then at Aseem. "Panditji cannot control the future, you know that. He can only tell you your purpose. Why you are important."

"But I made a mistake! I didn't realize she was from another time. I told her something and she disappeared before I could do anything. She could be in danger! It is a terrible future, Om Prakash. There is a city below the city where the poor live. And above the ground there is clean air and tall minars and udan khatolas that fly between worlds. No dirt or beggars or poor people. Like when the foreign VIPs come to town and the policemen chase people like me out of the main roads. But Neechi Dilli is like a prison, I'm sure of it. They can't see the sun."

Om Prakash throws his hands in the air.

"What can I say, Sahib?"

Aseem goes around the table and takes Om Prakash by the shoulders.

"Tell me, Om Prakash, am I nothing but a strand in a web? Do I have a choice in what I do, or am I simply repeating lines written by someone else?"

"You can choose to break my bones, sir, and nobody can stop you. You can choose to jump into the Yamuna. Whatever you do affects the world in some small way. Sometimes the effect remains small, sometimes it grows and grows like a pipal tree. Causality as we call it is only a first–order effect. Second–order causal loops jump from time to time, as in your visions, sir. The future, Panditji says, is neither determined nor undetermined."

Aseem releases the fellow. His head hurts and he is very tired, and Om Prakash makes no more sense than usual. He feels emptied of hope. As he leaves he turns to ask Om Prakash one more question.

"Tell me, Om Prakash, this Pandit Vidyanath, if he exists – what is his agenda? What is he trying to accomplish? Who is he working for?"

"Pandit Vidyanath works for the city, as you know. Otherwise he works only for himself."

He goes out into the warm evening. He walks toward the bus stop. Over the chatter of people and the car horns on the street and the barking of pariah dogs, he can hear the distant buzzing of bees.

At the bus stop, the half–familiar young woman is still sitting, studying a computer printout in the inadequate light of the street lamp. She looks at him quickly, as though she wants to talk, but thinks better of it. He sits on the cement bench in a daze. Three years of anticipation, all for nothing. He should write down the last story and throw away his notebook.

Mechanically, he takes the notebook out and begins to write.

She clears her throat. Evidently she is not used to speaking to strange men. Her clothes and manner tell him she's from a respectable middle-class family. And then he remembers the girl he pushed away from a bus near Nai Sarak.

She's holding the page out to him.

"Can you make any sense of that?"

The printout is even more indistinct than his. He turns the paper around, frowns at it, and hands it back to her.

"Sorry, I don't see anything."

She says: "You could interpret the image as a crystal of unusual structure, or a city skyline with tall towers. Who knows? Considering that I'm studying biochemistry and my father really wants me to be an architect with his firm, it isn't surprising that I see those things in it. Amusing, really."

She laughs. He makes what he hopes is a polite noise.

"I don't know. I think the charming and foolish Om Prakash is a bit of a fraud. And you were wrong about me, by the way. I wasn't trying to … to kill myself that day."

She's sounding defensive now. He knows he was not mistaken about what he saw in her eyes. If it wasn't then, it would have been some other time – and she knows this.

"Still, I came here on an impulse," she says in a rush, "and I've been staring at this thing and thinking about my life. I've already made a few decisions about my future."

A bus comes lurching to a stop. She looks at it, then at him, and hesitates. He knows she wants to talk, but he keeps scratching away in his notebook. At the last moment before the bus pulls away, she swings her bag over her shoulder, waves at him, and climbs aboard. The look he had first noticed in her eyes has gone, for the moment. Today, she's a different person.

He finishes writing in his notebook, and with a sense of inevitability that feels strangely right, he catches a bus that will take him across one of the bridges that span the Yamuna.

໒ᘒ

At the bridge, he leans against the concrete wall looking into the dark water. This is one of his familiar haunts; how many people has he saved on this bridge? The pipal tree sapling still grows in a crack in the cement – the municipality keeps uprooting it, but it is buried too deep to die completely. Behind him there are cars and lights and the sound of horns, the jangle of bicycle bells. He sets his notebook down on top of the wall, wishing he had given it to someone, like that girl at the bus stop. He can't make himself throw it away. A peculiar lassitude, a detachment, has taken hold of him and he can think and act only in slow motion.

He's preparing to climb on to the wall of the bridge, his hands clammy and slipping on the concrete, when he hears somebody behind him say, "Wait!" He turns. It is like looking into a distorting mirror. The man is hollow-cheeked, with a few days' stubble on his chin, and the untidy thatch of hair has thinned and is streaked with silver. He holds a bunch of cards in his hand. A welt mars one cheek, and his left sleeve is torn and stained with something rust-coloured. His eyes are leopard's eyes, burning with a dreadful urgency. "Aseem," says the stranger who is not a stranger, panting as though he has been running, his voice breaking a little. "Don't...." He is already starting to fade. Aseem reaches out a hand and meets nothing but air. A million questions rise in his head, but before he can speak the image is gone.

Aseem's first impulse is a defiant one. What if he were to jump into the river now – what would that do to the future, to causality? It would be his way of bowing out of the game that the city's been playing with him, of saying: I've had enough of your tricks. But the impulse dies. He thinks instead about Om Prakash's second-order causal loops, of sunset over the Red Fort, and the twisting alleyways of the old city, and death sleeping under the eyelids of the citizenry. He sits down slowly on the dusty sidewalk. He covers his face with his hands; his shoulders shake.

After a long while he stands up. The road before him can take him anywhere, to the faded colonnades and bright bustle of Connaught Place, to the hush of public parks, with their abandoned cricket balls and silent swings, to old government housing settlements where, amid sleeping bungalows, ancient trees hold court before somnolent congresses of cows. The dusty bylanes and broad avenues and crumbling monuments of Delhi lie before him, the noisy, lurid marketplaces, the high-tech glass towers, the glitzy enclaves with their citadels of the rich, the boot-boys and beggars at street corners.... He has just to take a step and the city will swallow him up, receive him the way a river receives the dead. He is a corpuscle in its veins, blessed or cursed to live and die within it, seeing his purpose now and then, but never fully.

Staring unseeingly into the bright clamor of the highway, he has a wild idea that, he realizes, has been bubbling under the surface of his consciousness for a while. He recalls a picture he saw once in a book when he was a boy: a satellite image of Asia at night. On the dark bulge of the globe there were knots of light; like luminous fungi, he had thought at the time, stretching tentacles into the dark. He wonders whether complexity and vastness are sufficient conditions for a slow awakening, a coming-to-consciousness. He thinks about Om Prakash, his foolish grin and waggling head, and his strange intimacy with the bees. Will Om Prakash tell him who Pandit Vishwanath really is, and what it means to "work for the city?" He thinks not. What he must do, he sees at last, is what he has been doing all along: look out for his own kind, the poor and the desperate, and those who walk with death in their eyes. The city's needs are alien, unfathomable. It is an entity in its own right, expanding every day, swallowing the surrounding countryside, crossing the Yamuna which was once its boundary, spawning satellite children, infant towns that it will ultimately devour. Now it is burrowing into the earth, and even later it will reach long fingers towards the stars.

What he needs most at this time is someone he can talk to about all this, someone who will take his crazy ideas seriously. There was the girl at the bus stop, the one he had rescued in Nai Sarak. Om Prakash will have her address. She wanted to talk; perhaps she will listen as well. He remembers the printout she had shown him and wonders if her future has something to do with the Delhi-to-come, the city that intrigues and terrifies him: the Delhi of udan-khatolas, the "ships that fly between worlds," of starved and forgotten people in the catacombs underneath. He wishes he could have asked his future self more questions. He is afraid because it is likely (but not certain, it is never that simple) that some kind of violence awaits him, not just the violence of privation, but a struggle that looms indistinctly ahead, that will cut his cheek and injure his arm, and do untold things to his soul. But for now there is nothing he can do, caught as he is in his own time-stream. He picks up his notebook. It feels strangely heavy in his hands. Rubbing sticky tears out of his eyes, he staggers slowly into the night.

Tamai Kobayashi *was born in Japan and raised in Canada. She is the author of* All Names Spoken *(co-authored with Mona Oikawa, Sister Vision Press),* Exile and the Heart *(Women's Press) and* Quixotic Erotic *(Arsenal Pulp Press). She is also a screenwriter and videomaker. "Panopte's Eye" is an excerpt from her novel-in-progress. She lives in Toronto.*

Panopte's Eye
Tamai Kobayashi

The Panopticon towered, cyclopean, encircled by the honeycombed cells of the city. Below its surveillance lay the marketplace with its shanties and cesspools, the vendors of roasted rats and charred gulls, the hand trade and blackbarter. The cells themselves were carved out of the Wall, baked in the heat, and the wavering air writhed, itself a creature that slithered out of the stinking orifices of the Wall. At the four point towers, the sentries gazed outward: against the torch gangs, or caravans of plague, or the rush of the coming flood. West lay the rubble, East, the parch, and between them, this city, this fortress, this prison.

The Panopticon towered, implacable in its slow revolution, but the Wall held its own, the residue of a thousand years, stratus of crushed cars, helios, side beams, electrical boards, a steam engine, the ruins of a crushed tower, maybe even the Rosetta stone. It was an architecture of failure, an archeology of defeat. What wasn't crushed into the Wall was burned, even in the high heat, for fuel. Beyond the Wall, the desert lay in the Dry, the high flood in the Wet, caravans of tuberculosis, bubonic encephalitis, ebola, trich, and rot, the venal and trade. Along the crest of the Wall, the Corpsmen stood, their glittering laser guns stabbing at the heavens. Death from the sky from dart ships. Even the stars were enemies. Caravans were life and death, hope and dread. And the Panopticon saw all, a massive eye; the Corpsmen were its arms, its legs; the shanties, its floating bowels. Yet the mind … and the heart.

United Corpsman Corazon Altzar was a woman, ranking gunnar, third class. She stood against the high wind, her black hair cropped close as she carried the ammo packs, the patience of arms, shift, the graceful swing, from hip to shoulder, passing hand to hand in a row of grunts. As gunnar, she fell into the class of mezas, the kickass poor who'd clawed their way up to the bottom rung, and hung there, ready to grasp whatever opportunities came their way. She was a grunt at heart, a meza of African and Indian blood, who'd never make it out of the shafting ranks, not like the Bluebloods, who worked in the Tower itself. Not like the Techs, who combed their way through the fabled tunnels, through distant hills, their collars winking in the dark. But a gunnar grunt, eating, breathing, shitting dust in the shadow of the Eye.

"Heads up, Altzar!" Corp Sargent shouted.

Altzar spit crow and looked up at the sky. No tell–tale black streaks, no dart ships here. She turned back to Corp Sargent. But he was running up the ramp, to the crest of the Wall, shoving aside the sentries, who were pointing and shouting. The ammo line disintegrated in the chase for weapons as Corpsmen poured along the top of the Wall. Altzar ran to the tower, clipped on her eye shield and mask, and peered into the dust whirl on the horizon. Kage, her second, trailed after her. Without armour or mask, Kage looked like some rag twisting in the wind, something small and feral that slinked through the cracks. Altzar's chest shield grated against the stone cornice as she glanced at the horizon. A raid, or sand devil, she didn't know which was worse. Caught outside, on the perimeter, the whirl of sand devils could cost you your eyes.

"What is it?" Kage peered into the sky. "It's too early for the Flood. Not even a crazy lord would attack without darts."

Altzar could hear the click of the binocs in the tower beside her, the beeps of the ecolock. She rubbed her fingers beneath the eye shield, blinked away the grit. When she looked again, she could see them, a writhing mass, like some great lumbering snake, caught up in its own tail. Caravan. A shout from the soldiers, even if it meant quarantine duty. Caravans meant riches, trade, and adventure. Caravan meant there was a way out of this rathole.

Altzar whooped, but her finger never left the trigger. She clicked mag on her eyes and saw the trail, mostly slavies, haulcarts, billowing trawls.

She bit her lip, clicked mag, clicked mag, scanning the trade. Sometimes the gangs would jack a caravan, hiding under the tails, their guns sheathed in tradelocks and just roll through the gates – trojan cargo. "Looks clear." She glanced at Kage, the tightness of shoulders, that unnerving stillness. Kage, who looked like blood, the pure ones, but Asiatic, not the Blue. "You'll be going to the shanties tonight."

Kage bowed her head. "Request permission to –"

"Ah, go on," Altzar cuffed her off, and Kage scuttled away.

Kage always took first crack at the Caravans; she was a good second, one of the best. She had slipped through the Tech ring, but always returned, looping back to the backstalls, searching, searching in Caravan's tail. She was always good for a scramble of rum, a contraband clip on the disc, or a forbidden trancer, no questions asked. Favours that had greased the wheels for Altzar at Command, favours that were the streamnet, when that bottom rung broke. As Kage descended, above her, Altzar clicked again. A scrawny lot for a caravan this size. Heavy dues, maybe, from gangs in the Parch. But there wasn't much competition, the last caravan run had been two months ago and everyone relied on the runs. Caravan. Life and death. A sliver of hope in a wasteland.

✿

What the caravans meant to Hurston was dust, and more dust. No masks for the slavies here, no, just breathing, eating, shitting dust. Sleep dust was what could kill you, drowning in dryness as it filled your lungs. Dust that lingered underneath the tongue, dust crumbles shaking out of your nose, your ears. No end to dust here. Dust. And ashes.

Now Hurston could see the city, but she felt no better. The chain chafed at her ankles, the collar scratched at her throat, and the prod zaps were becoming more frequent as the pace quickened to a murderous beat. They would be there in no time. If they stayed alive.

Beside her Cranston stumbled, his thin frame crumbling into a sprawl. Linked as they were, he took Hurston down with him.

"Up, come on, you can do it." Hurston grabbed his rags, pulled him to his knees. She squatted down, slipped a hypo against his neck. Cranston's eyes snapped open. He smiled weakly. "What?" his lips cracking, "you haven't given up on me yet?"

"Don't just sit there, goddamn it. Let's get going."

"Hurston –"

"Save your breath. Now, on the count of three. One. Two –"

She dragged him up.

She could see the gate, glimpsed the black uniforms, the red crest. So they were still United, even after the fallout. This far north, some cities had returned to pre-annexation union or independent citystate. But the black uniforms and red crests. Hurston craned her neck. If the city was United, then there must be…. She stared, her heart sinking at the sight of it.

Black, in the centre of the city. The Eye.

"Oh, fuck."

Cranston looked up. "What?" And saw the orb. "Delete it. Just keep your head down." He squinted. "Think they'll do a D-scan here?"

"Who knows. Tech looks run down. Their guns aren't even humming. My guess is this place is running to shit."

"And what the hell does that make us?"

Cranston grinned.

The line shuffled to a stop, but Hurston could not take her eyes off it. "You know, they call it a panopticon. It can see you, but you can't see it seeing you. So maybe it's watching all the time. Or maybe not. It gets under your skin. Makes you watch yourself just in case it's watching."

The line slunk forward. They were at the gate.

Cranston tugged at her sleeve. "Pass the hypo."

Hurston passed it without a word. The scan was coming up and both knew the odds: if they found it on him, he'd be traced as Tech, slapped with a collar, and Hurston would never see him again. But then again Cranston was forty years old; on the line he was an old, old man. The scanner buzzed and crackled, but no, nothing. Cranston and Hurston shuffled down, into the shanties, herded by the prod zaps into the barter quarter. Hurston stared at the crumbling partitions, the dust, the rock, the rusting shell. Rags and filth. She'd been in better hellholes, seen fatter rats.

But there must be something here to give this cesspool life, or at least some kind of promise of what passed for life. Mining in the rubble, or a chainlink for United, in this quadrant. And the Wall, the detritus of a thousand years.

Cranston jabbed her, nodded at the trader walking by. Hurston watched him look them over. She knew what that meant – no chow, there was never any chow before a barter. No rest, either.

The trader looked over the herd for the first skim, pointing the barters as his second raced to scan them in, the laser beeping as it ran across the hand.

"You, you, and you," the Trader pointed at Hurston, only a moment for a nod from Cranston, and she was on another line, another future. The scanner flashed, bright red. Cranston smiled his goodbye, and she caught it, his broad face, brown wrinkles, brown eyes, his dreads falling to his shoulders over that terrible thinness. Then the links dropped as the prod zap flared and she stumbled on, without a chance to even say her thanks.

Kage walked among the stalls, watching the traders set their wares. Each trader had a different method, a different tactic. Sometimes there was the big enticement, then the smaller hook, or planted "bumpers" to hike the prices up. Sometimes it was the muscle that did the talking or the gold liquor weighed by a slanted scale. But it was the slavies that Kage saw, torn shawls and bloodied feet, the scan on the back of the hand, the averted eyes, the lines and lines of misery. By the end stall, she slipped a biscuit into a child's hand. *I'll try and come for you*, but knew she could promise nothing. She clipped on her goggles and slipped between the stalls, into the crowded backhall.

The backhall was barely a metre wide, jammed with bodies yet to go on stall. The stench curled in Kage's nostrils, pinched at her eyes. As she blinked clear, Kage scanned through the stock, glancing off the shufflers, those close to gone, the walking dead. Where she could smell the fear, she stopped. Fear could mean many things, she knew, and felt it twisting in her gut. The pit was too familiar, and these faces. She'd stood in their place five years before, before Altzar had picked her for her second. She always wonder why Altzar had chosen her, had fought her Corps for a skinny slavie, but Altzar had never told her. Altzar was a mystery. It was a pity Kage didn't trust her.

But Altzar never asked any questions, so Kage didn't need to tell lies. Kage could have done worse, far worse.

Kage paused, her goggles buzzing. She turned to the corner. The woman was wiry thin, but Kage could see the strength beneath the fall of the tattered robe. Shoulders stooped, not out of habit, but in defense, the alert cock of her head, how she held her hands hidden, poised. Her dreads were pulled back and her brown skin was dusted with a coat of sand. Kage guessed she had been on the line for a only a couple of months. Kage glanced at her, handsome face, strong lines, and paused – *she is hiding her hands*. Kage's heart began to pound. The woman was subtly submissive, calculatingly so.

Kage called out to the Trader. "How much for this one?"

Crudely, the Trader studied Kage, gauging what he could grab. "Twenty."

"Twenty? Do you think I'm blind? Thin as a bone and about to drop. Ten tops."

"Eighteen or you're robbin' me."

Kage haggled down to thirteen. As she counted out, she tried to stop her hands from shaking. The woman had not said a word. As the scanner winked over the woman's hand, Kage saw it: a small protrusion on the wrist.

Kage waved her down the hall. "What's your name?"

The woman jolted and Kage remembered; on the line you were nothing – just a scan away from oblivion. But the woman recovered fast; the parch rot had not taken her voice. "Hurston."

Kage put out her hand. "Kage."

Hurston shook, hesitant.

"You're not a slavie anymore, Hurston."

"No D-scan?"

"No D-scan."

Hurston paused. "What am I?"

Kage looked her up and down. How easily she shed the links. "You're my second. I serve under United Corpsman Altzar."

"United."

Was that a challenge already? They hadn't even left the backhall.

"Yeah, United." Kage dropped her voice. "In hell you learn to dance for the devil. Come on, I'll show you the quarters."

ⵣ

Corpsman Altzar's quarters were in the top rung of the soldier's enclave, right below the guns. These quarters were the first trans that Kage had swung for Altzar, with Kage's subtle nudge, an exchange for twelve trancers and no questions asked. The climb was high but the security was worth it. As they rose upshaft, Kage quelched the urge to glance behind her. Let Hurston study her, the beginnings of trust; it was the least that Kage could give her. Kage herself was full of questions, but she could wait. She had been waiting for years.

As Hurston climbed the shafts, she noted the towers, the placement of the quarters; they were in the corner pocket – harder to scan for the Panopticon. Beneath the guns, there would be some interference with the hummers. Hurston observed that the corners were the weak points for the Eye: circle squared. Had this place been chosen for this purpose?

And Kage: who was this little rat's pup slinking from shadow to shadow, from backhall to sentry post? Altzar, had Hurston been bought for him? She shivered. And how could a grunt hold two seconds in a pit like this? Hurston looked behind her. She could see the unblinking eye of the Panopticon and, below, the shanties, the labyrinthine bowels of the marketplace, the backhall, the shithole of the stalls. End of the line. Hurston thought of Cranston, his wracked body, hollow sighs. Too late. Hurston shunted him from her mind. Her body count was way too high.

They stopped below the guns and Kage waved her into the corridor. The transition was sharp and Hurston stumbled, from the brightness of the shafts to the darkness of the hall. A small hand on her arm and Hurston knew it was Kage guiding her, but she was beginning to make out the glow strips floating along the floor. Hurston counted her paces against the sudden panic of blindness. Twenty-two and they were at the door. The lights fluttered and Hurston could see the quarters, luxurious in her eyes. A dent room, barely enough for two to turn around in, with an upright, probably Kage's and beyond, Altzar's rooms. Nothing fancy, nothing unusual, too nondescript for words, as if to say to the passing eye *move along, nothing here to see.* "So what's the story?"

Kage swung around, surprised, but just opened a console and placed a ration square in Hurston's hands. She let down the bunk slab and gestured to Hurston.

"Eat first."

Hurston sat and devoured the meal. Kage looked away. It seemed unbecoming to see such desperate hunger. And Hurston, she could tell, needed her pride. Had she been the same way, coming off the line, that need to hide her weakness, the sham of self preservation? No, Kage had been different, a bundle of fear that had frozen that desperate instinct to flee. Kage remembered that she had hidden under the bunk slab for weeks. Altzar had been the patient one, coaxing her out with treasures of food. Altzar the master, Altzar the enemy.

"Eat this one slowly." Kage held out another ration in her hand, along with a cup of water.

Hurston looked at her and chewed. As Kage ruffled through the storage box, she handed to Hurston what looked like treasures: a protein cube, soy spread, and miracle of miracles, a hard boiled egg. Kage smiled as Hurston struggled to hide her surprise, surprise and relief, her solid realization that she was safe for now – you don't waste a meal on a dead skivvy.

Kage turned and busied herself with a wire console in the corner, careful with her movements. *Close enough to keep an eye on, far enough for privacy.* Always a balance when the world's spun sideways, coming off the line. *Space enough and this one will come to me.*

"So who is this Altzar?" Hurston, her cup empty, her food eaten.

Kage sat down beside her. "Altzar is a gunnar in United. I am her second."

Hurston nodded, taking it in. "So Altzar is a woman," she murmured.

Kage continued. "We're in the third Quadrant; it's still pretty much United, although we do get raids, torch gangs mostly. Sometimes an

Alliance of citystates, they get together, give us a go. You see, United has control of the mining in the Rubble, where the mountains used to be." Kage filled Hurston's cup. "Altzar is decent. She'll give you no trouble. Besides, you're my second."

"Your second? Where do you get the chops for that?"

Kage smiled, waved her hand around the room. "This may not look like much, but it's better than most in the shithole. Now you, where do you come from?"

Hurston's eyes fell. "East. I got taken in the east. Around the salt flats. We were surveying for potash."

Kage sighed. *This old game. We play as if our lives depend on it. And they do.* "You're a Tech, aren't you?"

Hurston, the slightest hesitation, as she answered, "Nah, just a horse, trucking equipment here and there."

Kage sat back. "You know, we could waste a lot of time –" She thought of slapping a scan on her, but no, lose her now and she'd be lost forever. Kage gestured for Hurston's arm. *Careful, she may just bolt.* Hurston's face, like stone but her fist held out, fingers curled, defiant. *She's thinking it's another link, but it's now or never.* Kage traced the protrusion on Hurston's wrist. "You're Ark." Kage held out her arm, pointing to the jut on her own wrist, a small, circular cicatrice. "Like me."

✧

Ark VI

Kage sat on the hillock, running her hands through the long meadow grass. Green, green, she watched the sway of willows by the riverside, above her, the darting swoop of swallows, a burst of finches, yellow and red, roosting by the raspberry bushes that covered the Observation Station. For as far as she could see the lush woodland spread out before her. Tomorrow they would release the higher mammals from the cryolock: four wolves, two black bears.

Integration was going well, yet it seemed a shame; the place was a paradise, but Kage knew the balance of the ecosystem: predators were a necessity. She had had the same argument with Zhang, the entomologist – were mosquitoes really vital? What about those aphids? – and had gotten a lecture for her troubles. Yet she enjoyed arguing with her, Zhang's passion, her precision, that frisson of – what? Kage sighed. Here, so many miles below the embattled world, they were allowed these flirting distractions. Yet the Ark was still under the protection of United Corporation and it was best to be cautious. The reports coming from topside were ominous. Cities collapsing, armed resurrection. Kage thought, *I should be out there, overthrowing this monstrous regime.* But here she was, safe and secure, in the belly of the armoured beast, doing its bidding. *Well, not the belly, some useless appendage.* Project Ark, a subsidiary of United. She sighed. *And what could I do, I'm only a scientist.* She was the youngest on board, lucky to be sent here, lucky to be chosen.

The Project at least held some promise. Ten underground libraries, scattered throughout the northern quadrants, biospheres of natural habitats, like they had been before the uc Weather Umbrella Initiative. Kage shivered. At least she didn't have anything to do with that catastrophe. Like the frying pan into the fire, seed clouds to ease the drought brought on by the global greenhouse effect. Rains that washed out the continental agricorps, followed by a blistering drought that tore off the remaining topsoil. Kage pulled up a handful of grass, let the blades fall. But then, that's what you get when the world is carved up by Corporations.

But here, Kage leaned back, hands behind her head, looked up to the wispy vapour swirls that passed for clouds, under this artificial sun. She could smell the blossoming lilacs, hear the drone of bright and bumbling bees nestling among the buds. The Ark. Like life before the Corps, before the devastating environment regulation. But here, the birds, the flitting birds, the call of frogs in the riverbed, the chase of chipmunks in the orchard, everything in balance.

Except they weren't allowed to live in paradise. Maintenance, yes, and research, but limited impact. What did it mean, when they couldn't stay in the biosphere, that their human presence undermined the very harmony which they worked so hard to preserve? Outside the bubble, they catalogued and controlled, guarding the seed libraries, upgrading the cryolock. Stanton had petitioned for a community garden, but Kiran, sticking to her rulebook, had overruled all the scientists. The sphere would not be contaminated. Which reminded her.

Kage sighed, began to shamble towards the quarters. The air, so calm, so lush, not like the antiseptic, iron–tinged drafts pumped in from above, filtered and flushed, but here, a warm, living creature, tendril caresses. Kage grabbed a handful of grass, sprinkling it around her. She froze. The blades of grass had fallen but not scattered. She looked up. The trees, so calm, not a leaf fluttered. The river, too, had stilled.

She turned, breath clutching her chest. The birds. Kage burst into a shouting run, jabbing at the comlink on her arm. She was rounding the air shafts when the explosion hit her.

When Kage woke, her clothes were singed, the grass burning. Red

Crested United uniforms swarmed around the river, pumping water topside, but she had not been spotted, not yet. She brushed her damp forehead, her hand bloody, comlink smashed beyond repair. She blinked, her temples pulsing with a dull, insistent pain. She'd been blown into a hollow, the tall grasses obscuring her from the soldiers. UC military – hostile takeover – they must have overrun the research branch, Kage thought, why else this carnage. And the others – Kage crawled to the service tunnel below the Observation Station. She could feel the earth beneath her shaking, the rumbling blast of a field detonator. *Why? We have no weapons.* If the others had made it to the evacuation checkpoint, there'd be some chance of saving something. Maybe they'd overlook the cryolock, if this was just a raid to line some commander's pocket. A chamber breach could be sealed off and the biolab saved. But as Kage scrambled through the darkness of intersection five, she stumbled, sprawling, foot caught on –

Kiran lay below her, comlink blinking.

Relief flooded Kage, her choke of tears. Kiran, the architect of this sphere, she'd know where to go, where the others would be. Kiran, with her clicks and rattles, her protocols and procedures, she would know what to do. If they hid, they could wait out this battle, start over when the dust settled.

Kage grabbed her by the arm.

"Thank God –"

But Kiran's arm wasn't there. Kage's hand came away bloody. She held it against the light. The light, falling so dimly, she could barely see – half of Kiran's face had been blown away. Kage scuttled back, legs kicking, thrashing, a scream crushed down in her chest. Kage, panting, sweat stinging her eyes, shaking, as she dragged herself beneath a buttress. They were a scientific ob station. Non–military. It didn't make any sense.

A blast shook the tunnel, obscuring her vision. Kage brushed off her tears. And ran.

ev3

"I ran and ran and ran. Ran so long, dodging soldiers, fire, ran so I didn't have to sit still." Kage passed Hurston a bottle. "Eventually I hid in the air shaft, one of the auxiliary tubes, until the smoke cleared. They didn't stay long, the soldiers, just another snatch and burn operation. We didn't know, in the Ark, we didn't know how bad it was topside. I mean, the civil war, the linkup just talked about containment. Bullshit." Kage shook her head.

"I went back in. They were all dead, some blasted, some shot running. The rest they just lined up and pulled the trigger."

"Yeah," Hurston spoke in a monotone. "They came down through the freight tunnel, blasted through the chambers. They torched our seed libary, slaughtered our bio reserves. Then they wiped their asses with our field data. What a waste." Hurston took a swing of the bottle, winced.

"Easy on that," Kage cracked. "Even rocket fuel doesn't have a cleaner burn." She turned to the console.

∿

Hurston studied Kage, this little rat's pup. Everything about her was small. Feral and furtive, she had survived, twisting through the bowels of this city, right under the Eye. Hurston just had to ask. "So how did they catch you?"

Kage looked away. "I made it topside, pretty banged up, half starved, half scorched. Smoke was billowing out of all the shafts. Red flag for miles, you know, for scavangers, a trawl. Got caught by a torch gang, slumped the line to the eastern board, then I was traded to Caravan. Dragged here. Altzar bought me when I was barely skin and bones. But she doesn't know about this."

Hurston leaned forward. "She knows you're Tech."

"Yeah, but she won't sell me out." Kage smiled. "I make her life too easy." Kage paused. There was more to it than that, she knew, but this wasn't the time nor the place. "Like I said, she's okay, but I don't tell her anything. She's smart, but none too bright." Kage faced her, her eyes flickering over Hurston's face. She placed her hand on Hurston's shoulder. "You should sleep." Kage stood.

"Altzar –"

"I can handle Altzar. Rest."

No way I'll be able to sleep, Hurston thought as she leaned back on the bunk. She watched Kage retreat to the console in the corner. Hurston took a deep breath, feeling her ever–present weariness surge to the surface. She clawed back, her mind snapping clear, a habit of survival: on the line you never slept. But here? How much could she trust this little pup?

Hurston's eyes fluttered. The world spun heavily, her legs sinking into the mat, her head, swamped by churning fears that exhausted themselves in the battle for supremacy, she floated, desperately hanging on to that edge, until finally, eyes closed, stomach full, she sank into a clear, uncluttered sleep.

∿

As Hurston slept, Kage's mind raced. What she needed: clothes, rations, Ident scan. She'd have to keep an eye on Hurston. It wasn't unknown that the traders snatched back their goods before taking off to the next market. But after that they'd be free and clear.

Then the work would begin.

What would she tell Altzar? Her impulse, as always, was for the truth. She laughed inwardly. Suicide, the easiest way out of this cesspool. Yet Kage was not so sure. What was it about Altzar that made her trust her? Altzar never asked questions. What kind of soldier was she? But a soldier never asks why, just points a gun and blasts away.

It was more than that, Kage knew. Altzar had been the first human face she had seen since the destruction of the Ark. On the Caravan, Kage had only been barter, a piece of meat traded, trucked from post to post. Altzar had chosen her, saved her from death on the line. She didn't beat her or rape her, not like some of the other Corpsmen with their seconds. Altzar's demands seemed reasonable, a benevolent master, yet still a master. Kage checked herself. She mustn't forget that. Not when someone has the power to swap you to the fleshbowls in exchange for promo or trancers, or sell you down the line. Kage was still a slave, always a slave. But this place, the mindfuck of this place, you needed an emotional retreat, or a stable if not safe anchor. This prison stripped you of everything you were and what you took was what was given. Identification with your captors. The Eye, the fucking Eye, chipping away at your soul. Kage realized she depended on Altzar's silences, her distance, her stony self-sense. That and the promise of the Ark.

What would she tell Altzar? Something she would understand. For Kage had spent years watching that meza third class gunnar. She would give her a sliver of the truth. That Kage was lonely. And that she had chosen Hurston.

SECTION III
ALLEGORY

The following two stories are largely allegorical. "The Grassdreaming Tree" by Sheree Renee Thomas is a twist on the tale of the ever-familiar schism between parents and children, told from the point-of-view of a group of black colonists. "The Blue Road: A Fairy Tale" by Wayde Compton shows the contorted shapes we become as we're forced to live according to the dictates of the powerful.

A native of Memphis, **Sheree Renée Thomas** *is the editor of the anthology* series Dark Matter, *winner of the World Fantasy Award and named a* New York Times Notable Book of the Year. *Her short stories and poetry appear in* Mojo: Conjure Stories, Role Call: A Generational Collection of Social and Political Black Literature & Art, Bum Rush the Page: A Def Poetry Jam, Meridians: feminism race transnationalism, 2001: A Science Fiction Poetry Anthology, Obsidian III, Cave Canem, African Voices, Drumvoices Revue: 10th Anniversary Anthology, *and* Renaissance Noire. *She is a 2003 New York Foundation of the Arts Poetry Fellow and recipient of the Ledig House/LEF Foundation Prize in Fiction for Bonecarver. Her work was also nominated for a Rhysling Award and received Honorable Mention in the* Year's Best Fantasy & Horror: Sixteenth Annual Edition. *She teaches at the Frederick Douglass Creative Arts Center in Manhattan and the Center for Black Literature at Medgar Evers College, and is currently leading Eldersongs, an oral history poetry project, and other works designed to uplift, engage, and enlighten the community. For more information, email* wanganegresse@yahoo.com.

The Grassdreaming Tree

Sheree R. Thomas

That woman was always in shadow; no memory saved her from the dark. True, her star was not Sun but some other place. Nor did she come from this country called life. Maybe that's why she always lived with her shoulders turned back, walked with the caution of strangers – outside woman trying to sweep her way in. The grasshopper peddler, witchdoctor seller, didn't even have no name, no name. So folks didn't know where to place her. For all they know, she didn't even have no navel string, just them green humming things, look like dancing blades of grass. They look at her, with her no name self, and they call her grasswoman.

Every morning she would pass through the black folks' land, carrying her enormous baskets. These she made herself, 'cause nobody else remembered. And they were made from grass so flimsy, they didn't even look like baskets, more like brown bubbles 'bout to pop. What they looked like were dying leaves dangling from her limbs, great curled wings that might flutter away, kicked up by a soft wind. Inside the baskets, the grasshoppers fluttered around and pranced, blue–green winged, long-legged things. The *click-clack, tap-tap* of the hoppers' limbs announced her arrival. A tattoo of drumbeats followed the grasswoman wherever she went, drumbeats so loud they rattled the windows and flung back shades:

Mama, the children cried, *Mama, look! Grasswoman comin'!*

And the hoppers would flood the streets. Their joy exchanged: the grasshoppers shouted and the children jumped, one heartbeat at a time. The woman would pull out her mouth harp and put the song to melody. The whole world was filled with their music.

But behind curtains drawn shut in frustration, the settlers suck–teethed dissatisfaction. They took the grasswoman's seeds and tried to crush them with suspicion, replacing the grasswoman's music with their own dark song – who did that white gal think she was? Where she come from and who in the world was her mama? Who told her she could come shuffling down their street, barefooted and grubby–toed, selling bugs and asking folk for food? The white ought to go on back to her proper place. *But the bugs are so sweet*, the children insisted. The parents shut their ears and stiffened their necks: No, no, and no again.

But the children didn't pay them no mind. The grasswoman's baskets were too full of songs to forget to play. One little girl, hardheaded than most, disobeyed the edict and devoted herself to the enigmatic grasswoman. Her name was Mema, a big–eyed child with a head like a drum. She would wake early, plant her eyes on the cool window pane, waiting for the grasswoman to walk by. When the woman would come into view, Mema would rush down the stairs, *skip hop jump*. Bare feet running, she'd fly down the road and disappear among the swarm of grasshoppers spilling from the great leaf baskets. The Sun would sink, a red jackball sky, and still no word from Mema. Not a hide nor a hair they'd see, and at Mema's home, her folks would start pulling out their worries and polishing them up with spite.

Running barefoot, wild as that other.

Her daddy picked his switch and held it in his hand. Only her mama's soft words brought relief to the little girl's return. Hours later in the fullness of night, her daddy insisted on a reason, even if it was just the chalk line of truth:

Where she stay? Did you go to her house? Do she even have a house?

Her dwelling was an okro tree. She laid her head in the empty hollow of its great stone trunk. Mema told them the tree was sacred, that God had planted its roots upside down so they touched sky.

Daddy turned to his wife, pointing the blame finger at her. *See, the white's been filling her head. That tree ain't got no roots. Whole world made of stone, thick as your head. Couldn't grow a tree to save your life.*

The girl spoke up, hoppers hidden all in her hair. *It's true, Mama, it's true. The tree got a heart and sometime it get real sad. The old woman say the okro tree can kill itself, say it can do it by fire. Even if nobody strike a match.*

Mama just shook her head. Daddy roll his eyes. *Stone tree dead by fire?*

Child say, *It's true.*

What foolishness, the mama say and she draw her daughter close to her, tucking her big head under her chin, far and away from her daddy's reach. Then the man left, taking his anger with him, and he handed it over to the other settlers. At the lodge, they all agreed: the grasswoman's visits had to end. They couldn't kill her – to do so would offend the land and the children and the women, so whatever was done, they agreed to give the deed some thought.

Next day, the grasshopper seller returned. The drumbeats–of–joy wings and legs swept through the air. Even the settlers stopped to listen. Spite was in their mouths, but the rhythm took hold of their feet. After all, that white was bringing with her such beauty none had ever seen. None could resist her grasshoppers' winged anthem, nor their blue–greened glory, shining and iridescent as God's first land. The sight was like nothing else in this new and natural world. They'd left their stories in that other place and now the grasshopper peddler was selling them back.

The folk began to wonder: where in the name of all magic did she get such miraculous creatures? Couldn't have been from this land where the soil was pink and ruddy, and no grass grew anywhere save for under glass–topped houses carefully tended by the science ones. They had packed up all their knowledge and carried it with them in small black stones that were not opened until they'd settled on this other shore with its two bright stars folk just looked at and called Sun 'cause some habits just hard to break.

And where indeed? Whoever heard tale of grasshoppers where they ain't no grass? Where, if they themselves had already brought the most distant of their new land to heel?

The grasshopper peddler only answered with a chuckle, her two cheeks puffed out like she 'bout to whistle. But she don't speak, just smiling so, skin all red and blistered, folk wonder how she could stand one Sun, let alone two. They began to weigh their own suspicions, take them apart and spread them in their hand: Could it be that white gal had a right to enter a world that was closed to them? And how she remember, old as she is, if they forget? But then they set about cutting her down: the woman lived in trees, nothing but grasshoppers as company, got to be crazy laying up there with all them bugs. And where they come from anyway?

Whether it was because folk couldn't stand her or they was puzzled and secretly admired her strangeful ways, the grasswoman became the topic of talk all over the town. Her presence began to fill the length of conversations, unexpected empty moments great and small. The more people bought from her, dipping their hands in the great leaf baskets, the more their homes became filled with the sweet songs of wings, songs that made them think of summers and tall grass up to your knees, and bushes that reach out to smack your thighs when you walk by and trees that lean over to brush the top of your hand, soft like a granddaddy's touch, land that whispered secrets and filled the air with the seeds of green growing things.

Such music fell strangely on the settlers' ears that bent only to hear the quickstep march of progress. In a land of pink soil as hard as earth diamonds, it was clear that they held little in common with their new home. And could it be that the grasswoman's hoppers were nibbling at the settlers' sense of self, turning them into aliens in this far land they'd claimed as their own? Or was it that white gal at fault, that non–working hussy who insisted on being, insisting on breathing when most of her seed was extinct, existing completely outside their control, a wild weed of a thing, and unaware of the duties of her race? The traitors who traded her singing grasshoppers for bits of crust and crumbs of food hidden in pockets, handed out with a side–long glance should have known that after all that had been given, as far as they had travelled, leaving the dying ground of one world, to let the dead bury their dead, there was no room for the old woman's bare–toed feet on their stone streets.

The head folk were annoyed at such disobedience, concerned at the blatant disrespect for order and decorum, blaming it on the times and folks giving in to the children's soft ways, children too young to remember the hardness of skin, how it could be used like a thick–walled prison to deny the blood within. Too young to remember how the sun looked like wet stars in morning dew, and how it walked on wide feet and stood on the sky's shoulders, spreading its light all over that other place. How it warmed them and baked them like fresh bread, until their brown skins shone with the heart of it.

But the grasswoman was overstepping her bounds, repeating that same dance, treading on sacred ground that she did not belong to. Not enough that her folk had stolen the other lands and sucked them dry with their dreaming, not enough that they had taken the names and knowledge and twisted them so that nobody could recall their meaning, bad enough that every tale had to be retold by them to be heard true, that no sight was seen unless their eyes had seen it, no new ground covered unless they were there to stake it, no old herb could heal without them finding new ways to poison it, now she had stolen their stories, the song–bits of self, and had trained grasshoppers, like side show freaks, to drum back all the memories they had tried to forget.

Even the children, thanks to her gifting, were beginning to forget themselves. They hummed strange tunes that they could not have remembered, told new lies that sounded like cradle tales of old, stories about spiders they called uncle in a language nobody knowed, and hopped around like brown crickets, mimicking dances long out of step. They were becoming more like children of the dust than of the pink stone of their birth, with its twin Sun and an anvil for sky.

And a small loss it was. They had traded the soft part of themselves, their stories and songs, the fingerprints of a culture, for what deemed useful. Out went the artifacts that had once defined a people. Only once did they yearn for the past, when creatures could be swept away depending on their appearance. The grasswoman had even took hold of their dreams. The parents were determined to stop this useless dreaming. They knew if they were to live again, to plant new seed, they had to abandon all thoughts of their past existence. What they wanted were new habits, new languages, new stories to mine in this strange borderland in the backbone of sky. So the command was clear: the stone streets were off limits. You couldn't go out anymore. Curtains were drawn and the houses shut their great eyelids.

ᴄᴡᴏ

Order seemed to rule again, but it didn't last long. That's when things began to happen. Doors covered with strange carvings and cupboards filled with stones. Furniture was arranged in circles and drawers were mismatched and swapped round.

At the Kings' house:

Who been in this cupboard?

No one, none had. Grandmama King got mad: everybody in the house knew that her teeth were kept there. Now the little glass dish was full of stones, and from every shelf the stones grinned back at her like pink gums.

At the Greenes' house:

Who scattered grasshopper wings 'cross my desk?

No one, nobody, not anyone, none was the reply. Daddy Greene choked back disgust. *Grasshoppers all in my cup,* he muttered, *damn crickets.*

At the head folks' offices:

Who let them bugs in?

Nobody had. The bugs had filled the bottoms of file drawers and hid in official-looking papers, fresh piles of pellets and grasshopper dung on settler documents stamped with official seals, the droppings among the deeds for land with their names scrawled across them like spider webs.

On the tail of all this, a general uproar gripped the settlement. The settlers held a straighten-it-out meeting, hoping to make a decision. They'd held off on the grasswoman's fate for too long, and now it was time to come to the end of it. They assembled at the home of Mema's daddy. The girl slipped out of her bed and stood at the door, listening to the groans and threats. She didn't even wait for their answer. She rushed off down the stone streets and slipped through a crack in the glass, in the direction of the grasswoman's stone tree. There, she found the old woman settling herself by the okro's belly, a dark stone cavern that swallowed the light. Her great leaf basket rested in her lap. Another one at her side toppled over, empty.

They gone get you, the child say.

Mema was gasping for breath. The air was much thinner outside the settlement's glass dome. But the grasswoman didn't act put out. She seemed to know, and had gathered her two great baskets and released the blue-green winged things. But Mema could not see where they had gone and she wondered how they would survive without the grasswoman tending them.

The little girl tried harder. She scratched her drumskull and tilted her head, staring into the old woman's face with a question. Never before had the grasswoman meant so much.

Run away, the child cried. *You still got time.*

But the grasshopper peddler just set herself at ease, didn't look like she could be bothered. Her hair and skin looked grey and hard, like the stringy meat on a bone. She pushed the baskets aside, pressed her palms into the ground and rose with some effort. She stood, sucking a stone, patting her dirt skirt and smoothing the faded rags with gentle strokes. Her hair hung about her eyes in a matted tangle. She seemed to be looking at the horizon. Soon the Sun would set and only a few night stars would remain peering through a veil of clouds.

Go on, child, the grasswoman said. *Fire coming soon.*

Mema hung back, afraid. She glanced at the grasswoman, at her tattered clothes that smelled like the earth Mema had never known, at her knotted hair that looked like it could eat any comb, and her sad eyes that looked like that old word, *sea*. If only the grasswoman could be like that, still but moving, far and away from here.

Why don't you run? They gone hurt you if they catch you, Mema said.

The old woman stood outside the hollow of the tree, motionless as if time had carried her off. She stared at the child and held out her withered hand. Mema reached for it, slid her fingers into the grasswoman's cool, dry palm.

Mema, there is more to stone than what we see. Sometime stone carry water, and sometime it carry blood. Bloodfire. *Remember the story I told you?* Mema nodded. The grasswoman squeezed her hand and placed it on the trunk of the stone tree. *In this place you must know just how and when to tap it. Only the pure will know.*

The girl bowed her head, blinked back tears. The tree felt cold to her touch, a tall silent stone, the colour of night.

Now you must go, the grasswoman said. She released Mema's hand and smiled. A tiny grasshopper with bold black and red stripes appeared in the space of her cool touch. Its tiny antennas tapped into her palm as if to taste it. Mema held the hopper in her cupped palm and watched the old woman, standing in her soiled clothing among the black branches of the tree. To the child, the grasswoman's face seemed to waver, like a trick in the fading light. Her skin was the wax of berries, her tangled hair as innocent as vine leaves.

Mema pressed her toes against the stone ground, reluctant to go. She looked up at the huge tree that was not a tree, as if asking it for protection, its trunk more mountain than wood, its roots stabbing at the sky, the base rising from what might have been rich soil long ago.

Can you hear the heart? asked the old woman.

The child recalled the grasswoman's tale. The heartstone was where the tree's spirit slept, in the polished stone the colour of blood, the strength of fire. Whoever harmed the okro tree would bear its mark for the rest of their life. Mema stood there, her face screwed up, shoulders slumped, as if she already carried the okro's stone burden. With gentle wings, the grasshopper pulsed in her cupped hands.

☙

The settlers began their noisy descent. They surrounded the stone clearing, outside their city of glass. The little girl fled, her heart in her drum, hid, and watched from the safety of a fledgling stone tree. She saw the grasswoman rise and greet the folk with open palms, an ancient sign of peace. The curses started quick, then the shouts and the kicks, then finally, a stone shower. Tiny bits of rock, pieces scraped up in anger from the sky's stone floor were flung up, a sudden hailstorm. The old woman didn't even appear to be startled and her straight back, once curved with age and humility, showed no fear. The stones came and the blood flowed, tiny drops of it warming the ground, staining the black stone. They crushed her baskets with their heels and bound her wrists, pushed her up the long dark road. A group of settlers followed close behind, muttering, leaving the child alone in the night. The girl hesitated, her drumskull tilted back with thought, her neck full of tears. After a long silence, she stepped forward, facing the empty stone tree. Then it happened: the heartstone of the okro crumbled, black shards of stone shattered like star dust. She stepped gingerly among the coloured shards. The dark crystals turned to red powder under her feet, stone blood strewn all over the ground. With a cup–winged rhythm, the hopper pulsed angrily in her shaking hand.

Suddenly, the child made up her mind. She dashed off through the stone clearing the children now called wood, crushing blood–red shards beneath her feet. The hopper safely tucked in her clasped hand, she noiselessly scurried behind the restless, shuffling mob of stonethrowers. Her ears picked up the thread of their whispers. They were taking the grasswoman to a jail that had not been built. *The well*, someone had cried, a likely prison as any. Mema shuddered to think of her friend all alone down there. Would she be afraid in the cold abandoned hole that held no water? Would she be hungry? And then it struck her, she had never seen the grasswoman eat. Like the hoppers, she sucked on stone, holding it in her mouth as if it were a bit of sweet hard candy. What did she do with the food they had given her, the table scraps and treats stolen and bartered for stories woven from a dead–dying world?

The grasshopper thumped against the hollow of her palm as if to answer. Mema stroked the tiny wings to calm its anxious drumbeat. Maybe the hoppers ate the crumbs, the child thought as she crouched in the blackness beside the old woman's walled prison. The well had gone dry in the days of the first settlers, and now that massive pumping stations had been built, the folk no longer needed stone holes to tap the world's subterranean caverns. Hidden in darkness, the grasshopper trembling in her palm, Mema began to suffocate with fear. The grasswoman had taught her how to sing without words, without air or drum. Was there any use of dancing anymore, if the grasswoman could not share the music? If the world around her had been stripped of its beauty, its story magic? And in the sky was silence, just as in the stone tree, no heartstone beat its own ancient rhythm anymore.

The grasswoman's voice reached her from within the well, drifting over its chipped black stone covered with dust. Now Mema could see the soft edges of her friend's shape, her body pressed in a corner of darkness. If she peered closely, letting her eyes adjust to the shadow and the light, she could just barely make out the contours of the old woman's forehead, the brightness of her eyes as they blinked in the night. Voices made night is what she heard, felt more than saw, the motion of the old woman's great eyelids blinking as she called to her. The grasswoman's voice sounded like a tongue coated in blood, pain rooted in courage, the resignation of old age. Mema drew back, afraid. What if someone saw her there, perched on the side of the well, whispering to the unhappy prisoner in the belly of night? Footsteps called out, as if in answer.

Quickly, the child jumped off the wall and fell, bruising a knee as she crawl-walked over to hide behind a row of trash cans. One lone guard came swinging his arms and shaking his head. He leaned an elbow on the lip and craned his neck to peer into the well.

May I? the grasswoman asked, and she put her stone harp to her lips and tried to blow. But the notes sounded strained, choked out of her bruised throat and sore lips, where the settlers had smacked and cuffed her. The guard snorted, became suspicious. *Throw it up*, he ordered, and the harp was hurled up and over the well's mouth with the last of the old woman's strength. The guard tried to catch it, but it crashed on the ground, and the dissonant sound made Mema gasp and cup her ears. *There'll be no more music from you till you tell us where you come from*, the guard said, and the well was silent, but in his heart, he didn't really want to know. Truth was, none of them did. They feared her, the grasswoman who came like a flower, some wretched wild weed they'd thought they'd stamped out in that other desert and fled like a shadow, disappearing into their most secret thoughts. The guard glanced at the little broken mouth harp scattered on the street. They'd probably want him to get it, as evidence, something else they could cast against the old woman, but he wasn't going to touch it. No telling where the harp had been, and he certainly didn't want nothing to do with nothing that had been sitting up in her mouth. So he turned on his heel and headed for the dim lights down the street, leaving the grasswoman quiet behind him.

No, not quiet, crying? A soft sound, like a child awakened from sleep. He shook his head in pity. He didn't know what other secrets the folk expected to drag out of their prisoner. She was just an old woman, no matter her skin, and anyway, what could they prove against the street peddler, guilty of nothing but being where being was no longer a sin.

When the guard's last echo disappeared in the night, Mema crept back to the well and picked up the stone harp's broken pieces. She held the instrument in her free hand and released the grasshopper on the well's edge. She half expected it to fly away, but it sat there, flexing its legs in a slow rhythmic motion, preening. She clasped the harp together again, sat down on her haunches, and began to blow softly. As the child curled up in the warmth of her own roundness, she set off to sleep, drifting in a strange lullaby. She could vaguely hear the grasshopper accompanying her, a mournful ticking, and the grasswoman softly crying below, the sound like grieving. *Maybe,* she thought as her lids slowly closed, *maybe the grasswoman could hear it too and would be comforted.*

∽

She awoke in a kingdom of drumming, the ground thumping beneath her head and her feet. The hoppers! A million of them covered the bare ground all around her and filled the whole street. Squatting and jumping, the air was jubilant, but the child could not imagine the cause of celebration. *The grasswoman is free!* she thought and tried to rise, but the grasshoppers covered every inch of her, as if she too were part of the glass city's stone streets. All around they stared at her, slantfaced and bandwinged, spurthroated and bowlegged. It was still night, the twin Sun had long receded from the sky and even the lamps of the city were fast asleep. Nothing could explain the hoppers' arousal, their joy or their number, why they had not retreated in the canopy of night. Not even the world, in all its universal dimensions, seemed a big enough field for them to wing through.

Mema carefully rose, brushing off handfuls of the hoppers, careful not to crush their wings. The air hummed with the sound of a thousand drums, each hopper signaling its own rapidfire rhythm. They seemed to preen and stir, turn around as if letting the stars warm their wings and their belly. The child tried to mind each step, but it was difficult in the dark and finally she gave up and leaned into the well's gaping mouth. *Grasswoman?* she called, and stepped back in surprise. The drumming sound was coming from deep within the well. She placed her hands above the well's lip and felt a fresh wave of wings and legs pouring from it, the iridescent wings sparkling and flowing like water. The grasswoman had vanished, the place had lost all memory of her, it seemed. Mema called the old woman, but received no answer, only the drumming and the flash of wings.

She decided to return to the okro, the stone tree where for a time the grasswoman had lived. There was no longer any other place where she might go. There was some that pitied the grasswoman, but none enough to take her in. No street, nor house, only the stone tree's belly. As Mema walked along, the hoppers seemed to follow her, and after a time, her movements stopped being steps and felt like wind. It was as if the hoppers carried her along with them, and not the other way around. They were leading the child to the okro, to the stone forest, back to the place where the story begin.

Mema arrived at the grasswoman's door, and looked at the stone floor covered with blood-red shards, the heartstone ground into powder. The okro was no longer dull stone, but was covered in a curious pattern, black with finely carved red lines, pulsing like veins. She stood at the door of the great trunk, and entered, head bowed, putting the distance between herself and time. Was there any use in waiting for the old woman? Mema blinked back tears, listened for the hoppers' drum. Surely by now, the grasswoman had vanished, taking her stories and her strange ways with her, a fugitive of the blackfolk's world again. The child took the stone harp and placed it to her mouth. She lulled herself in its shattered rhythm, listening with an ear outside the world, a place that confused her, listening as the hoppers kept time with their hind legs and tapping feet. She played and dreamed, dreamed and played, but if she had listened harder, she would have heard the arrival of a different beat.

There she is! That old white hefa inside the tree!

Spiteful steps surrounded the okro, crushing the hoppers underfoot.

It's the woman with her mouth harp. Go on, play, then. We'll see how well you dance!

They tossed their night torches aside, raised their mallets, and flung their pick axes through the air. The hammers crushed the ancient stone, metal teeth bit at stone bark. Inside, the girl child had unleashed a dream: her hair was turning into tiny leaves, her legs into lean timber. Her fingers dug rootlike into the stone soil. The child was in another realm, she was flesh turning into wood, wood into stone, girl child as tree, stone tree of life. Red hot blades of grass burst in tight bubbles at her feet, pulsing from the okro's stone floor, a crimson wave of lava roots erupting into mythic drumbeats and bursting wingsongs. Somewhere she heard a ring shout chorus, hot cry of the settlers' voices made night, the ground fluttering all around them, the hoppers surrounding the bubbling tree, ticking, wing-striking, leg-raising, romp-shaking vibrations splitting the stone floor, warming in the groundswell of heat. And from the grassdreaming tree, blood-red veins writhing, there rose the grasswoman's hands. They stroked crimson flowers that blossomed into rubies and fell on the great stone floor. Corollas curled, monstrous branches born and released, petal-like on the crest of black flames. The child's drumskull throbbed as she concentrated, straining to hear the grasswoman's call, to remember her lessons, how to make music without words, without air and drum, and her thoughts floated in the air, red hot embers of brimstone blues drifting toward the glass–walled city.

And as the ground erupted beneath them, the settlers stood in horror, began to run and flee, but the children, the children rose from tucked–in beds, the tiny backs of their hands erasing sleep, their soft feet ignoring slippers and socks, toes running barefoot over the stone streets and the rocks, they came dancing, *skip hop jump* through the glass door into the stone wood, waves of hoppers at their heels, their blue–green backs arched close to the ground as they hopped from stone to hot stone, drumming as they went, bending like strong reeds, like green grass lifting toward the night. And that was when Mema felt the sting of blaze, when the voices joined her in the song of ash and the stone's new heart beat an ancient rhythm, the children singing, the hoppers drumming, the settlers crying.

And when the Sun rose, the land one great shadow of fire and ash, the hoppers lay in piles at their feet. They had shed their skins that now looked like fingerprints, the dust of the children blowing in the wind all around them. And that night, when the twin Sun set, the settlers would think of their lost children and remember the old woman who ate stones and cried grasshoppers for tears.

Wayde Compton *wrote* 49th Parallel Psalm *(ArsenalAdvance, Arsenal Pulp Press, 1999) and edited* Bluesprint: Black British Columbian Literature and Orature *(Arsenal Pulp Press, 2002); the former was shortlisted for the Dorothy Livesay Poetry Prize. A new book of poems,* Performance Bond, *is forthcoming in 2004 (Arsenal Pulp Press). With Jason de Couto, he is one half of The Contact Zone Crew, a turntable-poetry performance duo. He is also a founding member of the Hogan's Alley Memorial Project, an organization established in 2002 to preserve the memory of Vancouver's original black neighbourhood. He lives in Vancouver and teaches English literature and composition at Coquitlam College.*

The Blue Road:
A Fairy Tale
Wayde Compton

The wind bloweth where it listeth, and thou
hearest the sound thereof, but canst not tell
whence it cometh, and whither it goeth:
so is every one that is born of the Spirit.
– John 3:8

How the Man Escaped the Great Swamp of Ink

The man had lived in the Great Swamp of Ink for as long as he could remember, and for as long as he could remember, he had always lived there alone. The swamp was made of the deepest and bluest ink in the world. The man's name was Lacuna.

One night, just before dawn, Lacuna tossed and turned,

unable to sleep. He sat up against a tree and wept. He was hungry and thirsty, but all there ever was to eat in the Great Swamp of Ink were bulrushes, and he was forced to drink the bitter-tasting ink to survive. He dreamed, as always, of leaving the terrible swamp. As he cried, he noticed the swamp brightening. Lacuna looked up to see a large glowing ball of light as bright as a sky full of full moons. He stood up rubbing the tears from his eyes, and stared at the ball of light that hovered above the blue marsh.

It spoke.

"My name is Polaris," said the ball in a bottomless voice. "I live in this swamp, but I have never seen you here before. What are you doing in my home?"

"I beg your pardon," Lacuna replied, barely keeping his composure in the face of this very remarkable event. "I don't mean to trespass. Are you a ghost?" He was terribly afraid of this talking ball of light.

"I am Polaris!" the ball shouted. "I am a will-o'-the-wisp, the spirit of this bog. And I ask you again, what are you doing in my home?"

Lacuna was very frightened, but he was also very clever, and he saw an opportunity to escape the swamp.

"I'd gladly leave your home, Mr Polaris, sir," he said carefully, "but I'm afraid I've lost my way. Since I can't remember which direction is home, I guess I'm just going to have to stay here."

The will-o'-the-wisp grew larger and pulsated.

"You can't live here!" Polaris roared. "This is *my* home. You must leave immediately or I will shine brighter and brighter and blind you with the light of a thousand suns!"

"Now look here, Mr Polaris, there's no need to get angry." Lacuna spoke soothingly. "If you'll tell me the direction that I need to go to get home, and lead me to the edge of the swamp, I'll get out of here forever and let you be."

"And you'll tell all the others like you to stay out of my home?" the will-o'-the-wisp persisted.

Lacuna, who was very clever, realized that other people may some day find themselves here in the Great Swamp of Ink. He thought very quickly of an answer that would not get them into trouble with the will-o'-the-wisp because he was not a selfish man, and he did not want others to be blinded.

"I'll be sure to tell people to stay clear of your swamp," he said sincerely, "but when I tell them about how big and shiny and pretty you are, I'm sure some of them will want to come and see you for themselves."

Polaris' glow softened.

"Really?" he said wonderingly. "You think they might come into the swamp just to see me?"

"Oh, of course they will! When I tell them how bright and sparkly you look, just like a star fallen loose from the sky, a few of the brave ones are bound to come just to catch a sight. They won't be wanting to stay, though – just to catch a sight and be on their way. I'm sure you can understand that?"

The will-o'-the-wisp was quiet for a moment, and Lacuna held his breath waiting for his answer.

"Well," the will-o'-the-wisp said slowly, "I can understand how some of your people might want to come and see me. I *am* rather dazzling, especially on clear nights like tonight. But if they come, they cannot stay! They can only catch a quick glimpse and then I will escort them immediately to the edge of the swamp! This is *my* home and no one else's. Surely you can understand the sanctity of one's home?"

Lacuna nodded gravely.

"And now it's time for you to leave. You have witnessed my beauty for long enough. Now tell me: which direction is your home?"

Lacuna had successfully tricked the will-o'-the-wisp into leading him out of the swamp, but now he was faced with a question that confused and confounded him more than any other: which way *was* his home? He didn't know. He visualized the four directions in his mind as if they were on a wheel, and in his mind he spun that wheel; the point was chosen.

"North."

"North," the spirit repeated. "I'll take you to the northernmost margin of the Great Swamp of Ink."

The will-o'-the-wisp picked up Lacuna and flew into the sky in a grand and luminous arc.

∽

The Thicket of Tickets

Polaris gently set Lacuna down at the edge of the swamp, at the bottom of a steep grassy hill.

"Here is where we part," the will-o'-the-wisp said. "At the top of that hill you will find a vast briar called the Thicket of Tickets. If you can find your way through the thicket, they say there is a Blue Road that leads to the Northern Kingdom. There you will find others like yourself, and you will certainly live a better life than living in my swamp. Good luck."

"Goodbye," Lacuna said as he watched Polaris float back into the murk of the Great Swamp of Ink.

Lacuna climbed to the top of the hill and looked back in the direction he now knew was south: the vast swamp stretched out as far as he could see. He jumped up and clapped his hands together, then he did a little dance, because he realized that he was out of the inky wilderness forever. He looked at it and laughed out loud before turning northward, forever turning his back on the horrible swamp. He then noticed what faced him.

The Thicket of Tickets, as Polaris had called it, was the most dense briar he had ever seen. It stretched out to his left and right all the way beyond each horizon. There was no way to go but through it, or back into the swamp. He walked up to the thicket and examined its tangled mass.

The thicket consisted of coil upon coil of paper tickets, little squares of every colour, each with the words

Admit One

stamped on its surface in a stern black font. The coils were so tangled they reminded him of his hair when he did not comb it for several days; to pry it apart became a painful and daunting task. He reached his left arm in and found he could push the paper aside quite easily, however, so he stepped into the thicket with his entire body.

Lacuna soon found that he could walk through the Thicket of Tickets if he ripped the paper coils whenever he got too tangled. The only problem was that he could not see where he was going. He could not even see beyond his next footstep. He kept walking in faith but worried that at any moment he would step off a cliff, or into a tree or a rock. He stopped and pondered his situation after he had gone a dozen or so steps into the thicket.

"I can't go any farther," he thought, "because I don't know if I'm walking in a safe path or a dangerous one. I also can't be sure if I'm even heading north or not." He thought and thought, because he was a clever man and he knew all sorts of tricks that had helped him survive worse situations than this.

Finally an answer came to him.

"I'll go back to the edge of the thicket and make a fire. Since this is only a paper briar, it will burn easily and quickly, and when all the tickets are burned up, I'll be able to see and walk all the way to the Blue Road and on to the Northern Kingdom!"

Lacuna started to walk back in the direction he had first come. After he had walked for what seemed like the same amount of time it took him to get this far into the thicket, he realized that he was not yet out. A wave of panic swept over him; he could not tell if he was actually walking in the same direction he had come because he could not see where he was going! He started to run, frantically ripping through the tickets, but by the time he ran out of breath, he was still nowhere near the edge. Or perhaps the edge was but a few steps away – he couldn't tell! For all his cleverness, the Thicket of Tickets had swallowed him up and he realized that he would just have to take a guess and walk in some random direction.

He walked for what seemed like days. He was hungry and thirsty and he even missed the horrible swamp because at least there were bulrushes and ink that he could eat and drink. He walked and walked, and his legs were painfully tired, but he knew he had no choice but to continue. Lacuna lost all track of time; he didn't know whether it was day or night. He could only hope that he was heading north, and in his desperate state he began to wonder if north was even the best way to go anyway. Lacuna began to miss the old swamp desperately, and cursed himself for leaving it in the first place.

"Surely I could have tricked Polaris into letting me stay," he thought. Lacuna wanted to cry, but he was so thirsty and dry no tears would come, which made him even sadder. His feet and legs ached. The edges of the tickets cut his skin in a thousand tiny slices. He was tortured.

Just when he had resigned himself to the idea that he would soon die, but at least he would die walking until he collapsed of exhaustion, the coils of tickets got thinner and thinner until suddenly he found himself in the open air.

He emerged from the thicket at the top of a grassy hill. It was sunny and bright, and his vision was blurry from spending so long in darkness, and he tried wearily to focus. At the bottom of the hill, he could make out what looked like trees. Weakened and half-blinded by the full light of day, Lacuna started down the hill. His aching legs gave out, and he fell, tumbling down the slope in a jumble of arms and legs and bruises.

When he finally stopped rolling, Lacuna's cheek was resting on the cold, hard ground. He realized it was not grass, but stone. He sat up slowly and stiffly and found himself on a dark blue cobblestone road that ran from the bottom of the hill off into a dense forest. The faint sound of running water could be heard from beyond the trees, and he knew he had come out on the far side of the terrible thicket. Perhaps there would be fish in that stream, he thought.

The bricks of the road were a beautiful sight, bright and rich, though they were startlingly close to the colour of the ink in the Great Swamp of Ink. Although Lacuna was very happy to have found this Blue Road to the Northern Kingdom, he couldn't help but wish it were a different colour.

After a day of resting and regaining his strength, he turned his thoughts to the Thicket of Tickets.

"If people find themselves trying to cross the thicket like me, they won't realize how easy it is to get lost in there. I was lucky to survive, let alone make it to the right destination. I had a good idea to burn it, but I thought it too late." Because he was not a selfish man, but one who often thought of others, he decided to go back and set fire to the dangerous thicket.

Lacuna took a burning stick from his campfire and proceeded up the hill. He cast the stick into the tangled mass of tickets. As he had suspected, the paper caught fire instantly and burned fiercely. He had to retreat down the hill to avoid the intense heat of the fire. From the edge of the forest, he watched the entire Thicket of Tickets burn to a pile of ashes. For a moment, he felt a strange sadness seeing such a curious thicket destroyed by his own hand, but he knew it was for the best.

"Now," he thought, "no one will face the troubles I had to face if they make it this far."

Satisfied, he set out on the Blue Road.

The way through the forest was long but pleasant. The road was well-kept and food was more plentiful and infinitely more nourishing here than in the Great Swamp of Ink. On his journey, he picked fruit from wild trees, fished in streams, and gathered dark berries. Lacuna was still lonely, but he consoled himself with the knowledge that the Northern Kingdom was at the end of this road, and even if it were far, the travelling was easy. He sang songs to himself as he walked, to make himself feel less lonely; he sang songs about his loneliness. He dreamed of a place where he could settle down. He tried to imagine what the Northern Kingdom would be like, but the thought of it frightened him a little. Lacuna was very clever, and he knew that kingdoms were not always good. "The Northern Kingdom" *sounded* wonderful; the words felt good on his tongue. But what did he really know of this place he was seeking?

Up until now, Lacuna had drunk water straight out of the stream, but he decided to fill his canteen so he could sip the river water while he walked. When he pulled the canteen from his back pocket and opened it, he realized it was full of the ink that he used to drink when he had lived in the swamp. He smiled, thinking about how he would never have to drink ink again, but he decided he would keep the canteen full of it as a souvenir and a reminder of where he had come from. This way, he would never forget his past.

Finding the canteen full of ink caused Lacuna's thoughts to drift to the swamp. He thought about Polaris and how he had tricked that old will-o'-the-wisp. Although he had flattered Polaris to trick him, he now realized for the first time that Polaris really was pretty. His brightness *was* dazzling and beautiful, but somehow, in the telling of his trick, Lacuna had not even realized the truth of this.

∽

The Rainbow Border

As he walked and thought, Lacuna noticed a small booth beside the road up ahead in the distance. When he got closer to the booth, he also noticed a strip of seven colours painted across the Blue Road; it looked like a rainbow cutting across his path. An old man in a blue suit and a blue hat sat next to the booth on a wobbly two–legged stool. The old-timer only had one leg. A strange–looking crutch leaned against the wall of the booth next to him.

"Hello," said Lacuna to the old man. "I'm on my way to the Northern Kingdom. Are you from there?"

"Am I *from* there?" the old man snapped in an angry voice. "No, I'm not *from* there. You don't know much, do you?" He stared at Lacuna without a trace of humour in his eyes.

Lacuna felt annoyed at this unprovoked attack. He quickly decided that since this old man was not from the Northern Kingdom, and was not very friendly, he would just be on his way.

"I have to be going," he said curtly, and started down the Blue Road once more.

"Hey, wait a minute, wait a minute!" the old man shouted frantically, jumping up out of his seat, which promptly fell over. Lacuna stopped still, startled by the man's sudden outburst. The old-timer limped onto the road with the aid of his strange–looking crutch.

"Don't you see what's right in front of your eyes, boy?" He was pointing at the rainbow painted across the Blue Road.

"Yeah, so?" Lacuna said indifferently. He wanted to get going.

"That's the *border*. You can't just up and cross the border like that. What's the matter, have you lost your mind?"

"So what am I supposed to do?" Lacuna said impatiently. He began to wonder if the old man was insane. He wanted to be on his way northward.

"Listen to me, boy, because obviously there's a whole lot you don't know about this world. *That* is the *border*," he said, pointing again at the rainbow painted on the road, "and I'm the Border *Guard*. You can't cross the border until *I* say so." He shifted his weight from his good leg to his crutch.

Lacuna, now that he was up close to the Border Guard, could see that his crutch was actually a huge skeleton key.

"There are rules involved," the Border Guard added cryptically. "I'll need your ticket," he said, holding out his hand.

Lacuna immediately remembered the Thicket of Tickets he had burned to the ground. He felt a sinking feeling in the pit of his stomach.

"I don't have a ticket," he said quietly.

"You don't have a ticket?" the Border Guard snapped. "Then you can't pass. That's the rules: no ticket, no road."

"But I have to go to the Northern Kingdom," Lacuna said, trying to keep the sound of desperation out of his voice. "How am I supposed to get there if I don't keep following the road?" He was angry and frustrated, and wondered if he should even listen to this strange Border Guard with his crazy skeleton key crutch. After all, how did he know that the Border Guard had any real authority over the Blue Road? Polaris hadn't told him anything about this. But then again, perhaps Polaris didn't know about the border. Lacuna considered crossing it without the Border Guard's permission; he was only an old man with one leg, and he wouldn't be able to stop a young man like himself. However, perhaps the Border Guard worked for the Northern Kingdom, and not following these rules would get him into trouble when he finally got there.

"Isn't there some way of continuing on the Blue Road, Mr Border Guard?" he asked politely. "I really desperately need to go to the Northern Kingdom. I have nowhere else to go."

"Well," the Border Guard said slowly, "according to the rules, there is a way for people who don't have a ticket. But it isn't easy." He grinned enigmatically. "Have you ever seen a dance called 'the limbo'? Two people hold a stick a few feet off the ground and the dancer leans way back and shuffles underneath the stick."

Lacuna nodded. He knew the dance.

"Well, if you can limbo under the border, you may pass freely. That's all I can do for you."

Lacuna looked at the border again: it was painted onto the road. There was no way anyone could limbo beneath a painted border.

"Oh, and you can't dig underneath it," the Border Guard added, "you have to dance under it, you have to limbo underneath the border. It's nothing personal, son. I'm just following the rules."

Lacuna could barely contain his anger, but he knew he needed to remain calm and think of some way out of this situation. He carefully considered his circumstances. He knew that no one can limbo beneath a painted border. He thought and thought but could see no way out of his predicament.

There was nothing else to do but set up a camp beside the Border Guard's booth and wait until an idea came to him.

∿

How the Man Limbo Danced Beneath a Painted Border

For four days, Lacuna camped beside the Border Guard's booth. During these days he passed the time by playing cards with the Border Guard. Once, while they were playing cards, he noticed a tiny starling flying low to the ground; it was heading north towards the border. Just as the little bird was about to cross the place where the border was, the Border Guard leapt from his two-legged stool (which promptly fell over), hopped on his good leg towards the bird, and chopped the bird in half in mid-flight with the edge of his skeleton key crutch. He did this all in one dazzlingly swift motion, whereupon he returned to his two-legged stool to continue their card game. Lacuna was dumbfounded at the unlikely speed and agility that the Border Guard showed, not to mention the horror of seeing the tiny bird sliced in half.

"Sorry about the interruption," the Border Guard said, "but no one can cross the border without properly observing the rules."

"Not even birds?" Lacuna asked incredulously.

"Nobody at all," the Border Guard answered firmly. He went on to explain that his skeleton key crutch also doubled as an axe. In fact, according the Border Guard, it was the sharpest axe in the world, capable of slicing easily through any material. Lacuna realized that now, more than ever, he had to think of a way to limbo beneath the painted border.

On the fourth night of camping, while he tossed and turned unable to sleep, he finally came up with a plan.

When he awoke in the morning, Lacuna stretched for a while, then stood pondering the sky. He carefully studied the clouds and the horizon. He then breakfasted with the Border Guard.

That afternoon, while they were playing cards over lunch, Lacuna periodically looked up and observed the sky. When night fell, he bedded down and slept soundly until the morning.

This pattern continued for three more days. On the third day after Lacuna had had his idea, the Border Guard finally asked him what he was going to do. It had been raining all morning, and the two of them sat at the table inside the booth playing their afternoon game of cheat. The sun was just beginning to emerge from behind the coal-coloured clouds.

"So what are you going to do, boy?" the Border Guard asked him. "You can't stay camped here forever, although I suppose there's no rule against it. I don't mind the company, but I just don't think you're ever going to be able to limbo underneath that painted border. It just can't be done."

While he talked, Lacuna was staring out the window and into the sky.

"Are you a betting man, Mr Border Guard?"

The Border Guard eyed him cautiously. "Well, that depends on what the bet is, doesn't it?"

"Yes, it does," Lacuna said seriously. He thought about how he had burnt the Thicket of Tickets to help the people that might follow him, without knowing that they would need those tickets to get across this border. Now he would make up for his mistake.

"I'll bet you your skeleton key crutch that I'll limbo beneath the border today. If I don't succeed, I'll give you all of what little money I have."

The Border Guard shook his head.

"That's a stupid bet to make, boy. It can't be done. I'd be taking your money, as sure as you're born."

Lacuna held his gaze steadily. "Will you bet me or not?"

The Border Guard scratched his head and wondered at the younger man's stupidity.

"Why not? If you want to give your money away, I'll take it. Sure. Why not? But if you walk down that road without limbo dancing beneath the border like I said, I'll have to cut you in half just like I did that bird. I hope you understand that."

Lacuna nodded.

"I'm going to go pack up my campsite. When I'm finished, you'll watch me limbo beneath the border."

The Border Guard shook his head in disbelief as Lacuna left the booth to pack up his gear.

While he was outside of the booth, Lacuna examined the sky once more. Satisfied, he went to his campsite and rummaged around in his knapsack until he found the canteen filled with ink from the Great Swamp of Ink. He then went to the Blue Road and poured the ink over the painted rainbow border. Since the ink was the exact colour of the Blue Road, the painted border was completely blotted out. He finished packing up his things and returned to the Border Guard's booth.

"Well, I'm ready to limbo beneath the border. And remember: if I succeed, you have to give me your skeleton key crutch."

"And *when* you fail, you'll have to give me all your money. And I'll most likely have to chop you in half."

The two of them went to the spot on the Blue Road where the border had been, but the border was nowhere to be seen. The Border Guard was panic-stricken.

"But where is it?" he shouted. "The border's gone!"

Lacuna smiled and pointed into the sky.

Both men looked up to see an arcing rainbow far above them among the shifting clouds and sunlight.

"There it is," Lacuna said sharply.

The Border Guard stared silently at the rainbow, completely baffled by this unthinkable turn of events. He looked back at Lacuna, utterly perplexed, but could not think of a single thing to say.

Lacuna slung his pack over his shoulder, bent backwards ever-so-slightly, and limbo danced a few steps down the Blue Road, beneath the rainbow that hung fast in the sky above them. He then turned around and held his hand toward the Border Guard.

"I did it. Now give me your skeleton key crutch."

The Border Guard's mouth hung open. He still could say nothing, but he looked at his crutch. Without it, he would no longer be able to properly guard the border.

"Give me the crutch," Lacuna persisted. He thought for a moment about something the Border Guard had said to him. "Listen: we made a deal. I'm just following the rules."

The Border Guard reluctantly handed him the skeleton key crutch, which Lacuna snatched out of his hand. He immediately turned his back on the Border Guard, laughed, and headed down the Blue Road, and on towards the Northern Kingdom.

If he had turned around to look, which he didn't, he would have seen the Border Guard balancing on his one leg, with his mouth still open in disbelief. The Border Guard stared first down at the road, then up at the rainbow, then down at the road again. He continued to do this until long after Lacuna had dropped out of sight in the distance.

✧

The Gates of the Northern Kingdom

Once past the border, Lacuna's journey was easy. He reflected upon the incident with the Border Guard and felt confident he had done the right thing. He used the skeleton key crutch-axe as a walking stick, and cheerfully sang to himself as he walked the Blue Road.

After several days of uneventful travel, Lacuna at last saw a great city looming on the horizon. As he got closer he could see that the Blue Road led straight to its gates, through a high alabaster-coloured wall that surrounded the city. Lacuna knew from its magnificence that this had to be the Northern Kingdom itself.

As he approached the gates, Lacuna passed several people, some going in or coming out of the city, others selling goods by the side of the road. He marvelled that the people looked just like he did, but were all shapes, sizes, and ages. He was overwhelmed at seeing so many people in one place after seeing so few for so long – and this was only the outskirts of town. His mind boggled when he thought about how many more people there would be inside the vast metropolis.

He noticed several Gate Keepers checking people's bags and letting them through the massive portcullis. When it was Lacuna's turn to enter the city, a Gate Keeper stopped him.

"Your papers," the Gate Keeper said tersely.

Lacuna wasn't sure what to do. He remembered the Border Guard; perhaps he was supposed to have gotten papers that would allow him passage into the Kingdom from the Border Guard.

"I don't have any papers, sir," he said to the Gate Keeper. "I'm not from here. I come from the, uh, south." He had begun to say that he was from the Great Swamp of Ink, but decided that it might not make a very good impression; he wanted to erase his past forever and start again as a northern person, so he decided right there that he would mention the swamp as little as possible from now on.

"Go over there," the Gate Keeper said, pointing to a small stone gatehouse. He proceeded to inspect the next person's papers.

Lacuna approached the gatehouse and knocked on the door. Another Gate Keeper opened it and let him in.

"What can I do for you?"

"Well, sir, the man at the gate asked me for my papers and I told him I don't have any papers. See, I'm not from here, I'm from the south. Was I supposed to get my papers at the border?"

"The border?" the Gate Keeper said with a frown. "I don't know what you're talking about. He was asking you for your papers of citizenship. You have to have papers to prove that you are a citizen of the Northern Kingdom to enter, of course."

Lacuna felt despair welling in his chest. He had come so far, only to be denied.

"What am I going to do?" he asked desperately.

"Don't worry," the Gate Keeper said, beginning to grasp Lacuna's situation. He shook his head and moved his hand as if to wave away Lacuna's worries like so much smoke.

"Have a seat. Listen, I have the authority to issue you papers immediately. All you have to do is register here, and sign some forms."

The Gate Keeper pushed a stack of papers towards Lacuna.

"It's just so we know who you are. If you sign the papers and become a citizen, you can come and go as you please. You can leave the Kingdom and return any time you want. We welcome new subjects. All you have to do is fill out the forms and sign on the dotted line, and you'll be an instant citizen."

He passed a quill pen and a small pot of blue ink across his desk to where Lacuna sat listening intently.

"There's only one rule that I have to inform you of before you sign."

As he spoke, the Gate Keeper's eyes strayed absent-mindedly to the wall of his office. Lacuna followed the man's gaze to a portrait that hung there depicting a stern-looking man wearing a crown full of enormous sapphires. The Gate Keeper cleared his throat and continued without taking his eyes off the portrait.

"Citizens like yourself are required to take possession of a special mirror, which they are to carry on their person at all times. Now listen carefully: *as long as you are within the gates of the city you must never take your eyes off this mirror.* The mirror is magical, and if you look away from it for even a second, you will feel a sharp pain that will grow in intensity until it eventually kills you; all this will only take a matter of minutes. However, if you close your eyes entirely, you will not feel any pain. But as long as your eyes are open, you must be gazing into the mirror. That way, you may sleep at night quite normally, provided you do not open your eyes until the mirror is in front of you when you wake up."

Lacuna could not believe what he was hearing. A magical mirror from which he wasn't allowed to break his gaze?

"This is insane," he protested. "How will I get around? How will I hold a job or even walk down the street if I always have to look into this magical mirror? Does everyone in the Northern Kingdom have to do this?"

The Gate Keeper sighed as if he had explained this far too many times to feel altogether sympathetic.

"Only people who were not born in the city are assigned mirrors. Those who were born here do not need them. As for getting around, I assure you that the Mirror People – as we call citizens like yourself – do just fine. They manage to hold down jobs and raise families, and they get around the best they can. Believe me, it may seem strange now. but you'll adjust in no time. And if you can't, well, you can always go back where you came from."

Lacuna felt a horrid mixture of disappointment, anger, and frustration. He wished he had gone west or east or south: anywhere but here. But he had come so far that he was determined at least to see this great city with all its people. He reached for the papers, dipped the quill pen in the pot of deep blue ink, and signed on the dotted line. Immediately afterward, the

Gate Keeper brought forth a large golden-framed mirror from beneath his desk and handed it to him. It was heavy and unwieldy, as wide as Lacuna's shoulders, and square. He took it grudgingly and returned to the gates with his freshly-validated papers.

∽

The Mirror People and the Mirrorless People

Once inside the city, the first thing Lacuna noticed was that he had to strap everything onto his back, including his skeleton key crutch-axe, because it took both of his hands to hold the magical mirror in front of his face. He also noticed that the Gate Keeper was not lying about the intense pain that came to him when he glanced away for merely a moment to take in the city; the pain shot like lightning through his temples, and out of necessity he quickly returned his gaze to the mirror. He noticed, however, that there were several people on the streets who held mirrors up to their faces, although the majority of the people in the city did not. He saw that the Mirror People walked backwards, using their mirrors to see over their shoulders which direction they were going. It looked like many of these people had been doing this for years because they seemed very skilled at walking backwards, talking to each other, and even reading words in books or newspapers backwards, all by angling the mirror in the right direction. They looked awkward, but managed as best they could.

He spent his first day walking around the city, trying to get used to walking backwards and with his mirror as his guide, looking for somewhere to stay and places that might hire him for work. He felt foolish with his mirror, especially when he was around people who did not need mirrors.

At one point, he had to ask directions of a man who also carried a mirror, and for the first time realized that such a conversation meant that they had to stand back to back, each holding his mirror so as to see over his shoulder into the other person's mirror. He did not actually get to look directly into the man's face, but rather he was seeing a reflection of a reflection of the man talking to him.

After several days of orienting himself, Lacuna started working shining mirrors on a street corner for pocket change. He polished mirrors for the Mirror People who were busily going to and fro in the great city. He also found a cheap rooming house that he could afford, and spent his days working hard and wondering what his future would bring.

"I'm happy to be here," he thought to himself as he shined an old woman's mirror, "and I know this is better than the Great Swamp of Ink, but it isn't what I expected at all." His thoughts circled around in his mind like seagulls over a low tide, but they would not perch at a conclusion. He was not happy, nor was he entirely sad; he was puzzled.

"You're awfully quiet there, young man."

The old woman's voice caught Lacuna's attention. He looked up at her: she was a dignified-looking woman, and she sat in the little chair he had set up for customers, her eyes closed as he was busy polishing her mirror.

"I was just thinking about the Kingdom," he said to the woman. "I'm still trying to get used to these mirrors, to tell you the truth, ma'am."

"Don't you worry about it, youngster," she said kindly. He could hear in her voice that she cared and understood how he felt. "It might take a while, but you'll get the hang of it. Soon you'll barely notice that you have that mirror. It becomes like a friend after awhile."

"I still don't understand why we have to have them at all," he said.

"Now, that kind of talk is foolishness," the old woman retorted. "It's just the way things are. The King wants it that way, and this is the Northern Kingdom, right? There's no point in not understanding something as simple as that."

When he finished polishing her mirror, Lacuna put it into her hands. She opened her eyes and examined how well he had cleaned the glass and, satisfied, reached into her purse to pay him. Her eyes, in the angle of her mirror, fixed on the skeleton key crutch-axe which lay at Lacuna's side. He had gotten into the habit of carrying it around with him wherever he went.

"What's that?" she asked.

"It's a crutch. And an axe, sort of." He realized that he wasn't very sure what to call it. "It's mine," he offered finally.

"It's pretty," said the old woman. "I've never seen anything like it. It's unusual. I bet you could make an interesting costume for the Festival around something that unusual."

"What festival?" Lacuna asked.

"What do you mean, 'What festival?' *The* Festival. Only the biggest event of the year. You really must not be from around here. Once a year we have a celebration called the Festival of the Aurora Borealis. The great Aurora Borealis comes out and lights up the whole sky above the Kingdom. It's an unbelievably dazzling light show, and everyone wears strange and unique costumes for the occasion. We all look up into the sky and at midnight the Aurora Borealis arrives in all its glory. The Festival is only a month and a half away. You watch, business will pick up around the time before the Festival. Everyone will be getting their mirrors polished so they can see the lights best."

With that, the woman paid Lacuna, thanked him, and went on her way.

For the next few nights, he found it difficult to sleep. Thoughts circled in his head like his hand circled with its cloth when he polished someone's mirror. He realized that since he had come to the Northern Kingdom he had barely spoken to a Mirrorless Person, and the only Mirror People he knew were those he met as he worked. Amazingly, he still felt lonely even though he was surrounded by people. He hated carrying his mirror around all day, and it took all his patience to keep from smashing it every time he thought about how foolish it all seemed. He wondered if he would go on forever at this job, living in a tiny room, and feeling alone. But the Festival of the Aurora Borealis was something to look forward to. Surely the Aurora Borealis would be at least as beautiful as Polaris. Lacuna wondered if he should really make a costume using the skeleton key crutch–axe as the old woman had suggested. Perhaps he would dress up as the Border Guard. He thought that it would be such a pity that he and all the Mirror People would have to watch the Aurora Borealis through these stupid mirrors. He had had the experience of witnessing Polaris up close with his own eyes, and he didn't realize what a privilege that had been until this moment.

With these disjointed thoughts spinning in his head, Lacuna drifted off to sleep.

෴

The Festival of the Aurora Borealis

He woke abruptly out of a startling dream, and immediately opened his eyes by reflex; instantly, the pain rushed in. He groped for his mirror, which lay beside the bed, and looked into it. By the time the mirror was safely in front of his eyes, he realized that he had already forgotten his dream.

Later in the day, while polishing an accountant's mirror, Lacuna suddenly remembered what his dream had been about.

He had dreamt of a vast sheet of ice. Lacuna wore a pair of skates and glided effortlessly across the ice. He felt as if he were flying; he felt just as he did when Polaris carried him through the air out of the Great Swamp of Ink. Lacuna skated in large figure–eights, looping a broad curve, then arcing back across his previous path. His skates cut a massive figure into the ice that looked like this:

He skated and skated around and around on the ice. That was all.

When he remembered this dream, Lacuna stopped still in his polishing. An idea had finally come to him.

With his mirror, he looked up at the accountant sitting in the customer's chair; the accountant wore a pair of wire-rim glasses. Lacuna quickly checked his pockets to see how much money he had on him. He handed the accountant back his mirror, so that they could see each other.

"Listen, sir," Lacuna said, "can I buy those glasses from you? I'll give you this." He held out a week's earnings to the accountant.

The accountant frowned and looked at the money, then back at Lacuna.

"That's a lot of money. Why would you want to buy my glasses? If your eyesight is bothering you, you ought to go to the optometrist. You need to get glasses that work for you specifically. They're unique that way, you know."

Lacuna shook his head and thrust the money at the accountant.

"No, no, I don't need them for that. Please take my money, it's more than enough to buy a new pair. I just need your glasses right now."

"Are you feeling alright?" the accountant said suspiciously. None of this made sense to him, and, after all, he had only wanted his mirror shined.

Lacuna was getting impatient and blurted out, "Look, I'm fine, I'm fine. Will you please sell me your glasses right away? Please? I mean, if you don't want the money, I'll find someone else."

The accountant was reluctant, but he knew that the money was enough to buy a newer and better pair, and he really didn't care much if a crazy mirror polisher wanted to throw his money away on foolish things. He took the money, and gave Lacuna his glasses, but waited around to see what this crazy mirror polisher was going to do with them.

Lacuna took the accountant's glasses and immediately smashed the lenses out of them. The accountant shook his head, certain now that the poor boy had lost his mind. But then Lacuna carefully picked all the glass out of the frames of the spectacles until there was nothing but the wire rims. He lay his own mirror on the ground and picked up the skeleton key crutch-axe, which was at his side as always. He paused for a moment, remembering that the Border Guard had said the skeleton key crutch-axe was the sharpest blade in the whole world. He carefully pressed the blade of the axe against the glass of his mirror and cut out a small circle. The blade sliced easily through the glass, as easily as if he were dipping it into water. He gently lifted up the small circle of mirror and fitted it into one of the frames of the wire rims. The accountant watched speechlessly, and a small crowd began to gather. Lacuna put the small circle of mirror into the frame so that the mirror faced inward. Then he put on the glasses. His left eye stared directly into the mirror, while his right eye scanned the crowd, the buildings, and the sky directly; there was no pain because he had not broken eye contact with the piece of mirror with one eye, while his other eye was free to see the world plain.

The crowd grew until the whole corner was buzzing with people. The ones who had been there to witness the event were telling the newcomers, and people were talking to one another excitedly. Everyone was visibly awed, and some actually gasped when they heard the news that this young mirror polisher had figured out a way to see with one eye on and one eye off his cursed mirror.

The accountant, who had watched the whole spectacle, said, "Boy, will you make me a pair of glasses like that? I'll give you double your money back."

Suddenly, everyone pushed forward, some waving money at Lacuna, dozens of Mirror People asking him to make them a pair of the miraculous glasses. Right there on the street, he set about to making dozens of pairs of glasses for those who had the money and the frames. In less than an hour, he had made more money than he had ever dreamed of. The accountant offered Lacuna his financial services, which he accepted because he was too busy making glasses to handle the great crowd. The accountant organized the excited Mirror People into a line-up. By the end of the day, Lacuna had made enough money to live in leisure for years.

In the next few weeks, Lacuna opened up a shop and hired the accountant as his personal assistant. He used his idea and his skeleton key crutch-axe-glasscutter to accumulate for himself a small fortune. In the days leading up to the Festival of the Aurora Borealis, business, as the old woman had predicted, boomed. Everyone wanted the new glasses; everyone wanted to see the world directly with at least one eye, and without the medium of their cursed mirror. In time, he knew, other people would take his idea and start their own businesses with ordinary glasscutters, but he had already firmly established himself.

On the eve of the Festival of the Aurora Borealis, Lacuna and the accountant dressed up for the event, the accountant in a dazzling rented costume of silver and gold, Lacuna in a tailored blue approximation of the Border Guard's uniform. The two partners strutted out into the night to join the greatest celebration of the year in the Northern Kingdom. As they walked through the crowd, Lacuna thought about how fortunate he had been. Many of the Mirror People walked around in the glasses that he had made for them, excited to see their first Festival inside the city with one good eye. It was true that there were Mirror People who still held the old, large mirrors – those who couldn't afford to buy his new innovation – but he generally avoided looking at them. There were also the ones outside the walls of the city. He had learned that it was a tradition for many Mirror People to leave the city on this night to watch the Aurora Borealis from the countryside where they didn't need their cursed mirrors. There, some Mirror People had always gathered together to create their own Festival. He wondered about them, and he wondered about the ones who still held their large, cumbersome mirrors. He even wondered what the Mirrorless People thought about all the recent changes he had sparked. He wondered about these things, but his thoughts just circled in his head, round and round like the alabaster walls of the city.

At midnight, the Aurora Borealis arrived. It was beautiful, and everyone in the crowd gasped and cheered at its wavering colours. The lights danced and weaved across the sky, and everyone, in their brilliant and bizarre costumes, began the traditional dances that imitated the vacillations and the shimmer of the Aurora Borealis itself.

Lacuna stood still, among his people, looking up, gaping at the motion of the lights with one half of his vision, staring at his own open eye with the other.

SECTION IV

ENCOUNTERS WITH THE ALIEN

The largest grouping of stories centres on encounters with the alien. "The Forgotten Ones" by Karin Lowachee explores questions of vengeance, dispossession, and land settlement through the perspective of the struggle of a small group of freedom fighters. The title of Greg Van Eekhout's "Native Aliens" captures the paradox at the heart of his story as a Dutch Indonesian boy in the present and a Brevan-Terran boy in the future both face relocation. Celu Amberstone picks up the theme of relocation in her story "Refugees" during a planet-wide apocalyptic future. "Trade Winds" by devorah major is an examination of the two very different world-views of the exchange of goods and services. Carole McDonnell's "Lingua Franca" explores the cultural gains and losses when a new society faces the powerful economic force of the Earthers. And Ven Begamudré's "Out of Sync" gives us a widow's transgressive yet hopeful love on a planet facing a looming bloodbath between humans and aliens.

Karin Lowachee *was the winner of the Warner Aspect First Novel Contest in 2001 with* Warchild, *which was also a finalist for the Prix Aurora Award and the Philip K. Dick Award. She was a finalist for the John W. Campbell Award for Best New Writer in 2003 and her second novel,* Burndive, *a sequel, was published that same year and debuted at number seven on the Locus Bestseller List. Her third novel,* Cagebird, *will be released in 2005. She was born in Guyana, South America, and grew up in Ontario, Canada.*

↺

The Forgotten Ones

Karin Lowachee

In the twilight, my brother Hava's eyes glow red. Before the old women of Rumi village were washed from this life, they said it was the spirit of blood in him, my twin. I do not have such spirit. I am the silent breath, the old women said, she who walks behind the blood and is last in the sand before death. Death is the final hand that smooths your tracks beneath the waves. And before death there is the silent breath, and before the silent breath there is the blood. And my brother's eyes glow red with it.

In the twilight, hidden by broad leaves that bend over the shore and give shadow, we wait. We lie on our stomachs, Hava and I and all of our twenty soldiers, chins to the dark earth, smelling the spring richness of new growth. The wind plays a song above us in the trees. The scampering feet of the little animals up and down the trunks and across the floor of the forest are a low drumbeat, a thudding of tiny hearts. I could go to sleep here, like I used to do with Hava on the fallen trunks of lightning–struck trees. Before the Lopo came and killed our parents. Lopo from across the waters.

When I first saw them with their guns and their tall hats, I was afraid. But now I have seen them without their hats. I have taken their guns and felt the power of their shouts like a storm come in from the sea. The power in my hands, from their guns. And though the Lopo sit in our villages and sharpen their knives on our stone and rest their boots on our tables, I have seen them at my feet, in blood, and it flows as dark and thick as what runs out of me in that week of womanhood.

The Lopo keep coming from across the waters, and though we are half their size, barely thirteen strides along the sands of life, we drive them back. We, Hava and I and our twenty soldiers, have forced the Lopo to huddle in our villages, to sharpen their knives on our stone and beat their boots on our tables in frustration. Eventually, Hava says, their blood will flow to the waters and become one, until nothing will be left but the waters. And us, the children of the dead ones. We who have been here for as long as the old women remembered. We who were here first.

oMo

"Sister," Hava whispers to me. "Go tell Umeneni to climb the father tree. I think I see them on the waters."

I slither backward, deeper into the forest, until the glow of moonlight on the water disappears. The earth is damp beneath my knees as I scamper to the left, where Umeneni waits on his belly, chin to the ground. Broad chair-leaves arc over his back and narrow shoulders. The black mud in his deep red hair smells like starberries. We crush the sour buds into the earth until their juices create the paste. For a moment I think of our morning together and the feel of his coarse hair through my fingers when I twisted them with mud. He sat on a rock and cleaned his killing knife and the sun was strong on his brown shoulders and the back of my neck. His eyes are not spirit red, but blue like the waters. My father would have liked Umeneni. We would have had a child by now, if not for the Lopo.

Tonight he might die and I hate the Lopo. When I look at Umeneni and think of the children we do not have, I can kill the Lopo as viciously as Hava. I can slice their skin from their sinew and throw them to the sharks. My bones are tired with the feeling of it.

"Ara," Umeneni whispers, his breath against my cheek.

"Hava says to climb the father tree. The Lopo might be on the waters now. You must count how many, and where."

I see his mud-locks bob up and down in shadow, and then he is gone, leaving nothing behind but the twitch of a sheltering leaf and the scent of starberries.

෴

We do not know why the Lopo came. We do not know why we were forced to flee our homes as children and hide among the trees, prey for the big cats and the Lopo alike. One morning when Hava and I were only ten strides across the sands of life the Lopo landed on our shores with their long boats and their guns and their tall hats. Their shiny booted feet left deep imprints in the ground that filled up with rain but never washed away. The old women in our village, the ones who were there to remember and to carve, cursed at the Lopo and called them by names I had never heard. And the Lopo said, "That was long before our time and the agreement means nothing." Somehow they knew our language. And I understood them perfectly, though their words made no sense.

But it did not matter. Their weapons were their words.

෴

I wait beside Hava. The waves roll into shore like a mother's gentle breath, rippling the skin of the earth. Moonlight flitters on the waters as if it is calling for the fish to surface. Yet it calls the Lopo and when the Lopo come they bring only ruin. They row in as silent as the forest when a hunter is on the prowl. And all the world knows that death sits among it.

"Something is wrong," Hava says. I see the moon line of his profile in the near–dark. The corners of his eyes are red as though he bleeds tears. But it is only the glow of his blood spirit.

A hand touches my heel and I look back over my shoulder. Umeneni crawls up between us and lays down on his belly. His shoulder touches mine and it is warm from his climb on the father tree. Mine is cool from the night.

"There are lights," he whispers. "Far out along the horizon. But they come closer and they are fast."

"How many?" Hava asks. "How fast?"

Umeneni's voice is a shudder. "Too many and too fast."

Umeneni has the best sight among us. He has always spied far and wide. Once he saw a line of five Lopo hunters winding furtive and silent through the path of the big cats, covered in leaves and soil. Yet Umeneni saw them.

My brother says, "Maybe they come in different boats. Maybe they have new boats."

"Maybe," Umeneni says.

Hava knows the Lopo. He's tasted their golden blood.

"We will wait," Hava says. "And hide."

Umeneni says nothing, but I feel his gaze in the dark just as close as his skin. The disturbance in my brother's voice wafts through me like a shiver.

∽

Before our attacks on the Lopo, Hava would always draw our positions in the sand, in the earth. We and our soldiers, fifty strong as they once were, and even now when they are twenty, we all gathered around this map of our close futures and Hava would take his finger and trace patterns in the ground. His touch glided through the fine grains like the gods must sift our lives, separating some, pushing others together. We knew at some time the waters or the rain would wipe these marks away, but we never stayed long enough to see it. And so the lines of life that Hava traced in the earth would remain in our minds, marked deep and true. And we took them with us into battle. Lines like the grooves on the skin of our palms. Lines like the veins that run beneath our skin.

Blood paths.

And I would think, always, Is this the path of my children, if ever I should have them? Would their feet ever imprint on sand that does not wash away after two turnings of the moon?

∽

The lights scud toward us like falling stars, rolling through the surface of the waves. Impossibly fast. Faster than any Lopo boat. The closer they come, the clearer we see. Not just Umeneni and his far sight. We all see.

The lights do not touch the waters. They fly above it.

"Not the Lopo," Umeneni whispers, in fear. Umeneni who has killed a hundred Lopo and yet with me his touch is gentle. He fears little. He doesn't even fear my brother.

I feel our soldiers shifting behind us. What do we do? Run? Scatter?

"Stay," Hava says, loud enough so it branches through the trees and quiets the others.

The lights come silent. They pour day onto the shore, the trees, our hidden forms among the forest floor. White day. The lights bring wind and heat like a summer breeze, and the shake and growl of a thunderstorm, but only in passing. Only in nearness, like you hear someone breathe in sleep if you are the only one awake.

The lights sweep over our heads like birds and disappear.

And in a flash, my brother chases the beat of their windless wings through the feet of the bowing trees.

∞

I run, Umeneni by my side, our soldiers around us. We follow Hava and the storm of the lights as they skate the top of the forest. If these are Lopo, we must track them. We must get to them before they join the Lopo in our villages and become one.

The ground stabs my feet. The forest is alive with the snap and crack of our fiery path, cut by my brother.

These Lopo fly.

The three words beat a rhythm in my breath. The loud drumming of a death dance.

I want to grab Hava back and keep him still. I want to hold Umeneni to my breasts and say, Wait.

The blood can wait.

These Lopo fly.

Yet if the Lopo had such ability to fly among the clouds like birds, surely we would have known it. Surely you cannot go from water to sky in just a few turnings of the moon. The Lopo are not gods. They bleed, though their blood is golden like honey. But their spirits are not red like my brother's.

"Hava!" I shout. I don't care. The lights drown all but the closest noise.

But he doesn't stop. In his hand flashes the silver of his killing knife. He hunts the lights.

"Rumi village," Umeneni says, on a gasp. Running as I run.

I recognize the path, even in moonlight and the dying blaze of the beasts overhead.

We are going home.

∞

My brother stops on the edge of our village. What was once our village, where the old women sat outside their homes and braided long leaves into mats for our beds. Now the Lopo lie on our mats, still stained by the blood of our mothers.

Hava crouches at the feet of the trees. Our soldiers gather around in a line of attack, the positions of habit. I barely gather breath enough to speak before Hava turns to me, the red now so vibrant in his eyes that I barely see the white.

"They are friends of the Lopo," Umeneni says, his voice harsh, his teeth bared.

The lights touched ground in the clear spaces of the village. They are shaped almost like boats, almost like birds. Strange inbetween creatures that bellow the white of bright day over all the scattered homes. Yet the mud roofs don't melt and the grass of the walls do not burn.

"But the Lopo do not come out," I say. "Where are their brothers, if it's true they are friends?"

"The Lopo hide," Hava says, resting the tip of his killing knife in the earth. "See the shadows move inside that house? They do not come out. They are afraid."

There is no fear in Hava's voice. He stares at the inbetween creatures.

A door opens on the belly of one of the creatures. We wait, silent, but no Lopo emerge from the homes to greet the open door. Not a stirring.

A tall figure walks from the creature's belly, but it isn't clad in tattered Lopo grey. It wears stitchless black. And it is the shape of us, with arms and legs. But big like our mothers and fathers had been.

Hava sheaths his knife and reaches to his other hip. Soon he holds a Lopo gun and aims it through the trees. Tracking. Umeneni does the same, but I don't move.

Things that travel inside a flying creature. How will guns help? Better to sneak up on them. Better to jump on their backs and bring them down one by one, and then use the knife.

More figures emerge from the creature's belly. I lose the count at fifty. Soon the entire village is filled by these black-clad people. They are beetle-shaped on the head and about the eyes, as though they come from insect kin.

A voice calls out. It sounds like language, but not ours. Lopo words. Calling to the Lopo who hide in our houses.

But the Lopo do not come out. They are cowards.

So the beetle people swarm into the houses. Noise erupts, shouting, gunfire, flashes of light and the shake of violence. Some of the beetle people wait outside, not speaking. Not helping. They stand like trees.

Soon the rest of them reappear. The lights from their inbetween creatures reflect on their insect heads.

They hold the Lopo by their long spindly arms. Lopo warriors, men and women, some of them bleeding. They are ugly clean, and uglier in blood. They make a sticky yellow visage and their too-long legs bend deeper than normal, driven to kneel by these beetle people. The beetle people set the Lopo in the middle of our village, like the Lopo had once done to us, and make them sit on the earth. They hold the Lopo guns and they do not say a word. Yet they all move in agreement as though they can read one another's minds.

Enemies of the Lopo, yet Hava does not twitch or give us a command. Are these beetle people here to return our villages to us? Or will they push us to the ground, smoothing it with our blood?

My hands are cold with the thought. I touch Umeneni's back to feel his warmth. We must hide. We must pretend we are not here and when these beetle people leave with the Lopo, we will have our villages back. And we will grow old under the sun like the women who weaved and carved and remembered.

But my brother does not move.

One of the beetle people walks away from the others. The insect head faces the trees, turns toward us. It raises an arm. I see now that it has five fingers on its hand. On both hands. It is very much in the shape of our people. Except for the insect head.

But then it removes its insect head, like you would remove a hat. The black eyes go with it too and beneath it all is a face much like Umeneni's. Like mine.

A woman.

"Come out," it says, toward the trees. To us. Somehow it speaks our language even though the lilt and sigh of the words are unfamiliar, like when the Lopo speak. Yet we understand. It says, "Come out now, children."

⚬◊⚬

I want to grip Umeneni's hand, and my brother's, but instead we hold our weapons. Hava stands and looks over his shoulder at me.

"Stay," he says. "All of you."

"No, Hava." I try to catch his arm, but he walks out alone toward the beetle people. Toward the one who has a face like mine, and speaks our language, though she flew to us like a bird.

Umeneni tries to touch my shoulder, but I run out after my brother.

The beetle people swivel to face me. I stop, planting my feet, feeling the night air breathe cold up my bare legs. Hava turns.

"Ara!" He gestures sharply. "Go back!"

"No," the beetle woman says. Closer and I see she is like my mother was, beneath the smooth clothing. She has a woman's breasts and she is tall like one, broader than me about the hips. Her voice, free of the insect head, is the gentle trickle of river water. "Let her come too. Both of you."

Hava frowns at me. But he offers his hand. So I take my brother's hand and we approach.

"You look so much alike," the woman says. "You must be brother and sister."

Up close, they don't smell like Lopo. They smell like our knives after the rain has washed them clean.

The Lopo on the ground watch us with hatred in their small white eyes. We have killed many of them. They recognize us.

Hava looks at them once, then up at the woman. "What are you?"

They haven't taken our weapons. They called us children, though we have been without parents since our tenth stride across the sands of life. Maybe they have come to steal our forest from us, to steal our beaches and our near waters, like the Lopo stole our villages.

"What are you?" Hava asks again, louder.

"We are your fathers and mothers," the woman says.

"Our fathers and mothers are dead," Hava says. He points to the Lopo. "They killed them. They came from across the waters and wiped the shores of our homes. They let our parents' blood run with the waters and the rain. Is that what you are here to do?"

My brother's voice is a kitten mew compared to the smooth strength of the woman's. She is tall enough to pick him up by the back of his neck like the big cats do with their little ones. Yet Hava doesn't waver. And I grip his hand to feel him, not for him to feel me.

"No," the woman says. "You were lost for too long. Now we've remembered."

"How is it that you speak our language?" I ask. "How do your boats fly? Where do you come from, if not from across the waters?"

"There is too much to say," the woman says, like a sigh. She holds her beetle head in her hand. It is hollow inside, and padded with a strange cloth, one that shines like the moon on the waves. She says, "You must come with us now, children."

"Come?" Hava says. He lets go of my hand.

"Yes," the woman says, and lifts her chin.

The other beetle people start to move in, silent like a footstep on the sand.

I see the Lopo sitting on the ground, weaponless. Overtaken. So swiftly, like we have never been able to do for all our attacks and killings. The Lopo just kept coming from across the waters, like fishes spawned from an endless egg.

But now they sit, and can do nothing.

The beetle people are many. Soon they will block our sight of the forest's edge, where Umeneni and the others wait.

But now Hava raises his gun and that is the signal, and all of our twenty soldiers attack.

oⅣɔ

Though we fire our guns and stab with our knives, the beetle people do not bleed. There are enough of them to keep the Lopo encircled and still bat us away. They flick us away as though their arms are tails and we are nothing but rodents on their backs.

Soon we are all on the ground beneath the daylight of the inbetween creatures. I ache but I don't know how I was hit. I remember lightning, though there is no storm, and the sound of it was louder than a summershock. Beside me, Umeneni cradles his wrist in his other hand. It is broken. Some of us cry, little voices in the silence.

But not my brother. He kneels on the ground looking up at the woman. And the lines of his spirit make marks down his cheeks, in red.

The woman's eyes glow like stars.

"You must understand," she says. "You cannot stay here. This world now belongs to the mothers and fathers of these people." She points to the Lopo.

"You say you are our mothers and fathers," Hava spits out. "Then you should help us kill the Lopo. This is *our* village. This is *our* forest. The sands are *our* sands." He drives his fist into the earth. It leaves a mark.

"No," the woman says. "You never should've been here."

She speaks our language, yet I cannot understand her words as they are pressed side by side.

"Where else would we be?" my brother asks.

They have taken our weapons. There is nothing to do but sit.

"You need to be with us," the woman says. "We are of the same blood. Look in my face. The fathers and mothers of the Lopo will come. This is their world now. We were fighting, and had forgotten, but now the fighting is over and we have found you. And you cannot stay here anymore."

"Why not?" Hava says. Almost shouts. For this woman's words are like the wind. As it passes our ears, it makes a noise and yet we cannot hold it.

"We have given this world to the fathers and mothers of the Lopo," the woman says. Her face pinches as if she tastes something bitter, and she looks to the side, toward another beetle person. Not one of them has removed their insect heads. Only her. "The Lopo will never destroy any more of our villages. I come from a village too, but one that sits among the stars. My brothers and sisters –" She motions to the other beetle people who stand so still, and do not bleed or speak. "They were born among the stars. You were not meant to be born here. Your ancestors and the ancestors of these Lopo fought, and fell to this world, and were forgotten amidst the fighting. We fought as well, as you fight them here. But now it is over and now the Lopo are ours. Here they will all be kept."

"But this is *our* village," Hava insists. I can see in the woman's unblinking eyes that somehow she does not understand us either, though we speak the same words. "You talk nonsense!" Hava says. "How are we to believe these words? They are written in the air."

"It's impossible to sit among the stars," I say. "Our blood is of the sand. We walk upon the sand and when we can no longer walk, the waters will wash us away."

But our words fall like crystal grains through our fingers, weightless against these insect kin and their daylight boats.

Another beetle figure steps up and removes the shell of its head. Underneath he is a man with the strong bones of my father. His hair is the dark red of a sunset, like Umeneni's. His face is bare and there is a scar above his right eye that shines like a blade, not like the puckered pink of healing skin.

And his eyes are Hava's eyes. Under the bright lights that push back the night, I can see the spirit of blood in his gaze.

This man says to my brother, "There are more years on this world than what passes when we are among the stars. Do you understand?"

"We will understand if you speak with words that stay together," my brother says. He points to the man's face. "How is it that you have the eyes of blood?"

I do not know why, but I begin to shake.

The man looks down at Hava. He reaches to his hip and I see a knife there, but it is long and glowing, like his eyes. Like Hava's eyes. Red.

He pulls it from his side and I am too far from my brother to warn him, or protect him, and Hava does not move. He watches the blade. I want to cry out. Umeneni lets go of his broken wrist and grabs my hand. He won't let me run ahead again. There is nothing in my grasp but the earth, nothing to fling at these beetle people but my words which they do not understand.

The red-haired man crouches in front of my brother. His black body shines with the light of the false day. He turns his knife blade down and sticks it in the ground. The red glow pools on the brown, as though the earth did bleed.

"You lead your warriors," he says to Hava, "like I lead mine. So now you must lead them to their true home. It is my home too."

My brother is silent for a long moment, looking at the ground. His hair falls forward like a wing and covers his eyes. He has led us through so many battles with the Lopo and never feared. Now he puts his finger into the earth and draws. I step closer to see, but only as far as Umeneni's grip allows. I will not let go. My brother draws a familiar pattern in the earth. It is our forest, the edges of the trees, our shore and the waters.

"This is our home," Hava says, looking up now. Red with strength. "We will not leave it."

I feel Umeneni's hand, how warm it is, surrounding mine.

I feel all the blood of our children, the children we may yet have, waiting to be born but afraid to be spilled. I feel it as though it is growing from the roots of the trees and twining through my bones from the planting of my heels on the ground.

Then the red-eyed man takes the flat of his blade and wipes it across the lines my brother made.

Once.

The blood path of our close futures, gone.

I cannot breathe. There is nothing but silence. Nothing but the smooth step that treads behind the blood. Not even Hava speaks. He is a small body beside the large black shell of this beetle man. He never looked small beside the Lopo.

Around us, blazing with light, the inbetween creatures open up their bellies. Some of the other beetle people begin to walk inside. Most of them surround us and the woman behind the red-eyed man points into the belly, where it shines an unnatural blue.

And I feel it as I feel Umeneni's hand around mine.

My children will never know the warmth of sand beneath their feet.

"Enough of this," the beetle man says. "You are children of our ancestors and you are coming home."

And with the tip of his red knife, he carves it deep into the earth.

After spending most of his life in Los Angeles, **Greg van Eekhout** *now lives in the suburban deserts near Phoenix, Arizona. His stories have appeared in* Magazine of Fantasy and Science Fiction, Starlight 3, Fantasy: The Best of 2001, New Skies, *and a number of other speculative short fiction venues. He maintains a website at* sff.net/people.greg, *and a frequently updated online journal at* journalscape.com/greg.

ಬ

Native Aliens

Greg van Eekhout

1945

As Papa stands between the two rows of men holding rifles, he stands as a Dutchman. His shirt is starched white, tucked neatly into khaki trousers with creases sharp enough to cut skin. It is not especially hot today, but sweat pools under his arms and trickles down his back. The Indonesians with the guns are sweating too.

Papa's skin is as dark as the Indonesians', naturally dark and baked tobacco brown from years spent hammering together chicken coops and pigeon hutches in the backyard. He is a good carpenter, and people come to him for help and advice. But carpentry is not his job. He works as a bookkeeper for Rotterdamse Lloyd, the Dutch shipping company. He is a Dutchman with a Dutch job.

The men with rifles stand in two ragged rows, facing one another, before the entrance of the school where we learned our lessons, which now serves as a prison for enemies of the Indonesian revolution.

It is the imprecision of the Indonesians that angers Papa, their sloppy spacing, their relaxed and slovenly postures. They hold their guns as though they were shovels or rakes or brooms, and the Indonesians have no interest in hard work.

He recognizes almost all of them. This one sells satay in front of the train station. Papa's money has helped him buy the shoes on his feet. Another, Rexi, has actually been in our home. When he was a young boy, not so long ago, he slipped on the rocks by the river and hit his head, and when we told Papa of this, Papa carried him in his arms and laid him down in the sitting room until the boy's grandfather came for him. He has sipped water from our well, and now he waits for Papa with a gun slung lazily over his shoulder.

A hand shoves Papa in the back, and Papa, slightly built, pitches forward and goes down to one knee in the dirt. He uses this opportunity to mouth a very quick prayer before being yanked roughly back to his feet.

The man who pulls Papa up is one of those he does not know. He is one of those who pounded on our door in the night and demanded we all assemble in the front room of our sprawling house built on the hill. "Are these the only men?" he asks, indicating Papa and me.

Mama explains that, yes, we are the only men. Ferdinand remains in Tokyo, where he has mined coal for the Japanese since his unit's capture. He mines coal no longer, though, because he was freed when the Japanese surrendered. When he is well enough to travel, he will return home. And there is Anthonie, the next eldest, but he is not here either. He is dead of tuberculosis, contracted in a jail cell of the Japanese occupation army.

And there is Papa. And there is me.

I am eleven years old. Later, there will be a camp for me and Mama and my sisters. But for now, they take only Papa.

The man steadies Papa, who is shaking now, who is so afraid he cannot stop shaking, who hates himself for shaking, who should not have to fear his own neighbours. "I am a bookkeeper," he says. "What have I to do with this?"

"You are a Dutchman," says the man. "Isn't that what you always insist? At your office at Rotterdamse Lloyd? At the train station where you buy your Dutch newspaper? At the cantina where you drink your coffee? At the swimming pool where only the Dutch can swim. At home, where your servants cook your food and clean your house and raise your children? 'I am a Dutchman. My family is a Dutch family.' Isn't that what you always say?"

Three generations ago, a Dutchman came from the Netherlands and married an Indonesian girl. There have been Indonesians and Dutch–Indonesians in our family for three generations, but no one from Holland.

"Yes, I am a Dutchman."

"Yes. You are," the man says to Papa. "And now, you must run."

Papa is not the first to receive this command today. He knows what's expected of him.

The men with rifles change their stances. They spread their legs to shoulder width. They bend at the knees. They raise their guns over their shoulders, inverted with the rifle butts held before them, and they wait.

The dirt at the feet of these men, his neighbours, is dark with blood and vomit and urine and shit. This is the entrance to a new prison.

Papa hopes that if he runs fast enough, maybe only a few of the rifle butts will strike him. Maybe not too hard.

He makes the sign of the cross and takes a step forward.

☙

2367

At school, they tell us about Preparation. It's almost all we talk about. For the last three months, we haven't read stories. We haven't done logic problems. We haven't learned songs or sculpted in clay or played games or done swim-dances. All we talk about is Preparation.

In three months time a ship will arrive, and all 879 of us Brevan-Terrans will board, and we will spend the next four years travelling to Earth.

We need Preparation for the journey, and we need Preparation for the arrival.

At the beginning of the year, our teacher was Mr Daal, a Brevan-Terran like my classmates and me. But after the Re-Negotiation Si Tula, a Brevan man, with eyes so blue they seem to glow even when he shuts his lids, replaced him. He speaks in a deep-horn voice and is very nice.

In a circle, we sit on the floor in trays of warm brine, watching the pictures Si Tula projects before us. There is a planet of blue and white and brown, and I already know this is Earth, because I've been seeing it for months and months now. It's been on the news. Mama has been showing us books about it. Opa has been reading pamphlets about Earth.

Si Tula begins every lesson by showing us Earth. "This is your home," he always says. And then he raises his arms, his long fingers slowly fluttering as though they were underwater, and we know what to say: *This is Earth. This is where we come from. This is where we going. It will be good to be home.*

After that, the Preparation lesson is always a little different. We have seen the cities of Earth, which are big, sprawling fields of light. We have seen the animals of Earth, which are kept inside the cities in houses of their own for all to see. We have seen the great oceans, so much broader and deeper and more powerful than our little lakes on Breva.

"Your home is a mighty world," Si Tula says. And he flutters his fingers, and we respond: *Breva is too small for Earth.*

This is something the Brevan said a lot during the Re-Negotiation. It's the reason why all us Brevan-Terrans must go.

I have a question, so I raise my hand, and Si Tula bows respectfully towards me, his rib-arms lowered. It is odd, seeing my teacher bow to me. It is not something our old teacher would ever do. But Brevans are taught from childhood to bow to Brevan-Terrans.

"You may speak, Dool," he says.

I click my valves. "We have seen Terran habitations and Terran animals and Terran planetary features."

Nervous – and not knowing why – I shift in my tray, water sloshing over the sides. Si Tula nods encouragement, so I continue. "But ... when will we see Terran *people*?"

Si Tula makes an appreciative click. "Thank you, Dool. I am pleased you asked. For what now follows is the most important part of Preparation. All else is merely knowing. But this, what we are about to learn, will require doing. It will require doing from you. It will require doing from the Health and Wellbeing Authority. It will require doing from all."

The Health and Wellbeing Authority is a new organization formed after the Re-Negotiation. Only Brevans sit on the Health and Wellbeing Authority.

Si Tula moves his hands, and a new projection appears in the middle of the circle. It is a pair of creatures. They are four-limbed – two thick limbs upon which they stand, and two thinner, upper limbs which end in things that look very much like hands. One of the creatures has a large pair of teats in front. The other has much smaller teats, and a penis. Their faces are flat and unexpressive. I have seen enough pictures of Terran animals to know that these creatures would live on land.

The projection progresses, and the creatures now wear clothing of sorts, and they move about in various settings. Here, they fold their legs beneath them and sit on the ground, planting a tree. And then they are in a structure, putting food into their tiny mouths. Here they are holding a baby creature, and despite their alien faces, it is clear they are happy. These are intelligent creatures, perhaps. More like me than like animals.

"This is you," Si Tula says. "This is you. These are Terrans, and this is what you are. This is how you were when you came to Breva. This is how you will be again."

Si Tula pauses. When he does this, we know we are to remain quiet and think about what he has said. This is us, he has told us. This is me. This is how I was.

After a suitable interval, I raise my hand.

Si Tula bows.

"I don't understand," I say. "How can these creatures be us? They have no rib–arms, no dorsals, no valves. They are land creatures. How can this be me? I don't understand."

He smiles, his eyes very blue. "Your confusion is not surprising to me. It is a new concept. It is a new concept for all of you. But you will get used to it. Given enough time, one can get used to anything."

⚭

1949

They had told us we'd be coming to a place of colours. There would be fields of tulips, white and pink and yellow and red, a celebration of colours against the blue sky. There would be wonders – windmills and canals and lanes alive with bicycles. This would be a home. We were not Indonesian, we were Dutch, they told us, and this would be our home.

What we find here is stone. The buildings are blocks of neatly stacked stone, and the streets are stone and brick, fitted together, tight and clever. They had told us it would be cold, and it is. They had told us we would get used to it, and they were lying, because how can I get used to this? Even in my jacket, which weighs as much as I do, and the wool hat that scratches my scalp, and the gloves that prevent me from feeling anything I touch, I am cold. "You'll get used to it," they tell us.

 We are home. The third floor of a narrow stone building is our home. There is a small sitting area, and we can all sit together if we keep our legs tucked close. There is a room for Mama and Gerda and Anki. Because I am the only boy – the only male in my family who survived the Japanese occupation and the Indonesian revolution – I have a room to myself, shared with the two steamer trunks we brought from Jakarta.

When Mr Kaarl, the landlord, was showing us the apartment, he realized it was quite different from what we were used to. "The water closet is down the hall," he said, jingling a ring of keys. "That'll be different for you, but you'll get used to it. They make a lot of noise, but it's more privacy than you had in your other life."

Gerda peers down the hall skeptically. "More privacy? But we have to share it with everyone else on the floor."

Mr Kaarl laughs. He has a very friendly laugh. "But it's covered and indoors, at least. No prying eyes."

Gerda frowns, not understanding.

I, however, understand very well.

Mama casts me a sharp warning look, but I don't mind such looks. At fifteen, I am the man of the house.

"Mr Kaarl believes," I explain to Gerda, "that back home we used the river as our lavatory."

When I see terror, rather than anger, in Mama's eyes, I feel a small pang of regret. There have been many moments in the last few years in which the wrong word has had grave consequences. She still thinks Papa is dead because of all his bragging about being a Dutchman. But many of our neighbours are dead, and they weren't all the braggarts Papa was. There was a war, and once the Japanese were defeated there was a revolution, and the Dutch were cast out. Many people died, of course. Blood of all kinds soaked into the ground.

But my comment was spoken in Indonesian, so Mr Kaarl only smiles a happy, puzzled smile. "Chattering monkey," he says, winking. "I'm renting to a lot of chattering monkeys lately. I should have invested in trees instead of buildings." And he laughs, his cheeks very pink.

∾

2367

When Preparation finally happens, it happens in a dry, silver room. It is unlike any room I've ever been in. There are no mollusks clinging to the walls. There is no soft carpet of moss beneath my feet. There is no gentle trickle of water.

I am alone. I am here with only a Brevan doctor, his green–and–black mottled chest blinking with medical devices.

"This is the kind of room Terrans build," he says.

I tell him no, that is wrong, that my ancestors were Terran, and they built no dead rooms like this.

And I am told, Yes, oh, yes, they did. But Breva remained Brevan, and over time, Terran rooms became Brevan. The Terran rooms were changed, sometimes deliberately, to adapt to the Brevan environment. And sometimes Breva simply took what Earth brought into its embrace, and then transformed it. But too often, Brevan rooms were made into Terran rooms, and many Brevan rooms died forever. "Earth is mighty, indeed," says the doctor. "But there is more than simple might, is there not? Is there not also patience? Is there not also resolve? What lasts longer – a heart that beats hard, or a heart that beats gentle?"

This particular room has been drained of water. In this room, the mollusks have been scraped away. In this room, herbicide has killed the moss. This room is once more a Terran room, and it must be this way, says the doctor, for the Preparation.

In the centre of the room is an oval table, shaped like an altar in a bulb-temple. "Recline upon it," says the doctor.

I look at the table. I look above it. Hanging above the table is a cluster of silver arms, dangling down like jellyfish tentacles. Blades glint in the silver room.

The doctor's eyes are blue as Si Tula's, but not at all kind.

And I run. I run towards the door, towards the cool wet air of outside, away from this dry and silver room, away, away, towards home.

I don't get far. The doctor lashes out with his rib-arms, and though I struggle and beat at his arms and try to pry loose from his suction with my soft fingers, he is too strong, and he pulls me in and lifts me and sets me on the table. And once on the table, I cannot move.

"How do you feel?" the doctor says.

"I feel nothing."

He moves his hands, and the silver arms overhead descend.

"Good," says the doctor. "We can begin now."

He begins by severing my rib-arms.

When I scream out – not in pain, but in something else, something worse – he adjusts the table and I am silent.

"Yes," he says. "That is good. Your life has been good and comfortable, and it will be so in continuance. You have no cause to cry."

∽

1969

It occurred to me some time ago that my backyard is a re-creation. The chicken coop, with the half dozen Leghorns and Rhode Island Reds, is a plywood attempt at something Papa might have built. Only, he was a carpenter, and I just began playing with wood and nails seven years ago, when we came to California. My work is a mess of crooked surfaces and ill-fitted joints, but it keeps the chickens inside, and that's what's important. I fear once the pigeon hutch is done, only the fattest and stupidest cats will fail to find a way in.

But this is my backyard. In Holland, we shared a courtyard. Here, we have something: A rambling, cluttered, wild backyard that I can think of as home.

To have a home of your own – something that can't be taken away – this is no small thing. We rent now, but someday, perhaps, it will be ours.

Of course, anything can be taken away. Even here, in this country, anything can be taken away from any person.

It's important to keep that in mind.

I turn satay kambing on my barbeque grill while across the fence, the neighbour flips hamburgers on his. Between the pickets, I see the neighbour's boy watching me. He wrinkles his nose as if he smells something foul, and I say, loud enough for him to hear, "Mmmm. Good dog. Good, delicious dog." Even louder: "Say, I wonder where Ranger is?"

Ranger is the boy's sweet-faced mutt.

The boy runs to complain to his father, and the neighbour scowls at me.

I smile and wave.

ঔ

2371

To be Terran is to walk without water. Earth is a wet world, but our home is a dry building. There is water in the walls – sometimes I can hear it course through pipes – but it comes out only in faucets, and it can be collected only in small vessels. There is a tub in the bathroom, roughly the size of a coffin, but it is dead water and I will not stay in it.

My family is fortunate. We have been located near the sea, only twenty minutes by rail, and I have a job on the shore. I sell tourist items to those who visit the water. They like to buy clothing and sensations that remind them of their travels. I sell these items well, and someday, perhaps, I will have a business of my own. I often wonder if people who come to the sea might like to have sensations that don't remind them of where they've been, but instead show them where they cannot go.

In the shop's changing room is a mirror, and I always volunteer to clean it. It is not pleasant to examine myself, but doing so is like the kind of meditation we did back home in the bulb-temples.

My body is made for work. My two arms are stronger than my rib-arms ever were, which were made for sculling. My lungs don't take in as much air as they used to, but I get enough oxygen by inhaling often. Sometimes I stand and look at myself as I am now, and then I try to imagine myself as I was. Neither body seems quite right. My new body is alien to me, and my old body is alien to this world. When I clean the mirror, I see a puzzle that cannot be solved, or an out-of-place object that has no place.

In times that are not busy, I can look outside the shop, out over the ocean. The surf can be violent here, and the waves boom against the sand, fingers of white foam reaching out and grasping, as if the ocean were trying to pull itself up on the land. Twice a day, the ocean gets as far as it can go, but then it recedes. Despite its strength, the ocean must always return to itself.

∽

1969

Last night, we went to the Moon. Three men were packed like the last pairs of socks into an overstuffed suitcase and then they went to the Moon. I didn't stay up to watch, but Anthony did. From down the hall, I could dimly hear the voices from the television, and the sound of Anthony clapping and bouncing in the squeaky–springed chair.

He's a dreamer, my son. He believes in better places.

He comes out of the house and I hand him an unseasoned lamb skewer. Satay kambing should be made with goat, but nobody eats goat here.

"How are your spacemen?"

"Astronauts," he corrects. "I don't know. Mama made me turn off the TV. She thinks I need more sunlight."

"The spacemen can get by without you watching them."

"The most important moment in the history of humanity, and Mama's worried about my Vitamin D."

I bite my lip to keep from laughing. He's a funny kid, my son. And smart. Much smarter than I was at twelve. Or smart in other ways, I suppose. By the age of twelve, I'd lost two brothers. I'd seen Japanese Zeroes fly over my house. I'd seen my father taken away by our neighbours to die. Not much time for jokes when I was his age.

"So, first we walk on the Moon," I say. "And then what? We come back home? We use what we learned to build better adding machines? New and improved vacuum cleaners?"

He gives me a look that, had I ever given to my Papa, would have earned me a slap across the face. And I let it pass. I have learned to let so much pass. It is a better way of getting through life, I think.

"It's not about … *things*," Anthony says. "It's about going places. There's so much out there, Dad." About a year ago, he stopped calling me Papa and started calling me Dad. I understand why – it's what American boys call their fathers – but I have yet to get used to it. I will, in time, but not yet. "We can't stay here forever. First, the Moon. Then, by the time I graduate college,

Mars. Then the asteroid belt, maybe. And the moons of Jupiter. By the time I have kids, the stars. There'll be other planets. Other worlds. Maybe with intelligent life. We have to go there."

"We can barely live on the Moon," I argue. "Billions of dollars and space suits and thousands of people to make it happen. And the Moon is just next door, isn't it? It's just a few thousand miles away."

He gives me that look, and I chide myself for baiting him. The Moon is 240,000 miles away. I've been following everything too.

Anthony clamps down his molars on a chunk of lamb and tears it from the skewer. "Things'll be different by the time we get to the stars," he says. "We'll be different. I read a story about it. If we find life out there, we'll change ourselves to be more like what we find. We'll make our bodies and brains different. We won't even have to come back home. We'll be so well adapted that we can survive wherever we land as efficiently as the native aliens."

Native aliens.

I let the paradox pass.

Removing the satay from the grill, I lay the skewers down in neat rows on a plate. "But, what if the life we find out there doesn't want us? What if they see us as a threat? People come to a new land, and they want to change it. They want to make it like the place they came from, and they want to be top dog. Visitors who refuse to go home aren't really visitors."

"We'll be welcome," he says, with so much confidence that I feel my heart fissure, "because we'll come with peaceful intentions."

This is a moment, now. This is a moment in which I could press the issue. I could bring to bear my thirty-five years of life experience, of scratches and bruises and scars and calluses. I could strip away every one of my son's naive sentiments and make him see the world as it is. I have seen blood in the dirt. I bet I could make my son see it too.

I hand him the plate of satay. "Bring this to the kitchen. And then watch your spacemen walk on their rock."

"Astronauts," he says, taking the plate. "And it's not just some rock. It's a world."

I pierce more lamb chunks onto skewers. "Okay. Have it your way. A world. Tell me if the astronauts find something good on their new world."

He gives me his look and takes the satay kambing into the house.

I stay in my backyard and look to the sky.

There's nothing to see there, but I look on my son's behalf, praying that he'll never have to see what I see.

Celu Amberstone *was one of the only young people in her family to take an interest in learning Traditional Native North American crafts and medicine ways. This made several of the older members of her family very happy, while annoying others. Though legally blind since birth, she has spent much of her adult life avoiding cities. She has lived in the rain forests of the west coast, a tepee in the desert, and a small village in Canada's arctic. Along the way she also managed to acquire a BA in cultural anthropology and an MA in health education. A teacher of cross-cultural workshops and traditional Native ways, Celu loves telling stories and reading. She now lives in Victoria, British Columbia near her grown children and two grandchildren.*

⌀

Refugees

Celu Amberstone

Awakening Moon, sun-turning 1

This morning I arose early and climbed to the Mother Stone on the knoll above the village. The sun was just rising above the blue mists on the lake. The path smelled of tree resin and flowering moss. I took in a deep breath and sang to the life around me. I was shivering by the time I reached the Mother Stone and made the first of my seasonal offerings to Tallav'Wahir, our foster planet.

I cut open my arm with the ceremonial obsidian knife I carried with me, and watched my blood drip into the channel carved into the stone for that purpose. Blood. The old people say it is the carrier of ancestral memories, and our future's promise. I am a child from the stars – a refugee, driven from my true home. My blood is red, an alien colour on this world.

161

But I am lucky because this planet knows my name.

ᴄᴎᴐ

Awakening Moon, sun-turning 2

I should rejoice in the renewal of life, but with this Awakening Moon my heart is sad. Always before one of my daughters has been with me to share this special time. Now they are all gone. My youngest daughter married last harvest and moved to a village across the lake. I miss her. My dear old man, Tree, says I should be glad to be done with that cycle of my life. But if I still crave the company of children, he is sure that my co-wife Sun Fire would be happy to share. He says this with a smile when he sees my long face, and truly the children left in the compound are more than a handful for us. But though I love them all – including my widowed sisters – it isn't quite the same. I pray that Tukta's marriage will be a happy one, and blessed with healthy children. Oh Mother, how we need healthy children.

ᴄᴎᴐ

Awakening Moon, sun-turning 7

Today our Benefactors confirmed our worst fears. Earth is now a fiery cloud of poisons, a blackened cinder. When it happened, our ancient soul-link with Earth Mother enabled us to sense the disaster even from this far world across the void. Tallav'Wahir felt it too. But we told our foster planet mother that our life patterns were sound. Our Benefactors would help us. Such a tragedy would never happen here. There was a great outpouring of blood and grief at the Mother Stones all over the world. The land ceased to tremble by the time the ceremonies ended.

ᴄᴎᴐ

Leaf-Budding Moon, sun-turning 3

The star shuttle arrives with our new wards tomorrow – twenty-one of them for our village. What an honour to be given so many. Dra'hada says that the crew won't awaken them from cold-sleep until just prior to their arrival. When they are led out, they will be disoriented, and we will have to be patient with them. Dra'hada has assured me that our implants and theirs have been attuned to the same frequency so that we can communicate easily, and that is a relief. I wonder what these new people will be like. I am excited, and maybe a little afraid too. All the wars and urban violence we've heard about, I hope they can adjust to our simple ways. It's been a long time since our Benefactors have brought settlers to Tallav'Wahir to join us. We desperately need these newcomers. Tallav'Wahir is kind, but there is something in this adoptive environment that is hard on us too. We aren't a perfect match for our new home, but our Benefactors have great hopes for us.

⠶

Leaf-Budding Moon, sun-turning 4

It is moonrise, and it's been an exhausting day for all of us. I was near the front of the crowd when the shuttle set down on the landing pad. I thought I was prepared for anything. How wrong I was. They are so alien. It is hard to believe we are the same species. The situation on Earth deteriorated so fast that the ship was forced to gather what survivors were available without delay. There was no time to select the suitable. The sorting will have to be done here, I suppose, and that is unfortunate. Culling is very stressful for everyone. Most of the people assigned to our village were dazed and confused, but some were angry too. Maybe they were afraid of our Benefactors, and that might account for their rude behaviour. Filthy lizards indeed. They are an unsettling addition to our village, and the land feels it too.

⠶

Leaf-Budding Moon, sun-turning 5

Dra'hada says, even though they look and act so differently, they all come from a large city called Vancouver. We have three staying in our family's compound. When I first saw the young woman given to us, my heart pounded like a drum. I'd caught only a glimpse of her in profile, and I thought my daughter Tukta had returned to me. Then she turned to face me and the resemblance vanished. It was an unsettling experience nonetheless. Her features at times still remind me of Tukta's, but in no other way are they the same!

This girl is of medium height, golden–skinned, and very, very thin. She was wearing tight black pants, and black boots with high heels that make her walk funny. She also had on a black shirt, very sheer – I could see her tiny nipples pressed against the fabric. Over that she wore a black leather jacket with lots of silver chains. Her hair is short, spiky, and blue. She has a ring in her nose and several in her ears, and a pudgy baby that cries a lot. She told us her name was Sleek. Jimtalbot, one of our other charges, says that isn't her real name, just a "street name." I'm not sure what he meant by that, but I'll wait and ask him later.

Jimtalbot is one of the few older adults left in our care. Unlike Sleek, he has pale skin and grey streaks in his short brown hair. His face is a bit puffy, and his belly soft. Dra'hada says we will have to watch him because his heart is weak. Jimtalbot told me that he was a professor at the university. He has lively blue eyes and is very curious about everything. I like him the best of the lot.

Our third fosterling, given into Tree's care mostly, is a sullen, brown-skinned youth whose "street name" is Twace. He wares a bright-coloured cloth tied around his head and baggy striped pants. I don't like his angry eyes or the colour of his aura. It is filled with red and murky grey patches. When he looked around our compound and saw the neat round dwellings with their sturdy mud walls and mossy roofs, the thatched stable for our woolly beasts, and the shady arbor where my loom sits, his mouth curled in contempt.

They are abed now – finally. Tomorrow we will have to get them suitable clothing and bring them to the Mother Stone on the knoll. I hope they won't be too frightened by the adoption ceremony.

⌗

Leaf-Budding Moon, sun-turning 6

We tried to prepare our fosterlings for the proceedings, but no amount of assurance on our part seemed to ease their minds. All were anxious, and some had to be dragged screaming and cursing to the Mother Stone while an elder made the cut for the required blood offering. Sleek was one of the worst. She kicked and clawed at the men who brought her forward, and no amount of assurance on my part could calm her.

When we returned home, Sleek was a mess. Her arms and face were bloody, and her alien clothes were ruined. I saw my neighbours' pitying glances as we took her away. My widowed sister and my co-wife, Sun Fire, helped me strip off her clothing and get her cleaned up. I was so ashamed for our family.

"Ignorant savages, cannibals, leave me alone, goddamn you!" she shouted at us as we washed her.

"It's all right, daughter, calm down. Come now, it was only a little blood; it didn't really hurt to make the gift. No one is going to eat you. The blood was given to the Stone so that our foster planet mother could taste you. Now She will know you as one of her own. We all make such offerings; it is one of the ways our Benefactors have taught us to commune with the soul of the land. Such traditions were practiced on Earth once – didn't you know that?"

"Screw traditions – and the lizards," she snarled and threw the new dress I was trying to hand her to the floor. "I want my own clothes – what have you done with my things, bitch?"

"Don't talk to your foster mother like that," my sister said. "Show her more respect."

Sleek opened her mouth to reply, but I spoke quickly to forestall another outburst. "I'm sorry, Sleek, but it was necessary to get rid of those alien things. They aren't in harmony with life here. You must wear and use the natural things provided by *this* planet now. Their manna will help you commune with Tallav'Wahir. These ways may seem harsh to you at first, but they are important. Our elders and our Benefactors know what is best for us – truly they do."

Sleek gave me a withering look, but took the simple dress I handed her. While the fabric was over her head, I heard her mumble something about ignorant savages talking to dirt. "Our Benefactors know best," she mimicked as her head cleared the opening. "Well, they're not *my* benefactors. You people are pathetic. Damned lizards have you humans living like primitive savages while they fly around in their spaceships."

Her words were meant to cut, but I thought I saw tears in the corners of her eyes, so I bit back my angry response. "We know about the high technologies," I told her quietly. "We use what you would call computers, air cars, and other technical things too. But to help you make the repatterning, we decided that a simple lifestyle would be best for all of us for a time. There is no shame in living close to the land in a simple way, daughter.

"Our Benefactors teach us that technology must never interfere with our Communion with the Mother, lest we forget the Covenant, grow too greedy, and destroy our new home."

Sleek's face flushed a deep crimson, and she probably would have said more rude things to me, but at that point her baby began crying in the yard outside, and she took that as an excuse to leave us. When she was gone, my sister Sun Fire and I looked at one another in exasperation. Her behaviour could try the patience of a stone.

∽

Flowering Moon, sun-turning 7

The planting is over. It was a nice change to play with the children on the beach today. The water in the lake is already warm enough for a swim. Sleek and I played with them for hours in the shallows by the shore. Her face relaxed; she looked younger and seemed so happy, and that made me happy too. Maybe she and the others can adjust to our ways after all.

✧

Flowering Moon, sun-turning 9

Jimtalbot rubs his fourth finger when he thinks no one is looking. Like the others he was forced to give up everything from his past, including the narrow gold ring that used to be on that finger. Just now when I went out to relieve myself, I heard someone sobbing quietly in the shadows under the te'an tree. When I went to investigate, I saw Jimtalbot. I sat down beside him and took his hand. "What's so wrong?" I asked him. He sniffed and tried to pull his hand out of mine, but I held on and repeated my question.

"Nothing really – I'll be all right … I was just thinking about home – and my dead wife. She was visiting her mother in Toronto when it happened. The whole eastern part of the country was annihilated, from what Dra'hada told me."

"Such thoughts are more than nothing, Jimtalbot. I can't imagine losing so much; it must be terrible. I think you and the others are very brave."

He shook his head; I could see the gleam of unshed tears in his eyes by the lantern light. "Not brave at all. Your *Benefactors* gave us no choice."

There was such harshness to his voice when he said those words that I shivered and wrapped my shawl tighter around my shoulders. "They are your Benefactors too," I pointed out to him. "Would you rather have had them leave you to die?"

He was silent for a long time. Finally he said, "I don't know, Qwalshina. It is all so different here – I don't know if I have the courage to live in this place."

Surprised by his confession, I raised his hand to my lips and kissed it. "Surely you can; we are all here to love and help you. You aren't alone here – and if you wish a new wife –"

At that point, he disentangled his hand from mine and stood up. "Thank you for your concern, Qwalshina. You are very kind. I think I shall go back to my bed now. Good night."

I went back to my own bed with a troubled heart. The little ring was such a small memento. Did we do right to make them give up everything? Our Benefactors advised it, but....

∽

Flowering Moon, sun-turning 25

Last night, there was an argument down by the beach that ended with Sand Walker and one of the new men being injured. Everyone is so upset today, and Dra'hada was furious when he heard about it. He told me that such violence wouldn't be tolerated. Why can't the new ones see how lucky they are? These people were saved from death; why are they so angry? I don't understand them. I wish they'd never been brought here.

No, that isn't true; we need them....

∽

Korn-Growing Moon, sun-turning 11

I had to make a difficult decision yesterday about Sleek. Her baby was suffering. She would shout and curse the babe more often than she would feed or care for the boy. Today the women's council came to take the baby away. She cursed us in the vilest terms. Judging by her behaviour later, however, I think she is secretly relieved to be rid of the child. The council gave the little one to Aunty Shell to foster. Granny Night Wind says the boy is doing better already.

I look at Sleek's hard eyes and I wonder what is wrong with her. Can't she feel any emotion but anger? How could she be so indifferent to her own child's welfare? I remember how it was when we lost my oldest daughter's first born. Poor unfortunate mite – we were all distraught when he had to be culled.

∽

Korn-Growing Moon, sun-turning 16

Our medicine woman, Granny Night Wind, thinks we will have a good crop this harvest season. Tallav'Wahir, we live in harmony with Her cycles. She feeds us, Her spirit helpers protect us, and in return we bury our shit and our dead in her rich gray soil so that She can absorb our essence, swallow our memories, and enfold us in the oneness of Her living soul. My daughter Tukta's face comes into my mind – she is so young, and so happy. Will the land love and bless her, make her one of Her favoured ones? Oh, I pray it will be so.

◌◌

Berry Moon, sun-turning 2

There was a great bonfire down on the beach last night. We baked fish on sticks, and ate berries cooked with sweet dumplings till our bellies grew hard and round. In the long green twilight, we played running games. Then someone brought out a drum and that started everyone singing and dancing. Our Twace and two boys in my cousin Rain's compound can drum very well. I danced till I thought I would fall over from exhaustion. Later Tree, Sun Fire, and I crept off to a quiet place by the spring where we made sweet love under the stars. Some time during the night Tree's unmarried brother Sand Walker joined us and that was good too.

◌◌

Berry Moon, sun-turning 9

When I was working at my loom this evening Sleek came over unexpectedly and sat down beside me. She seemed curious, and maybe a little interested. None of my other children have the talent to be a master weaver. It would be a shame for the family to lose such a skill when I become too old for the craft. Some of our Benefactors pay high prices for our art back on their Homeworld. I let her watch for a time, then I asked, "Would you like me to show you how to do this?" She shrugged, but didn't get up and leave. Best not frighten her away, I thought, so I just continued on with my work.

After a while she volunteered, "My grandmother used to weave – it looked something like that."

Startled, I stopped my work and turned to face her. "Really? That's very interesting. What kind of things did she make?"

"I don't remember exactly; I was pretty young when she died.... I remember one thing she made, though. It had bright colours; I used to tangle my fingers in its long fringes." She smiled at the memory, and added, "It was probably something ceremonial, a dance cape maybe. A lot of the old women in our tribe used to make them for the potlatch ceremonies."

"Pot–a–latch." My tongue stumbled over the unfamiliar word. "Was this a ceremony of your people held to honour the Earth Mother?"

"I don't know; my mom never took me to one."

I went back to my weaving at that point. I could see she was becoming nervous by my questioning. *Be careful, Qwalshina, or you will frighten her away*, I told myself. But inwardly I smiled as I twined the yarn back and forth between the rope strands on the loom. Truly our Benefactors are wise. Dra'hada knew how much I was missing Tukta, and gave me a new daughter of the same racial stock as my own. At that moment I felt very good about knowing that. It made me feel a little closer to her.

On impulse I asked her, "How old are you?"

She seemed startled by my question, and her eyes narrowed with suspicion at first, then she relaxed. "The lizards didn't tell you?"

"No. I never asked our Benefactors. Is your age a secret? Would you tell me?"

She gave me another shrug. "No secret. Eighteen. Why?"

"I was just curious." Eighteen. I forced myself to go back to my weaving. *Gently, gently, Qwalshina*, I told myself. "You are about the age of my third daughter. She got married recently and moved to another village. I miss her. I'm glad you are here to take her place."

Sleek snorted. "I don't have much use for *mothers*, so don't get your hopes up about making me your new daughter – or teaching me that silly string stuff either."

She made me angry then, and I allowed my evil tongue to say something cutting in return. "Maybe if you had been more willing to be *mothered* you could have done a better job of being a mother yourself, instead of abusing your baby."

Sleek jerked back as if I'd slapped her – which in a way I had. I saw the hurt in her eyes for just a moment and then it was gone, replaced by her habitual sullen anger. She stood up and glared down at me with such contempt that it made my bones shiver. "You people make me sick," she spat back.

"You think you're so wonderful and know what's best for everyone, don't you? Well, let me tell you about *my* mother. She was a drunk who let her boyfriends fuck me whenever they wanted; then told me it was my fault for being a slut. I never wanted to be a mother – fuck mothers – all mothers. Who needs any of you?"

I stared after her with tear-filled eyes. Why had I said that? I'm so ashamed. Now I understand a little more why she acts the way she does, but that doesn't excuse my behaviour. I must go to the Mother Stone, make an offering, and try to regain my internal harmony. Like a disease, these people are destroying our peace. And, if I am honest with myself, I must admit that Sleek and the others frighten me. Her questions and her anger make me uncomfortable. Is she right? Are we too complacent and judgmental? I have to go help Sun Fire with the children.

∾

Korn-Ripening Moon, sun-turning 17

The entire village is in an uproar after what happened last night. Someone stole some of Granny Night Wind's uiskajac. It was fermenting in a big wooden barrel at the back of her compound. When Sand Walker went to check on the brew, he found the barrel only half full. Granny Night Wind was furious. She threatened to give the persons responsible a bad case of "the itch" when she finds them. Whoever did it is either very brave – or crazy. She is a powerful shamanka; the spirits obey her. Still, it was funny to see her stomping around, looking under everything – people leaping out of her way – or jumping to do her bidding.

∾

Rain-Comes-Back Moon, sun-turning 2

These young ones, so corrupted by poor food and alien drugs, have grown up spindly, like unhappy plants shaded from the sun. The last human crop of their tormented, polluted world is a pitiful one indeed. Will their life–patterns be suitable to mingle with ours? My people need the flow of new genes or we may perish in spite of all our Benefactor's efforts. I am so afraid for my children. The birth defects and terminations are so many. I fear for my daughter Tukta. She is so young and so happy with her new man.

Ah, but Dra'hada says not to give up hope. We will salvage what we can from this last harvest. And if that is not enough, our Benefactors will collect the seeds of other worlds and crossbreed them with ours. Our descendants may not be the same in appearance as we are, but some part of us will survive. And the land will always remember us. Our bodies will lie in the cool ground until the blood memories of our species have passed into the crystals of the bedrock itself.

∾

Rain-Comes-Back Moon, sun-turning 4

Jimtalbot and Bethbrant were troubled by a crazy rumour they'd heard, and came this evening to ask me if it might be true.

"One of the guys from Earth living at Black Rock Village said that Earth isn't really destroyed," Jimtalbot told me.

I looked into their troubled faces and felt a shiver run down my spine. "What? Why would he say such a thing? Of course the Earth Mother is gone. Why else would our Benefactors have brought you here?"

"Why indeed, Qwalshina?" Jimtalbot said. "Could the – uh – Benefactors be planning some weird experiment? Something that they need live humans, or human body parts for?"

I was shocked, speechless. "Experiment? No, of course not. That's preposterous. Who said such a thing? I must tell Dra'hada; who is it?"

Their expressions became closed at that point. Jimtalbot mumbled that he didn't know the man's name, but I was sure he was lying to me. He looked at Bethbrant and they started to walk away, but I stopped them. "Please wait. If you don't wish me to tell Dra'hada, Jimtalbot, I won't, but listen to me. There is no truth to this rumour. I felt Earth Mother's death agony myself – through the Communion – we all did. The pain was almost unbearable. Truly She is gone. And, there is no planned experiment. Our Benefactors only wish us well."

"If your people were also a part of their design, you might not be aware of the experiment either," Bethbrant said.

"No, we would know if they were using us in that way. We have been here for generations. My father was a man of the Tsa'La'Gui people. His ancestors were brought here when pale-skinned invaders from across a big ocean came and took their land. My mother's people came here long before my fathers. They were Crunich and lived on the island of Erin before the black-robed ones with their dead god came and stole the island's soul. There are others from Earth Mother here too, rescued from disaster as you were. Our Benefactors wish only good for us. And, no matter our origin on Earth, we are all one people now, the children of Tallav'Wahir. There has never been any experiment. Please believe me."

When I finished talking to them, they seemed convinced that it was all a crazy, made-up lie. But later the children told me that a group of our charges walked down the beach together to talk something over in private. Did I do right to promise not to tell Dra'hada? This is very troubling. I must go to the Mother Stone and tell Her my concerns.

☙

Falling Leaves Moon, sun-turning 5

Sleek's tattooed friend and six other youths have developed a terrible case of "the itch." No common healing remedy has worked. Poor lads – I know they're miserable – and I shouldn't laugh at their misfortunes, but it *is* funny to watch them trying to scratch all those hard–to–reach places. Rain's twins were in on the scheme. One of them finally broke down and confessed. About half of the stolen uiskajac was brought back. Granny is keeping the offenders in suspense for one more night, but she told me privately that she would forgive them, and give them a healing salve tomorrow.

∽

Falling Leaves Moon, sun-turning 25

Sleek and I took the children for a walk on the knoll today. We piled up great mountains of leaves and had fun jumping into them. I tired before they did, but felt so good just watching them. I think my new daughter loves playing like a child when none of her Earth friends are around to ridicule her. She is recreating the happy childhood she didn't have on Earth, and it is a joy to see her so.

Later we gathered siba fruit and roasted it on sticks over an open fire, and everyone sang songs. I found myself wishing Tukta could have been there to share the day with us. When we were heading home the children raced ahead as usual, but Sleek waited for me on the trail and fell into step beside me as I passed. I smiled and she returned the gesture.

In the dappled light under the trees, her face suddenly seemed to metamorphose into that of an ancient. Expressing wisdom far beyond her years, she said to me, "I had fun with you today, but I'm not Tukta, Qwalshina. Please try to remember that." There was no anger in her voice for once; the smells of tree resin, spicy siba, and a lazy afternoon had drained her of hostility.

Startled, I paused on the trail and faced her. "I know.... I had fun today too, and I'm glad you are who you are. I wouldn't want it any other way."

"Mmm.... Then stop calling me Tukta."

"I don't," I protested.

She gave me a reproachful look, her eyes luminous and sad. "You're not even aware that you're doing it, are you?"

Was I? Oh Mother, was I confusing her with my daughter in the physical world as well as in my mind? "I'm sorry, Sleek, I *didn't* realize I'd been doing that. Do I do it often?"

She made a noncommittal sound which I took to be acceptance of my apology. "Not often, but sometimes – like today – you forget." She shrugged, looked away, and brushed her hand across a feathery tree branch. We'd chopped off the dyed blue parts of her hair some time back, and now soft brown waves hung down past her shoulders. Up ahead, one of the children called to her at that point, and she raced down the trail to catch up with the others.

I kept walking at a slower pace, thinking. I hadn't realized I'd been doing that. Her gentle rebuke caused me to question my own insecurities. It wasn't fair to Sleek if I was indeed trying to mold her into another's image for my own comfort. Why did I continue to cling to the past? Why couldn't I go on with my life – what was I afraid of? I will have to guard my tongue and my thoughts more carefully in future. I must go see Granny Night Wind; maybe she can guide me through this difficult time.

cℵɔ

Frost Moon, sun-turning 15

It's getting very cold at night now. We arrived back in the village by the lake yesterday afternoon, our pack beasts heavy–laden from the annual hunt. Soon we will hold the last harvest feast. Everyone is excited. After the festivities we will pack up everything important and leave this exposed, stormy beach. When the blue snows pile up outside, we will be safe in our warm underground lodges up the sheltered valley in the hills.

cℵɔ

Frost Moon, sun-turning 28

I walked to the Mother Stone today to say farewell till our return in Awakening Moon. The seasons have turned and the dark time is upon us once again. In the shadows along the path specters of other races that once lived here too materialized, and watched me with solemn red eyes. Their voices whispered to me on the cool wind, but I couldn't understand their alien speech. What happened to those born to this world? Our Benefactors don't know....

Along with my blood, I poured out to the Mother my hopes and fears for the future. I hope She heard and will bless us. We are all that is left of humanity now. Can we survive? Or will this land one day absorb us back into itself as she has others who have walked these hills? Such thoughts deepened the chill in my bones, and I hurried back to the warmth of my family's compound. I want us all to live, and be happy.

The last harvest feast is tonight after the communal prayers. I'm resolved to set aside my dark mood and be happy. My pregnant daughter and others from across the lake are coming for the festivities. Oh, it will be good to see her. I mustn't waste any more time, Sun Fire needs help with the baking.

☙

Cold Moon, sun-turning 1

I am a little achy this morning – too much good food, dancing – and definitely too much uiskajac. What a wonderful party. I danced till I thought my feet would fall off. It was too cold for lovemaking under the stars, but the sweet pleasure under our warm blankets was just as good. I want to laze around in bed today, but the village will begin the packing for our move. And I have to say farewell to our departing guests. My daughter looks radiant – she is due in the Awakening Moon. What a good omen. I will miss her though. I wish I could be with her during this time. I hope she waits till I can come to her to have the child.

Sleek has disappeared again – just when I need her the most....

☙

Cold Moon, sun-turning 12

During the good weather, we were able to distract our charges with work and games played down on the beach in the evenings. Now that the blue snows are here, some of them have started whining about computer games and videos again. I talked to Tomcowan today about a theatre project. Maybe that will help keep them amused.

☙

Cold Moon, sun-turning 14

As a compromise, Dra'hada is willing to send for some of the high tech equipment now in storage. If our new charges agree to study in our school, they will be allowed limited time on the equipment for entertainment pursuits. Twace and the others are dubious about the schooling part, but Dra'hada was firm with them. The Long Sleep Moons are a strain on everyone; I hope the play practices and Dra'hada's machines will help it pass in tranquility.

ᴄᴧɔ

Ice Moon, sun-turning 2

We are teaching those who wish to learn the discipline of "The Communion." In the long nights when the snows are heavy on the land above, we journey underground, to the warm cave of the Mother. There we lie together on the floor of a large chamber, our limbs touching, and we slide into the sweet reverie that is the Deep Communion with Tallav'Wahir. We leave our bodies in the warm darkness and allow our spirits to swim upon the Great Starry River. We journey to other worlds and visit with friends light years away. None of our charges can travel so far, but for those who are willing to try, we have hope that someday they will master the technique well enough to join us.

ᴄᴧɔ

Ice Moon, sun-turning 7

Tomcowan's play was a success. It was written and performed by our charges. And I am so proud; my new daughter is such a good actress. She seemed to shine like a jewel when we offered her our praise. Our fosterlings told us the story of their lives in the lost city of Vancouver. Parts were funny, and some things were sad. Much of it I didn't understand, but in spite of that, the performance was very moving. The elders will tell stories of our own history tonight. I hope our fosterlings will like them. There is so much for us to share and weave together if we are to become one people.

ᴄᴧɔ

Ice Moon, sun-turning 15

In the aftermath of Tomcowan's play, an air of desolation has settled over our charges. It is very disheartening. The long, gloomy days indoors have given the memories of their lost home an unexpected poignancy. More fights today.

Just now I found Jimtalbot staring moodily into the flames of our fire. I sat beside him and asked why he and the others were still grieving for such a horrible place.

He looked at me with his sorrowful blue eyes and said, "It wasn't all bad there, Qwalshina. My wife and I lived comfortably in a nice house by the ocean. Along with the bad, there was a lot of good too. Art, music, fine literature, advances in science and medicine – we had a lot to be proud of. As hard as it was for people like Sleek and Twace back home I think they miss it as much as I do."

"Yes, I'm sure they do, and I can't understand that either."

He shrugged. "Home is home, no matter how bad it is, and you can't help caring when it's gone – if it's gone."

If it's gone? I didn't want to get bogged down in that conversation again, so I began a new topic. "Caring? Why didn't the people of your city care enough to protect suffering children who starved on your city streets? Why didn't they care enough to honour the Earth Mother and not destroy her gifts to you? Can you honestly say that life here has been so terrible that you would wish to go back?"

He was silent for a long time, just staring into the flames. Finally he tossed another stick onto the fire and shook his head. "I don't know, Qwalshina."

"Don't know?" I was confused and upset myself by then so I left him. Vancouver sounded like such a terrible place. How could they possibly miss it and want to return?

ᴄᴍᴐ

Ice Moon, sun-turning 19

The rumours about Earth have surfaced again, and this time I'm sure Dra'hada has heard them. Perhaps the play wasn't such a good idea after all. Everyone is getting tired of the cold and the confinement. The books have been read and reread, lessons and amusements are boring, and food and drink grow stale. Tempers are short. I try to sleep as much as I can. For us, this time is a natural phenomenon to be endured. For our charges, it is a torment beyond belief. Our warm dark homes anger or depress them. The snow is too deep, not the right colour, too cold – the litany is endless. I'm going back to my bed.

ᴄᴍᴐ

Sun-Comes-Back Moon, sun-turning 7

When I lie upon my communion mat and close my eyes, I can feel the deep stirring in the land, and my body responds to it gladly. The sap is rising, and the snow melting, and my daughter tells me her belly is nearly bursting. The sun is warm on my back when I collect the overflowing buckets of sap from the trees in the sugar bush. And, wonder of wonders, our Sun Fire is pregnant again. Tree is taking a lot of teasing for starting a new family at his age, but we are so pleased. This time the baby – all the babies – will be healthy, I just know it.

ᘯ

Sun-Comes-Back Moon, sun-turning 28

One of the great ships from the Homeworld is coming. Dra'hada is ecstatic. Poor creature – this past year–turning has been so hard on him. What with all the villagers' and fosterlings' complaints to sort out and the unease of the Mother's Spirit Guardians to placate, it is no wonder that our Benefactor has aged visibly. It will do all of us good to have Benefactors from the Homeworld here for the renewal ceremonies. Perhaps they will be able to put those rumors about Earth's survival to rest once and for all.

The ship will be here by the time the snow is gone, so Dra'hada tells me. I wonder if they will bring a new mate for our dear teacher? It will be a great celebration; other villages are coming to join us. Everyone is excited, even our young fosterlings.

ᘯ

Awakening Moon, sun-turning 4

We are back in our village by the lake again. Our compound survived the storm season without needing many repairs. That is good because the ship will be here soon and there is so much to do before our guests arrive.

During all the confusion, Sleek went missing again. When she crept back into the compound just before the evening meal, I was so angry I shouted at her. She of course shouted right back. Why, oh why, does she continue to be so irresponsible! I'm trying not to compare her to Tukta, but it is so hard.

ᘯ

Awakening Moon, sun-turning 10

My heart is on the ground. The village is overflowing with guests. I'm trying very hard not to let my personal tragedy spoil the festive mood for others. My daughter's baby was born deformed and was – oh, I can't even write down the words…. The tragedy happened the night before last; her husband's aunt told me when she arrived today. Tears blur my vision as I try to write this. Oh, Mother, how could this happen – again.

Tukta, my dear sweet Tukta! I want desperately to go to her, take her in my arms, and kiss away the pain. But I can't, not until after the ceremonies are over. What am I thinking of? She isn't a child anymore. I can't make this terrible hurt go away by my presence. And I have obligations to the People that take precedence over personal concerns. I must stay; I must be here to greet our Benefactors when the ship comes tomorrow. The Renewal Ceremony at the Mother Stone this year will be very important.

৵৲

Awakening Moon, sun-turning 11

When I looked into the faces of our guests from the Homeworld today, I felt such a rage building up inside me that I could hardly breathe at times. Granny Night Wind sensed my disharmony, and made me drink a potion to settle my spirit. This new emotion I feel frightens me. What if we are living a lie – what if the people from Earth are right? I hate them! Why did they have to come here? Maybe they should have been left to die on their god–cursed world!

৵৲

Awakening Moon, sun-turning 12

Our compound is quiet tonight; we took in no guests for the feasting. I can hear the sounds of merriment going on around us as I write this. The little ones don't understand. Sun Fire has taken them to the fire down on the beach. I am glad. My old man Tree is resting in the bedroom behind me. His nearness right now is a comfort.

To my surprise, Sleek hasn't joined the revelers. She was standing in the doorway when I looked up from my pad. I wanted to say something encouraging to her, but I feel too dead inside to make the effort.

She watched me for a long moment in silence, then said, "I–I'm sorry about your daughter, Qwalshina. Sun Fire said something went wrong and the baby's dead. Is that true – or did the damned lizards kill it?"

Her unspoken thought seemed to ring in my mind: filthy lizards, I told you they couldn't be trusted. Suddenly I felt my anger leap up like oil poured onto flames. I hated her at that moment with all my heart, and maybe she felt it, because she staggered backward and grabbed the doorpost for support. Why was she here – and healthy? Why had she, an unfit mother, had a healthy baby, when my dear sweet Tukta could not? Tukta loves her new husband, I thought, and now our Benefactors will probably want her to choose a new mate – it is unfair.

When I gave no answer and only glared at her, Sleek's expression crumpled, and she disappeared back into the night.

After she was gone, Tree came out of the bedroom. He didn't reproach me for my cruelty; he only took me in his arms and led me to our bed. I lay down beside him, buried my face in the warmth of his chest, and cried.

When I could control myself enough to speak, I said, "I'm so ashamed. The one time she tried to comfort someone else, I was unkind to her. Like a mean–spirited hag I pushed her away. Why was I so cruel to her, Tree? I don't understand her or myself anymore."

"Hush now, my flower," Tree soothed. "You are tired, and grieving. People say and do things that they don't truly mean at such a time. I know you care about her, and she does too. I will speak to her tomorrow. Go to sleep, my heart, all will be well."

I drifted into sleep, as he suggested, but deep in my heart I knew all would not be well – not for a long time – and maybe not ever again.

oⱱꜱ

Awakening Moon, sun-turning 13

The most terrible thing has happened. Oh, it is so terrible I can hardly think of it without bursting into tears all over again. Sleek is dead, and so are ten others, one of them a native man from Cold Spring village. Tallav'Wahir, forgive me. I saw her sneaking out of our compound, and I did nothing to stop her. Did I drive her into joining those foolish people with my hard looks and resentment? Was I just another mother who failed her?

It was late in the afternoon when it happened. Most of our visiting Benefactors and other guests had taken air cars down the lake to visit Black Rock Village. I was just helping Sun Fire settle the children for their naps when a loud rumbling whine brought me and most of the adults still in the village racing to the shore. The great ship resting on the sand was making terrible noises, and trembling violently by the time we arrived. From within its opened hatchway we heard screaming – human screaming.

We looked at one another, our eyes round as soup bowls. Then all the noise and trembling stopped as abruptly as it started. We waited, but nothing further happened. Finally Granny Night Wind and I walked to the stairway and called out to the crew left on duty inside. At first no one answered, but when the old woman started up the stairs, a weak voice from within warned her to come no closer. We exchanged glances, and then I said to the people in the ship, "Honoured Benefactors, is something wrong? Can we help you?"

"No, you can't help. Come no closer – it may kill you too if you try to enter."

Kill us? I was taller than Granny; I peered into the dimness of the open hatch. My nose caught the metallic scent of blood before I saw it. There on the floor, blood – red blood. The benefactor's blood is brown. I shivered, a claw of fear tearing at my heart. What had happened in there? Oh, Mother, where was Sleek? I turned back to Granny. Had she seen the blood on the floor too? I stepped down off the stair, my mind in shock. People called to me, but I couldn't answer. I heard the sound of the air cars returning, and then people running past me. I swayed and would have fallen, but suddenly Tree's arms were around me, hugging me to his chest. "Qwalshina, what's happened?"

He was warm and solid, smelling of budding leaves and smoky leather. Against his chest, I shook my head. No words could get past the aching lump in my throat.

The visiting Benefactors rushed into their ship, and soon after Dra'hada appeared and told us to return to our homes. He wouldn't answer the shouted questions put to him. "Everything is in order now. No need to fear. Go back to your homes. Tonight at the Big Sing I will tell you all that has happened."

Granny Night Wind added her own urging to the gathered people and soon most drifted away. I stayed; I refused to let Tree and Sun Fire lead me away. When Dra'hada came over to us, I clutched his scaly hand and begged, "Please, honoured teacher, tell me what has happened."

Dra'hada's headcrest drooped, and he patted my hand. "Go home, Qwalshina. You can't do anything to help here. Go home with your family."

"Damn you, I'm not a child. Tell me what's happened. Is Sleek in there?" I heard Tree and Sun Fire's gasps of surprise at my disrespect, but I was too frightened to care. I had to know.

For just a moment Dra'hada's headcrest flattened and I saw the gleam of long teeth under his parted black lips. I shuddered, but stood my ground.

I had to know. Then he let go his own anger and looked at me solemnly. "I never assumed you were a child, Qwalshina; I am sorry if you think that. All right, I will tell you. Yes, Sleek is in there – dead."

I continued to stare at him, willing him to finish it. He sighed and finally continued, "It seems that the rumour about Earth still existing took root stronger in other villages than it did here. All during the harsh weather this cancer has been growing among the new refugees. A man named Carljameson wanted to take our ship and go back to Earth. There were others who helped him try. What they didn't know, or couldn't understand, is that the great ships from the Homeworld are sentient beings. They aren't shells of dead metal like the machines of Earth. When our crew was threatened, the ship itself responded by killing the intruders in a most painful way."

Dra'hada refused to tell me the details. He could sense how upset I was, and told Tree to take me home. Later I learned Carljameson and his war band forced their way on board the ship with the help of the man from Cold Spring. They stole weapons from somewhere and injured one of our Benefactors during the struggle. With so many new people here, and everybody celebrating, no one took note of the conspirators' odd behaviour.

Ah, why didn't I go after Sleek when I saw her leave? I was selfish and careless. I was grieving for my daughter, and I was so tired of fighting with Sleek. I blame myself in part for her tragic death. Could I have done more to make her a part of our family?

᠀

Awakening Moon, sun-turning 14

There is a great council being held among our Benefactors aboard the ship. Communications with the Homeworld have been established. Because of the man from Cold Spring's involvement, not only the newcomers' fate, but also our own, will depend on the Council's decision.

Some of our Benefactors claim that we are a genetically flawed species. We should all be eliminated, and this world reseeded with another more stable species. Others like our dear Dra'hada counsel that that is too harsh a decision. We have lived here the required seven generations and more. We are not to blame for the assault. They counsel that those of us who have bred true to the Ancient Way should be allowed to continue on either as we are, or interbred with another compatible species to improve our bloodlines.

They are meeting on the ship now.

Around me, the land continues to sing its ancient song of renewal. The Mother will not intercede for us with our Benefactors. She is wise, but in the passionless way of ancient stone. In the darkness last night the people met in the village square to sing the Awakening songs, as we have always done. Tears in my eyes, I lifted up my voice with the rest. I was afraid – we all were. Just before dawn I climbed to the Mother Stone.

What will the day bring to my people, life or termination? I lean my head against the stone's solid bulk and breathe in the smells of new growth and the thawing mud in the lake. Blood. The old people say it is the carrier of ancestral memory and our future's promise. The stone is cold. I'm shivering as I open a wound on my forearm and make my offering. My blood is red, an alien colour on this world.

devorah major *became the third Poet Laureate of San Francisco in April 2002. She is a poet, novelist, spoken word artist, arts educator, and activist. Her most recent poetry books are* street smarts *(Curbstone Press),* where river meets ocean *(City Lights Publishing), and* with more than tongue *(Creative Arts Books 2003). She has two novels published,* An Open Weave *(Seal Press) and* Brown Glass Windows *(Curbstone Press) and is currently working on her third novel. Her poems, short stories, and essays are available in a number of magazines and anthologies.*

Trade Winds

devorah major

1.

"We are always home," Enrishi said. Her instructions were very precise on repeating the welcoming three times.

"We have much to learn from one another," Jonah smiled as he stretched out his hand, a white glove encasing the lined red–brown fingers she had seen in the transmission. His face, though, was close to the same colour, a red–brown not unlike the asteroid rock her grandfather had given her, but his skin shone in a way that was not evident in the video feeds, and now she could also see thatched fine lines at the edges of his eyes and mouth, similar to those on her sacred meditation stone.

Enrishi wore a thin cloth that fell down her soft stretched frame. She was just under two metres tall, with a soft green skin that reminded him of banana leaves. As she stepped out of the ship's final inspection chamber, she threw back the shimmering cloth that covered her entire face. She shook her head very slowly, bowed slightly, and then as her chin scooped forward, the cloth fell open smoothly and settled across the top and back of her head.

The envoy wore fine gauze pads over eyes that glowed in a soft amber behind the barrier. The voyagers, as they called themselves, lived in a much darker environment. Official protocols did not allow the light to be dimmed below 1,500 lumens, so this was a hastily created solution.

"We are always home," the envoy repeated.

"Welcome to our space station," the translator replied, knowing his voice was trembling with excitement. This was the third group of extra-terrestrials that he had worked with in his twenty-five year career as a universal translator, and the first face-to-face exchange.

"We are always home." She hoped he would make a suitable response. The air in the chamber was quite heavy and she needed to either sit or leave.

"Welcome to our home," he countered, still holding out his gloved hand and smiling all the while, but his eyes were wide as if making mental notes for later entry in his impressions journal. Close enough, she thought, and very slowly moved into the room. Space station engineers had reduced the artificial gravity, but the station's air still pressed her limbs down with much more weight than was comfortable. She was used to being able to almost fly around a space cabin; being anchored to the ground was a new challenge.

Jonah could not see the webbed fingers from under the cuff of her sleeve. Only the edge of the creamy green fingers showed. He wondered if he should keep his hand out or let it fall.

Gold fluttered across her lips. It was time for the second salute of welcoming: "We give and are given."

Jonah was flustered. He knew this was a ritual greeting, but he also knew that there were required answers. The conversation wouldn't progress until he gave the correct answer. And it seemed that although more than one answer could work, most answers were wrong. What was he to say now? He repeated, "We have much to learn from one another."

Now, tiny gold cilia stood out from her lips and seemed to dance around.

"Yes, we are always home. Yes, we have much to learn from each other."

He could not see her ears or head. The ears, he knew from early photographs and the first transmissions, were like the openings of a conch, and the pate not unlike the head of a peacock, smooth, iridescent blues and greens changing colour with the speaker's mood, which he had once witnessed as she laughed in delight when they had finally found common ground with words such as home, land, peace, universe.

Jonah could barely contain himself. He was actually talking with an extra-terrestrial. He was about to shake hands with an off-worlder. For the past ten years, he had lived on the space station with this as his one hope. He had forsaken his family, his beloved ocean beachfront home, solid land, for this chance. And now here she stood, Enrishi, one of the Voyagers. Oh, they had met through transmissions dozens of times over the last year. It had taken quite a bit of time before they could create a common vocabulary. His team had adjusted mathematical languages and tried human, dolphin, elephant, and the recently translated kiwi to build a communications matrix. It wasn't until he was able to produce the twelve sound chimes that he had learned in his first encounter with the extra-terrestrial culture of Auralites eighteen years earlier that progress had finally been made.

Enrishi did not speak again. She stretched out her hand as she had practiced repeatedly in the weeks before. Her entire crew had learned to do so, hand sideways instead of flat, prepared to barely touch the fingers of the other. She touched Jonah's gloved hand and was stung by the bleach in the fabric. She drew back and spoke slightly louder, enunciating each syllable with care. "We-are-al-ways-home." It seemed to Jonah like she was almost crying. She unfolded her palm until the star shape became a flat saucer and then folded up its ends until it looked more like a rosebud.

Jonah immediately realized the problem and tore off his gloves. He heard the station doctor scream through the tiny earphone he was wearing: "You idiot. We haven't completed bio-screens. You are facing isolation. Damn it, I knew we needed to get a regular business negotiator." Jonah knew he now faced at least three months of isolation He did not care. This was a chance of a lifetime.

"We welcome you to our station. I hope that you will soon be able to come to the surface and see our home planet. It is very beautiful."

"Life blooms," she answered.

Jonah was half a metre shorter than Enrishi, built square and sturdy, and moved like a thick-legged spider. He had learned yoga, how to play the flute, balafon, talking drums, and sarangi as a part of his translation training. Finally, after twelve years of schooling and eighteen years of three satellite station postings, moving from support translator, to primary translator, Jonah had become an interspecies emissary of introductions. The Auralites had spoken in music; the Soldaties only screamed. But here was a being who communicated, who lived in ways he could imagine, in ways he could understand. And this time they could talk, they could share more fully than any two species ever before, and they could do it in person.

"Is this not your home?" Her hand indicated the station.

"No. I mean, yes. Well yes, I live here, so it is my home in that way. But my home, my real home, is on the planet Earth."

"You are not always home?"

"There is home and there is home. Like your spaceship is your home, but your home planet, the place you came from, that is home too."

"I have never been on a planet. I am forty-two life cycles away from my ancestors who *knew* a planet. I have never been off the home that is our ship until today."

"You really have lived on a spaceship all your life?" Someone on the team had come up with this conclusion earlier but Jonah had resisted the idea. He thought that these beings must have a home planet. He thought they simply wanted to keep its origins concealed. The Voyagers never told much about themselves. They had a family structure not unlike Earth's more open families – multi-generational, elders usually given deference. It seemed to be non-hierarchical, led by a central council whose members got their positions by proving themselves in areas of translation, navigation, and mediation. Enrishi, he had learned, was the youngest of her species to be allowed to translate, and she was over a hundred Earth years, yet she looked as if she could have been a teen-aged Earth girl, except for the green skin and webbed hands.

"We are Voyagers."

"All of you? I mean, of course you all are on a journey, but none of you has ever seen your home planet?"

"We do not know a planet that is home. We are always home. It is our job to see and map and learn languages and stories and carry them from place to place."

"For who?"

"For who?"

"Yes, why do you map and learn languages and stories?"

"To carry them from place to place."

Jonah sighed. This interspecies translating was so strange. It was more than simply changing words to words. It was conveying the social constraints behind the words. He rephrased the question.

"Do you do this mapping for the people of the planet where you once lived?"

"I have never lived on a planet."

"I mean where your ancestors once lived?"

Enrishi was silent. She had worked through the ideas of ancestors, back through to the Hall of the Being and the Tunnel of Passage. "Ah," she said as she realized that he stretched his ideas to the first ripples of the ship. That was why the coven agreed to meet with Jonah, and only Jonah. He seemed to have a small idea of generations. "You must mean the ones who stayed. Land–bound souls? Oh no, we do not map for them. Why would they need charts? They don't leave the planet." She laughed softly as if repeating a family joke.

"Well then, for the captain of your ship? For science? Why do you do this?"

"Do you not travel?"

"Oh, I love to travel. I have visited every major country on Earth and colonies on Mars and the Moon. I have not been home, I mean to my home planet, in ten years. Travelling is in my blood."

"So you are like us."

"In a way, but I don't actually pilot, so I don't read or use star charts."

"On your station is there no one who needs maps and charts?"

"Yes, of course."

"Well, then, we do it for them."

"But you didn't know we existed until we made radio contact two years ago."

"We knew that life streams cross."

"So we are a life stream?"

"As are we? We meet streams as waves crest, we cross, perhaps we...." She had to be careful; here the wrong words could close the transactions. "Perhaps we find soil that is good to grow."

Now it was Jonah's turn to smile. "Soil does not grow. Plants do, but not soil."

"What does soil do?"

"It is the bed of seeds. It helps the plants to grow."

"Ah, perhaps we find seeds that we may grow."

"And what do we get in return?" He could tell by the immediate tightening of her cheeks that he had erred. Why had he ignored the most basic of business protocols? Hadn't the corporate bosses spent the last three months training him in trade potentialities? He knew when to be aggressive, when to lay back and let the best trade offer show itself, and most of all when to be patient. He had a list of minerals they wanted, and of course, water was the highest priority. Indeed, the space station was short of water due to the crash of a space freighter and failed delivery two years earlier. It would be a year before another freighter got that far from Earth – they were close to desperate for water and hoping to trade. No one bathed with water, only food plants were given the liquid, and most food was eaten dry. Strict rationing and recycling of all fluids, including body fluids, was the rule of the day. Jonah knew from earlier conversations that the Voyagers had a huge store of water and were willing to trade. The only question was what it would take to get some.

"As we give, so we are given." She was embarrassed. One was not to speak of trade so early in a meeting. It was completely wrong. "I've never been on a planet. None of us have. You and your stream have. We hope we can have new soil." She faltered, took a breath, and began again. "We hope to have new seed that we may grow. We will leave some seed that will help you to grow."

"I am afraid that we do not allow any kind of extra-terrestrial plants to reach our planet, spaceships, and stations until several generations have passed."

Enrishi nodded her head sadly. "Our words are trapped in rocks." She left the room and went back to the shuttle that took her to her home ship.

∽

2.

A month later, Jonah came out of his isolation chamber to once again meet with Enrishi.

"We are always home," she started.

"Welcome to our home," he answered.

This time, Enrishi said nothing. She waited for him to open a space.

They said nothing for close to an hour. Finally, Jonah spoke again. He was told to avoid trade issues. His job was to instill trust, build trade routes. He had warned her that he had questions. Jonah realized she was probably just waiting for him to begin. "Have you ever wanted to land on a planet?" he asked.

"If it is our season, we land. If not, those who come after will alight. Sometimes it is two, three, or four generations between planets or even asteroids. They say the first ones went twelve family cycles before landing again. When they did, half of those on the ship chose to stay. My grandfather once walked on an asteroid that was hundreds of kilometres around. His generation is the last ripple to have known land. But forgive me. I am letting my words burn like too many stars."

The envoy tipped her head and smiled again. She had trained all her life for this yet she was skipping so many of the rituals. It had been fifty-seven years since they had decided she was to be a star talker, learning all the languages known so far. She had worked with her council, continuing to build translation models and to simplify protocol, first for passing ships that had the ability to anchor and exchange hosts, or for those who for a time would share an asteroid. In her mother's time, she would have sung the stories of memory. That was supposed to be Enrishi's path. It was painted on the ship's Tunnel of Passage. But she had sat herself under grandfather Simetra's feet and listened to his stories.

"I never did get the chance to cross plant tongues on an asteroid; the one we came to was deserted. But there was evidence of another landing, and I walked land, child, walked land. We have passed seven ships on my life wave, child, and docked with two. So I have had the chance to meet other life streams. We have planted, traded song and time channels.

"Your grandmother does not believe there are planets in this crest. She does not believe there are others who can speak with us in a way that has worth to us. I have shown her the shadowed glass that holds the ship drops of those we have passed, but she thinks they were created in the craft module. She has forgotten the truth of our travels; her mind is locked in soil piles. She sees our stories as some painter's fantastic dreamscape. It is a sadness, the space sickness. A sadness when we lose our anchor in time." Her grandfather's eyes had filled with tears. He caught one drop on a fingertip and pulled Enrishi close and pressed it into her lips, where it instantly was absorbed.

"But, Enrishi, forty-three generations from the leaving, a thousand from the settling, I believe – no not believe, know – that the time is coming near. I know it the way you know a tongue after hearing it fold and unfold only three blood cycles, know its weight and direction." And he had been right – here she was. Enrishi's stomach quivered. She hoped the folds of her dress would conceal her excitement. It was not good to be too obvious in negotiations, or so she had been taught by teachers who had never had to negotiate.

As the translator and the envoy stood across from each other in stillness, Enrishi felt her grandfather's spirit speak into her air, telling her again as he had done so often in the last eddies of his cycles, "It was my grandfather, your great-great grandfather, who landed on the Ice Pinnacle and met the Muhabs." He was so much older than the oldest of Earth people, about 230 Earth years, far beyond Jonah's vision. It had taken so long to get Jonah to understand that her people did not count age in individual segments. Their birth year was always acknowledged by the generation. She was the forty-third of forty-six life cycles that had lived on the ship. Her number was forty-three on the day she was born and would be so on the day when she left, just as her grandfather's was forty-one, from birth through passing, and his grandfather's thirty-nine. For Enrishi, her grandfather had always been the mouth of the ancestor. His limbs had tired of the cabin pressure and now he floated above his bed with wind jet support and she sat solemnly next to him on a cushioned ledge.

At one time, he was the youngest of seven strands that had actually crossed life streams. But generation after generation died and he was the last who had seen any other beings.

She would ask him again and again, "Tell me, Grandpa. Tell me about the first ones."

"It is painted on the Tunnel of Passage, child."

She would begin to pout and he would start again. "The first crossings, the beings could not bear the weight of air and quickly left, crippled and shrieking."

"The wind walkers."

"Yes, child. And after that, light seekers. They came and gathered around each of the children. I remember how it was so bright that we all started to cry, and when they realized this, began to turn to a dark blue shadow. I wasn't much more than an air scruncher then, but I swear I remember. I know, child. I know there are others who can speak, who will speak stories we can carry forward."

Years later, after she told him of her acceptance into the Translator's Academy, he had counseled her frequently. "You must learn the ways of knowing we have carried from the planet-bounds and join them with our fate as a voyager. This ship has lived through forty-three generations, child. You will be the one who walks on land-tied dirt. I know it. I can feel it, child. It will be you who speaks first words with the planet-bound. Remember, they will be afraid. They are like children who have only explored one corner of their nursery, yet are convinced they know the world. They are like our ancestor seed who sent us outward but trembled and cried as we left. Remember, Voyagers and Stayers always make each other uneasy. Be slow with your words, and quiet. Do not tell them what they are not ready to know. But learn words we do not have, learn them well so they can be painted in our halls."

"And so it became," Enrishi thought.

Jonah reached out with his ungloved hand. Of course, they were a people of great rituals. He must be the same every time. He lightly touched her webhand. The earphone hissed, "No skin contact!" but Jonah ignored the transmission.

"You are only –" Enrishi reached back through the pictures, through the sounds. "– bark."

"Skin," he said, grasping her hand a bit more firmly and lightly curling his fingers around her web.

"The shadow is bark that does not burn."

"Brown. Brown skin. And no, it will not burn you. No chemicals."

"Shadow bark is brown skin." Enrishi reached out and barely touched the tips of his fingers.

"Yes."

"Life blooms," Enrishi smiled broadly, and bowed her head before opening her arms and letting a soft fabric fly from her sleeve, sending the gentlest of breezes around Jonah's face. He had begun to sweat from a mixture of fear and excitement. The breeze took his breath and sent him rocking back on his heels. He bent his knees slightly to shake off the cramp that had been growing.

"So you are an intergalactic nomad?" Jonah asked.

"We are Voyagers. Have you not wanted to join the waves and eddies that link the stars?"

"Well, yes, there are times I have wanted to just take off and see where I go."

"So you understand. You are like us, Jonah. If you would sit, we would sit. If you must stand, we will stand. If you would sleep, we will sleep near."

She smiled again and opened her over-robe to reveal a thinly rolled mat. He barely saw her long fingers undo the twine and could not believe how large it became as she spread it on the floor between them. The docking port was usually quite cold, but he felt heat rising up from a small mound at the center. His legs became heavier and heavier.

"I would sit." Jonah shivered despite himself.

Enrishi thought that it was all going quite well. She tried not to feel too smug. The coven would not take to her inflating herself or her role, but she had achieved so much. She knew trust was building. Perhaps in a little more time they could trade seed.

"It is good," she smiled. "As you would have it." As she spoke, she let the hood fall from her head. Golden strands stood on end and reached out. They seemed to be travelling towards him. He held his hands overhead and she retreated to the far wall. Only two of the strands landed. But they were like the touch of a smile, and suddenly he felt foolish.

"Excuse me," Jonah tried to apologize. Nothing more was said that day. It was two weeks before they met again.

∽

3.

Jonah was preparing for the third meeting. The science officer and galactic corporate trade commissioner barked orders at him from behind a protective glass barrier. His superiors were angry at him for touching an alien, angry and afraid. He had spent the past weeks in the space station docking lounge, isolated, communicating only through television screens. All the tests that had been run showed no untoward microbes, nothing to be afraid of, but everyone worried anyway. Jonah knew he would have to make a very good arrangement in order to get back into the main part of the station. He knew that the isolation was not only because of conservative attitudes about extraterrestrials, but also because of his ongoing habit of defying small orders.

"You are correct, we have not found any biological dangers, but there is an incubation time. I told you: no skin-to-whatever-they-are-covered-with contact."

"They call it skin. Their skin is green, mine is brown, yours is – well, it was creamy, but now it is kind of red." Jonah held back a chuckle.

"That kind of insolence is getting us nowhere," the commissioner cut in. "The next meeting you must ask questions about minerals and fresh water."

Jonah knew that a wrong step in the trade negotiations could cost him his career. He would be back in an Earth-side college, teaching and lecturing, not out here, not meeting beings like Enrishi.

Jonah had some power, though. The Voyagers would not allow anyone else besides him to meet with Enrishi. "I have gone over all of your notes and memorized your questions and the suggested terms of trade," Jonah replied flatly. He had memorized the basics and knew that the earphone would feed him the finer points during negotiation. After training for decades for this job as head translator, he hoped he would get it right. He knew twelve root languages and fifty-seven dialects of the planet Earth. He had decoded four radio transmissions of extra-terrestrials and gone on one space journey that involved a orbiting around a ship filled with a biped species that had no eyes but bodies covered in sensors. They spoke with notes and gestures and did not read or write text. It was quite amazing, the team had thought, that they were able to travel at all. How did they learn the mathematical configurations that kept their ship going? They had hologram maps that sang out when they placed their hands over them. They sang and their walls lit up with familiar star charts. They had a live video feed that led him around what seemed to be the bridge. They would sing the names of the stars and point him towards their home. It was a week before Jonah could sing the correct tones for "Good morning," "I would eat," and "Thank you." Another three before he understood their measurements for time and distance.

Once, while inadvertently insulting an offer of octave partnering, which he later discovered was a ritual of welcoming, he found out why the Earth sensors could find no sign of weaponry. Their only weapons were their voices. The eight members unfolded their limbs from each other and from him and begun to stroke as they sang, creating a high–pitched whine that left him shriveled and crying on the floor. One member who had been his guide was soon apologizing. They had not known how sensitive Earth ears were, that he had no internal modulators.

Jonah insisted they continue, but wore earplugs to muffle the sounds, but they still pierced through and he found himself again screaming out in pain. His harsh protestations had caused their skin to burn as well. He was shown the welts. In time, everyone recovered. The beings decided they would not leave the station and land on the planet itself. They simply used their own recording devices to absorb the music of earth. They called it eating. For four years, he spent hours with them as they laughed and cried while listening to Indian ragas, jazz symphonies, Chinese operas, Moroccan love songs, European concertos. They requested many singers and musicians be brought to them so they could converse. Only a half-dozen agreed.

There had been only one item traded that session. The Auralites had offered a tonal instrument that seemed to have the ability to numb the senses. It was an effective analgesic and showed promise in the medical field. In time it would yield great profit, or so it was thought. However, in the seventeen years since the trade, only one musician had yet been able to master it and she could only keep the tones playing for periods of thirty minutes to an hour. It was enough for minor surgeries, but no more. No one was angry, since the Auralities left with only a compendium of recorded Earth music. They seemed quite pleased with the value of the trade. Indeed, one of the envoys apologized repeatedly, feeling that the Auralites were cheating the Earth people. Jonah's superiors, on the other hand, were quite sure that they had gotten the better of the deal.

Jonah hoped this session would go as well. He thought it would. Enrishi was convinced that they shared the same root spirit, the same direction. Jonah was sure he could make a good trade deal.

∽

4.

"We can share life's breath," Enrishi said, offering a small flask to him.

They sat on the mat on the floor. He was cross-legged. She sat with her feet curled around her hips. This time she did not reveal her head. Jonah would have preferred a chair. Enrishi would have preferred her own ship. They both tried to look at ease.

"I cannot." Jonah was almost rude in his response, but quickly recovered. "Forgive me. I may not take before I have given." The water had to be tested. They had drank asteroid water before, indeed miners had drained the ice from a passing asteroid six years ago. It was fine. But still the science officer insisted that the water be analyzed in case the Voyagers had enhanced the liquid.

"We are home," she answered. "This is," she paused looking for the word, "asteroid water. Our supply was replenished on the asteroid we call Deep-with-ocean. I believe on your star charts it is Artemis. The water there is sweet without the fire of star or the dust of comet."

"Perhaps another time." Jonah felt his cheeks become hot. Enrishi loosened the scarf around her head, and a soft breeze flowed. Jonah caught his breath and tried to keep his voice even. "Perhaps you would have some of our water. We could trade. It's been purified by River's Return."

"River's Return? It comes from a water road, then?"

"Well, maybe once. I mean maybe, because maybe it is desalted ocean too. You never really know, but the company that markets it ensures it's purity. They are named River's Return."

"Where did you find this River's Return water?" She was genuinely confused.

"We didn't find it. We bought it from a passing supply freighter. They tour the satellite stations and give us food, water, entertainment, supplies."

"You make a value exchange for water?"

Now the man paused. "You mean do we buy it? Yes."

"If water is given, what is returned?"

"Credits."

"Credits?"

"Money."

"Ah." She nodded that she understood. "A contract of promise."

"No, not a contract, just credits, and then whoever gets the credits can use them to buy something else, say clothes or fuel or to pay a worker's salary."

"What is a salary?"

"We all work and we are given credits for our work, for our time. My time now is paid by the Xavier Mineral Retrieval Incorporated."

"Your time is not your own."

"Not during work hours."

"So right now you are a slave."

Jonah chuckled. "Some would say so."

For the first time, Enrishi was afraid. The coven had deduced that they were slavers, but Enrishi refused to believe. They were so advanced, she told them. Listen to their music, look at their communication modes. They had spaceships and stations. But the coven focused on the weapons. Only slavers need so many munitions, they warned.

Jonah stared. Her skin was changing from green to grey. He knew that this was not good, but he did not understand the problem.

"No, no, I was only joking. Some people joke that we slave for our wages, our credits, but it is not real slavery. I work for credits and then buy whatever I need."

"Are there those who do not have life's breath, I mean, water?"

"Some have more, some have less. Some water is better, some is not as good. But all humans must have water to live. It is as you say, life's breath."

"Then how do you make value exchange?"

"Everything has its cost, its price, its worth."

"We only know the giving."

"But when you give, you expect a return. That is all we do. We buy water, the company gets credits. They give the credits to a worker who takes them and buys whatever he or she needs."

"Water?"

"Sometimes."

"So you sell water so you can buy water? Why do you not simply have the giving?"

Jonah paused. How could he answer the question? His earphone buzzed and then the commissioner's impatient voice hissed out, "That is not the way of capital."

"That is not the way of capital," Jonah said, echoing the voice that spoke into his ear.

For the past two weeks, the Voyagers had debated moving closer to Earth and possibly landing. The history of the planet was one of discord and a distrust of differences. Although it looked beautiful, most of the old ones felt it was far too dangerous. It had been generations since the ship had neared a hospitable planet. Some Voyagers wanted to land, to see. Others felt nothing but destruction could come of it. It would be three Earth years of travel before they reached the Earth's atmosphere. Finally they had come up with a compromise. Enrishi hoped Jonah would welcome the trade.

She spread her arms and he heard the familiar rustle that her clothes always seemed to make. "Water is a small part of our home. But you are home in water, home of water."

She put her hands on his which were spread softly across his thighs. She turned them over and flattened her star palms close to his. They were dry but soft, almost like a piece of raw silk. She lifted her hands up and the rustling sound came again. Jonah realized it was her, like autumn leaves of the oak tree in the park where he played as a child. When she lifted her hands from his, a drop of his sweat hung from the glistening tip of one finger. He realized his palms were bone dry. In only a moment, she had absorbed all of the sweat from his palms. His mouth dropped open.

The earphone hissed. It was the doctor. "Damn you. She could be safe one day and dangerous another. *No* contact." Jonah rubbed his ear and the plug popped out.

"You are home of water," Enrishi said, seeming not to notice the small device that had fallen to the floor. She touched him again. He tried to pull his hand back but she had already wrapped her palm around his, enclosing it like a banana leaf wrapping sweet rice and mango. He felt moisture like a smooth lotion move into his palm. She lifted her hand and let it blow in the breeze.

"Water is life, and we can use some more life around here," Jonah answered. Suddenly he heard a voice yelling from the floor, but could not discern the words. He knew the essence of the comment thought. The need for water was the one thing he wasn't supposed to mention. He could express desire, but not need. How could they bargain now? How could they not lose too much? Jonah hoped he could repair his mistake.

"We would share life with you." Enrishi poured a thimble full of water into a translucent cup. She quietly passed it to Jonah.

"Don't drink, you fool!" The voice came out of a wall speaker.

Enrishi jumped. Jonah drank.

"It is so sweet. Our water is recycled many times and tastes stale. I mean on the station, at home it is another thing."

Jonah smiled weakly. Enrishi seemed not to care about the monitoring. She had regained her composure and was smiling.

"Why are you not home on the station?"

"I am at home. But not the same home."

"Home is always the same. Only the –" Enrishi thought of the picture she should make. "– only the river changes, but the water is still always water."

"Yes, but sometimes salty and sometimes sweet."

"Sometimes cloudy and sometimes clear, but always water. That is life's crossing."

"Yes," Jonah answered.

"Yes." Golden tendrils danced on Enrishi's lips. She covered her mouth with her hands. "You have given stories and we have received. We have given stories and you have taken."

"You have let us see star charts and our scientists are very pleased. We would like to know how we can repay you."

"We would have you in our home."

"Excuse me?"

"We would have you in our home."

"You want me to visit."

"We would share a stream for a time. We give and are given."

"One cannot trade life stream for water."

"But do you not sell each other?"

"No," Jonah said calmly as if speaking to a child. "We do not sell each other. Long ago we did. On my birth continent we had slaves into the twenty-first century, but not now. We are all free now."

Jonah realized that he was out of his depth. He found the earplug and put it back in his ear. He hoped he had been discreet.

"You are an idiot!" the commissioner yelled. Then a spew of angry epithets followed. "Get a price that we can negotiate. This is no time for a history lesson," the commissioner screeched, "Get a price, don't accept it, just get it."

"Your ear whines. I see it run colours. Perhaps you would cross tongues with those who cut roadways."

Enrishi got up to leave. Jonah jumped up after her. "Did I offend you?" he asked.

"No, Jonah," Enrishi spoke very softly. "But the one who lives in your ear crackles and hisses and does not share home."

He scrambled for the right words. "I am sorry, but I do not know how to negotiate trade, so they are helping me. I am a translator, not a trader."

"We are all traders."

"Not on Earth."

"All is trade, Jonah." Enrishi moved towards the door.

"We have," Enrishi unrolled a note hidden in the cuff of her sleeve and read, "one metric tonne of water. The coven has written out the details of trade."

"Damn." The commissioner was laughing.

"That's what I want to hear." The science officer chortled.

Jonah's eyes grew big as he began to read the paper. Enrishi said nothing as he read, just stood at the door. Then she resumed: "These are the seeds we would trade. We want no more or less from this sharing."

Enrishi turned and left the chamber.

∾

5.

Jonah sat grim-faced. He had been on the Voyager's ship for hours, maybe days. The last thing he remembered were the harsh words of the commissioner before he went to sleep. They were repeated for hours: "duty … responsibility … desperate measures … hero … no choice … only choice." He had stopped listening after a while, heard the phrases only as discordant chords that irritated his spirit. Jonah left the meeting with the word "no" emblazoned in his stance, on his lips. He had, in fact, quit the project. When he went to sleep, it was in his own cabin. When he awoke, he was in a strange room with weights wrapped around his ankles and wrists that let him lie softly on the bed. There was also a shelf protruding from the wall and a computer console. The light was muted, as if it were dusk. There was a window that showed the stars, a window that showed his space station as a small green blinking dot in the corner of the oval frame.

Jonah was surrounded by crates that he at first thought were trade goods. He was surprised because there had been no discussion with him. He thought the Voyagers had indicated that he would be the only translator. Who on the team had arranged this transfer? The air was dry and cool. He got up to move and found himself much lighter than he had been on the station. He bounced around the room, hovering a few inches from the floor on each large stride. He began to open the boxes.

The first one was full of foodstuffs. What a surprise! What would the Voyagers want with dried apricots and marinated artificial meats? How could they digest grains, and what in the world would they do with fine cognac? Jonah began to tremble. He opened a third crate. He found his books and music disks, instruments and hologram portrait book, clothes and toiletries, and a communications radio.

There were six more boxes. He did not bother to look. What did it matter? It was obvious the trade had been made. He was sold for water. He was alone on an alien ship that never docked.

Jonah heard a soft chime and then saw a door open. Enrishi entered the room.

"Jonah, you have awakened. It is good. We are, excuse me, welcome home." She saw that he was stiff and did not offer the handshake.

"This is not my home."

"We are always home." She bowed her head and let the cloth fall off her. He saw that she was frowning, that soft red tendrils glistened close to her scalp.

"It seems I am never to be home," Jonah replied, his lips dry and cracked.

Enrishi carried a jug with five litres of water. She placed it at his feet. "We are always home."

"This is kidnapping, you know," Jonah sullenly responded.

"If you would drink, we would drink. If you would fast, we would fast."

Jonah needed the water, but did not move.

Enrishi opened the squat jug and daubed the corner of her sleeve into the water. He saw it turn from a pale yellow to a deeper saffron. She then moved to him and put the cloth on his mouth.

"You are home to water," she smiled. Then she put a small ladle into the jug and put the rim at Jonah's mouth. He opened his lips and let it in. He had dreamed this water the night before, dreamed it as melting snow that he had rolled in, as a cresting river that he had rode, as a rainstorm that he had walked in open–mouthed, clothes drenched. Not one drop was wasted. When he emptied the ladle she refilled it and again fed him. Jonah could not resist. It was so sweet, slightly chilled without a trace of chemical aftertaste.

"Enrishi, I am a translator. I have trained for years. I am not a Voyager, I am a scholar. I have lived on the station for years. I don't stay on a ship. In fact, I was to return home on the next freighter. I had given up my position. You understand, I was going home. I don't want to be here, but there are others who would love to go with you. We have a captain who can navigate. We have a ship's doctor, we have a –"

"We carry stories. That is our purpose. We need one who unfolds tongues. We need you."

"How could you make me an object of trade?"

"There is always a giving. We have given a metric tonne of water to the station. We have given a communications device that will work so that you may talk to your friends for several Earth years. We have given star charts. We have asked only for you. Only for another with a tongue that can carry stories. It is a good trade. We have made a doorway for you. You have said that your blood is made of travel. Now, you do not have to work for credits. You are truly free. What you need we will give."

"I was already free."

Enrishi ignored him. "We will fill the Hall of Being with your stories. Our artists will braid your tales into the ship. You would become the forever of our journey. In time you will be engraved on the Tunnel of Passage."

"Are there others on your ship who are not Voyagers?"

"We are all Voyagers."

"Others who are not from the planet of your homebound?"

"We have traded for forty-one generations. We have known others. We have welcomed others."

"Now? Now are there others?"

Enrishi again ignored him. "Our ship has been tethered for months. Our people grow restless for the swells of the sky winds. They want to move on. It has been decided. Do not worry, we will cross other life streams. If you choose you will join them and leave us. Perhaps one will be an Earth ship again. As the wave rises, we rise too."

"So I am the sacrifice for the station." Jonah spit out the words.

"What do you sacrifice?"

"My home, myself."

Enrishi shook her head. A few of the red tendrils drifted and landed on Jonah's cheeks, prickling him slightly. "But we do not take your home, we give one. Come, let me show you around. We will meet with my grandfather. Did I tell you he walked on an asteroid once, as a child? And wait until you see the Hall of Being. I believe you will like it. You and I are already there."

Enrishi reached out and took his hand. He looked out the window and saw that the beacon light from the station was becoming smaller and smaller. "Come, Jonah, let me show you home."

"Home?" Jonah began to cry.

"Yes, yes. It is so. We are always home."

Carole McDonnell *is an essayist, fiction writer, and writer of devotionals. Her book and film reviews appear online at* thefilmforum.com, compulsivereader.com, *and* curledup.com. *Her devotionals appear in Christian online and print magazines and also on* faithwriters.com. *Her short stories and essays have been anthologized and published in publications including the essays "Oreo Blues" in* Lifenotes: Personal Writings by Contemporary Black Women *and "That Smile" in* Then an Angel Came Along. *She is putting the finishing touches on an SF novel called* The Daughters of Men *and on Father Gorgeous, a Christian horror-romance. She is also currently finishing a Bible study called* Scapegoats and Sacred Cows in Bible Study. *She lives in upstate New York with her husband Luke (an illustrator) and their two sons.*

࿋

Lingua Franca
Carole McDonnell

Mist removed two large coins from the blue money box on the counter and walked outside her shop. Closing the door, she reached for the ideograph placard which read, "Closed, but unlocked. Take what you need and leave your payment in the coin box." The signboard in place, she stuffed the "D" volume of her interplanetary *Webster's Dictionary* into her quilted backpack, strapped it on her back, and walked into the dusty bustle of the open-air market.

The market still basked in the heat although First Dusk had already come and Second Dusk had begun rolling across the sky. Using her marriage scarf to shield her face from the dusty streets, Mist headed towards the fruit stands where the Federation-approved traders sold exotic foods gathered from across the galaxy.

In the distance, near an ormat tree, four Federation off-worlders with ear-caps on their heads talked among themselves. One man carried something long and metallic on his shoulders. Another had a metallic box with a glass tube on one side. The only woman among them was looking through a metallic tube at the reddening sky. For several seconds, Mist studied the movement of their lips, but could decipher nothing.

The purple warning lights of the market flashed: three slow blinks, then two long ones. Mist felt a cold chill run down her back. A dread unsettled her mind and she glanced nervously at the Town Square stage. Two women with children strapped in chest-sacks raced past her.

I'm getting old, Mist thought as they rushed past. Fifty. Even with children on their chests, they fly past me. But age comes to all of us. The Creator was hard on me. But, at last, I had my child. Only one. And at forty, when most women are past their prime. That child, though, is a true blessing. Worth a million others. Flowers-in-the-Sun has extended my youth. Before her birth, I was a "ghost" – a childless woman.

Two more women raced past Mist. She caught a bit of their signed conversation. Their hands spoke of the cutting, about mouth-speech. To her left, two young mothers with small children strapped to their chests were also signing about the implanted children and the encroachment of the mouth-speaking Federation.

"These Earthers are not like the other off-worlders," one woman signed. "They do not accept us as they find us. Look at them. Not content with fixing our 'problem', now they say they're 'fixing' our air. As if anything was ever wrong with our air. Why do the elders allow it?"

The other pointed in the direction of the Town Square stage and signed, "Today and tomorrow a News Carrier will bring us troubling stories about these meddlers."

Mist looked up at the wallaou tree where the nearest lights were strung. The pattern of the warning lights had changed. Now three slow flashes followed one long beam. The News Carrier was already here and would begin soon.

I'm not too old to keep up with news, Mist thought. But Flowers-in-the-Sun has looked sad lately. News will have to wait. Something from the fruit stand will cheer her up.

When she stopped at the fruit stand of her favourite vendor, something orange caught her eye. The name of the fruit was written in the three regional ideographic dialects in addition to the lingua franca of the Federation: the English language. The "English" letters o-r-a-n-g-e took up more space than all the ideographs combined.

"Brother," she addressed the old vendor, "the Earthers actually named a fruit after its colour?"

The grey-haired old man whose name was Smoothed Stone smiled back.

"Try it, Sister," he signed. "It's good. Your Sweet One has a sweet tooth. She might like it."

Mist smiled. "Yes, Flowers-in-the-Sun does like these foreign sweets."

"Only three coins each. Not a lot to pay for fruit from the far side of the universe."

"She's probably home from school by now, being spoiled by Ion's unmarried sisters, or by his brothers' wives," Mist answered with fake petulance. "From the day of her birth, Flowers-in-the-Sun has been the family favourite. The girl is too spoiled. Why should I spoil her even more by bringing her expensive foreign fruits?"

Smoothed Stone smiled. "Perhaps because she expects it. And because she still plays and jokes with her elders."

Mist raised her right eyebrow and clasped her hands in front of her mouth. The old man placed his clasped hands to his mouth too, but signed nothing. The old man obviously knew about recent events in her mother-in-law's house where all the children, except Flowers-in-the-Sun, had been given the ear and throat implants. Lately, her implanted nieces and nephews had stopped signing. Now all they did was mouth-talk among themselves, indulging in "sounds" which the rest could neither hear nor understand.

Mist made a quick mental assessment of all the servants in her mother-in-law's household and tried to figure out which was the old man's liaison. She would have liked to know. An ally – even a servant – was always helpful. She would also have liked to gossip with him about the situation at home. But Ion's family was extensive and prominent. To sign the family's dirty laundry in public would not help her already troubled reputation. Nevertheless, Mist knew she had an ally and that the old man understood her.

She picked up two oranges and tried to fit them both in her backpack, but the dictionary filled the bag and only a small space remained. Mist was not about to be seen walking through the town square carrying something in her hand, like those women one couldn't converse with in the streets because they had no servants to carry their ling-carts on shopping days. "I'll take this fruit with a colour as a name," she said. "Tomorrow I'll get another."

"The fruit is segmented," he signed, as if reading her mind. "It will serve many." Then he smiled and stretched out his hand for the payment.

Mist felt around in her dress pocket. Then she winked and smiling, gave Smoothed Stone two small coins instead of the three he had asked for.

Smoothed Stone took the coins and smiled conspiratorially. "You always were a girl with an eye for a bargain, Sister."

Mist shrugged. "I might be married to someone outside the trader caste, but I haven't lost my skills."

When she returned home to Ion's family's compound, she was greeted by Ion's mother and Flowers-in-the-Sun.

"Daughter Mine," Ion's mother, Shadow-of-Light-Turning said, "Flowers-in-the-Sun has been telling me about her day."

"What about your other grandchildren?" Mist asked. "Don't they have news also?"

"They keep to themselves," Shadow-of-Light-Turning responded. "They're practicing mouth-to-ear."

"I don't see why they have to practice mouth-to-ear," Mist answered. "We can't hear them anyway. Are they hiding things from each other now?"

Shadow-of-Light-Turning made the gesture which meant Mist was being argumentative and unreasonable as usual. "My dying wish is that my granddaughter will not be poor and isolated as her mother is," she signed, casting a disgusted glance at Mist's blue marriage scarf. "Can't you wear the scarf of our caste?" Shadow-of-Light-Turning asked. Although Mist had used the green embroidery thread of the science cast throughout the scarf, her husband's mother was still not appeased. "Aren't you ashamed of yourself for being so strong-willed? And look at your daughter! The girl has no bracelets on her arms, no caste-cap, no jewellry around her calves, no gems around her neck and ankles. When I see her coming home from school capless, like an outcaste child, I cannot bear the shame."

This woman has nothing else on her mind, Mist thought and signed, "She has not decided yet what caste-cap to wear."

Her husband's mother didn't say the obvious, that a child should not have to choose her caste.

Ninety-eight people lived in the family compound, including servants – none of whom belonged to Ion. As a mere superintendent of standards and weights in the agricultural department, and that only because of his mother's influence, Ion was not well paid. His family had tolerated his love-match marriage to a woman not of his work caste, but his co-workers had not. Neither the traders nor the scientists he worked with considered Ion truly qualified for the inter-caste job – in this case, a position which was both scientific and trade-related. And neither did the sub-caste of regulators consider him part of their network. He found peace and acceptance, however, among his family.

Mist, on the other hand, was accepted by the other traders. (Traders, being expedient, valued networks and friendships.) But she was grudgingly tolerated by her mother–in–law's household who continually reminded her that Ion had given up an advantageous marriage to a woman of the science caste to marry her.

It didn't help matters that because of the initial upheaval in both families, Ion and Mist flatly refused to accept monies or gifts from their relatives. Such were the dangers of love–matches.

Shadow–of–Light–Turning finished listing Mist's many flaws and walked away without the requisite gesture of respect. Mist and Flowers–in–the–Sun exchanged knowing glances and Mist thought to herself, My little sunshine. My only female ally among my enemies. A minute later, the green entry lights of the family compound gates flashed: three long beams, two quick ones, then six quick ones. Ion's pattern: he was home. Waiting to surprise him when he entered their area of the house, Mist stood by the door of their family apartment holding the orange in her outstretched hands.

But Ion did not immediately come up to their apartment. When he finally arrived upstairs, he told Mist his mother had intercepted him.

"She believes Flowers–in–the Sun should get the implants," he signed. After a pause, he added, "And I agree with her."

Mist could not answer him: the orange was in her hand. But she glared into his dark eyes until he turned his face away.

Mist put the orange in the food closet and walked over to her husband, slowly and deliberately. She forced him to look at her by raising her hands directly in front of his face. They were so close they almost touched his nose. Then she made the signs which meant, "No. Once again, my opinion does not matter."

"Your mother has taught you many things," Ion signed. "Chief of all is how to be an alarmist. The operation will not harm our daughter. Already she is alone, even among her cousins."

"Because I worry about our daughter, I'm an alarmist?" Mist exclaimed. "Isn't our heritage important to you?"

Ion made a gesture with his right hand that took in the entire house. "Compare," he signed, "Mother's house and Mother–in–Law's house. Do not the compartments of our siblings overflow with riches? Have not both families gotten even richer since their implants? The universe is getting smaller. English is the common language of the Federation universe. And it's 'mouth–spoken,' not signed. Of what use are traders who do not speak the lingua franca? Shouldn't the thing be done?"

"You sound like your mother."

"It is the only time I have ever sounded like her."

Mist nodded. Ion had always stood by her in family quarrels. "But why agree with her now?" she asked.

"My agreement is not with her," he signed, raising his eyebrow.

It dawned on Mist what Ion was saying. "Flowers–in–the–Sun requested the implants?"

Ion held his wife's hands tightly and gently pulled them away from his face, towards the ground. He then released them, kissed her, and signed, "Children come of age."

Mist pulled her hands from his. "But when she was here with your mother," she told him, "she smiled at me as if she agreed with me. How could she change her mind so quickly?"

"Obviously, she's been thinking about it for a while. You know how she is. She's like us and yet not like us. She thinks as we do, but she likes fitting in." He grinned. "Should not traders learn to 'accept change'?"

For a moment, Mist was confused. Ion had used the Aqueduct sign which meant "coin" instead of the one which meant "alteration." Then she remembered the various meanings of the English word 'change.' It was an effective bilingual pun which only a student of English would understand. And the joke only proved her point. The Aqueduct people, to whom Ion and Mist belonged, were linguists par excellence.

"You see," she signed. "Look at your joke. 'Change' and 'change.' Does this not show that we are good at adapting, that we are an intelligent people, that it's not necessary to implant and mouth–speak? Has not our culture taught us how to survive in a world of sound–speakers?"

Ion kissed her fingertips. Then he signed, "What can be done? I have given up my birth–livelihood. We have lived by integrity and we have been happy. But we have not been successful in our financial lives. Let our child live her life. Mist, my love, think: Don't you want Flowers–in–the–Sun to find her place in the world?"

"Our world, yes. Not theirs. Flowers–in–the–Sun was born here, not on Earth."

"She's a smart child. She says she wants to show the Federation our knowledge. She says she will use their ways to show them our ways. Can you not see her wisdom in this?"

"But why should she cut her throat?"

With one dismissive gesture, Ion indicated that his wife was being unduly worried. He signed that he had seen enough implanted people. The cutting was a small thing, nothing for her to get so worked up about. He repeated again that he and Mist had been dreamers, that they had sacrificed their lives to love. But the child wanted what the child wanted and shouldn't children receive what they ask for?

"Dreamers should not sacrifice their children," he signed. "If we do the cutting now, when she becomes a young woman she will have great skill in mouth-speaking. She will truly be multilingual. Be reasonable, my love. Mother Mine says that if you insist on doing things your way, Flowers-in-the-Sun won't even fit in with her own family, much less with the rest of our world. Already, the other children leave her out of their mouth-to-ear practice. And yes, she wears no gems, no jewels. We should not harm her any more than we already have."

Mist threw her arms in the air. "So it's all about fitting in, is it? These children, mouthing and mouthing and no one can hear them."

"It's a new language. Like a new toy. Let them experiment."

"It makes my heart boil to hear you talk like the others in this house. Don't you see how strange it is for us, the people on our planet, to laugh-talk-sing through the mouth? In our world, mouths were made for eating only."

"And for kissing too, I hope," Ion signed, giving her a coy look. "Or are we going to bed angry?"

"Be serious. For millennia, we have known that other humans in the universe understood 'sounds.' But we accepted it. It was what made us unique to the creator. We never thought there was anything wrong with us until Earthers came along. Why should we change to please these upstarts? Why must, from this day to that forever day, our children, our grandchildren be cutthroats? And simply for money and to fit in?" She headed towards the door. "I will speak to the council about this."

"Mother Mine will not like it if you speak to the elders. She speaks for our family, not you. Know your place, Wife Mine."

Mist stopped in her tracks. Ion was right. It would not look good at all for her to go over her mother-in-law's head and talk to the elders. It would only make her seem even stranger than she already seemed, a woman without gem anklets, in a mixed-caste marriage without servants to carry her ling-carts, who allowed her daughter to go capless.

"Don't you trust your mothering skills?" Ion asked. "Do you not believe our daughter loves us? Mouth-to-ear in front of her parents is not something Flowers-in-the-Sun would do."

"Who knows what people will do?" Mist signed back. "Look at you: disobeying our Creator's laws against flesh cutting."

Ion smiled. "You're using the more literal interpretation."

"Since when did you consider that interpretation 'literal'? 'No cutting into flesh!' Period. The ideograph is clear enough. And don't give me any talk about it meaning *no meat* and *no murder*. It says what it says."

"The Creator understands expedience," Ion responded.

Mist glared at him. Then she walked downstairs to the family garden.

In the farthest corner near the wall, the implanted nieces and nephews huddled together speaking mouth-to-ear. Sitting near her aunts, Flowers-in-the-Sun looked on.

When her mother entered the garden, she said, "Mother Mine, my cousins cover their mouths to hide their thoughts from us."

"They're practicing to control their new voices," Mist answered. "So they don't offend the Earthers when they speak."

"I know what is on your mind," Flowers-in-the-Sun said. "You have been talking to Father Mine."

Mist nodded.

"The Earthers don't speak to us unless they are contracting business," Flowers-in-the-Sun explained. "They think our life-knowledge is not equal to theirs."

"They're right. We don't know how to kill cultures or cut throats. May we never learn."

"I want to show them how smart we are," Flowers-in-the-Sun signed. "I will be a great scientist when I grow up and I will show them how high our knowledge really is. I will –" She stopped short. Across the garden, some of her cousins were laughing at her. She pulled her mother inside the house. "They think it's funny that everyone knows what I'm saying."

"They won't think it's so funny when they get infections from getting their throats cut," Mist answered. "I hear people never really heal from that." Mist had not really heard that, but she felt no qualms in saying that she had. "So," she continued, "you want to work in the sciences like your grandmother's family?"

Although children followed in the caste-careers of their mothers, Mist was untroubled by her daughter's choice of her father's caste. "You have the mind for it," she said. "And you were not raised in a trading household, but in the house of a science-caste grandmother." She smiled. "I'll have to make you a green cap. Perhaps I'll wear green too, to help you fit in."

Flowers-in-the-Sun smiled. "Thank you, Mother Mine."

"Will you study the scientific assessment of standards as your father does? Or will you choose another science?"

Flowers-in-the-Sun nodded. "Father has a perfect inter-caste job. It's the right job for me. I will show the Earth traders that we know how to measure the purity of foods, that we are more than receivers of their tainted money."

Mist stroked her daughter's hair, her heart overflowing with pride at having such a wise daughter. And as Second Night rolled into First Morning, she found green fabric from which she made a cap for her beloved daughter and a new marriage scarf for herself.

Her husband's mother smiled approvingly when she saw Mist the next morning. "Will your trader friends accept a trader who wears green?" she asked.

"Those who know me will," Mist answered, smiling. "The ones who don't know me will think I'm new to the trading game. It will be interesting to see how this 'change' affects a trader's purse."

On the way to her shop, Mist saw the four off-worlders again. Again they had their instruments pointed at her beloved sky. As she studied them, she saw a light flashing from the corner of her eye. It came from Smoothed Stone's fruit stand. He was signaling her.

"Sister," he said, when she arrived in front of his stand. "How goes your study of the Federation Lingua?"

"Their English lingua has many words, brother," she signed back, and wondered why he had called out to her. "But it isn't particularly complex. Lip-reading, however, is hard. Not as hard to decipher as the guttural clucks of the Towans, for instance. But challenging nevertheless. Many unruly vowel sounds. Inconsistent."

"Very hard to lip-read," the old man agreed, and yet even as he agreed with her, it seemed as if he had something more urgent to say. "The people of our world have always loved challenges," he said at last.

"True," Mist answered. "Their 'alphabet' is something of a challenge." And then as proof of her studies, she slowly finger-spelled in English, "Me not good Lingua talker yet. Go their English School maybe?"

"We Aqueduct people are smart. Whoever heard of going to school to learn languages? Hey, you want them to cut your throat?"

"Not me," she said and added, "Many people are getting the implants. In many homes. All because the Earthers think it's best to speak by mouth."

Smoothed Stone sighed. "Some of them tattoo the implants, embroider them with floral patterns, as if to cover their guilt. Worse, the more brazen among us leave the cut marks untattooed, uncovered, for all to see; braggarts, as if the cutting were an improvement to the Creator's work. In our youth, if such a thing were told, who would believe it?"

"Did not our Creator forbid flesh-cutting?" Mist signed rhetorically.

"Those who get the implants grow richer and stranger," the old man continued. "Sad it is, but true. I have seen it said that the Earthers are helping our economy with these implants."

Mist's only answer was a facial gesture which meant, "I have so much to say, but not here."

He answered. "And I too. But whether from fear, fatigue, helplessness, or grief, one must be quiet."

Mist nodded. The flickering purple lights along the wallaou tree indicated that the News Carrier had arrived: six quick flashes and one long one. Just in time she looked up to see her brothers' wives walking ahead of her.

How richly dressed they were! How round and well-fed their bodies! Living in her husband's family house, she rarely saw her mother's family. But she had heard that her mother's family, too, had chosen implantation and had prospered greatly in doing so. Mist studied her scrawny brown jewellry-less arms jutting out from under her full yellow sleeves. Her dress was made from Yona plant fiber, but her sisters-in-law wore Federation "silk" embroidered with Federation "gold." Unsure if they had seen but purposely ignored her, she watched as they took seats near the podium. In the days before her marriage, she too would have sat in those places of honour. But now she hid in the back row among the women of the servant caste, dutifully dragging their mistress' ling-carts from one vendor to another. She hoped no one from her mother's house would see her.

The News Carrier who wore the wide tribal pants of the people of the land beyond the Two Hills took the high seat in the center square.

"My mothers, my fathers, my sisters, my brothers, my daughters, my sons," the woman began. Her gestures indicated a Two Hills accent. "Life has changed in our village since the Earthers came with their cutting. I have heard your elders are contemplating mandating this matter. Please warn them not to. Already I have seen" – and here the woman from beyond the Two Hills stared impolitely at Mist's sisters-in-law – "that already some of your own people are cutting themselves and their children."

Mist watched to see what her brothers' wives would do. She remembered well how they had mocked her when she chose to marry out of the trader clan. Their cruel hands had sawed at her like daggers. Her brothers' wives were not the types to be challenged. But neither would they disagree with a stranger in the town centre where everyone could read their business.

The News Carrier approached them and signed "Traitor!" in an angry sweeping gesture.

In response, they stood up. They walked away from the crowd, their gold-threaded blue silk marriage scarves trailing behind them. Mist hid her face when they passed by, but she could easily imagine their faces, arrogant and expressionless as if the insult were nothing more than vapour in the air.

The woman from beyond the Two Hills continued. "Already the children of our village no longer dance to the light at our festivals. They insist on 'Sound-dances,' preferring 'music' to light. They hide their natures, clans, and status. They do not wear their clan colours. Some of our marriageable young girls refuse to wear the courtship tassels. They refuse to give the world knowledge of themselves. It's a perverse game they play. Yesterday, at the beginning of the Mother–Infant Festival, some children insisted on mouth–singing, even though their parents could not understand a word they said. And when they talk, they hide their conversations, imitating the mouth–speakers' mouth–to–ears talk, what the Earthers call" – this she finger–spelled in English – "'whispers!'"

Mist thought of her nieces and nephews huddled together in their groups, doing mouth–to–ears and hiding their conversations. She remembered the family's excuses: *Children must explore and discover. They're practicing using those implant things right. Children play endlessly with their toys until the novelty wears off. They then outgrow them.* Mist had always thought her husband's brothers' wives were foolish women with no foresight. These latest events only proved their short–sightedness.

"And many other new things have happened," the News Carrier continued. "Now the young married youth move from the family house. They live by themselves. 'Husband and wife family house,' they call it. Who has seen such a thing? But worse things happen: They disappear and are not seen, then they suddenly re–appear for an afternoon. To 'visit,' they call it. They come when they want something. And many want to create speaking temples in order to worship the Creator. The world has crashed around us." The News Carrier went on to list all the alarming troubles caused by cutting. She ended with the warning, "One law falls and all others fall with it."

Mist's eyes met those of another woman in the crowd. They exchanged looks and then glanced backwards at the off–worlders in the distance with their strange metallic equipment. Mist and the woman shook their heads.

"Surely the News Carrier is stretching stories," the woman signed. Mist hoped the woman was right. Surely, these were only tales.

After the town meeting, she returned to her book shop. Many Earthers were coming in and out, marvelling at the "primitive" lifestyle of the "locals," buying dictionaries and planetary histories. In the old days, she did not mind them. But now she grew impatient with them. They made her sad. Even stranger, they made her tired. The more Earthers she saw in the marketplace holding their ears like princes holding their noses, the more fatigued she felt. If the Earthers don't like it here, she thought, why do they walk among us? Mist spent the rest of the day suspiciously reading their lips and feeling unusually tired, and later when she left her shop, she locked the door securely and carried the key home with her.

Returning home, she saw more Earthers, two men and a woman, standing in the train station. She watched them for a while, standing there with those two ear-caps sticking out on the sides of their heads. She had thought them funny when she first saw them. But now she considered them offensive, small intrusive weapons against her culture.

Several Aqueduct families were to the left and right of her. From their shells and floral holiday dress, she knew they were awaiting the Festival train which would take them to Living–Water–White Light, the town where the largest Mother–Infant parade occurred.

One young woman in the tribal cloak of the people of the Solitary Hills wore a baby carrier across her chest. The baby's face was buried in its mother's holiday cloak, a cloak trimmed and edged with "gold," the signifier of a new mother.

Her first time in the festival, Mist thought. I remember when I was newly–married, childless and young, and so wanting to join all the mothers in the parade. I waited so long. And then Flowers–in–the–Sun came. What a joy that was. To be a mother at last.

The woman's face was turned in the other direction and Mist could not gesture a greeting. The baby twisted and shook in its carrier, obviously uncomfortable and agitated. Mist watched the woman from Solitary Hills take the child from its little pouch in order to comfort it. As the woman lifted the baby, Mist saw the tell-tale patterned tattoos on the baby's neck. No wonder she can wear "gold," Mist thought. Her family is one of the mutilated. Then, startled, Mist realized that the people surrounding her all had the tattoos. Tears stung her eyes. She glanced at the Earthers speaking among themselves at the far end of the track.

How smug they are! she thought. And she wanted to tell them so. What will I say to them? Will they even listen to me if I tell them they are destroying my culture?

Mist had seen ideographs which told the stories and histories of the Earthers. A war–like lot, to be sure, bent on their own glory, "paying lip-service" – she loved that English phrase – to Cultural Respect, but not really caring about it. She walked towards the Earthers.

"Coming to see our festival?" she signed when she reached the woman Earther.

The woman Earther turned to look questioningly at a male Earther to her right.

Very rude, Mist said to herself. Even if she doesn't know our language, she should know that turning the face away is not done. That's basic body language.

The male Earther, who had black hair and dark brown skin like Mist's people, reached into a sack and picked up a book of ideographs. He signed, "Do again. Sign again."

He had not preceded his conversation with the "Please" sign, which made his conversation seem abrupt and pushy. But Mist reminded herself that linguistic etiquette was complicated.

"Watch me," she signed. "Sign 'Please.' Or bow twice whenever you tell anyone to do something. So you don't offend people." She signed slowly, word by word, until he bowed twice and she knew he understood her.

"What's your name?" the dark-skinned Earther asked. "Mine is Ray." He finger-spelled the English name, then signed "Sunlight Beam."

"Sunlight Beam?" Mist answered. "You must have been a blessing to your mother."

Ray grinned surreptitiously at the Earth woman, then bowed twice to Mist. "Tell me the question you asked our woman friend."

"I asked if she was going to our Mother-Infant festival," Mist answered. "It happens every year at this time. It is our greatest festival and it lasts the whole month. If you go there, you will understand our culture and see our heart."

Sunlight Beam answered, "We don't usually go into your towns unless we have to. Business or something. Your towns are very loud, you know. You don't know it. But they are. Maybe that's why you people ended up with atrophied eardrums and vocal cords. The air density causes any kind of sound to…."

How dare he judge my planet with those stupid hearing things of his! Mist thought and interrupted his analysis of her culture with a purposely impolite remark. "We have heard that your towns are very ugly, lacking colour."

Sunlight Beam made a gesture with his shoulder which Mist interpreted as "I don't know" or "I don't care" or "Your thoughts don't matter." "Towns are towns," he signed.

"Then what are you doing here?" Mist asked and bowed twice to indicate she was merely being curious, not intrusive or rude.

"Waiting for the train to the coast," Sunlight Beam answered. "We have a community there. And a school for bilingual education. You speak English?"

"I heard about your school," Mist finger-spelled in English. "Lingua Franca good. Cutting? Not good. Cut people there all-you? Implants put in?"

Sunlight Beam made the same shoulder gesture again. "I just teach you people our ways," he signed. "Funny, but you people are the only humanoids we've met in all the galaxy who don't really use their ears."

Mist could not quite figure out if he meant to praise their uniqueness or if he thought they were freaks. Either way, she found the Earther rude.

Turning, she walked away without giving him the customary goodbye gesture. What would such a gesture mean to rude Earthers anyway? Had he really said that he was teaching her people his ways?

She walked back to where she had been previously standing and studied the "implanted baby" who was holding its small hands in a clenched fist. Tears streamed down its little brown cheeks. Its tiny feet kicked at the air. Mist wondered if an infection had set in. She almost hoped it had. Perhaps if there were rampant infection, the women of the council would stop the procedure for medical reasons. Not that she wanted the baby to suffer, but one or two deaths here and there might not be such a bad thing after all.

The green lights flashed, indicating that the train was on its way. Beside them, Mist noticed, were "speakers" attached to the eaves of the train station. The Earthers had touted bi-lingualism and had convinced many elders of many towns to create some kind of communication system that ears could respond to. But lately, Mist told herself, the "speakers" were proliferating to a dangerous degree. She thought of the long tube and of the off-worlders "fixing the air." If the dense air makes things loud, aren't there technical problems with having speakers and other sound-based technologies? she asked herself. She grew nervous. What are they going to do with our atmosphere?

Mist pondered again the Earther's words. Teach our thousand-year-old culture? She thought. Those Earthers think highly of themselves, don't they? Our families have roamed the starry seas for centuries. Others accepted us; they saw our gifts, not our lack. But these Federation Earthers are used to seeing things their way, so they change everyone else's way of seeing.

Her downcast eyes saw four flowers blooming in a small shaded corner near the tracks. She thought of Flowers-in-the-Sun.

My child, my life, she thought. You are living in a time when another planet's sun overshadows yours. I hope you will change your mind about the cutting.

She reminded herself that she and Flowers-in-the-Sun would both be revitalized by their visit to the Mother-Infant festival later in the week.

Arriving home, she found Flowers-in-the-Sun in the family gathering room surrounded by her aunts. Flowers-in-the-Sun had been implanted. When Mist entered her apartment, the aunts and cousins rose almost as one and formed a barrier between her and her daughter. The Earth doctor and a woman of the medical caste stood beside the sedated patient. Their lips were moving and they were giving Ion a small bottle of tiny balls with writing on it.

Shadow-of-Light-Turning looked immensely pleased. "Can't you see?" her mother-in-law signed. "Your daughter is no longer being isolated by her cousins."

Ion's face was turned toward the ground and not once did he lift his eyes to look at her. Not even as she sank into a chair near the door, too shocked and amazed at the conspiracy and betrayal to speak.

Her old self might have spoken. She had been a warrior woman once. The chief of barterers, the villages had nicknamed her. Now, she could hardly lift her hand to argue. Her emotional and physical strength failed her. She looked up at Ion and thought, what use is fighting if my family, my husband, and my village won't fight for me? What was the use of fighting what could not be undone? She felt old, like a living ghost.

A day or two later, after she had taken enough of the little white pills, Flowers-in-the-Sun began to smile in that sweet way she always had. Seemingly gone was the sadness that had accompanied her when the cousins ignored her. Seeing her daughter's happiness, Mist's anger melted into resignation and grief and lost its edge. And yet she felt old. But she was not truly old, not yet.

That happened at the end of the month, when Flowers-in-the-Sun was fully healed and Mist took her and a niece to the Mother-Infant festival.

Mist was one who always tried to mind her own business and so she did not ask her niece why her mother had not accompanied her to the festival. Besides, few of Mist's sisters-in-laws had attended the festival this year. No doubt the lack of interest in celebrating children was because of the increasing tension caused by children ignoring their elders. Mist wished her mother-in-law would call a family meeting about it. As it was now, a brooding "silence" hovered in the house.

Mist, her daughter, and her niece disembarked from the train at its terminal in the Valley of Living-Water-White-Light. The flashing multicoloured lights pulsated in rhythm to the choreographed water fountains. Dancing young girls in ribbons marched gaily beside their mothers who walked regally behind, their clothing proclaiming the number of children they had borne. Mist was dressed in the green science caste colours, shells, and flowers. And Shadow-of-Light-Turning had crowned Mist's plaited hair with a floral wreath and adorned those arms that had once held a child and given a new immortal soul to the Creator with gems and semi-precious stones. Her mother-in-law's kindness to her was a new thing. And she felt young again. New birth and change were everywhere.

The parade route followed the river valley, meandering through the hilly cliffs. Visiting Earthers stood atop the ridges or near the ridges with their VID-machines in their hands, giggling and recording the festival as if the people on Mist's planet were some strange backward civilization. She tried to ignore them.

She reached towards Flowers-in-the-Sun. "The procession of the older mothers is about to start. In ten years you'll be married with your own children and I won't be able to come to the Mother-Infant festival anymore. You'll be all grown up."

Flowers-in-the-Sun looked at the festival-goers and at the Earthers with their VID-recorders. Her eyes stared pensively out at the passing villagers.

"Mother Mine," she began, then paused.

"What is it, Daughter Mine?" Mist asked, staring at the tattoo on her daughter's neck. "The implants have healed, have they not? You aren't in pain, are you?"

"It's very loud," Flowers-in-the-Sun signed. "Everywhere. It hurts my ears. We are a very loud people."

"By whose standard?" Mist asked, annoyed. "I hear the Earthers are fixing our air, making the world less noisy for you implanted ones. I doubt, though, that the air density can be changed." She extended her hand towards her daughter. "Coming?"

Flowers-in-the-Sun did not take her mother's hand. She glanced at her cousin, then turned to her mother. "Perhaps," she signed, "we should not hold hands."

"We must hold hands," Mist answered. "It's part of the festival. The Mothers and Daughters walk the procession together until we reach the town square. Then we do the responsive dance."

Flowers-in-the-Sun shrugged. "Mother, look around. The Earthers are watching us. And the girls my age aren't holding their mothers' hands."

Mist lifted up her eyes and studied the crowd around her. It was true –true and strange – the mothers of older children were definitely not holding their children. They weren't even walking with them. In fact, the mothers all seemed lost, forgotten, childless as they stood on the edge of the road, their backs against the high walls of the cliff. Their lost eyes watched dejectedly as their children chattered on in animated mouth-talk with other children.

In her new green dress and green marriage scarf, Mist stood in the middle of the road glaring at Flowers-in-the-Sun. "Am I to be like those women?" she asked. "Standing on the sidelines like a childless woman, while your life passes me by?"

She grabbed Flowers-in-the-Sun's hand and the child stared up guiltily into her mother's eyes and began walking by her mother's side. But as her mother marched ahead, she looked behind at her cousin, smiled, and whispered something her mother could not hear.

Ven Begamudré *was born in Bangalore, India, emigrated to Canada when he was six, and has lived in Mauritius and the United States. His six books are* The Phantom Queen *(2002),* Isaac Brock: Larger than Life *(2000),* Laterna Magika *(1997),* Van de Graaff Days *(1993),* A Planet of Eccentrics *(1990), and* Sacrifices *(1986). His half-dozen appointments as a writer-in-residence include the Canada-Scotland Exchange. An earlier version of "Out of Sync" appeared in* Laterna Magika *(Oolichan Books).*

တလာ

Out of Sync

Ven Begamudré

They were at it again. I listened closely, and I knew. It was more than just the wind.

I must be the only adult in Andaman Bay who falls asleep unaided. Sometimes, though, when the wind rises in pitch and windows shudder, or when it slides down the scale and walls rumble, I flick on the white noise. Its soothing hiss can block out everything, even thoughts of the Ah–Devasi, out there in the aurora. No one wants to believe the aurora is alive. That's only a tale, we claim, invented long ago to keep children from wandering too far. Especially north, where the mountains rise so high an entire search party can lose its way in the canyons. I sighed, got out of bed, and pulled on my robe. From the doorway of the children's room I listened to the twins' breathing, the rise and fall of their breath out of sync. I'm sure they dream of birthdays. They're hoping for a Khond magic show at their upcoming party, and how can I refuse? But, oh, that Cora! She must have been teasing during all that talk about the Khond murdering us in our beds. Teasing even when I asked her point–blank:

217

"Could you really kill me and the twins?"

"Oh no, Miss," Cora said. "I could never kill the family I work for." She put breakfast in the oven. "But someone else's children –"

"That's enough!" I ordered.

"Yes, Miss."

Now I closed the door to the children's room and slipped their breathing monitor into my pocket. Like me, they rarely need white noise to sleep. I double-checked the alarms before leaving the flat, and the lift arrived at once. Inside I pressed the button for the dome lounge. Even through the whine of the motor, I could distinguish two sets of breathing. It comforted me, as it does even now.

Leaving the lights off in the lounge, I sank into the padded observation chair and strapped myself in. I raised it until the lights on the arm shone dimly in the top of the dome. Around us rise the domes of other buildings, forty-seven in all. More are under construction. In another ten years, the population of Andaman Bay will double. Architects call this planetary sprawl. A hundred kilometers to the east, the lights of Tonkin Bay twinkled in the night. I turned the chair south. Here I could see a faint glow. A cloud of ammonia crystals reflected the lights of Corinth Bay. I turned the chair west and saw nothing. There's no bay out there. Not yet. Then something flickered in a corner of my eye, so I turned the chair north. I was right. It was more than just the wind. The Ah-Devasi were at it again.

The aurora hangs in the sky like a drape spanning the spectrum from yellow to blue. Its shimmer hides the stars in the whole quadrant from northwest past north into northeast. The aurora begins fifty kilometers up and falls in strands. They weave in and out, sometimes even braid, but only for a moment before waving free again, reaching out, curling up, crossing yellow on green. I watched the blue. Sometimes, where the aurora dips below the Pyrrhic Range, I'm sure I can see a strand pull away: one that glimmers in blue shading to indigo. Violet. I wait for shades of violet. I think I saw a violet last month, there at the end of Bight Pass. A violet so faint it verged on ultraviolet. I couldn't be sure, though, since earlier that day we had cremated Cassie Papandreou. We were all upset.

☙

Cassie's husband, Spiro, pleaded with the coroner to rule her death an accident. Anything but a suicide. The coroner did, for her children's sake. Everyone understood. For who could deny Cassie had been troubled? We'd seen it each time she'd said, just as she had the week before:

"I'm telling you we don't belong here. *They* don't want us here."

"Then there's no argument," Zhou Feng said. "We don't want to be here either." Most of the guests laughed with him because he sits on the bay council. Other guests laughed at him. He doesn't care. The main thing is to make people laugh since he has his eye on the governor's suite.

"Don't patronize me," Cassie snapped. "You know what I mean." Spiro looked past her at an empty crystal goblet on the sideboard. The goblet reflected light from the chandelier. I wasn't the only one who sensed his unease.

Still, Zhou Feng couldn't let things rest. He called down the table to our chief of maintenance, the lone Demi on the bay council. "Harun al-Rashid," Zhou Feng called, "do *you* want us to leave?"

When Harun smiled, everyone looking directly at him protected his or her eyes. "Sorry," he said. The glow faded with his smile. "Cassandra, dear lady," he insisted, "it is not a question of leaving or staying. Your people have been here for nearly a century. Your parents were born here, no?" He made his voice a pleasant bass to reinforce his gravity. Most times it's difficult to know when he's being serious because his natural tenor carries the strong, laughing lilt of his people. The Demi are famous for their sense of humour.

"That's just what I'm talking about," she cried. "Every time I have to deal with a Khond it looks right through me as if I'm not even there. I know exactly what it's thinking. 'Why don't you people leave?' Not you, Harun. You're not really one of them. I mean...."

"I know exactly what you mean," he crooned. "These same Khonds call me a diamond when —"

"A what?" Spiro asked.

Oh, that Spiro! Sometimes I wonder whether he takes his eyes from his spectrometer long enough to notice the colour of the sun. I told him this once, when he asked for advice about Cassie, but he didn't want to hear he might be neglecting her. "Sometimes I wish you'd keep your eyes on the spectrometer more," he said. "But I suppose you're too busy trying to guess what colour the sun will be."

It's been some time since people coddled me for being a widow.

"Like the gem itself," Harun was saying, "though I am one of the few privileged to savour its beauty." He nodded at Zhou Feng's wife, Zhou Li.

She was fingering her necklace. She basks in knowing she's the only woman in Andaman Bay wealthy enough to own such a necklace. Small things keep her happy.

"They call me a diamond," Harun continued. "Dull on the outside like a human, blindingly bright inside like —"

"Like your Khonds?" It was Zhou Feng again, trying to be humorous.

The Khond are Harun's only on his father's side.

Everyone except Cassie and I laughed. She was staring at her hands, clasping and unclasping them on the damask tablecloth. I was raising mine to my ears. I wanted to be ready for what might follow. It did, and I was. The moment Harun opened his mouth to laugh, a dazzling light flooded the room. The moment he did laugh, china rattled and the chandelier swung in the shock waves. The empty crystal goblet burst. After he stopped laughing, all of us lowered our hands and blinked to clear our vision. He shrugged an apology to Zhou Li for breaking the goblet.

"It's nothing," she said.

"I can tell you," Harun said at last, "what I tell the others. Humans gave us form." Raising his left hand, he tilted it to display its translucence. "You gave us time, even if most Khonds are rarely on time for anything. But then it is not always easy for a Khond to synchronize its existence with yours. Unlike we Demi, the Khond are born out of sync."

Again, everyone except Cassie and I laughed. He can be such a show off sometimes.

"We were spoiled," he said, meaning those on his father's side. "We thought time did not exist the way it does in the rest of the galaxy. We thought we were immortal."

"Aren't you?" Spiro asked. "I mean, aren't *they*?"

"In some ways, yes," Harun said. "In other ways, we are created and destroyed just as humans are born and die. Or in your case," he said, addressing me, "reborn. You are still a practising Hindu, I believe?" Everyone knows I am, to some extent. Harun continued: "By bringing us the concept of time, you brought us the realization we were not the only beings in the galaxy. It was a hard lesson to learn but with it we also learned –" He wiped his lips with a serviette, then studied its brocade. "– to love."

"Come again?" Zhou Li asked. It's her duty at these gatherings to ask questions no one else can ask unless they want to look gauche.

"I simply meant," Harun said, "that when there is no urgency of time, there is no urgency to love. Your long-dead Bard of Avon put it so well." Harun's voice dropped lower in pitch so there was no mistaking the gravity of his words:

> *This thou perceiv'st, which makes thy love more strong,*
> *To love that well which thou must leave ere long.*

Zhou Feng applauded softly.

Spiro complimented Harun on his gift for recalling obscure literature.

Harun reminded Spiro that, as everyone knows, the Demi are famous for their inability to forget. "It comes from having to live so long," Harun said.

When Cassie slammed her fists on the table, her place setting rattled as violently as when Harun had laughed. "You're not listening!" she cried. "Damn you," she said, looking at the rest of us. "Damn you most of all!" she added, glaring at him. "We have to do something before the Ah–Devasi help the Khond destroy us! We have to leave while there's still a –"

Spiro tried to uncoil her fists. "You're just tired," he said. "The aurora beings –" He paused. "The Ah–Devasi just want their land back."

She began to laugh, a laughter others joined nervously until hers became a cackle. "You fool," she hissed, "they don't need land. They don't even have *bodies*."

"That's enough," Zhou Li said. Her necklace glinted when she turned. "Cassie, dear, you've been up in the dome again. Spiro, you're still listening to fairy tales. The beings you're both talking about don't exist. The aurora is not made up of the spirits of this planet's ancestral –"

"No?" Cassie demanded. "Haven't you ever listened to the wind? I have. Haven't you ever watched the way the strands dip down behind the mountains and the blue breaks away into indigo? I'm telling you people, one day that glow is going to roll down Bight Pass and the whole of the plain will be red. With our blood!"

No one dared to laugh then, just as no one laughed a week later at the cremation. Cassie had driven her Morris up into the Pyrrhic Range. The search party had found her two days later, halfway through Bight Pass, with the Morris on its side and her life support system drained. No one wanted to believe what really might have happened: that she'd gone out there to speak with the aurora. Only I believe it, just as I'm the only one who knows the fatal error she made. She hadn't been driven by a desire to make contact. She'd been driven by fear.

✺

I unstrapped myself even as the observation chair lowered me from the dome. The vinyl creaked uneasily. What was I doing, staying up so late again? If I'm not careful I'll end up as obsessed as Cassie, whose ashes Spiro scattered to the wind. Now he's trying to raise the children with help from his new domestic. Cora's sister. Is that how they'll do it? Will Cora kill the Papandreou children and her sister kill the twins? I found myself wishing the lift could go faster. Downstairs, even as I entered the flat and reset the alarms, I heard the wind rising. I pocketed the monitor and checked on the twins. No one will hurt them. The plain will never be red with blood. Not theirs.

I decided to make some Horlicks. But halfway to the kitchen, I stopped. I'd left my bedroom door ajar and the blackness around it glowed. I crossed to it and eased the door fully open.

Harun floated near the ceiling. He lay on his side with his head propped on a hand, his elbow casually propped on thin air. Not thin to him. When my eyes met his, he trilled on a make-believe flute. He does this when I look annoyed. I told him once about my favourite incarnation of Lord Vishnu: Krishna Gopala, the cowherd who played his flute for *gopis*, those cowgirls of Ancient Indian Earth. I closed the door behind me and locked it. Then I switched on the white noise.

Harun grimaced, but no one could hear us now.

"How did you get in?" I demanded.

He tapped the ventilation grille.

"And what do you think you're up to?" I asked.

"Tsk, tsk," he replied, shaking his head. "Don't you know?"

It's a game with us, a re-enactment of the first time he appeared like this, unannounced. As he did then, he floated down to offer his hands. This time, though, I threw off my robe and flung myself onto him. We rolled across the bed, and I clung to him so I wouldn't fall off the edge. Then he pulled me back, over him. While I pressed his left hand onto my face, the hand grew even more translucent, and I breathed deeply. I tried to breathe particles of his very fabric into myself. He smells like jaggery, the palm sugar I loved to eat as a child. When I raised his hand to kiss his fingers, they grew opaque.

Everyone knows what the Demi are famous for: their sense of humour and inability to forget. But few humans have discovered what the Demi should be famous for. I like to think I'm the only woman, perhaps the only human, who has ever made love to a being of another species. I know this isn't true. Where did the Demi come from, after all, if not from the union of early settlers and Khonds? Now humans love only humans. Most of them. The Khond reproduce as only they can. And the Demi? They claim they have little use for others. Not my Harun. When I'm alone with him, no white noise can shut out the wind as well as he can. He can shut out the world.

He wrapped his arms around me and lifted me off the bed. He always does this. Provided he doesn't let go, and he never has even in jest, he can slip my nightgown up and over my head more easily in midair. More easily than when my elbow or thigh pins the fabric beneath me. The nightgown felt suddenly heavy. I pulled it away and tossed it into a corner. We floated down onto the bed. I nudged him onto his back and felt him grow opaque to support me. Then he rolled me onto my back and grew translucent so I could breathe. Translucent everywhere except on top of my thighs, where I like to pull the weight of him down. His clothing always seems to evaporate. One moment it's there, the next moment his flesh quivers on mine. I clamped my legs over the small of his back and pretended to draw him in. I still need to pretend he can enter me there first. He began to glow. The more he glowed, the warmer he felt. The warmer he grew, the farther I could draw him in. And not just there. He filled my body. His flesh pushed up under the surface of my skin. Finally, when every particle of our bodies mingled, he laughed. The room filled with blinding, violet light. I squeezed my eyes shut, I clasped my hands over my ears, and I shrieked.

When he tried to draw out of me, I said, "Not yet." This is the best part: lying together afterward with his body in mine. Knowing that nothing which happens outside this room or this building or this bay matters.

He drew himself out slowly, one particle at a time, one part at a time. First a finger, then a toe. He pulled out his arms and his chest and his trunk and legs until I could feel only his head inside mine. I stifled a moan when he pulled out completely. He slid his arm under my shoulder and his arm grew opaque. My head rose and he cradled it on his chest so he could toy with my hair.

At last he said, "I watched one of your old dramas. This is where they smoke."

I laughed, and so did he. When light poured from his mouth, I kissed him to block the light. To stifle the sound in his throat while his chest quaked. The light also tasted like jaggery. I drew away and pressed his lips together. Trying to flex them, he made soft, protesting sounds.

"Shh," I warned, "you'll wake the children."

He became serious then. He pulled away and said, "Can't have that, can we?" His voice was a grave bass.

"That's not what I meant," I said. I rose and found my nightgown inside out. I fumbled it outside in. Even as I pulled it over me, I said through the now comforting fabric, "No one should know, that's all. Not yet."

"No one does know," he said. His clothing reappeared, and he sat up. "How've you been?"

"Same," I replied.

"Is it your friend?" he asked. "The one the others could never call Cassandra because of that prophet of the Ancient Mediterranean?"

"She wasn't my friend," I said. I lay down beside him and urged him to lie close. Once again, I rested my head on his chest. "Cassie was going mad. No one can be real friends with someone like that."

"Because you couldn't help her," he asked, "or because you were afraid you might become like her?"

"I read a book once," I said. "It was about the first law of space travel. It's not really a law because it can't be proven empirically."

"And it's not like you to change the subject," he said.

"No matter how far the human race leaves Earth behind," I told him, "we can never be completely at home anywhere else. I'm paraphrasing, of course." I sighed. "Maybe that's what Zhou Feng was trying to say the other night, at dinner, when he said we'd all like to leave."

"You can't go back," Harun said.

"Are you trying to tell me something?" I teased.

He pretended he hadn't heard, and I should have known better. He talks glibly about love except when we're alone. "Physically you can go back," he was saying, "but you were all born here."

"Try telling that to the Khond," I said.

He snorted, then smiled at allowing himself to become annoyed. It's all humorous to him, even annoyance.

Everyone knows the last thing a Khond or a Demi does before dying is to laugh. A loud, long laugh which empties its body of its spirit in the form of a light. The light begins with the red of destruction, races through the spectrum into the violet of creation, and fuses into a blinding, white light. So people say. No human has ever seen a Khond or a Demi die. When the time for this comes, they flee into the Pyrrhic Range.

"The Khond," Harun said, "dream of an age that never existed. It's true your coming brought them the notion of time but now they're weaving a fantasy of their past. 'Time without time,'" he scoffed, repeating the Khond chant. "'Form without form. Life without death.'"

I pulled away from him and sat up. "I wish you wouldn't mock your own people like that," I said. "I mean not your own people but –"

"I know what you meant," he said.

I turned with my jaw set and found a weak smile lighting his face. I kissed the spot where his navel should be. He grew translucent, and I moved my hand down.

He clasped my hand to stop it from sliding between his thighs. It still bothers him. He can make love to me as no man ever could, yet he's still not completely human. He moved my hand up to his chest, which rippled from translucence into transparence. My hand sank until I could feel his heart, there below his breastbone. His heart beat under my palm. He likes doing this to show his heart beats only for me. It's part of the wedding ritual of the Demi: to clutch one another's hearts for the only time in the presence of others. During those long nights when I still grieved, when I couldn't allow myself to make love to him, he would say, "Touch my heart." The night I could finally bring myself to do this was the night we finally made love.

"Once long ago," he now said, "before you were even born, I went up into the mountains. I forced myself to endure a ritual my father told me about. 'Spread yourself thinly,' he said, 'and when the sun eclipses, your ancestors will sing to you.' I don't think he ever dreamt I'd do it." Harun's face hardened. The light between his lips faded into a grey that might have been either sadness or anger. It must be sadness, I thought. He's incapable of anger.

"Then what happened?" I asked.

"The aurora appeared," he said. "The Ah–Devasi –"

"They do exist!"

"Of course they do," he said, "only not the way you think. And not the way the Khond think either. That's what galls them. I've heard of Khonds who go into trances and see the world through the eyes of the Ah–Devasi. And these same Khonds don't like what they learn about themselves because they've become, well, unworthy of their ancestors. Don't ask me if it's true."

"The ritual?" I prodded.

"The ritual," he said. "It was the middle of the day and the sun was eclipsed. It was cold. So cold. Then the aurora appeared and its beings really did sing to me." He reached for my hair.

"Well?" I asked.

"They cast me all the way to the other side of the world," he said. "'We are the spirits of the aurora,' they sang. 'The aurora of the spirits.' They? It was many voices. It was one voice. Maybe the Khond never did speak with one voice the way some of them like to believe. Just as some of them like to think humans speak with one voice. When a Khond looks at you, all it sees is a human. Not an individual, distinctive being. When they look at me, all they see is a Demi."

I shuddered even as his lips drew back. He was capable of anger, after all, if compassion failed him. If he saw the Khond exactly as he claimed they saw humans. The light from his mouth glowed red. Even his eyes glowed faintly red. He closed his mouth and his eyes. When he opened them once more, they looked normal, the irises a pale violet. He opened his mouth to speak, and the light from within looked normal, too. "I'm sorry," he said. He clutched my hand to his heart and it beat rapidly beneath my palm. "You see, I still have vestiges of the Khond in me. Too much for my own good. If only they could find a way to lose their anger, then their own eyes wouldn't glow so much. Do you know what happens to a Khond if it's consumed by anger? It goes blind." Harun smiled, and light flickered between his lips.

I couldn't decide whether to believe him. "Did the Ah–Devasi say anything else?" I asked.

"Oh yes," he replied. "'You are not of us,' they or it said. 'Nor are you of the humans,' they–it said. They–it sound like I do when I'm in public, like a character from one of your old dramas." He shrugged. "I went through all that to learn what I must've known all along?"

He smiled again, so brightly I kissed him to stop the light from flooding the room. The light no longer tasted like jaggery now. It tasted bittersweet. We made love again, less playfully than before, but I made him remain inside me a long, long time.

⌥

As soon as Harun left, through the ventilation grille as always, I glanced at the clock. It was the middle of the night and I still wasn't sleepy. I barely sleep on the nights he visits me and yet I never feel tired. It's as though he leaves a residue of his energy in me.

I left the flat once more and, this time, found the Khond at work. Silently. Few of them looked me in the eye. In the eyes of those who did, I saw a surly glow. When I reached the lift I found it out of order. I still punched the up button, then waited with my arms crossed. Through the large window, I watched the twinkling lights of Tonkin Bay far to the east.

A voice startled me: "May I be of service?"

I knew even as I turned that I would find a Khond. A faint smell of ammonia was filling the air. The Khond's head poked out through the closed lift doors.

This is why the Khond are so good at maintenance: they can go anywhere. Up to a point. The very oxygen we humans breathe gives them their form and they like this. They like feeling useful. But too long among humans and a Khond can never venture into the ammonia rich atmosphere. It's trapped inside and lives out a life shortened by oxygen. The Khond sneer at the Demi, who move so fluidly between our two worlds, and yet Khonds who are no longer useful slouch through walls if they can. Slouch against them if not. No Demi would ever slouch. I watched this Khond closely and waited for it to speak.

"I believe the stairs work," it said at last.

"No kidding," I said. I turned toward the flat. I wasn't about to walk twenty floors up to the dome.

"I believe kidding is for goats," the Khond said, "though I have never set eyes on such a creature." The Khond pulled itself farther out from the lift. "Might you have on your esteemed person a modicum of divine tobacco? It refreshes the weary and makes one sleep as soundly as a babe. Oh, if –"

"I'm sorry," I said, as politely as I could. "I don't smoke."

The light in its eyes barely flickered when it smiled. "Do not concern yourself," it said. "Tobacco affords a truly fetid and diabolical smell. It chokes the air…."

I let the Khond continue. I should say I let this particular being continue. It was an individual, distinctive being, not the representative of an entire species. But I knew exactly what it was doing: entertaining me with servitude. Ingratiating itself. Any other time, late in the day when I'm tired, I would have let my annoyance show. I do care, but I resent having my politeness used against me.

"Look," I finally said. The Khond stopped in mid–soliloquy. "I'll make you a deal. Let me up to the lounge, and you can come by later and help yourself to anything in my pantry." I raised my index finger. "Any one thing."

The Khond snorted. I expected the smell of smoke yet smelled only more ammonia. "A test," it said. "Nothing more." After it looked left and right, up and down to ensure there were no Khonds within hearing, it said, "If any of my kind inquires, however, pray insist you exchanged a gram of tobacco in return for my humble service. Irreparable would be the harm to my reputation, such as it is, should rumours begin to the effect that I bestowed my favour on a human." The Khond's right hand emerged from the lift door. "Okey dokey, liddle schmokey? Shake."

I reached forward but we never made contact. The hand pulled back through the door. Chortling, the Khond stepped completely out of the lift, then pressed a button on its work belt. The lift lights came on.

When I touched the up button, the doors slid open. I stepped inside and turned in the doorway so the doors couldn't close. "What's your name?" I asked.

Startled, it said, "Pray, why do you inquire?"

"So I'll know what to call you next time."

"I have long believed," it said, "that no member of your species could distinguish any member of mine from another. Except domestics, but familiarity also breeds –"

"Okay," I said. "Fine." I stepped back.

"A moment," the Khond cried. "I beg you!" It stepped forward and the doors slid back. "You require my human appellation or my original appellation?"

"I wouldn't be able to pronounce your original name," I said.

"This is true." It chortled until a faint light glowed in its eyes. "My human appellation is Henry – short for Henry the Fourth, Part One. My sibling, as you may surmise, was Part Two. Alas my sibling is, to all purposes, no more, having stiffened in a living death somewhere in Corinth Bay. My original appellation, however, might roughly translate as −" The light in its eyes dulled, and its shoulders sagged. "Even my comrades, my kith and kin, address me as Henry. Why is this?"

Before I could try to answer, it backed away and the lift doors closed.

I consoled myself with what I now knew. What most others, even Zhou Feng and Zhou Li, don't know. The Ah–Devasi didn't drive Cassie mad. It's avoiding contact that drives a human mad, and not simply contact with those we love. Or once loved. If we can't make contact with the aurora beings, we can at least make contact with Khonds. They're all around us and yet, just as most humans pretend the Ah–Devasi don't exist, so most humans treat the Khond as if they, too, barely exist.

Spiro, for one, but then he's so caught up in his precious work.... No, that's not fair. It is precious. We're trying to find a way to oxygenate the entire planet without killing off the Khond. As for the Ah–Devasi, Spiro cares about his children as much as I care about the twins, but I wonder if he could defend anyone with his life. If it came to this, if the violet glow ever rolled out of Bight Pass onto the plain, I would protect the twins with my life. I would even kill to protect them. What am I thinking of, though? There are likelier ways of dying than being murdered in our beds: meteor showers, quakes, vehicle crashes. Especially crashes. Life is full of danger even for the Khond. They simply have less to lose, or so people say.

The lift doors opened and I hurried to the observation chair. I strapped myself in and raised it. I turned the chair through north toward the northwest. Toward the aurora.

The strands hung down, even braided, then waved free and curled blue on green. Where the aurora dipped behind the Pyrrhic Range, a strand glimmered in blue shading into indigo. The aurora was resisting the rising of the sun. Before long, though, the aurora lost its battle. It retreats by day and surges back at night. Now it has faded, drawing into itself while the sun keeps rising. While its harsh, harsh rays wash out the lights of Tonkin Bay. The sodium content of the atmosphere has increased since yesterday morning, when the sun looked more blue. Today the sun will be a warm, yellow–orange.

I should go downstairs now to let Cora in. I should be there when the children wake. I think they will like Harun.

SECTION V
RE-IMAGINING THE PAST

The anthology closes with three stories that re-imagine the past: "The Living Roots" by Opal Palmer Adisa, Journey Into the Vortex" by Maya Khankhoje, and "Necahual" by Tobias Buckell. The Caribbean past of slave resistance and rebellion is the subject of Adisa's story but she brings in a whole other layer of meaning. Khankhoje's lyrical story links together pre-Columbian history and myth and contemporary Native American realities. And the natives in Buckell's story – who have had multiple dislocations from their homelands – play a more active role as yet again they face people who see themselves as carrying the white man's burden.

Opal Palmer Adisa *is always wrestling with a story in her head while she goes about her busy day juggling life, teaching, mothering, and loving herself. She is grateful to the places and people who grow large in her head, and hopes she does them justice. Her most recent poetry collection is* Caribbean Passion *(Peepaltree Press, 2004) and her forthcoming novel is* The Orishas Command the Dance.

The Living Roots

Opal Palmer Adisa

Dusk skipped in like a woman in haste to meet her lover. The sun, hiding behind the mountain, was the only witness as Essence's head emerged flat from the side of the cotton tree. She knew as soon as the air hit her face that she should have waited until night had crept in like a man returning from a clandestine affair, but she was impatient. She had told Tuba, who claimed the Maroon leadership after her father died, that they had been too long underground; that Piliferous Layer, although a safe haven for them, was only meant to be temporary. He saw her advice as a challenge to his authority; he believed that perhaps Essence, as daughter of the past leader of one the most formidable Maroon colonies, felt she should be the heir. But Essence was only amused by Tuba's masculine insecurity. She loved being a reconnaissance scout and had no ambition to be a leader. She had witnessed firsthand the challenges and sacrifices her father had made, and understood how leading and trying to be everything to everyone had worn him down. Besides, she fully intended, when she was ready, to woo Tuba to her bed and make him her husband; he had both the mind and body that was as close to an equal that she would get, and it didn't hurt that he titillated her. Perhaps that was why she was on this mission, defying his order, knowing he would come after her and provide her with the opportunity she needed for them to be alone, away from colony scrutiny – especially her mother's, a master strategist.

Before Essence could withdraw and blend fully into the tree, the woman spotted her, and cried out, "How duppy come out so early?" Instantly, the woman dropped the bags in her hands, cupped her palms together, blew in them, and then tossed her palms above her head as if throwing something away. Essence smiled. It was not the first time that an enslaved person thought she was an apparition. The woman gathered her bags loaded with fruits and ground provisions, glanced around at the tree, and took wide strides, her arms swinging vigorously despite the heavy bags that she clutched. Essence was tempted to call to her, but decided against it, as there was no urgency. Why scare the woman out of her wits, she mused. In due time, she would have the information she needed to report back to Tuba and the colony. Essence stayed connected to the trunk of the tree until night was fully dressed like a bride in a veil.

She separated herself from the tree trunk and wavered in the cool night air – flat, one-dimensional, compressed soil that slowly ballooned out until she was body and flesh. Her waist-length dreadlocks separated from the sap of the tree, and Essence coughed and stretched as she acclimated her system to the slave colony. Then she remembered what she always forgot: that the people of the world she was entering wore clothes, the unnecessary excessive fabric that hid the beauty and sensuality of their bodies. In Piliferous Layer they wore no clothes, had no need for such excess that impeded them from communicating with one another. Everything was through touch and taste; in fact, not to touch or lick another was an indication of animosity towards that person. That was why she knew Tuba was meant to be hers. He tasted like roasted sweet potato, but she had never told him this. Nor had he told her what her taste was. Essence put aside her reverie as she heard footsteps and squatted behind the tree, making sure she was out of sight of the voices. She had not yet mastered this human form that she hated; not because it was ugly, but because the enslaved world always infuriated her, with its control of human labour and restriction of their movements: "a complete degradation of the human spirit."

She identified two men, walking slowly, machetes slung across their shoulders, their voices loud and friendly. As they strode past, the shorter of the two craned his neck and glanced at the tree. Essence could feel his eyes scanning the tree and wondered how he knew she was there even though he could not see her. This had happened to Essence several times in the past when she visited the enslaved world. When she had mentioned these incidents to her father, he told her that even though some of the people were slaves, they were related to the Maroons, and could, if they really tapped into their ancestral memory, escape bondage by submerging below the surface of the earth to live freely as they once did. Essence suspected that this man was related to them and was either a subversive or his memory was damaged by the system of slavery. Still, it was not wise for her to call to him, because with his altered brain capacity, he might think that she was an apparition, or duppy. It was funny to Essence that some of these enslaved relatives of hers were unable to distinguish between the ancestors who had gone ahead and those who were still living in an evolved state among them.

The men moved safely out of sight until their voices were a distant sound like crickets speaking another language. Essence scanned the landscape to ascertain where she might find nondescript clothes in order to move among them without attracting attention. She felt that this time was different than the last time she was here. The air was not as constricted, and she smelled another fragrance – even in the men who had just passed and the woman earlier – that she hadn't smelled in them before. It was like thyme, but she did not know how to read that smell, or its meaning. It had been about five years since she had last visited this land they called Xaymaca. She and the other reconnoiterers had figured out that every one year of their life was equal to five years of their enslaved relatives. Her grandmother had known this from when she was prodded into a ship, pregnant with her first child. That was why in the dark and despair of the hold, rather than surrender to defeat, she had raised her voice, and called out to see who else was in training to be a priestess like she had been. Six other women had responded and despite the vomiting, tears, feces, and the sheer bewilderment that many succumbed to, they had plotted and planned how to transform themselves and escape their fate, paving a way for the life growing inside their wombs.

Essence's mother had told her the story many times about her maternal grandmother whom she had never met, and how the first inhabitants of the underground Maroon colony were all pregnant women, all former priestesses in training who had discovered that pregnant women had the capacity to survive underground and to train their unborn children to do likewise, that the source of their power was in their dreadlocked hair that were like roots that allowed them to breathe and receive all the nutrients that they required. That was why all the enslaved people, especially the men, were forced to have their hair cut short and even the women's hair refused to grow to any significant length because it was being tamed by the enslavers' comb. This was simply another way they were being trained to work for the benefit of others, and more importantly, they were also being trained to dislike and distrust their natural selves. But this was not the time to reminisce, she was on a mission, and if Essence wasn't careful to adapt to her environment, she could end up like her maternal grandmother, head shaved and doomed to live the life of an enslaved captive. Quickly, she identified a house about two miles from the cotton tree, where she would find clothes and cloth with which to wrap her hair and protect her power. Putting her ears to the ground to make sure no one was walking around in the immediate vicinity, Essence easily jogged to the farm house and found a stack of clothes folded in a corner in a small room. She selected the simplest sack–like dress, then digging through a basket, found several pieces of cloth. Selecting a smooth, brown, cotton piece, she wound it around her head, completely covering her thick hair that when left free brushed against her bottom. She was ready to move about and learn how her earthly relatives were making out, and how she and her people might continue to help them regain their freedom.

Morning found her in the market with the other women, as they were always the source of news.

"Howdy!" they greeted each other, their full voices like hampers loaded with ground provisions, their gestures free and intimate as the breeze flirting under the leaves of trees. "Howdy!" Essence joined the women in greeting, quickly scanning their bodies to try and discern which of them still had active memory. Once again she smelled thyme among them and then she remembered. It was the same fragrance she had detected the night she had wandered into the rebellion that left three overseers dead and several acres of cane–field smoldering. Could it be that these women had acquired their freedom? But how could that be, since she did not detect the memory in any of them. Confused, Essence floundered. She did not know if she could trust herself. This always happened when she covered her hair and wound it tight in a bundle to keep from being easily recognized; she received mixed messages, and wasn't quite sure if the information she was receiving was accurate. Desperate to regain balance, Essence pushed her way into the midst of a group of women and touched one on the arm. Very clearly she received the answer she sought: "Me neva gwane be anybody's slave," the woman's skin proclaimed. Just as Essence was about to let go and move away, she felt the woman's thumb and index finger circle her wrist.

"Is who yu?" the woman declared, pulling Essence closer to her and jerking up her arm. Essence slowed her heartbeat to synchronize it with the turning of soil as a seed takes root. Instantly the woman dropped her hand, alarmed.

"Do me know yu?" the woman asked, less self-assured now.

Essence looked at the woman and recognized her from the evening before, when in her haste Essence had emerged from the side of the tree.

"You belong to the Starch people, like me," Essence said, spreading her moist calm over the woman. "If you search your memory bank, you will recognize me as a cousin," Essence continued drawing strength from the woman, which allowed her to scan the woman's body more fully. She realized the woman was growing dreadlocks hidden beneath her head-wrap.

"Me see yu before," the woman replied as her mind travelled back in time. "Me se yu before, but yu was different," the woman ended, nodding her head as if to awaken her memory.

"We survive through our ability to disguise and adapt," Essence smiled, touching the woman's hand and immediately drinking in her warmth, like soil being sprinkled with water. "Can we go where we can talk?" Essence asked, feeling other ears prick up at their conversation.

The woman's eyes bore into Essence, trying to read her in a more obvious way than Essence was trained to do. Then she smiled, satisfied with what she believed she saw and knew.

"We guh afta me get a likkle piece a meat fi flavor de pot," the woman said, turning. Then she stopped and gazed once again on Essence. "Cousin," she said with full meaning, "de people call me Walker because me feets does know where to travel any time day or night, but me other name be Carmen. Carmen de Walker be me preference." She smiled broadly and began to move through the crowd of mostly women haggling over food and prices. Essence kept up, and with her mouth almost touching Carmen's ear, said, "I'm known as Essence of the Starch People."

Carmen de Walker nodded acknowledgment as she weaved with ease through the crowd, occasionally greeting others with both a nod of her head and a salutation which often involved inquiring about other members of their family. After more than an hour of this ritual, Essence deduced that the market was merely a meeting place to exchange news; shopping was the guise. The women's talk was about how sweet freedom was, even though the bacras still had their foot on their backs.

"But we will find a way round dem white people and dem meanness," said a woman selling carrots.

"Me done tell de one me lease land from dat fi him keep touching me behind, ah go fall down pan him and squeeze him to death," a rotund woman said with mirth.

"It nah gwane tek much fah you fi squeeze de day–lights out of dat maga, red skin bacra," said another, bearing a bunch of bananas of her head.

The women all laughed good–naturedly and moved on. Essence tried to understand their tongue that was slightly different from the language she spoke, but even more, she was trying to comprehend how they could claim to be free, and in the same breath declare that someone had a foot on their back. She listened keenly, trying to sort out all the talk, but always making sure she was close to Carmen's side. On more than two occasions, they were stopped, and once a woman who walked with a cane and whose face was filled with lines, searched Essence's face and asked,

"Is whe you from, girlie? Haven't seen you before."

Essence quickly thought of what to say, trying to bring to her lips the name of other estates over the island that she had visited, but Carmen came quickly to her rescue.

"Howdy Miss Tilda. Yu looking well, today. Dis here is me cousin Es. So what yu buyin'? Yu need any help, ma'am?"

Essence was impressed with the Carmen's swift and expert manner in deterring folks. As they moved on, Carmen remarked, "Miss Tilda okay. She mean well, but still one can neva be too careful. If anyone else ask, tell dem yu from Yarmouth Estate. Me 'ave people dere."

This confused Essence, although she did not say anything. If they were free, why did it matter where she was from? All was not what it seemed; there was a great deal more she had to learn before reporting back to Tuba and the Elder Council.

At last Walker purchased a small piece of salt pork and they were on their way to her home, four miles from the market, which they walked in well under an hour. Walker's name was appropriately suited, Essence decided as they made their way to her little round cottage, built with bamboo vines and covered with a thatched roof from coconut boughs and secluded in a grove.

Before they were inside the one-room cottage, Carmen de Walker reached for Essence's hand and said to her. "Yu nuh tell me eberyting. Yu know yu can trust me."

"Are you free or are you enslaved?"

"We claim freedom two years now. Whe yu been hidin out? Yu is one of de Maroon dem?"

So that was why she had smelled thyme. What had her mother told her about thyme again? "If you rub thyme into your joints, and behind your knees and under your arm-pits, it will make you invisible to the enslavers and the enslaved." Her mother's words seeped into her consciousness. Now she had to decide how much to tell Carmen the Walker.

"Yesterday evening you saw me at the cotton tree," Essence began, observing Carmen closely. "I was just coming up and had not filled my lungs with air yet."

"Yu is duppy?" There was alarm in Carmen's voice.

"I am still among the living," Essence hastened to assure her. "But you are right about me being a Maroon. There is a whole group of us Maroons who live underground." Before Carmen the Walker could interrupt, Essence pulled off her turban and shook her hair, which fell around her like tall, brown grass. "We breathe and survive through our hair. I am a reconnoiterer. I come up to learn how those who are enslaved are making out to gain their freedom. A few of us who came up were captured and enslaved when our hair, the source of our power and transformation, was cut off."

Carmen also pulled off her head–wrap, and her finger–length dreadlocks stuck up on her head. "We is indeed cousin, and me heard oonuh chatting plenty, but me moda tell me me a gu mad cause nu body kyan live inna ground like yam root." Carmen clapped her hands and the balls of her feet tapped the ground. "Yu can neva know how it feel fi know me nuh mad," she said, embracing Essence, who immediately licked her arms in joy. Carmen pulled away.

"Mek yu lick me like puppy?" she asked.

"That's how we greet each other down there," Essence apologized, remembering that this was not the way of the enslaved.

Carmen took hold of Essence's hand and pressed it to her stomach. Essence felt the child growing in Carmen's stomach. Both laughed, then held each other and danced around the small room. Essence realized she was suddenly tired. She yawned.

"Yu tired. Tek a likkle rest while me cook."

Grateful, and sensing she was safe, Essence stretched out on the small cot and pulled the colourful sheet, made from the scraps of many different cloths, up to her neck. Some of her hair, falling to the impacted dirt floor, instantly drank the nutrients. Her dreams connected her to her grandmother who was sitting on a hill looking down on a valley in which people, who appeared to be the size of ants, went about their daily chores. Her grey–roped locks were pulled over her shoulder almost to her ankles.

As Essence approached her grandmother, the old woman caught hold of her hand and licked her fingers. Essence returned her grandmother's greeting by licking her shoulder as both a sign of respect for her age as well as a symbol of deep affection. Essence sat beside the elder, who did not avert her eyes from the valley, but spoke as if she was merely continuing a story.

"Your mother has told you how I, along with six others, came to find Piliferous Layer and how I came to lose my claim to it. It has taken more than ten years, fifty in the world of the enslaved, to grow back my hair. Now it almost brushes the ground; this way I am always connected to the soil that sustains us.

"When I was on that slaver's ship, cuffed and chained, bewildered and bereft of hope like all the others, I heard the voice of my great-grandmother saying to me over and over, 'All is not lost, all is not lost.' I was trying to shut out her voice when I raised my own to ask who else beside me was a priestess in training. Others replied, and they too were being sustained by their grandmother's voices, telling them, just like my own who had already made her transition from our world, that all was not lost, and together we had the knowledge in our wombs to forge a new way to live.

"I cannot tell you how we did it, except that once the ship docked and we were relieved from our chains, we each ran, and to keep from being detected we buried each other, and in our desperation to be quiet, to keep from being detected, our bodies transformed and we found ourselves being pulled more deeply into the earth, as if through quicksand, until we sank to a latitude that had a floor.

"From there we learned what we had always been taught, that we could become whatever the occasion demanded, and the season of hostility and geographic realignment slated for our people required that some of us transmute and become one with the yams that had historically sustained us. We grew roots and dug more securely into the ground and gave birth, then one by one, rose to the surface to claim men and teach them to live like us.

"Our numbers increased and we learned to slow down our aging process considerably because we surmised that this season would be a long one, and our role was not only to be way-makers, but to survive it, as we were the keepers of memory and purveyors of tradition.

"At first we didn't think we would survive, partly because we were ambivalent. Our continent, that would become divided up and renamed Africa, was not perfect, but it was ours. Our needs were met. Like most people, we sometimes fought among ourselves, and often had to contend with kings who wanted to expand their territory, but it was home.

"The tears I shed for that place and the people lost to me is in the ripple of each wave. But every time I wanted to give up, my grandmother's voice would pound inside my head, 'All is not lost, this is a great journey-way that you are making. Go on and make of it something new.' And so I did with the help of Arrora, an Arawak woman, who did not die with the rest of her people, but stayed to help us who were coming. She was a mother to me; she had been a high-priestess of her people. She taught all of us how to breathe underground, how to become soil and use our hair like roots. She delivered our babies and showed us how to wriggle like worms to the surface of the earth. Mostly, she taught us the smell of the white man and how to stay safe from becoming one of his slaves. Arrora is your grandmother, too. You are a woman now, soon will be sleeping with a man. You must put water out for Arrora just like how you put water out for me.

"You are as good a scout as I was, better in fact. Once again the wind has changed course, but there are still battles ahead. Always remember that you are a purveyor of memory and tradition. You must always be able to live and survive anywhere. That is our claim. We survived when others did not. I was fifty, the age of your mother now, when the enslavers captured me and cut off my hair. I had been visiting several estates over the years, speaking to the women, teasing out their memory, helping them to set fire to the fields, showing them which herbs to grow to strengthen their and their men's bodies, which to use to weaken the bacras and make them worthless without killing them. I was doing well, but then I took up with a man on one of the estates. The woman I took him from got jealous and told the overseer that I was telling the cook how to kill him. I was too wrapped up in this man's love to be vigilant. I was tight in his arms, our legs intertwined when they caught me, and right there before him, my hair was cut off and my head shaved clean. That was true bewilderment; that and the sting of the whip. Thirty lashes with the cat-o'-nine-tails, but not a sound escaped my mouth or a tear watered my eyes. I knew my responsibility and kept my focus on the colony underground and on our people. I knew I would see them again."

Essence turned on the small cot and the back of her hand wiped the tears that spilled from her eyes. She was still asleep, but mumbled, "Fifty in our years, but 250 in theirs. Oh grandmother, you were such a warrior."

"We all are warriors, child, especially those who were enslaved and did not succumb to death, but kept believing and working to break the chains of slavery. My child, some of the greatest warriors simply kept faith."

While Carmen de Walker hummed a mento and cooked, Essence slept deeply, her grandmother dreaming her the memory she needed to fulfill her duties. She woke after the day had gone to rest. Her mother always cautioned her to wait until day was chasing evening before entering the enslaved world. She woke feeling powerful, and immediately her eyes located Carmen sitting just outside the cottage on a low stool and a man standing behind her massaging her shoulders. Essence rose quietly and walked to the door, but even before her feet were over the threshold, Carmen called to her.

"Yu was well tired. Yu sleep sound."

"Yes, your cot is very comfortable," Essence replied, her eyes scanning the man, the father of Carmen's unborn child; she detected that he was safe.

"Dis be Joint, also known as Sammy."

Joint smiled at Essence, and his eyes fastened on her like burr–burr, that thorn–like weed that easily attached itself to cloth.

"Me did know yu," he declared, moving from behind Carmen and walking towards Essence. "Me did know you from another time when memory flowed like river water."

"Joint was here before," Carmen interjected. "Him was here two times more dan me, but de both of we been here before."

"And are you free also?" Essence asked.

"Slavery days done!" Joint declared, spittle spewing from his mouth, his nostrils flaring.

A rush of excitement flushed Essence's skin. She wanted to rush back to the colony and tell Tuba and the others that they could come up now, that they no longer needed to live underground, but first, she had to hear the full story. She had to confirm what Carmen and Joint told her, and had to decipher the smell that clung to the colony. Essence walked up to Joint and licked his cheek and then his arm. She had to be sure; taste was the ultimate confirmation. Carmen reared up and Joint brushed Essence away gently.

"Dat's me oman dere," Joint said, pointing to Carmen who had her arms akimbo. "We be family. Me no want no more oman."

Realizing that her action was misinterpreted, Essence hastened to explain.

"It's only through taste that I can verify what you say. It is the language of the Starch people."

"Is who oonuh be?" Joint asked.

"Whe oonuh live fah real?" Carmen followed on the heels of Joint, now insinuating herself between Essence and Joint, and linking her arms with his.

Essence smiled at this gesture of ownership. How would Tuba react if she were to openly declare her intention to posses him by licking his soles and tracing his spinal cord with her tongue at one of their weekly public gatherings? Would he in turn circle her navel with his tongue and lick her eyelids to indicate consent and signal their union?

"Tek me whe yu live," Carmen de Walker stood in front of Essence, demanding of her. "Tek me; mek me see cause me is one of oonuh." Her voice was determined. Both feet were planted firmly on the ground and her arms were akimbo again. Essence could see that she would not be dissuaded easily, yet dare she take an outsider into their free colony?

"I cannot take you. You do not know how to transform and become a root."

"Me can become whateva me want. Jus tek me and show me how," Carmen de Walker insisted.

Essence knew she was cornered, but her mind quickly reviewed the first tenet of Piliferous Layer: Safety is the responsibility of all, from the youngest to the oldest, and no outsider must be allowed into Piliferous Layer without the approval of the leader, an elder, and two other members of the community. Essence respected this rule and knew that the colony had been protected all these years because everyone, including her great-grandmother who had been captured and made to live like a slave, honoured that code. She could not and would not break it, even though she believed Carmen de Walker was one of them, and wanted to show her how they lived. But before she could explain to Carmen why she could not take her, she felt a cool wind on her arms and legs, and knew instantly that someone else from the Maroon colony was approaching. Almost immediately, she smelled the sweet potato and smiled. So Tuba had come after her as she had hoped.

"The leader of my colony is approaching. You can make your request to him."

Tuba strode into their midst, his skin rich like wet soil, his muscles taut. Essence moved quickly to him and licked his knuckles in greeting as he ambled through the gate leading to Carmen de Walker's cottage. Immediately Joint stepped forward, his hands fisted at his side. With her peripheral vision, Essence glanced at Joint and smiled at the folly of men, free or enslaved; they amused her with their need to always lay claim, to establish their territory. Apparently Carmen was equally aware, because she moved quickly beside Joint and placed her hands over his fist, massaging it. "Him is not here to cause trouble," she said to Joint, although her eyes were on Tuba, drinking him in.

Essence felt like someone was yanking on her dreadlocks and her scalp prickled. She had not experienced this sensation before, but she knew enough to know it was her way of wanting to claim territory, indicate to Carmen that Tuba was hers, even though she had not yet made such declaration to him or the colony. "Tuba, I am glad that you have come after me. Slavery is over. Everyone is now free. This is Carmen de Walker and her man, Joint. They are free and she is carrying his child." She knew she had said more than she needed to by way of introduction, but she felt the need to establish Carmen and Joint as a couple.

Tuba nodded to the couple, but his eyes were fastened on Essence: she read both irritation and desire.

"I had to come, and for defying your order I will submit to your punishment," Essence said more coquettishly than she had planned. It was the general rule that when the leader was disobeyed, the violator had to spend every minute of two weeks shadowing the leader.

"There is to be no punishment," Tuba replied, smiling at Essence for the first time.

"No punishment!" Essence was incredulous.

Tuba moved closer and licked her neck. "I conferred with the Elder Council before I left. I told them I approved your mission because like you, I believed we have been underground too long."

Thrown off guard, Essence could only mumble as her mind raced ahead to try and discern if Tuba was laying a trap for her.

"But you always opposed me," she shouted.

"It might have appeared that way, but perhaps I was allowing you to practice your rebellion on me," Tuba spoke softly.

Essence felt as if all the wind and fight had been knocked out of her. Was Tuba more complex than she had thought him to be? He was certainly liked and admired by most, including the Elder Council.

"So Mr Leader, tek me and Joint so we can see whe oonuh live," Carmen de Walker interjected, jarring Essence.

"First we must experience this freedom that you have gained," Tuba said, focusing fully on Carmen. "My people have been waiting on this day, when they could come up and breathe in the sweet air of freedom. The drums will sound this news when Essence and I return. Then perhaps you can come and see where we live, but of course there will be no need now that you are free. Living in the belly of the earth was how we resisted slavery."

"Well, slavery done, but we still have fi struggle fi get the laws change," Joint, said circling his arm around Carmen's waist. "Some of the bacras dem still want treat we like we is dem slaves. Dem no want give us no land fi grow and plant and profit from me own labor. Dem no want we have any say in how de island fi run." By now Joint was worked up and going at full speed.

"We free, but yet still we not free," Carmen interjected. "Dem still flog people like dem is slave for de slightest ting. Dem nu want pay we what we worth. Dem is true bad-minded people, dem bacra people who chat like hot coal in dem mouth and skin red and blotchy like wild leaf dat yu boil fi wash sore foot."

The four laughed, feeling a warm cameraderie.

Tuba was invited to dinner and they ate and exchanged stories about their day-to-day activities in their respective homes. Although Joint and Carmen weren't sure, they believed that slavery had ended more than two years before. They insisted that Essence and Tuba tell them about Piliferous Layer, and they listened to all the details with their jaws agape and their eyes big. Essence and Tuba also sought more details from them about their new freedom, and the four agreed that they would travel the island over to make sure that everyone now enjoyed freedom. Carmen de Walker said she would lead the way as she had travelled most of the island, and had even witnessed some of the torching of the fields, as well as some killings. Still, she insisted that she wanted to visit Essence's colony and have her unborn child live in a place where people refused to be slaves. After yawning and declaring it was time to sleep, Carmen stretched out on the ground and pressed her ears to the soil. A smile covered her face.

"Me hear dem talking. Me hear dem, me always used to hear dem. Me is one of oonuh." She turned on her back and smiled up at the sky sprinkled with stars. Joint and Tuba reached down and helped her up. "Well, me tink we is all tired and must get some shut eye," Carmen started moving towards the cottage. "Es, you and Mister Tuba can take the cot. Joint and I will pass the night on de floor."

Essence wanted to ask Carmen why she called her Es, but decided now wasn't the time, and besides, she rather liked the sound of Es. And she had no intention of taking her bed and told her so. They argued back and forth for a while, then Carmen proceeded to spread bedding on the floor for Essence and Tuba. With the lamp out, the two Starch people stumbled toward each other, unsure of their next move. They could hear Carmen and Joint settling on the small bed. Suddenly, Essence felt Tuba's tongue circling her navel. Now twice in one day he had beat her to the punch, this time by declaring his affection.

"It does not count," she whispered in his ears.

"It does to me," Tuba rejoined, licking her neck. "When we return, I shall honour you in the appropriate manner, before the community."

Essence pulled Tuba to her and whispered in his ear. "You are my sweet-potato."

"And you are my cassava," Tuba said as they fell into a sound sleep nestled together, tongue against skin.

Maya Khankhoje *was born in Mexico City to a Belgian mother and and Indian father and studied in Mexico and India. Her essays, stories, and poems, which have won several awards, have been published in India, the U.K., Ghana, the U.S., and Canada in several anthologies and magazines including* Shakti, Herizons, Montreal Serai, Feminísima, *and* Toronto South Asian Review. *She recently retired after a 25-year career as interpreter and translator for the International Civil Aviation Organization in Montreal in order to write fulltime. "Journey into the Vortex" was first published in* Voices and Echoes: Canadian Women's Spirituality *(Wilfred Laurier, 1997).*

༄

Journey Into the Vortex

Maya Khankhoje

They told her she would come out on the third day. That is what the mediators of the Lords of Xibalba had led her to believe. At least, that is what they wanted to believe. The hunger of their hollow power could only be assuaged with their own lies and delusions. It is true that the war of the heavens is the opposition between night and day. It is also true that the stars have to be conquered and sacrificed, so that the sun can drink their blood and the day begin all over again. In order to keep the universe in movement, people have to spill their blood so that it does not perish. But she knew them to be wrong when they said she would be out in three days. She grasped this truth as firmly as she grasped and held on to her mother's breast soon after she was born.

Her birth was auspicious. She exited the real world of the void to start her journey through the world of illusion on 12

243

Baktun, 16 Katun, 8 Tun, 7 Uinal, and 5 Kin, under the round and radiant face of Ix Chel, the moon goddess who wanders endlessly through the dark night so that the sun, her consort, does not burn her into oblivion.

It is to Ix Chel's care that her own mother entrusted her, shortly before she was sucked back into the vortex of creation. Her poor mother, who paid for the honour of birthing her with a torrent of sacrificial blood that drained her body as her hungry child drained her breasts dry for the first and last time. At least her mother had been transformed into a lovely butterfly, the reward bestowed on a man who dies in battle or a woman who exchanges her own life for that of her newborn child.

This is one of the many truths that she understood but failed to accept: that men are rewarded for destroying life and women for creating it. But that seems to be in the nature of all dualities, for how can we see the radiance of goodness when there is no shadow of evil to set it off?

Birthing her was indeed an honour. It was written that this female child born under the sign of Ozomatli, the monkey who invented fire, was to be a great medicine woman. So the midwife swaddled the baby carefully in her mother's blanket, hurriedly buried the cord that tied her to her unborn twin in the very centre of the house, and stole into the night with a little bundle in tow. Under the complicitous gaze of Ix Chel.

The midwife had acted out of kindness, for she knew that power is a good and strong thing, but not before its time and not in the wrong place. Before its time, power can turn upon itself, which, in this case, would hurt the lovely child who would now be hers.

And when power is used in the wrong place, it can be misused by the enemy. For the midwife knew that she alone could pass on to this child the knowledge that she acquired from the Final Mother, without any interference from the child's father and his high-born clan.

So she was named Sac Nicte and was brought up in the neighbouring temple city of Tulum, where the breeze blows cool air from a turquoise sea and children grow big and strong. Sac Nicte grew to be as pretty as her namesake flower and as strong as its fragrance, although her secret name was to remain hers alone. It is in her secret name that she nursed her power while it grew and took shape, whereas her public name only held her outward appearance, which, by the way, enchanted many men and made the maidens envious.

But Sac Nicte paid scant attention to her body or her face. At least, not in the way it was expected of her. She was nursed by a kinswoman of the midwife until she was three, when she playfully started biting the very breasts that made her teeth so strong. Her nurse, who had many children of her own, was glad to wean this strange child and send her to her Tata, the midwife. Under her Tata's loving hand, she grew up to be wilful and sure of herself.

It is thanks to her Tata that no pebbles were strung from her soft baby head to a midpoint between her eyes, to make them crossed. Crossed eyes might be beautiful, but she needed to see straight for the arduous tasks that awaited her. Her teeth were also spared being polished with stone and water to make them sharp like the teeth of a baby shark. It was her Tata who refused to encase her forehead between two planks of wood, to give her the gallant elongated look of the temple friezes. For that, she was grateful. In any case, she did not intend to carry heavy baskets slung from her forehead over her back. She did not know why, but she sensed that the source of her strength and her understanding lay somewhere behind her forehead, in a point between her eyes. After all, she had observed that people fall into a deep dreamless sleep when they are hit hard on the head. And babies whose heads get stuck in their mothers at birth often grow up to be dull.

Sac Nicte was not vain, but she was sensuous. She liked to sit at her Tata's doorstep and allow the old woman to oil her hair and braid it into two long braids that fell below her waist. And after bathing in the sea, she would rinse herself in sweet water and anoint her body with pungent red resin which would start a fire in her loins if she happened to be thinking of him.

His name was Can Ek and he was a son of one of the Lords of Xibalba. Can Ek was as tall as she was full and his skin had the burnished look of a dying sun. His mother had burnt the roots of the scanty hairs on his face before he reached manhood and now his face was as smooth and soft as hers. His lips were round and red and his eyes were as black and as sharp as an obsidian knife. So was his rod.

He came from far away to visit his kinsfolk and to plunge into the jade sea. He plunged into her soft flesh instead and tasted the salt on her lips. The first time she felt him inside, she cried out in pain and the blood between her legs was not the blood that was preordained by the rhythm of the moon. After that, she marvelled at how he could be hard and soft at the same time, a lesson she, as a medicine woman, still had to learn. At times she imagined that what she held in her hand was a plantain that was not yet ripe; at others, she accused him of being like a slippery eel not wanting to be caught.

But his very beauty was her undoing. They said that he had an evil streak. How could it be that she, a medicine woman, had not detected it? They said that when he turned seven, he killed a butterfly, that could have been her own mother! And at fourteen he had killed a deer, merely to possess the gland which holds the secret of all life. But as a grown man he had met Sac Nicte and his eyes filled with tears. A man who could be thus moved was a man to cherish.

He was her undoing not because he showed the cruelty that was often mistaken for courage and expected of men, nor because their limbs entwined around each other like the roots of the mangrove tree, but because he was her kin. At least, that is what everybody thought, except for herself and her Tata, who knew that it was not so. It was carved in stone for eternity to see that no man or woman was to come together with a member of the same clan.

"You must be good at making corn bread," he said as he stared at her while she bathed in the river. "Those breasts ripe for children are only given to those who grind corn every morning of their womanly lives."

Sac Nicte smiled and stared back at him, not making any attempt at covering her private parts.

"I do not make bread at all," she replied earnestly. "I am a medicine woman. I can help women in childbirth, remove warts, and help people polish their shields against their enemies. I can call on Ashana to keep the evil spirits at bay. I am good at helping people find their secret twins to translate their dreams and visions. I can weave as fine a cloth as the gossamer web of a spider and fashion quetzal feathers into adornments fit for a queen. I can count in twenties and predict the movement of the heavenly bodies. I can do that and a lot more, but I cannot make bread. That is not my calling."

Can Ek remained silent. Knowledge is recognition and Can Ek recognized her and this is why tears streamed down his face like the first rains of summer. The Lord of Dualities decreed it so. A man and a woman must join each other just like the water of the earth ultimately meets the water of the heavens in the distant horizon. This was the woman who was his true opposite and the twin of his soul.

Sac Nicte recognized him too. She had seen him many times even without the help of sacred mushrooms or generous portions of the brew prepared by the goddess Mayahuel. She had seen him and she imagined the feel of his smooth skin but was not prepared for the richness of his voice or the headiness of his scent.

It was then and there that they had touched for the first of many times, before he even knew her name, before she had pulled him by the hand and taken him home to her Tata.

"I want the priest to tie our tlimantli and if he will not do so, I will do it myself," she announced in a defiant tone.

"Have you gone out of your mind!" her Tata scolded. "He cannot marry into our clan because he is a kinsman of my brother."

Sac Nicte smiled and, leaning towards her Tata, grabbed the old woman's feet and squeezed them gently. "Didn't you tell me that when my mother died you took me away from my father's clan because their rank would not have allowed a child of theirs to have become a medicine woman? Didn't you once swear to me that even though there was nothing more in common between us than the bonds of love and wisdom you were willing to spill your blood to spare mine? I'm not asking you to spill your blood for me. I am merely asking you to help me meet my destiny with Can Ek."

The old woman nodded. "If I reveal your origins, the priest might be willing to bless your union, but your father will claim you first. And then I will lose you and you might lose your man. You must go away, my child."

Sac Nicte held the old woman in a tight embrace. "You cannot lose me ever, Tata. You are the one who taught me that essential life and love can never leave you, because you are that."

Three nights after that conversation, Sac Nicte and her lover left Tulum and made their long journey to Chichen Itza, under the cover of a dormant Ix Chel. In Chichen Itza, they hoped to blend in with the crowds that had thronged the sacred city to celebrate that moment when the day and the night are of the same duration, before winter arrives. It is known that on that day, as the sun moves over the horizon, the shadow of the great plumed serpent Kukulkan, Father of all of the Maya people, makes his ascent in seven laborious segments up the steps of the main pyramid. When he reaches the top, the 365 step which marks the completion of a solar year, a new cycle begins.

So Sac Nicte arrived in Chichen Itza with her man and their meagre rations of dry bread and peppers and ground chocolatl and some honey and a gourd which they filled with the sap of the maguey cactus to quench their thirst along the way. And they stood there in front of the pyramid, marvelling at the sight of Kukulkan and dreaming of a new life for themselves.

But love made Sac Nicte drop her guard. It is there that the mediators of the Lords of Xibalba grabbed her and dragged her across the main square and took her through the paved road that leads to the sacred cenote of Chichen Itza. She did not need to be a seer to know what awaited her. Nor did she wonder about Can Ek's fate either.

Can Ek tried to stop the men from leading her away, but others materialized from nowhere and dragged him away too. Except that they took him up the pyramid, where Lord Kukulkan had snaked his way up in an eerie play of light and shadows, and gouged out his heart with a deft cut using an obsidian knife, as dark and sharp as his lovely eyes.

Sac Nicte stood before the cenote while the priests droned their drivel. She knew why she and Can Ek were chosen to propitiate the gods. They were recognized because of their uniqueness. She understood that to be different means to share the fate of kings, who are destined to taste the bitter drink of sorrow. So Sac Nicte and Can Ek were called to return to the whirlpool whence the powers of the universe have evolved.

She understood the hidden designs of nature and the eternal fires within all things. She also knew that the priests were wrong. They told her that she would return within three days but it was not true. Nobody ever returned from this cenote, which was a well so deep and green and airless that even the fish could not live within.

But Sac Nicte also knew how to count time and read the stars. She understood the circular nature of time. Time was really like a spiral, like a whirlpool, sucking you in and down until you resurfaced again, but in another form. When you measured time by the moon, you could count your holy days, and when you measured it by the sun, you could calculate the seasons of the harvest. But every fifty–two years, everything started anew. More than the sum of her age and that of Can Ek's but less than her Tata's.

Just as childhood and youth are the promise of form and old age the ruin of physical form, death is the fall into formlessness. Life begins with surprise and ends with a question. Would Can Ek's heart live on in an eagle or a jaguar? Would her formlessness take another form, and if so, when?

All these thought forms disintegrated at the very moment in which she was thrown into the green pool. Before she went back to the liquid womb of the Great Mother. Before she left the dry world of illusion to return to the liquid depths of the primal source.

The water was warm and soothing against her limbs. She swam forever in a wonderful underground grotto which was mottled with light from holes that opened up to an azure sky. The sea bed was carpeted with undulating coral which swayed gently as fish passed by. The colours were pink and yellow and blue and green, comparable only to those you get under an electron microscope. The vaulted ceiling of that grotto was dripping with stalactites that looked like the strings of sugar candy from her Mexican childhood.

She was glad that she had conquered her irrational fear of water and learned how to scuba dive. A holiday in Cancun without this vista of marine life was unthinkable, honeymoon or not.

They had finally made it, her Kanuk and herself. They had met at a sociology congress in Mexico City and it was love at first sight.

Marriage had really been quite beside the point. But the Mexican government did not issue work permits to foreigners unless they were married to Mexicans and her Kanuk often spoke longingly about his home in Oka and his job in Ottawa with the Council of Native Peoples. They decided to commute back and forth, like migratory birds, until the children arrived.

So they had married to please their respective tribes and meet official requirements. This is why they were in Cancun, in a pyramid-shaped hotel where the food was good and the crowds abominable.

Their one concession to their sanity was staying as close as possible to the sea and visiting the Mayan ruins.

So this is how Maya came to be swimming in a lovely grotto which formed part of a network that turns into subterranean rivers and feeds the cenotes.

She got out of the water, dried herself, and applied sunscreen to her body before lying next to Kanuk. It never failed. The slippery oil on her skin and the sun beating on her pubis always seemed to arouse her. She turned to one side and with her index finger started tracing the moon-shaped scar under Kanuk's left nipple. She then pinched his nipple gently, noticing that it had already hardened.

Kanuk stopped pretending that he was asleep. He kissed her hungrily and seeing that there were not many people around, he eased his shorts to one side and penetrated her right there near the ruins in Tulum. They then fell asleep in each other's arms, like the tangled roots of a mangrove tree.

When Maya woke, she scanned her surroundings. Her eyes lingered over the temple perched on a hill and then turned to the sea. A couple of billowing clouds floated lazily over the water. The beach was almost empty. Everything appeared the same and yet it was not. In her mind, jaguars swished past uninvited. Butterflies fluttered in her belly. Obsidian knives ripped her heart. The sound of long-forgotten drums reverberated through her body.

Kanuk stirred. Maya turned to him and started tickling his face with a flower that she found lying next to them.

"Stop it," he said, "or you will get me started all over again!"

"Thanks for the lovely flower," she whispered."I didn't notice when you got up to get it."

"I didn't. Someone else must have given it to you."

"You mean when we were making love? Or asleep? Look around you, the beach is almost deserted."

"It is a strange flower. I've never seen anything like it. What's it called?"

"It is called Sac Nicte," replied Maya. "They say there was once a Maya princess by that name who ran away with her lover to the forest of Peten, fleeing her father's wrath. When she died, this flower sprouted all over Chichen Itza, commemorating their love."

Kanuk sought Maya's eyes. "Why do you suddenly look so sad, Maya?"

"I just had a strange and haunting dream in which I recognized myself a long time ago. Kanuk, you've never explained how you got that scar under your left breast."

"Oh that. It's nothing, really. When I was a kid on the reserve, my friends were always pushing me to go deer hunting with them. I couldn't bring myself to kill anything, so one day just to show them I wasn't a coward I took a jagged can top and cut myself, hoping to gouge my heart out. I botched it up and the ambulance had to take me to a hospital in Ste Anne de Bellevue to get it stitched. Now that I've told you my secret tell me yours: who gave you that flower? Was it the guy who was ogling your breasts this morning?"

Maya kissed him gently on his round red lips and shrugged her shoulders.

"It was Sac Nicte herself," she finally said.

"Who?"

"Sac Nicte, my secret twin."

Tobias S. Buckell *is a Caribbean-born speculative fiction writer who now lives (strangely enough to him and through many odd twists of fate) in Ohio with his wife Emily. He has published in various magazines and anthologies. He is a graduate of the Clarion East Science Fiction and Fantasy Writers' Workshop, a Writers of the Future winner, and a finalist for the Campbell Award for Best New SF Writer. His work has received Honorable Mention in* Year's Best Fantasy and Horror. *His first novel,* Crystal Rain, *will be out from Tor Books in 2005. Visit TobiasBuckell.com for more information.*

⌒

Necahual

Tobias S. Buckell

We drop out of the wormhole towards a mess of a planet by the ochre light of a dying sun. From the cant of orbit, upside down and even then through virtual portholes, we can see tiny spots of white light blossom in the atmosphere.

Each one of those little blossoms of light is an impact. A chunk of rock with a controller vane on it, predestined for a certain target. It clears out the enemy's ability to hit back above the stratosphere.

We're liberators. And all the thousands and thousands of other pods dropping to their designated targets and missions all over this planet are liberators as well. We are like a deadly rain of flesh and metal.

I know from past experience that sunsets here on New Anegada won't be the same for a long while. On another planet, far away in both distance and time, I used to sit on a porch and watch magnificent sunsets just like the ones that would soon appear here. The League had liberated my own world then, and now I am here to do the same.

"Man, we're dropping the hammer on this backwater shithole," the man across from me says. His white and blue exoskeleton wraps around his body. He looks like a striped mantis. Right now the exoskeleton is plugged into the convex wall of the pod, charging up while it keeps him from bouncing around as we skate atmosphere.

A single bead of sweat floats loose from his bulbous nose and hangs in the air between us.

"You know much about the target?"

Everyone wants to any know juicy details about them.

"Historical info only," I say. "They call themselves the Azteca. But the Azteca of Mother Earth never even called themselves that. They were the Mexica."

I wonder if the black man to the right of me has skin-flauge painted on. Hard to tell under the blue and white he's wearing. It's hard not to look askance at him. No one like him on the planet I came from. But at least he's human, real human, and The League today will be adding another human planet, we're told. If there are any aliens here, we'll wipe them out, every last one, like they tried to wipe The League out.

"The warrior priests of Mexica were pretty brutal," I explain. "They used to induce hallucinations by piercing their foreskins" – all the men wince – "and dragging a knotted rope through the tear until they saw visions."

The woman to my left asks, "What is it going to be like when we hit?"

"I got the same report you did."

The large island continent of New Anegada on the planet was also the name of the planet. This was confusing for conversation. But no one had consulted with the original colonists, who were mainly Caribbean refugees from Mother Earth. Half the sole continent was called New Anegada and home to the descendents of the initial Caribbean refugees. The Azteca claimed the other half, a group of humans ruled by aliens who set themselves up as ancient Aztec gods. Large mountains split them down the middle.

The entire system got cut off several hundred years ago, a forgotten incident, a sidenote of history. Then the wormhole that connected New Anegada to the rest of the worlds opened up again several weeks ago and shit hit the fan.

We were ordered out to make sure The League got here first to offer these humans membership, before any aliens could get here. The Azteca attacked before any negotiations were finalized. Now things were messy. A rumour had spread that the Azteca were results of some alien human breeding program, recreating the culture in order to gain extraordinarily loyal and dangerous human fighters for their own use.

This is all I know.

All four of us are strapped across from each other in the pod, waiting as the heat builds up, looking past each other.

The virtual panorama on the floor screen flickers off.

The buffeting ceases. We're still alive.

"Hello," says a small voice deep inside my inner ear. It's the dry and bored monotone of an artificial intelligence transmitting its way into my mechanical armor. "I am riding shotgun for you. Got about a minute and thirteen seconds left until you hit dirt, and congratulations, you have just passed the highest probability zone of being shot down by automated Azteca fire."

Which is why it is just now downloading itself into my armor. No sense in its wasting its time on me until it knows for sure this body made it to ground.

"Name's Tai Thirteen Crimson Velvet. Call me Velvet," the voice says. "Lady on your left is Paige, man across is Steven. On your right is Smith. Smith has augmented ears for congenital deafness. If you get hit by anything with a good electromagnetic pulse, it'll wipe his hearing chips and he'll back to being deaf. Just so you know."

All the information we need comes to us from the Tais. Tactical artificial intelligences. Little cybernetic ghosts. They give us the real orders, the real info, so that if we get into trouble they can scramble, leave, and we won't be the wiser about the big picture. This is why we know so little about our part in this liberation.

These are tactics learned from many alien encounters. There were creatures that could just suck shit right out of your brain and figure out what your plans were. Humanity had to adapt. Tais were one of many different tactics The League used just to keep humanity alive in a hostile universe.

"Take a deep breath and close your eyes," the Tai orders. "Time to peel."

The pod explodes. The sides rip back and vaporize themselves. I open my eyes to see the actual island of New Anegada directly below me. My heart hammers as we plummet.

The green land rushes faster and faster toward me until the Tai whispers "Okay" and the chute slides out of the back of my exoskeleton.

There are no explosions, no shots fired at me; just a calm blue sky and lush green forest below my feet, the rippling blue ocean up ahead. The chute canopy overhead is invisible in a variety of spectra, including the visible.

A minute later, my feet hit turf.

I'm on the ground and I have no clue what's going to happen next.

⤙⤚

I'm expecting shots. But I only hear wind rustling through palm fronds and the distant foaming sound of waves breaking over reef. I'm expecting Aztec priest-warriors wearing gaudily coloured feathers to fan out and attack us. Instead, I'm facing a large three-storey concrete building painted bright yellow and pink.

It's got terracotta shingling.

I'm expecting anything, but what I get is a man with his back against a mango tree, chewing a stem of grass, looking straight at me.

"Is this a friendly?" I subvocalize to the Tai.

"Okay," the Tai says, ignoring my question. "Your regular weaponry is locked under my command. You have a tanglegun in your left pocket, if you need to use that. This is a police action, we're not here to kill anyone. There are no hostiles on this side of the mountain range. We're just here to talk and gather information from the New Anegada locals. HQ has brokered a meeting between some high level locals and an Azteca representative at this spot."

"This is a friendly, then?" I ask again.

"Yes."

I look down. The extendable cannon I have aimed at the man is primed, but useless because it will not fire in a friendly situation. So I let go of the trigger.

"Go ahead," the Tai orders. "We're here to gather information and any confirmations about who the Azteca are, where they came from, and what, if anything, these people can do to help us. I am recording everything back up to Orbital HQ. I'll prompt you as needed. If you do this well, you'll be promoted. So will I."

The cannon swings back up under my arm to fasten itself to the back of my exoskeleton armor. It's a smooth lubricated slide. A whisper. I hear the cannons of the other soldiers from the pod withdraw in similar fashion. They're all fanned out behind me, facing into the jungle, covering the man in front of me and glancing up at the sky, just in case.

The man by the mango tree pulls the stem of grass out of his mouth and stands up.

"So," he says to me. "We get invade, or what?"

I have no idea how to respond. I stand there, still, waiting for someone besides me to do something.

"You speak English?" The man asks. His brown eyes twinkle. He has a deep tan that is almost the colour of oak, and short, tightly–curled hair. He's wearing a cream–coloured suit. With no shoes on.

I nod.

"You looking for Bouschulte, right?" He says, the words so quick they blend into each and I stumble over the accent. He ambles over to us. Someone's booted feet shift just behind me. If anything goes wrong, I have backup.

I speak my first word.

"What?"

"You. Looking. For. Bouschulte." The man repeats himself as if I'm slow. He looks frustrated for a second. "He up in he house."

"What is…." I swallow, "a bouschulte?"

"It a name. Frederick Bouschulte. If you have a Azteca name like 'Acolmiztli' or some stupidness like that, and you hiding with us, you don't keep calling you–self 'Acolmiztli.' Seen?"

"Seen." I agree out of sheer panic. The Tai in my head is still silent. I wouldn't mind some assistance. The man's accent is hard and I still haven't been given any damned orders. "Tai," I subvocalize. "Damnit, where are you?"

The man reaches out to touch my face, then stops when I flinch.

"You eye them, chineeman: you do that to fit in with them?"

"It…." was done a long time ago. Far away. "An old tradition my forefathers continued." I'd been too young to protest the removal of my eye folds.

A tiger–striped cat tiptoes out from behind the building and sits down. It starts to lick its tail, working hard at ignoring the five people on the grass before it.

"What you name?"

"Kiyoshi," I say.

"Well, Kiyoshi, let we get on with this so–call invasion, eh?"

My Tai wasn't being quiet, I realize, it was gone. And looking around at the panicked faces of the three other soldiers with whom I fell out of the sky, I realize theirs are dead too. We're on our own. That was sudden. The Tais must have sensed an attack and bailed.

We might be just one step away from getting slaughtered.

The panicked feeling that follows that thought comes and goes swiftly. Old training takes over. Yes, the Tais make the decisions, but we have training. We're still mobile representatives of The League. We're still soldiers. We can still do something.

I grab the man's shoulder with one hand, aim the tangle gun right dead in the middle of his forehead with the other. At this range, the tangle gun is lethal.

"What's going on?" I hiss. "Tell me what is going on!"

He snaps loose of me, shrugging my armored arm aside as if it were only a nuisance. The motion is quick enough I have trouble following it. There is, surprisingly enough, a small knife now shoved up between the joints in my armor.

Smith aims his tangle gun at us, but it's an empty gesture. He's too far away. We no longer have superior weaponry to a barefoot man with a knife.

"You conquest failing."

"There is no fucking conquest," Steve snaps from behind me. "We're here to save you from the Azteca. "

"Yeah man, so I hear. But first thing: seeing that we been making do for a few hundred years already, you might wonder what we know that you ain't figure out yet. Second thing: you here to tell us what to do, right? Because you assume we don't know what we doing. You want tell us what to do, how to think. That is mental conquest, friend. Mental."

A boom shakes the air. Paige looks up at the sky. None of us can see anything, but I shiver anyway.

"Any of you able to contact anyone?" Paige asks us.

We all try. Shake our heads. We're cut off.

"Come inside with me now," our new host says. "Drop you weapon to the ground. You don't need them."

For some reason, without the Tais, the three soldiers are looking at me. Command structure has returned to our small unit. Ironic how we fall into the old patterns. This is what it would have been like in The League before the Xenowars. Only then it wasn't The League, just scattered groups of space-faring humans spreading throughout the wormhole systems.

I have a decision to make.

"Do you have any way that we can communicate to our superiors?" I ask.

The man nods.

"That we do," he says.

Into the rabbit hole, I decide, and nod. I give the order and we drop our tangle guns and the blade near my ribs disappears just as abruptly as it had appeared. I still want to know how it got under my armor.

"I name Jami," the man in the cream suit says, shaking my hand. "Jami 'Manicou' Derrick."

Jami turns around, and we follow the barefoot, dapper man into the concrete-block house. We troop past the cat, which is now working on cleaning an extended furry back leg.

✤

Jami asks us if we read much. He wants to know about some old book none of us have ever read, or heard of, or care about right now. He tells us it has an interesting moral to it.

He laughs gently at our ignorance, our focus on what is going on right now. He takes off his tie and suit jacket and hangs them off the back of a canvas chair.

"You going wish you know these things," he laughs at us. "You should have wait and talk with everyone longer. So now, it a mess. The League trying to come in and reshape everything to be just the way it wants, and it ain't that easy."

The door creaks open and we look straight into the face of the enemy.

✿

The Azteca reclines in a leather chair while an elderly black woman in a bright red and yellow patterned shawl carefully snips at his flat hair. Much to my amazement, her skin is even darker than Smith's, who still stands behind me, clearing his throat slightly to let me know he's there. It is an adjustment, I remind myself. Almost everyone on this planet is some shade darker than myself. I am the stranger.

A red cape drapes around the Azteca's knees where his hands rest, gently crossed over each other. The gold plug in his nose glints in the light streaming through a large opened window, and his jade earrings gleam as he slightly turns his head to regard us.

Blue eye shadow swirls around the crinkled edges of his eyes. His black–smeared lips twitch.

"The League has arrived," he pronounces, looking at our uniforms. "What do you think of our conquerors, Jami?"

Jami is leaning against the concrete wall, arms folded, looking at the small ensemble in the room. "Centuries ago the first conquerors of Tenochtitlan arrive in small numbers," Jami smiles sadly at us. "They had armor and superior technology. The League only got the small number and the armor."

"But this is not a group of Spaniards with gold lust and domination in their hearts," the Azteca says. "The League is here to save us. Is it not?" His eyes are piercing. Something has wounded him. He hates us. "The first conquistadors thought they were saving the savages back then too," he adds. "As you mistakenly think now."

I have nothing to say, but stand straight and return his restrained fury with a calm gaze of my own. I am a professional.

"You done then, Frederick?" Jami asks.

"I miss my true name," the Azteca man says.

Jami sighs.

"Acolmiztli, Frederick … I guess it don't make no difference what you call yourself now," he says.

"Done," the woman with the scissors says.

Acolmiztli stands up and takes the cherry bowl with his hair clippings in it from her.

"I'm not much of a believer," he says, "but the old ways are specific. You must have your hair cut in a way that does not lose *tonalli*. Or you risk losing the strength of your spirit." He takes a deep breath. "In times like these, I need all the strength I can get."

The door slams behind him as he leaves the room.

"He's bitter," Paige whispers to me. They've been taking my lead. I'm in charge. I'm their Tai.

"Acolmiztli *very* bitter. But the League shouldn't assume," Jami says, looking at the door with us, "that all Azteca go be your enemy. Some go be your friend."

"How would I know?" I snap. "We know nothing right now. All we *do* know is that the Azteca didn't exist on this planet when it last had contact with other worlds. We know you're in danger from the Azteca. That's it." I want to ask if the Azteca are ruled by aliens, who've bred them, but that's a rumour, and I keep quiet as Jami explains that there are what he calls Tolteca, reformed Azteca who have spurned human sacrifice and made great changes to Azteca society in the last hundred years.

My stomach flip-flops.

"Human sacrifice?"

Jami unfolds his arms.

"Acolmiztli tells me he only sacrificed snake, bird, and butterfly. He say," and Jami imitates Acolmiztli's voice perfectly, "because he so loved man, Quetzalcoatl allowed only the sacrifice of snakes, birds, and butterflies. As he was opposed to the sacrifice of human flesh, the three sorcerers of Tula drove him out of the city. The people of Tenochtitlan did not follow Quetzalcoatl. Instead, they followed the war-god Huitzilopochtli or Xipe-Totec: the flayed god. Then the fifth sun was destroyed and we lived in the sixth and it became a time of change."

It sends shivers down my spine.

"You said you had communications equipment." I fold my arms. The shivering continues. "We'd like to use it now."

I shiver again, my knees weak. Jami catches me under my arms as I drop to my knees.

"What's happening?" I'm disoriented; the walls of the room seem to bend in on themselves.

"Remember how I tell you you should have read Wells?" Jami says. "Come on." He helps me over to a wooden bench in the corner of the room and opens a cupboard. I vaguely recognize the device behind the wooden doors. It looks like a museum piece. But it responds to a wave of my hand and my voice.

Static is my only reply. There is accusation in my angry stare, but Jami gestures at the device.

"Try again. You feeling rough."

Sweat drips from my forehead, the shivers continue to wrack my body. This time I find a carrier signal and send a voice request up. Archaic. But they reply.

"Who is this? Identify."

I do, giving personal ID codes and answering questions until the voice on the other side is satisfied.

"We give nothing away by saying we're doing a retreat," it says. "All ground assaults have been infected with some sort of virus. We're losing this battle. We have your touchdown coordinates. Be outside in five minutes for a starhook. You'll be in quarantine upon return."

Then it's gone.

My three companions are sprawled on the floor, sweating.

Infected. Quarantine.

"When we saw you," I say, "you walked over to us, touched me." My hand goes up to my face.

"Acolmiztli gave it to me, and I passed it to you," Jami says.

"Is it fatal?" I ask.

He shrugs. "Better get back up to orbit and find out, right? I look alright, but I could have take an antidote." He smiles.

I purse my lips.

"Get up," I order everyone. It's been interesting being in charge, but I'm glad to see the end of it coming. Paige, Smith, and Steve struggle up. Smith leans heavily on Steve. "Get outside, now." Smith nods. He must still be able to understand me, which is a small comfort in the middle of this mess.

We're a pathetic group that pushes through the door with Jami following us. My knees wobble, but I manage a convincing stride through what looks like a bar.

Dim lights cast shadows, and from those shadows loom wooden tables where several men in khaki camouflage toast us with their glasses and sly grins. I see no weapons, but my stomach churns with the weapon they've already used to defeat us.

My gut spasms. The pain almost blinds me.

"Come on." I push my three soldiers on in front of me, shoving my hand against their hard armor, ignoring an unidentifiable chuckle from somewhere in the room.

I trip over a chair, grab the table to steady myself, and when I blink everything is blurry. I have no soldier-sharp senses, no wired edge for combat. The armor I wear to assist me do all that is failing as well as my body.

Right before me is an aquarium taller than I am and stretching half the nearest wall's length. Something moves sinuously through the tank and presses against the glass. I stumble closer and a woman stares back at me through the refracted water and solid glass with wide brown eyes. Sheets of her oak-coloured hair twirl behind her head. Her ultra-pale skin has an almost greenish tint.

The eyes hold me until my face presses right against the glass.

"Beautiful, isn't she?" Acolmiztli grabs my shoulder. "She was a present I inherited from one of my brothers. A gift from the Emporer Moctezuma the Ninth. One of the *teotl* created her for him."

Her smooth stomach fades into the singular muscle and pilot fins of her tail's trunk. The wide fins are splayed out. They're delicate, yet powerful enough to drive all six feet of her through the water with a flick.

Which she does. Out away from the glass.

"Created?" I ask. And then, "*Teotl?*"

She turns back, looks at me, and her hands flutter.

"Created just like we were," Acolmiztli whispers. "But unlike my countrymen, there is only one of her, and many, many of us."

We have to keep moving, he's just toying with me. I walk away from the tank.

"Keep moving, dammit," I say. Smith looks at me and frowns. He shakes his head, points to his ears. He doesn't understand a word. His hearing implants must have failed. Could a virus do that?

We keep walking, and pass out of the door into the sunlight. I lean back and look at the sky. Nothing yet.

"Why are you doing this to us?" I ask Jami, who is still right behind us.

"The Azteca doing it to you, not me."

"But you knew about it," I snap.

"Yes."

"And yet you did nothing. You collaborate with them."

"You the one that drop out the sky and land. We didn't force you."

Overhead I hear a roar, then a rumble.

"But all those deaths…"

"All because of you. Consider: before you came we were changing the

Azteca from the bottom up, and inside out. The Azteca a hornet's nest, and we blow some sweet smoke their way. Now you throwing rocks."

Thunder rolls and a small oval speck drops out of the sky. The long carbon filament trailing behind it is strong enough to reel us all up from the ground we're standing on into orbit and then into the hold of a waiting mothership.

"Snap in when it drops," I order everyone, voice husky. "Paige, make sure to help Smith, he can't hear what we're saying."

I turn and look at Jami, dizziness threatening to drop me at any second.

The pod slows to a halt and falls into our midst. Paige struggles over and snaps on, pulling Smith with her and making sure he got hooked in. Steve looks at me and follows suit. Three soldiers, ready to get lifted, the cable rising up into the heavens from between them.

"We have a minute, maybe two," Steve says to me.

I'm still staring at Jami.

He stares right back. "We study you. When faced with the other, when the hard times had hit, you choose to cleanse the aliens from all the human worlds. And right now you all still working on 'purifying' The League. Making it only human."

"There was no other choice," I say. "There were wars. Humanity was endangered. Dammit, I was four. You can't hold me responsible. It's different now anyway."

"You had start with war. Then deporting the rest from any human territory. But The League ain't stopping there, right? Now The League tries to manage the entire human bloodline, disqualifying humans with altered DNA."

"Like the Azteca," I say. That is why Alcolmiztli has no love for us. He knows The League doesn't recognize him as human.

"Yes. Listen, during all these years we been cut off here all of you all almost wipe yourselves out. Yet you come here to tell us what to do now? That's hypocritical."

"Drastic things were done," I admit. "But we never would have survived the alien attacks if we didn't do these things. We could never have matched their superior military skills and constant encroachment." And, despite the fever, I have a trump. "You talk hypocritical. Hypocritical is the mermaid," I hiss. "You let that Azteca keep his slave in a tank. How dirty does that make you?"

I might as well have struck Jami.

"The line is tightening," Steve yells at me.

"Maybe you right. Maybe them thing had to be done. But that don't mean you have to force it on all of us here," Jami said. "And think of this: your League only concerned about 'pure' humans, right? Then that girl back in the tank there, she ain't even considered human by them."

He's right.

I stumble towards the pod. In a second I'll be yanked out of here into the stratosphere, my suit bubbling out to enclose and protect me. Back to the warrens inside the depths of a troop ship.

But his words are resonating with me. I don't clip in.

"We ain't ignorant," Jami said. "When the wormhole had close, we was all left with each other. We made plenty mistake, but we have a history of adaptation. The alien *Teotl* who create the Azteca, and the Azteca, we all shared just this world uneasy at first. The Azteca had been create to destroy all of we, because during the first war we had almost destroy the *Teotl*.

"And that ain't what The League wants, right?" Jami spreads his hands. "The League want keep fighting, and fighting. It coming at all of we here, threatening things and too blind to see that we already figuring out how to make it work, balancing Azteca and *Teotl*, changing things. We ain't done yet, but we was well on the way before you came. So you a superior force, with bigger guns. And we had to go and use something you all didn't expect. The only way you can find out how to deal with the infection is to talk with all of us all down here. That's why we work with the Azteca on this, and get the antidote from them. Now we all go have to work together."

Jami is speaking mostly to me, but the message is general. Let's work together.

The people on this planet want to figure out how best to handle the new situation that just opened up in their backyard. The League will somehow need to help liaise between this tripartite mess it's found itself in, and certainly not in the dominant position it thought it would have.

I remember a small biological part of what being human is. The reason we fear the alien, death, and why The League fights so hard and maniacally against *everything*.

Survival.

I can see a way out of my infected situation that doesn't involve quarantine.

Smith signs something at me. A hand flutter, like that of the woman in the tank.

I turn to Jami.

"I would like to stay and help you talk to the League," I tell him. "But I want the same antidote you have, okay?"

Jami nods. "The very same. I promise you."

Paige recognizes what is happening.

"You can't desert," she shouts. "They'll deactivate you."

The rest of the objection is lost. The starhook goes taut and all three of them lift off the ground and accelerate towards space.

I drop to my hands and knees and puke. Tiny pieces of machinery I didn't even know were in me litter the grass along with the remains of pasty meals from the last day of eating.

With a deep breath, I stand up again.

Jami helps steady me.

"I have a condition," he says. "You have to help me free her." He's talking about the lady in the aquarium.

She's been in the bar for weeks, he tells me as he helps me back across the lawn. Ever since The League began its bombardment and invasion. Acolmiztli brought her here with him. He won't let her go, despite Jami's arguing for it. Acolmiztli's brother died a long time ago, and this is all he has left to remember him by.

Jami can't free her. If he were to set her free Acolmiztli would blame him, it would create a diplomatic stir in the middle of a delicate time. But a rogue League soldier with a soft heart, a human heart, could do it.

"Just give me the antidote, please," I beg. "I'll help you."

∽

Acolmiztli regards me with suspicion.

"He is still here?"

"He a smart man," Jami says, his voice soft and guarded. "He know when a battle turn."

The Azteca laughs, then folds his arms and glares at the men around him.

"The battle *is* turning. Soon I'll get to be going home, as things settle down."

"Lucky us."

"The antidote?" I ask Jami. "Where is it?" I'm scared of another attack, of puking something really important out.

"The antidote?" Acolmiztli asks. "Come on, Jami. Can't you give this poor man the antidote? Doesn't he know what the antidote is?" Acolmiztli laughs at me and the sound makes me clench my hands. "All those nasty little metal bits inside of you that talk to each other and to your ships, all those little ghosts running around inside your heads, those intelligent machines, they're all dead now. There is no antidote. You'll live. Oh yes, you're just fine. You just don't have any metal inside of you. You're just like Jami, or me, here. That's what he meant when he said we all have the antidote."

I'll live. But I know what the result in space will be. All those battle formations of space ships swarming back through the wormhole in retreat, their bows milliseconds away from each other, will collide and destroy each other.

There will be mass confusion. Systems failures. Anyone up in orbit was a sitting duck. Anyone whose life depended on advanced machinery was dead.

"There is a story I tell, that my father told, and his father before him," Acolmiztli says. Reflections from the wall of water behind me dapple the wall in front of me. "Horse and Stag came into quarreling once, long ago, and Horse went to a Hunter for help in taking his revenge against Stag. Hunter said yes, but only if you let me put this piece of iron in your mouth that I may guide you with these pieces of rope. And only if you let me put this saddle on your back that I may sit on you while I help you hunt Stag. The horse agreed and together they hunted down the Stag. After this, the horse thanked the Hunter, and asked him to remove those things from him. But Hunter laughed and tied him to a tree, then sat down and had himself a very good meal of Stag. You see what I am saying?" Acolmiztli looks at me.

"No, what are saying?"

The half-grin on his lips flitters away.

"Who's really riding whom here?" Acolmiztli asked.

Jami has sat near me, but at an angle so he can look at both of us.

"You drunk," Jami says.

"Do either of you realize how many people are going to die today?" I yell. I'm shaking, angry with everyone. I had been convinced I was here to land and perform a duty under the Tai's direction, stripped of that leadership, then told I was infected. I had thought I would die, but now I'm alive.

I'm a mess.

"Yes," Acolmiztli says. "I'm going to go outside and watch." He stands up and leaves the room.

Jami leans forward and grabs my forearm.

"Please," he hisses. "Tell me you still go help me."

I turn and look at the lady in the tank, who is staring back at me.

"Who is Acolmiztli, really?" I ask.

"He the brother to the Azteca Emperor," Jami says. "Here in case the Emperor get attack by you League. Now that The League falling, he go leave soon as he can."

I swallow.

"Okay. Where are we moving her?"

"She lives in sea water," Jami says. The ocean is not too far from here. "She knows that if we can get her out, that I have told people around the coast to help her out with whatever she needs."

He'll have a cart filled with seawater waiting for me outside. I just have to get her out and to the sea.

ᏇᎧᎧ

I know no sign language. I stand in front of the tank and wonder what will happen when I try to take her out.

"And," I whisper to myself, "how do I make you understand that I'm going to help you out? Set you free?" There is an ocean and a small beach nearby that Jami tells me is easy to get to. There is a dirt road that leads from this place straight to it.

"Will you even want to be free?" She has been in a watery cage like this for all her life. She might only be able to conceive of that being her world. Would it be right to set her free?

And if I do, am I not making enemies with the most powerful Azteca? I've seen what they can do. Can Jami's people do anything to protect me? I doubt it, but they've survived with Azteca so far.

Sound shakes me free. The pane of glass in front of her is covered in mud and silt and she writes something with her index finger.

I don't understand what it says.

She frantically scribbles another line.

It is meaningless to me. But she looks at me, clasping her hands together, pleading. That I can understand.

This is the right thing to do.

Through a gap in the silt on the glass I tap to get her attention.

"Get back." I mime the motion, waving her back. She disappears in the gloom of the tank.

I'm still wearing exoskeleton armor, and the helmet section slides up with a quick slap of my palm. The glass shards that hit me when I fire the tangle gun at point blank range don't slice me to shreds.

The lukewarm water and silt, however, drench me. She slides towards me.

She weighs more than I thought, or I'm weak. Her mossy hair drapes over my shoulder. The smell of seaweed fills the room. I stumble over broken glass with her in my arms and gently lay her into the cart filled with water that Jami has outside as he promised.

Then comes the pushing run towards the beach, water slopping out over the sides.

Occasionally she pokes her head out to look at me.

Palm trees rustle and shake. My feet crunch on dirt. A dog barks.

The trail turns down. The beach isn't far. I can hear the rhythmic surf, and the wind starts to lift sand into the air and into my eyes.

At the end of the trail I pick her up again, lift her out of the cart and run over the sand, almost tripping, until I'm wading into the salty water. She wriggles free of me.

For a second we stare at each other, then she's gone, a shadow beneath the waves. Was there gratitude? I don't know. It isn't important. I did what I did.

I strip off the exoskeleton, piece by piece, and throw the useless carcass out into the waves.

Overhead the rumble of engines makes me look up and see a machine climbing from the house into the sky. It is brightly painted with geometric shapes, much like I would expect an Azteca flyer to be. It speeds off into the distance like an angry mosquito.

ᴄⱴꙜ

Jami hands me a towel and a drink when I walk through the door. He sits down at a wooden table and looks at me.

"She leave?" he asks.

"Yes." I nod slowly.

"You'd hope she would stay?"

"I don't know. It doesn't matter. It's done. Acolmiztli?"

Jami smiles. "He gone back to his brother."

I take a deep breath and put my hands on the table. "What am I going to do now?" I ask Jami.

He grabs my hands.

"That one small act of liberation," he tells me, "that little bit of freedom you got her, will have more of an impact than all you ship, you missile, and all you soldier. Understand?"

No, I didn't.

"That lady, her name Necahual. It mean 'survivor.' All this time she been surviving, but that ain't good enough. Now she can have a whole coast, where fishermen will know to feed her. Because surviving not enough. You can't just survive, Kiyoshi. You must do better than that. And right now The League just surviving. Like you.

"So you just the beginning. The League, we have a lot to offer them too. Along with the Azteca. How to accommodate and incorporate. We been learning how to do this since Mother Earth when we were all islanders." He slaps the table. "And we get better and better. Most places, always they get caught up in ruling, dominating, becoming greater, and then falling apart." Jami leans forward. "We learn how to stay outside that, man. It ain't easy," he says. "Always a struggle. But for a much greater good."

I pull my hands free.

"So what do I do right now?" I ask. "How do we start all this?"

Jami leans back in his chair. "For now, just to talk to me, man. Don't look for information, or try to resolve anything, or figure it all out. Just talk."

I relax a bit. "And tomorrow?"

Jami smiles. "There's going to be a lot of work tomorrow. A whole lot of it. We go be very busy."

"Jami?" I remember something from earlier. "That old book you'd asked me if I'd read, what was the name of it again?"

War of the Worlds," he said. "By H.G. Wells."

I roll the name around. "Yes, that was it. You think it's important I should I read it?"

Jami looks up at the sky. "Maybe. You might appreciate it more now, I think."

There is one last thing I want to ask about. "And what of these aliens on this planet, the *Teotl?*"

"There aliens, yeah. But they belong here. The only real alien right now is you," Jami laughs. "And soon we go teach you how to belong."

I freeze my face. I'm nervous about this. All my life I've been scared of the other, fighting them, forcing them out of The League.

"Tomorrow," Jami says. "One step at a time, we show you how."

I breathe again, slowly, savouring the air.

It's more than just surviving.

Final Thoughts

Uppinder Mehan, co-editor

I had crossed de line of which I had so long been dreaming.
I was free; but dere was no one to welcome me to de land of freedom.
I was a stranger in a strange land.
– freedom fighter Harriet Tubman, describing the first
time she set foot on land where she was not a slave

Harriet Tubman's quotation above spells out an assumption that she, Moses, and Heinlein's Michael Valentine all might share when she refers to herself as a "stranger in a strange land." She may be free now that she has crossed the line dividing the North from the South in nineteenth-century U.S. but she has little sense of herself as a free person and of the free land she finds herself in. It strikes me that many of us who might call ourselves postcolonial are in a similar situation.

Perhaps the strictest definition of a postcolonial person is one who is a member of a nation that has recently achieved independence from its colonizers, but by shifting from the adjective "postcolonial" to the noun "postcoloniality" a more inclusive and I think truer definition comes into play. Postcoloniality includes those of us who are the survivors – or descendants of survivors – of sustained, racial colonial processes; the members of cultures of resistance to colonial oppression; the members of minority cultures which are essentially colonized nations within a larger nation; and those of us who identify ourselves as having Aboriginal, African, South Asian, Asian ancestry, wherever we make our homes.

Some of the stories in this anthology might be categorized as science fiction, some as speculative fiction, and some as fantastic but they all broaden their labels. The simple binaries of native/alien, technologist/pastoralist, colonizer/colonized are all brought into question by writers who make use of both thematic and linguistic strategies that subtly subvert received language and plots. One of the key strategies employed by these writers is to radically shift the perspective of the narrator from the supposed rightful heir of contemporary technologically advanced cultures to those of us whose cultures have had their technology destroyed and stunted. The narrators and characters in these stories make the language of the colonizer their own by reflecting it back but using it to speak unpleasant truths, by expanding its vocabulary and changing its syntax to better accommodate their different world-views, and by ironically appropriating its terms for themselves and their lives. Postcolonial visions are both a questioning of colonial/imperialist practices and conceptions of the native or the colonized, and an attempt to represent the complexities of identity that terms such as "native" and "colonized" tend to simplify.

Coming back to Harriet Tubman and company, postcolonial writing has for the most part been intensely focused on examining contemporary reality as a legacy of a crippling colonial past but rarely has it pondered that strange land of the future. Visions of the future imagine how life might be otherwise. If we do not imagine our futures, postcolonial peoples risk being condemned to be spoken about and for again.

Postcolonial writers have given contemporary literature some of its most notable fiction about the realities of conqueror and conquered, yet we've rarely created stories that imagine how life might be otherwise. So many of us have written insightfully about our pasts and presents; perhaps the time is ripe for us to begin creatively addressing our futures.

Toronto and Boston, March 2004